Raves for the novels of Marshall Ryan Maresca:

"Superb characters living in a phenomenal fantasy world, with a detective story that just sucks you right into the storyline. Marshall Ryan Maresca impressed me with *The Thorn of Dentonhill*, but *A Murder of Mages* has secured me as a fan."
—Fresh Fiction

"*A Murder of Mages* was another hit for me, a fantastic read from a new talent whose star continues to be on the rise."
—Bibliosanctum

"Books like this are just fun to read."
—The Tenacious Reader

"*[A Murder of Mages]* is the perfect combination of urban fantasy, magic, and mystery."
—Kings River Life Magazine

"Marshall Ryan Maresca has done it again. After introducing readers to Maradaine through the eyes of criminals in *The Thorn of Dentonhill*, he focuses now on the constabulary, the ones catching the criminals, in *A Murder of Mages*. . . . Another rollicking adventure of magic and mayhem."
—The Qwillery

"Maresca's debut is smart, fast, and engaging fantasy crime in the mold of Brent Weeks and Harry Harrison. Just perfect."
—Kat Richardson, national bestselling author of *Revenant*

"Fantasy adventure readers, especially fans of spell-wielding students, will enjoy these lively characters and their high-energy story."
—*Publishers Weekly*

NOV 2016

AN IMPORT OF INTRIGUE

A novel of
The Maradaine Constabulary

MARSHALL RYAN MARESCA

DAW BOOKS, INC.
DONALD A. WOLLHEIM, FOUNDER
375 Hudson Street, New York, NY 10014

ELIZABETH R. WOLLHEIM
SHEILA E. GILBERT
PUBLISHERS
www.dawbooks.com

First Printing, November 2016
1 2 3 4 5 6 7 8 9

DAW TRADEMARK REGISTERED
U.S. PAT. AND TM. OFF. AND FOREIGN COUNTRIES
—MARCA REGISTRADA
HECHO EN U.S.A.

PRINTED IN THE U.S.A.

Acknowledgments

The more I do this, the more I realize the depths of gratitude I have for the help and support I've received in the process. When I wrote *The Thorn of Dentonhill* and *A Murder of Mages*, it was literally an act of faith: night after night, typing away because I believed in what I was doing. Now I'm here with *An Import of Intrigue* and whatever comes next because that faith was rewarded. As much faith was put into me as I put into the work. So many people deserve a nod on this book.

- My family, who have been the magnetic north I set my compass to through this journey. My wife Deidre, my son Nicholas, my parents Louis and Nancy, and my mother-in-law Kateri have all contributed to this work being possible.
- Kevin Jewell, who reads rough drafts and is always ready to point out when I'm taking lazy shortcuts in the storytelling.
- Rebecca Schwarz and Melissa Tyler, for taking plenty off my shoulders when this needed to be finished.
- Amanda Downum, Marguerite Reed, Caroline Yoachim, and a score of other writers who have offered advice, encouragement, and fellowship in navigating this crazy career. Also Mark Mattson for his help in brainstorming the title.
- Stina Leicht. Always Stina Leicht.
- Mike Kabongo, my agent, for the faith and trust

he's put into the work.

- Sheila Gilbert, my editor, and everyone else at DAW and Penguin Random House who have put so much into making Maradaine a reality: Betsy Wollheim, Joshua Starr, Katie Hoffman, Nita Basu, and everyone else who contributed to all the Maradaine books.

- Paul Young, who has blessed me with wonderful covers.

- Finally Daniel J. Fawcett, who in addition to constantly being a sounding board for brainstorming and other madness, lent his linguistic expertise whenever I had random questions about phonemic inventories or pronunciation. My work is consistently enriched by his input.

AN IMPORT
OF INTRIGUE

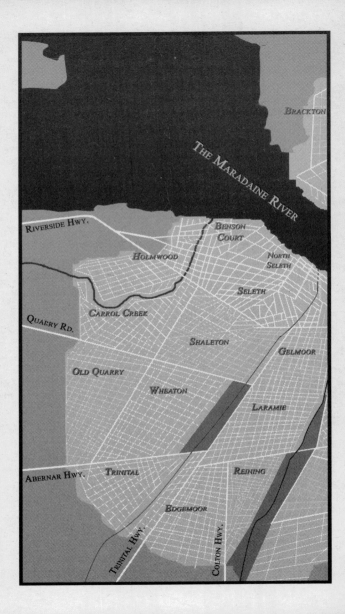

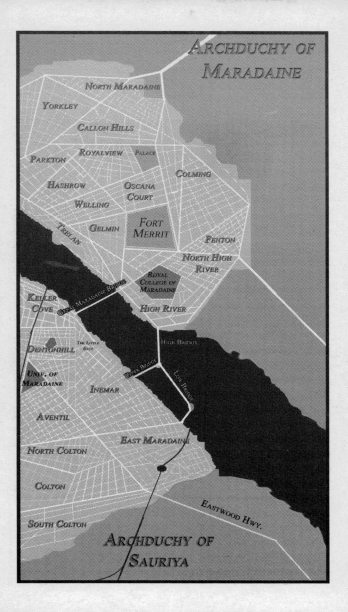

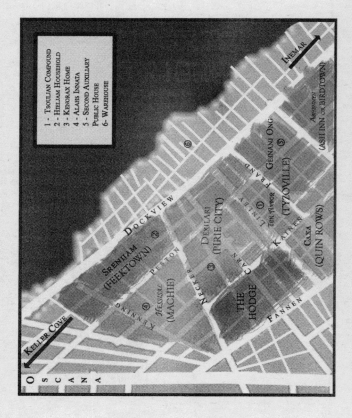

Chapter 1

THE DEAD MAN had no face.

All that remained where a face had once been was a gruesome mess of flesh, bone, and hair. The rest of his body was no better. Satrine Rainey was astounded that it was still recognizable as a man.

She was also astounded how, after two months as an Inspector Third Class in the Constabulary of the city of Maradaine, she had grown accustomed to sights like this. Too many of her case assignments involved dead bodies, and Captain Cinellan still delighted in assigning, in his words, the "strange ones" to her and her partner, Minox Welling.

Since Captain Cinellan was still letting her be an Inspector Third Class, and draw the salary she needed to care for her husband and daughters, she wasn't about to complain.

Inspector Welling responded to the sight by pulling his pipe from his coat pocket and stuffing it with his favorite Fuergan tobacco. "We were told this one was horrible," he said. "We were certainly not lied to."

Satrine stepped out of the refuse-strewn alleyway where the body had been discovered, finding little comfort in the busy streets of the Inemar neighborhood. Plenty of people were crowding a small distance away, held back by the footpatrol officers, gawking at the spectacle. Near the front of the crowd were a group of girls, around twelve or thirteen years old. Blouses with the sleeves torn off, most likely to deal with the sweltering summer heat, and tough smirks on their faces. Twenty-some years ago Satrine would have been one of those girls, trying to get a peek. There was always comfort in seeing that Inemar had chewed up and spit out someone else.

She turned back to the alley. "Based on the heat and the smell, he couldn't have been out here very long."

"Agreed," Welling said, crouching by the mauled body. "Whoever dumped the body here made little effort to even hide it."

"So our suspect is someone who would bring a dead body and dump it with other garbage in the middle of the day," Satrine said. "In other words, an idiot."

"Which are, unfortunately, not in short supply." Welling stood up and took a puff on his pipe. Looking at the cracks in the cobblestone, he added. "Almost no blood flowing from the body. The poor soul probably lost it all quite quickly." Satrine was amazed how calm he looked, not even seeming hot, despite still wearing his overcoat in this swelter. She had left her coat at the stationhouse, wearing just her inspector's vest and shirtsleeves. Even with that she was sweating up a swamp.

"Anything in the trash with him that helps you determine where he came from, who he is?" Satrine asked. Welling was gifted at making brilliant observations based on minimal details.

He shook his head and stepped out. "Nothing incriminating or remarkable. The past few days' worth of the *South Maradaine Gazette*, but all that indicates is it's probably from this neighborhood. Which I already presumed. Whoever dropped the body likely didn't go very far to do it. Probably no more than two blocks."

"Why do you think that?" Satrine asked.

"For one, as we've determined, idiocy. Second, the method of disposal hints at laziness. Whoever did this wanted nothing more than to get rid of the body with as little effort as possible. Come here with a wheelbarrow, drop it in the alley, and get away."

Satrine turned out to the crowd. "I don't suppose anyone saw someone come by here with a wheelbarrow? Maybe carrying a dead body?"

The girls in front chuckled, but no one gave a useful response.

"I suppose it was worth the effort to try that," Welling said.

Satrine shrugged. Inemar residents weren't particularly known for helping out the Constabulary. That had been the case in her childhood, and during her months serving here she hadn't seen anything to show it had changed.

A mule-drawn wagon approached the alley. The driver reined it to a stopped and hopped down. Leppin, the stationhouse's examinarian and bodyman, came over with a wide grin on his tiny head, looking all the sillier wearing the leather skullcap with various lenses in place over one of his eyes.

"What's the word, specs?" he asked in his thick northeastern accent. "Heard it's a real mangler."

"Quite," Welling said. "In fact, I doubt this was done by human hands."

Satrine thought on this. "Factory accident? That hurts your proximity idea." The closest works shop was over in Dentonhill. There were a couple sewinghouses in this part of Inemar, but nothing capable of threshing a man to this extent.

"It does." Welling puffed on his pipe a bit more.

"Though that is the sort of thing it puts me in the mind of."

Leppin had gone back to the alley and whistled low. "I ain't seen anything like this in a while."

Satrine came a bit closer. "All right, consider this. The body is horribly mangled, but casually dumped off. If this had been a true murder, someone who wanted him dead, they would have been as emotionally invested in getting rid of the body as they were in killing him. But if it's an accident . . ."

"Yes," Welling said, snapping his fingers. "Then there's no investment. The dead man is an inconvenience, as he mostly represents . . ." He thought for a moment. "He represents something dangerous they're trying to keep quiet."

"Like what?"

"Something with animals," Welling said. "Those injuries could be from an animal."

Leppin nodded. "Something vicious."

"Another dogfighting ring?" Satrine offered. "We've broken up a few in the past couple months."

"I don't think this was dogs," Leppin said. He pointed to one of the enormous gashes on the man's chest. "That's not a bite. Not of any dog I've ever seen."

Satrine's gaze moved from the wound to one of the bits of unsullied flesh. Near where the neck met the shoulder was a reddish-purple mark. "Leppin, clean off the blood by his neck."

"Eh?" He pulled out a rag and wiped it away. It was definitely purple, and not an injury from the mauling. "That's a birthmark, isn't it?"

"Pretty strange one," Leppin said.

"Of note?" Welling asked.

"Of note, indeed," Satrine said. Memory flared up. "I think I know who our dead man is, Inspector. And I have a suspicion that fits our theory."

Gregor Henk had been a few years older than Satrine. A boy always pulling a grift or a hustle, usually for his uncle, when he wasn't trying to get girls' skirts off. He was also one of those boys who thought the best way to get girls' attention was to walk around their corners with his shirt half open. That had never gotten Satrine's interest, but she couldn't deny that it worked on several of the neighborhood girls at the time.

Satrine could never even contemplate it, since she had always been repulsed by the ugly purple birthmark on his neck and shoulder.

"Gregor Henk," she told Welling as they walked down Selim. "A lot of mouth on that boy, and not much else. To be honest, I'm surprised he lived this long."

"You're certain of that?" Welling asked.

"That birthmark is quite the giveaway."

"So where are we going?"

"Giles Henk was his uncle. Kept a few tenement flops in one of the side alleys off of Selim. Was one of those guys who did his best to put crowns in his pocket by getting kids to work the streets for him. You know the type, gives them a place to bed down, but at a price."

"You ever?" Welling asked.

"I did a lot of things back then to stay warm and fed." She had done even worse as an agent in Druth Intelligence. Despite that, she had then been blessed with fourteen years of "normal" life with a doting husband in the Constabulary and two brilliant daughters. Everything had fallen on her shoulders when her husband was beaten and drowned nearly to his death. The work she was now doing, on her old streets, if that was her account coming due, she could live with that.

"So you're saying Giles Henk is our killer?"

"I'm saying Giles is probably who dumped the body.

A block away and incredibly lazy. So he was involved, or knows who is."

"Presuming he's still alive," Welling offered. "He'd be an old man now."

"I'm sure he is," Satrine said. "He's the sort of man who always manages to survive."

They approached the door, shabby and paint peeling, tucked away in a below-ground stairwell in the back of the alley. Some of Inemar had cleaned up over the years, but this part certainly hadn't. Even the backhouse was still there at the end, though it was little more than a rotten skeleton of wood and shingles. The slightest touch would likely collapse it.

Satrine wondered if that was the one she had been locked inside that one winter night. The memory of it happening was so clear, but now that she thought about it, she couldn't quite recall which backhouse it was.

Inspector Welling was already rapping his knuckles on the door.

"No response," he said after a minute.

"Let me try something," Satrine said. She gave a single hard knock, followed by six quick raps, and then waiting a moment, concluding with another hard knock.

"Really? A secret knock?" Welling almost looked offended.

"That's the kind of bloke this guy is," she said. "That's what he thinks clever is."

The door opened a crack, and a leathery face covered in white hair appeared. "That's an old code. Ain't heard it in years."

"But you remembered it," Satrine said.

"Course I did. Who the blazes are you?"

"City Constabulary, Mister Henk," Welling said. "We'd like to ask you a few questions about your nephew. May we enter?"

"Suppose," he said, stepping back. "What's that fool gotten into now?"

Satrine entered the place, which smelled like sewage and rotten meat. Her stomach rebelled for a moment, but she held it down.

The old man was still every inch Giles Henk, wearing nothing but dirty skivs, his scrawny body covered in a shaggy fleece of white hair. There was little furniture, and that which was there—a table and a couple chairs—Satrine would swear were the same ones from twenty years ago. The floor was covered in refuse—mostly newsprints, the kind often used to wrap potatoes or strikers or fish crisps.

Henk sat down at the table and poured himself a cup of vinegary-smelling cider.

Welling took the place in stride. "We've found your nephew Gregor, dead from multiple injuries, in a nearby alley."

"Did you?" Henk took a long drink and poured another cup. "Somebody get a jump on him?"

"It didn't seem to be someone—" Satrine started.

"Because he ran up debts, I can tell you. Someone was going to grab hold of him one day or another and make him pay."

"Could you name anyone who might have a particular grievance? That could help our investigation."

Henk screwed up his face. "Name anyone? I'd have to think about it."

"Don't hurt yourself," Satrine said.

"I know you, red?" he asked. Even with Satrine's uncommon hair color, he didn't recognize her. Maybe his eyes were going.

"We've met before," Satrine said. "I've been down here before." She pointed to the door in the back of the room. "I remember some of the things that happened back there."

"Oh, what?" Henk asked. "I don't know what you're talking about."

"So you don't have kids sacked out back there? Maybe a couple you can lend to your friends?"

"Aw, blazes, no. Been a long damn time since anything like that happened here."

The man had no shame about his past. She almost admired that.

"So what's back there now?" Welling asked, approaching the door.

Henk jumped out of his chair, quite spryly for an old man. "Some of my mates are, you know, sleeping off their cider. They'd be pretty cranky if you go back there."

Welling raised an eyebrow, and then pounded on the back door. "City Constabulary! Come out and be identified!"

A sound came from the back room, but it definitely didn't come from one of Henk's friends. Or anything human.

Henk was unfazed. "See, pretty cranky."

Satrine was on her feet. "You aren't keeping kids back there anymore?"

"No, no, red. I got nothing back there with kids. I tell you, I don't do that no more."

She looked to Welling. "Cause?" A complex question reduced to one word. Legally they had no right to charge into a private residence. Even having been invited inside to one room, they couldn't arbitrarily go through a closed door. The City Protector would throw out their arrest if they did that. Unless they had cause—a sincere belief that there was active crime or imminent danger that required immediate action.

Welling responded by drawing his handstick, which she took for agreement.

"Hey, you don't wanna—" was all Henk got out before they were at the door, pushing it open. Satrine pulled out her crossbow and took point. She'd been in this place before, after all. She doubted it could really surprise her.

She took only a few steps into the dim room before her foot slipped. She lurched forward, and realized that there was now a pit dug into what had been an earthen floor. She forced herself back, almost crashing into Welling.

"Saints," she muttered, and Welling's hand on her shoulder steadied her. "What is this, Henk?"

"I think we've found Gregor's killer," Welling said, pointing into the pit. Satrine couldn't see into it very well, but even in the darkness she could see something large and hairy moving about.

Then it bellowed up at them.

"A rutting bear?" Satrine asked.

Before Welling could respond, they were struck from behind, sending the both of them careening into the pit with the bear.

Satrine landed badly—her left leg still hadn't fully recovered from getting stabbed during her first case with Welling—but rolled with the impact. Her crossbow fired wildly, striking the bear in its leg.

Welling landed like a cat, and moved to Satrine to aid her to her feet.

"Good luck down there, officers!" Henk yelled from the lip of the pit. "He's probably not too hungry, so you might make it!"

The bear roared and charged at the both of them. Getting shot probably did not improve its mood at all. Its massive claws swept in at Satrine's head.

Before she could move away, the bear's paw slammed into a patch of empty air as if it were solid steel.

Welling's hand was held out in front of him, a blue nimbus surrounding it. The bear struck again, its paw again bouncing off of apparently nothing.

"Thanks," Satrine said. Welling avoided using his magic, since he was Uncircled—no Mage Circle would ever cooperate with the Constabulary or take an active officer as a member. It was dangerous for an Uncircled mage to do magic in public, with no legal protection against a mage-fearing populace. Also as an Uncircled mage, he was untrained, using his magical abilities mostly on instinct.

Sweat beaded up on his brow. "I cannot hold it back indefinitely," he grunted through tight teeth. The bear growled and pressed against the solid wall of nothing.

Satrine reloaded her crossbow, took aim, and fired. She hit, center of the bear's chest. It howled and slammed its paws against the force that Welling was holding up. Welling dropped to his knees, both hands held above his head.

"Takes more than that to kill a bear, red!" Henk yelled from the top of the pit.

Satrine grabbed Welling's crossbow off his belt. "Hold it still!"

"I will endeavor," Welling said. Making a noise like a wagon crashing, he came up on his feet and brought up his other hand. The blue nimbus shifted to an angry green, with sparks and snaps flying from his left hand. The bear flung back against the wall of the pit, its arms pinned by the green. Its great maw opened wide in a deafening roar.

Satrine took her shot.

The bolt buried itself deep in the back of the bear's throat. With a pathetic whine, it dropped to the ground.

Welling did the same.

"You all right?" Satrine asked him.

"Just need a moment," he wheezed out. "Mister Henk."

Satrine needed no further prodding. She jumped up on the rough wall of the pit—crudely constructed, easy enough to climb once there was no bear trying to maul her. In a matter of seconds she was over the edge of the pit and back in Henk's sitting room.

She had her handstick drawn, but Henk wasn't there. His front door hung open, swinging idly. Not that she could blame him for running. Trying to kill two Constabulary inspectors was going to get him many, many years in Quarrygate.

Satrine ran out into the alley. Her bad leg twinged, not wanting to work this hard. She ignored it as best she could and pressed on. Henk was stumbling his way toward the street, trying desperately to go as quickly as he could while pulling his pants on. He was carrying his boots in his teeth.

"Henk! Stand and be held!"

The old man gave a frightened cry, letting the boots drop to the ground. He tore off, barefooted, into the street.

Satrine sprinted down after him, pushing through the protests her leg was giving her. As she ran, she felt a small smile creep on her face.

She was going to enjoy this far more than she should.

Satrine closed the distance in moments—it wasn't hard to catch up to a barefoot old man in half-fastened pants—and brought her handstick down on his shoulder. As he tumbled down, she added another shot to his back. As soon as he was on the ground, she pinned him with her knee.

"Mister Giles Henk, you are lawfully bound," she said, pulling her irons off her belt. "You are accused of crimes and will receive fair trial." Shackling his hands behind him, she pulled him back up on his feet.

"Name my crimes," Henk said. This was the common response, and lifelong sludges like Henk were familiar enough with the rituals of arrest to know that the specific crimes they were to be charged with had to be identified.

Much of the law involved protecting common people from spurious arrests and Constabulary abuse, including this.

Welling came up, still looking pale and winded. "You are charged with harboring a dangerous animal in residence without license. You are charged with reckless care of that animal, resulting in the death of Gregor Henk. You are charged with attempting to kill two officers of the City Constabulary."

"Hey, hey," Henk said. "I never did nothing of that sort. I just bumped into the two of you, it was all dark in there, and you fell in the pit."

"Tell it to the City Protector's Office," Satrine said. "You are obliged to come without incident."

Henk shrugged and started to walk.

"You don't look well," Satrine said to Welling as they made their way back to the stationhouse.

"That was draining," he said. "I'll be fine once I eat something."

Satrine sighed. "I suppose there's always the fast roll cart outside the stationhouse. Though I honestly cannot fathom how you choose to eat those things. I still can't figure out what meat she's using."

"It isn't choice," Welling said. "It's necessity."

<hr/>

Minox knew it was patently absurd to order three fast wraps from Missus Wolman while Inspector Rainey waited to the side, holding their arrest at bay in irons. Not that Giles Henk was resisting in any way. Minox wasn't worried that Henk would attempt to escape. He was clearly far too afraid of Inspector Rainey's wrath.

Inspector Rainey herself clearly didn't mind the inconvenience, but she had grown accustomed to the eccentricities of their partnership, specifically with Minox's eating habits.

"Looks like you've got one there," Missus Wolman said as she seared the meat on her flat grill. "What'd he do?"

"That wouldn't be appropriate to disclose," Minox said.

"It's all a trump, lady," Henk said.

Inspector Rainey responded by smacking him across the head.

Missus Wolman scooped the meat onto fresh flatbreads, and rolled them into old newsprint. "He's getting what's coming to him, I can tell."

"That's for trial to decide," Minox said. He took the wraps from her, passing coins in excess of their cost. "Greatly appreciated."

She shrugged, "You're my best customer, Inspector. Even with that one giving me the eye."

"Sheep hearts, am I right?" Inspector Rainey asked.

"I could charge three times this for sheep heart!" Missus Wolman snapped. Inspector Rainey seemed to enjoy this little war she had with Missus Wolman over the contents of the wraps. At this point it was nigh impossible that Inspector Rainey had not accurately guessed the makeup of the meat mixture, but Missus Wolman held fast to her refusals. Thus Rainey made more and more outlandish accusations.

"You have a good afternoon," Minox told her. He put two of the wraps in his coat pocket and tucked into the third.

"Come along, Henk," Inspector Rainey said, pulling him with them toward the stationhouse.

"I don't suppose you could spare me one of those wraps, mate," Henk said. "I mean, who knows when I'll be eating something real again."

"Spare me your tears, Henk," Rainey said. "Both the holding cell here, as well as Quarrygate, will square you just fine. You won't go hungry. Unlike the kids you kept."

"Oy, red, that was ages ago. You really are grudging me."

Minox had put together a rough sense of what Inspector Rainey's childhood on the streets of Inemar had been, and from what he had gathered, going hungry under Henk's negligence was far from the worst of it.

They entered into the main work floor of the stationhouse, placing Henk on the bench for incoming arrests. "Bringing one in," Rainey said to the duty officer.

The duty officer kept his attention on his ledger.

Rainey slammed her hand on his desk. "One for you to process."

The duty officer looked up. "Sorry, Tricky. Didn't hear any Constabulary walk in here."

"Fine," she said, ignoring his rudeness. In her two months in the Constabulary, she had had to do that on a daily basis. As much as Minox disliked his fellow officers' attitudes, he understood why they behaved that way. The fact that Satrine Rainey had started her career in the Constabulary as an Inspector Third Class was more than enough to grind any patrolman's teeth. When it became public that her hiring had been the result of forgery and fraud, the rancor among the Green and Red turned viscous and vicious. Despite that, Captain Cinellan had kept her on at an inspector's rank, entirely due to her merit.

As far as Minox was concerned, Satrine Rainey was an officer of remarkable insight and skill, and deserved her position regardless of the unorthodox manner in which she had achieved it. She was the only partner he had been assigned who was worth his trouble. He owed her his very life, and was proud to have her by his side.

Of course, given his status as an Uncircled mage, something that was an open secret within the stationhouse, he wasn't much more beloved by the lower ranks.

She navigated the difficulties of the duty officer ably enough, and Henk was processed and taken off. She also had them send a few patrolmen to Henk's home to seal it up. She definitely took a bit of glee in telling them to take care of the bear carcass.

"That's right," she said. "A bear. It's a shame, but we had to put it down."

"You . . . killed a bear?" the duty officer asked.

She just winked at him and left for the inspectors' floor, Minox leaving with her.

Minox finished his second fast wrap in the meantime, and started to feel some small amount of recovery from his magical drain. He had been hard and sloppy, which was understandable in the moment, but he wasn't happy with himself. In the past two months he had been exploring his magical ability, and thought he had gotten more of a handle on how to control it. The messiness of today's magic, leaving him far more weakened than it ever should have, showed him that he still had plenty of work to do.

He flexed his left hand. Much of that messiness had come from there, and it was numb again. That had been a recurring problem in the past months, ever since the arm had been broken by one of Nerrish Plum's strange magic-sapping spikes. The break had healed—quite quickly and cleanly, according to the ward surgeon and Aunt Beliah—but his hand never felt quite right again. He wondered if the spike had had a residual effect on his magical ability, at least as far as his left hand was concerned.

Those spikes were somewhere in the stationhouse as evidence. Minox would want to investigate them further, but he didn't even know where to begin. He didn't have the knowledge base, and anyone properly trained would never speak to him about it.

The inspectors' floor was all but deserted, which was unusual, even in the middle of the afternoon. "Everyone out on call?" Minox asked Rainey.

Nyla Pyle—the inspectors' floor's secretary officer, as well as Minox's cousin—came out from one of the back rooms. "There you are. I was about to send pages out on an All-Eyes for you."

"We were on our assigned case," Minox said. Nyla walked past them both to her desk at the floor entrance. "Is something going on?"

"I don't know what, exactly," she said. "But it was big enough that the captain went out there."

Captain Cinellan rarely went out on the streets himself. The situation must be either dire or delicate for the captain to take direct action.

"Is it a murder?" Inspector Rainey asked.

"I think it is," Nyla said, though she addressed her response to Minox, never looking directly at Inspector Rainey. Nyla had taken the revelations of Rainey's subterfuge and fraud far harder than anyone else in the stationhouse. She somehow managed to perform her duties administrating the inspectors' floor while avoiding all direct contact with her. She even left Rainey's tea on her desk for her every morning without a word.

"And he wants us, specifically, to go out there?" Rainey pressed, despite Nyla ignoring her.

"Inspectors Kellman and Mirrell are already out there," Nyla said, still directing her eyes at Minox. "As well as Leppin and his team."

"Leppin has a team?" Rainey asked Minox.

"There's that boy who does the charcoal sketches," he offered.

"And a slew of patrol officers," Nyla continued. "Despite that, a page delivered a note from the captain telling me to send you two—by name—out to Peston and Linley as quickly as possible." She took the note off her desk and handed it over. Minox scanned the captain's note. It offered little more to elucidate the nature of the investigation, but it did make the urgency clear. They were to requisition horses from the stables and come up at whistle gallop.

"Did you tell the stables—" Minox started.

"Two racers at the ready for you," Nyla said. "Just head on down."

"Efficient as always," he told her as they went toward the back stairs.

"Don't you forget it!" she called after them.

"Peston and Linley," Rainey said absently as she restocked her quarrel of crossbow bolts. She must have grabbed them as they passed their desks. "That's up in the northern part of the neighborhood, right?"

"That's right," Minox said. "Deep in the heart of the Little East."

Chapter 2

THE LITTLE EAST wasn't part of Satrine's world when she was growing up in Inemar. Her corners were Jent and Tannen, down near the southeastern tip of the neighborhood, close to The Lower Bridge. Until she was fourteen, she'd barely ever gone north of Upper Bridge Road, or across the river. Even going west of Promenade had been a rarity.

The Little East had been little more than rumors and wild speculation amongst her people. A few kids she'd known would wander up Fannen, and come back with crazy stories. Multiple enclaves of foreign people, with their strange appearances, food, languages—Fuergans, Imachs, Racquin, and who even knew exactly what else, all living just a few blocks away.

Another world from her corners.

Four of them had grabbed her, as she had slipped down the alley to the backhouse. They had been waiting for her there, but they weren't the usual rats who hung about in Inemar. These were men. She gave them as much brawl as she could, but they moved quick and hard. A hood went over her head, her hands bound behind her, and then she was in a wooden crate. It all happened in a few clicks.

She could feel the crate being loaded into a wagon. She cried out, kicked and thrashed, but it didn't do any damn good. It was rolling off to saints knew where. She had heard stories like this. Girls her age being grabbed and dragged off to be doxy slaves. Enough boys in the neighborhood wanted her with her Waishen red hair, so she'd imagine the degenerates who bought young girls would be interested. Creeps.

She wasn't going to go easy, though.

In the dark of the crate, she took deep breaths and bided her time. Her hands were tied up, but that wasn't going to keep her. They hadn't done it all that tight, so she was able to work her hands free. Then she had the hood off. They'd open the crate and whoever was there would get a face full of her fist. Then she'd fight like blazes to get out, or make them kill her before she was ever sold.

The wagon pulled inside somewhere, she could hear, and came to a stop. The crate was taken down and put on the floor. She heard voices—men talking.

"You really think she's right?"

"It's uncanny, I'm telling you."

"Let's see."

The crate opened, and she drove her fist into the first stupid face she saw. She sprang out of the crate, jammed her knee into the same man's goods. He went down, and she pushed past him.

"Got some spunk in her!" said one man.

There were three of them at the door, clubs and knives at their hips. No windows, no other way out that she saw, save a dark back room. She wasn't going to go that way. She spun around and put the wall at her back.

"Easy, easy," one man said. "No one's going to hurt you."

"Right," she said. "Because you wouldn't want to damage the merchandise, right?"

"Merchandise?" the man asked, sounding genuinely confused.

"Your little gang of doxy slavers ain't gonna take me quiet, hear?"

The man laughed. *"You're right, Keeter. She's perfect. But it's gonna be a lotta work. What's your name, girl?"*

"They call me Tricky."

"What's your name?" He said it with a force that almost compelled her to answer honestly.

"Satrine."

"Satrine," he said calmly, *"We need your help."*

"Who's we?"

He chuckled. *"Your king and country."*

She couldn't help but laugh. *"Like either of those ever gave a blazes for me. I ain't your girl. Doxy or otherwise."*

"You're the only one who can help us, Satrine." He sounded so blazing sincere.

"A corner bird like me?" she asked. *"What the blazes can I do for you?"*

He turned to one of the other guys. *"Bring her out."*

Two men went into the dark room, and came back pushing a wheeled table. A table with a girl on it. A dead girl.

"Blazes, is this sewage?" Tricky asked.

"This is why we need you," the man said. *"Come take a look."*

Tricky stepped closer. Then she saw the girl was also Waishen-haired. Another step closer, and she could really see the dead girl's face. Her own face. Clean and fresh, but still the very face she saw in dirty shop window reflections. *"This some kind of sick rutting joke? Why you have a dead girl who looks like me?"*

"We need you, Satrine, because you look like her."

"Why?"

"Because no one can know that she's dead. That's where you come in."

Tricky laughed. *"What, am I supposed to fake being her?"*

"Yes, Satrine. That's it exactly."

The whinny of the horses pulled her out of the memory.

Welling had pulled himself up into his saddle like it was second nature. She knew he had started Constabulary in horsepatrol, and he took to riding like a robin to the sky. Satrine knew how to ride—one of the many bits of mannerly education crammed into her skull when she had to learn how to be a Waish *quia*. She and horses were acquainted with each other, nothing more. She never had the bond that Welling seemed to form immediately with any animal under him.

"Shh, shh," Welling said to his mount. "You're going to get to really run today."

"Whistle gallop?" Satrine said as she followed him out the stable on her own horse.

Welling flashed her a smile, which never looked quite natural on his face. But in this instance, it actually showed hints of genuine joy. "You're first time doing one, yes?"

"You would know, right?"

"Follow my lead, then." He pulled his Constabulary whistle out of his pocket, and Satrine did the same. "We'll take Ironheart to Fannen, and then take that north to Linley. Best to stick to the widest roads for this."

"Makes sense."

Welling was about to put his whistle in his mouth, then hesitated. "One bit of advice. If you should stumble—"

"I won't." She may not love it like Welling did, but she could ride.

"If you should," he stressed, "try to spit out your whistle. I've seen some gruesome injuries from a failure to do so."

"Fair enough," she said, and placed her whistle in her mouth. Leaving it there, held in her teeth, she took hold of her reins.

Welling nodded, and then let fly three long, shrill blasts. She followed suit. Having done that, he drove his heels into his horse's flank, and spurred it into a gallop. Satrine took off after him.

They pounded together down Ironheart, both blasting their whistles as they charged. People in the streets scattered out of the way, doing their best to clear the road. Pedalcarts and carriages pulled off to the side, and when things couldn't move fast enough, Welling steered around the obstacles expertly.

Satrine's own horse was well-trained, like any Constabulary horse would be, and followed Welling's lead. She mostly needed to hold on and trust her horse's instinct, trust Welling's skill to navigate through the crowd.

They turned up Fannen, a wide thoroughfare that had always struck Satrine as fancy and clean when she was a little girl. Now it seemed as dull and ordinary as the rest of Inemar, as the rest of all of Maradaine. Stone buildings, several stories high, with storefronts at street level. Iron grates over windows. Steel gates hanging open, so each store showed they were open, but could lock themselves away at a moment's notice. The people in the street were just as pedestrian, walking with tense caution. No one making eye contact, but everyone keeping their eyes on everyone else. Of course, with her and Welling racing through on a whistle gallop, all eyes went to them.

Traffic of oxcarts and carriages and pedalists seized up at the crossing of Fannen and High Bridge, as a footpatrolman, clearly having heard the whistle blasts, held the intersection open for them. He gave them a brief salute as they pounded through.

Past the large thoroughfare, which had once been the unofficial border of Satrine's life, they were out of an area that was instinctively familiar. The city was still much the same; nothing magical happened to the surroundings now that they were in the northern part of the neighborhood.

For another four blocks.

Then, on her right side, things changed. The buildings were built all the same, but the steel gates vanished. Signs were now symbols instead of Trade letters. People changed, with duskier skins and wide straw hats.

Welling turned right, onto Linley. A good Druth name for a street.

But she wasn't in Druthal anymore when they turned.

Grays and whites of the stone buildings were gone. Yellows and oranges on her right, a cacophony of color on her left. Signs on the right were symbols of one kind, completely different on the left, and yet further differences up ahead on Linley.

Even the windows changed, the bunting on the awnings.

And the faces. Suddenly the fair Druth complexions with tawny brown hair were a minority.

And people weren't moving out of the way for a whistle blast.

Welling came to a halt, and Satrine stopped short. She almost stumbled off the horse, but recovered before she would have had to spit her whistle out. Which was good, because Welling probably wouldn't have let her live that down for several weeks.

There was a man with a wheelbarrow far larger than he should be trying to push on his own—with his goods covered by raw canvas—blocking most of the road. The man—dusky skinned with thick freckles dotting his face, wearing a wide straw hat and a rough woolen blanket as if it was a coat—shouted something at Welling.

Welling, for his part, shouted something right back, and seemingly in the same language.

Satrine led her horse next to Welling's. "Kellirac?"

He shrugged. "Racquin. I know a few words from my mother."

"She's Racquin?" That shouldn't have been surprising, with his given name.

"Grew up somewhere over there in Caxa," he said, pointing vaguely into the canvas-tented alley to their right. He used the proper name for the tiny enclave, instead of the more common Quin Row.

They worked their way around the impasse, no longer able to race. They were only one proper block away from their destination, though, so it was no longer urgent to press quite as hard.

"So what did he say to you?"

"I'm honestly not sure. Something about too many of us."

"Constabulary, or Druthalians?"

"Maybe it's all the same."

The crossroads of Linley and Kainen was the strangest Satrine had seen. Each corner was completely different in style. They had just come through a Kellirac section, and cat-corner from that was recognizably Kieran. The other two were mysteries to her.

Welling seemed to pick up on that, pointing to the area on their left they had just passed. "The Hodge, they call that. Most of the blocks around here are pretty clearly defined. Dexliari, the Kieran enclave is there. The Tsouljan one, Tek Andor, is there. The Hodge is all a mix, mostly from parts of the world that don't have much presence here."

Tsouljan. That was where they were going, clearly, as several Constabulary regulars were holding a perimeter around one of the buildings. Satrine didn't know much about Tsoulja, even in the deep depths of her special training.

The Tsouljan buildings weren't painted, but their windows and doorways were all adorned with colored braids of ribbon, purples and whites the dominant colors, tied to wooden balusters with intricately carved spirals. Lines of bunting with similar ribbon braids ran down the stretch of Linley, culminating in a spiderweb of strings, right in front of the building the regulars were guarding.

The poor footpatrol stood out like blood in the street, and not just for their red and green uniforms. Their Druth complexion was notably paler than the nearly golden-hued Tsouljans in their rough robes, tied off with multiple sashes.

Of course, with the Tsouljans, the thing that caught Satrine's eye was their hair. Each one, man and woman alike, had their long hair in thick braids, so thick it made the hair stand up. The braids were dressed further with ribbons woven into the braids and then dangling down their shoulders. And the hair itself was dyed in bright, unnatural colors: red, yellow, blue, and green. The red was not Satrine's Waishen-haired shade, but rather the bright red of a rose petal, which no person would ever naturally have.

Satrine had heard—many years back when she first saw a Tsouljan—that their natural hair color tended to be very fair, almost white. But she had never seen it.

"Oy, specs," one of the footpatrol called. "Over here's the call."

Welling dismounted and handed his reins to the footpatrol. "We're shy on details. Has there been a murder?"

"Quite a murder." Captain Cinellan emerged from the doorframe of the building, which was clearly the largest structure in the Tsouljan part of the Little East. The gray-haired officer often looked worn out, but in this moment his pallor was more sallow than Satrine had seen it. He looked like he had lived five years since this morning.

"Big enough to have us race over, Captain?" Satrine asked.

"It's . . . I don't even know." He gave a chuckle, devoid of any amusement. "Remember how I threatened you two with the strange ones? This is where I make good on that."

———————— ◆◆ ————————

Minox felt like he had been transported somewhere utterly foreign—even in the context of the Little East—as he crossed the threshold into the Tsouljan enclave. If it weren't for the uniformed Constabulary officers, the illusion of leaving Maradaine would have been complete. The inside was not a building at all, but a sprawling open-air courtyard, a garden of pebble paths, finely trimmed shrubs, and small pools. A series of small huts—wooden domes—dotted the area. The most notable features were the trees, since they were clearly not native to Druthal. The leaves were so dark they almost looked blue, and they were in full bloom with bright violet flowers.

Two Tsouljans flanked the inside of the threshold, both with red-dyed hair and coarse robes. They bowed their heads upon each person's entrance, saying the same phrase each time: "Qhat nek dav."

Captain Cinellan waved them off as he passed. Minox nodded back to them, as did Inspector Rainey.

"I had no idea this was here," she said quietly. "What is this?"

"Near as I can tell, they call it Rev Tak Mel," Captain Cinellan said. "I think it's a temple of some sort. But I was hoping you'd be able to tell me more."

"Me?" Rainey asked.

"You're the only inspector I have who has any real experience with foreign matters. We almost never have calls out here, and . . ."

"We don't," Minox said. Full investigations, especially ones where they were made such a sizable presence, were highly irregular in this part of the neighborhood. "So that, in and of itself, is notable as odd."

"Everything about this is odd, Welling," the captain

said. "And, not to put too fine a point on it, you are my expert on odd."

"I will take the compliment."

One of the huts was clearly the location they were focused on, as the Constabulary officers, as well as the bodywagon men, were concentrated around it. Also Inspectors Kellman and Mirrell were interviewing a yellow-haired Tsouljan. From the looks on their faces, they were not pleased with how their interview was going.

Being in this place gave Minox a sensation he couldn't quite understand. He felt like the place itself was exuding calm—there was a quiet to the place, and every aspect of the garden seemed like it should lend itself to serenity. But what he was feeling was anything but that. Instead, he felt agitation and unease, and he had difficulty understanding why.

It was not unlike the moments when his magic slipped out of his control.

"Can you give us some particulars, sir?" Rainey asked. "Like you said, we don't get called out here much. Is this place an embassy? Are we on Tsouljan ground right now?"

"It is not," a slightly accented voice said from behind them. A green-haired Tsouljan, barely more than a boy, was on his hands and knees. At first Minox thought this was some form of supplication, but then he saw the truth: the boy was pulling tiny shoots of grass out from the pebble path. "This is a place of Tsouljan making, but it is every bit Druth soil."

"Well, that clears that up," Rainey said. She crouched down in front of the boy. "Your Trade is pretty good. How long have you been here?"

The boy looked up from his work. "I was born here."

"So what is this place?" she asked.

The boy scowled. "It is not my place to say. My place is to maintain." He went back to his work.

Cinellan pulled them a few steps away. "Jurisdiction is not an issue. In fact, it was the residents of this ... place who called us in."

Minox pointed to the yellow-haired Tsouljan being interviewed by Kellman and Mirrell. "He reported it?"

"That's right," Cinellan said. "Went to a whistlebox, brought a patrol officer over, and told him to summon the Inspector Captain. He knew what was going on was ... huge."

Rainey spoke up. "Sir, if I may, you're being needlessly vague. Beyond the murder occurring in this Tsouljan temple enclave, what is so unique about this murder?"

"The victim, primarily," the captain said. He pulled out his leather notebook. "Let me try and get this right. Hieljam ab Wefi Loriz lek Lavark."

"Fuergan?" Minox asked, recognizing the format. In his time frequenting his favorite tobacconist in the Fuergan section of the Little East, he had gained some familiarity with the culture. 'Hieljam' would be the family name, and 'Wefi Loriz' his given names.

"And that's the short version of his name, apparently," the captain said. "But the important part for us to note is the 'Lavark' part."

Inspector Rainey suddenly gasped. "That ... no, are you sure about that, sir?"

"Quite," Cinellan said.

"Enlighten me," Minox said. His experience had not taught him what "Lavark" meant.

"It's a rank of nobility—well, not exactly, because Fuergans don't have quite the same—that doesn't matter." Inspector Rainey whistled through tight teeth. "What matters is it looks like we have a Fuergan equivalent of an earl, murdered on Druth soil."

Chapter 3

MIRRELL AND KELLMAN STORMED AWAY from their interview and closed the distance to Minox and Rainey, but their focus was purely on Captain Cinellan.

"These blasted tyzos aren't giving us a damn thing we can use," Mirrell said. It was no shock to Minox that a man like Mirrell would call the Tsouljans here "tyzos." He gestured vaguely to the man they had been talking to. "That one is the only one even telling us anything."

"And who is that, besides our prime witness?" Minox asked.

"That's Burekuti," Mirrell said, glancing at his scratch pad.

"No, no," Kellman said. He put on an exaggerated Tsouljan accent. "Bur Rek-Uti."

"Some decorum, gentlemen," Minox said. "He's the one who found the body and reported it to Constabulary. We should be grateful."

"Very grateful," Mirrell said. "These tyzos kill a feek, and then tell us about it."

Mirrell was, as always, an inspector with no knack for investigation. He came to immediate conclusions and held to them with rock-solid certainty. When a case was clear-cut, he was usually correct, but he saw every case as clear-cut.

Minox spoke up. "In your estimation, someone in this enclave is responsible for the death of Hieljam?"

"Makes sense," Kellman said, stepping forward in a vain attempt to intimidate Minox with his height, as was his usual pattern. "Who else is around here? Blazes, the only ways in have got a couple red-hairs—sorry, Tricky— red-hairs bowing and muttering every time someone enters. They'd have seen anyone else coming in. But they ain't talking."

"They haven't talked to us," Rainey said. "Probably because we haven't asked the right questions."

"Which are?" Mirrell asked.

"For one, how do we know the dead man is Hieljam ab Wefi Loriz?" Rainey remembered the Fuergan name perfectly. "Does he have his Papers of Transit on him or something?"

Mirrell smirked. "Blazes, do any of these tyzos have their papers on them, I wonder."

Rainey continued, "And why was he even here?"

The gardening Tsouljan, still close to them, made a small noise. When Rainey looked at him, his attention appeared to be fully on his work.

Mirrell's face turned smug. "That I can tell you. One of the few things we got out of Burekuti over there. He had an appointment to meet someone else here."

"Near as we understood," Kellman said, gesturing at the various huts, "that happens a lot in these things. People meet each other here because it's neutral ground. Supposed to be safer, I suppose."

"Supposed to," Mirrell said. "So Heejib shows up for his meeting . . ."

"Hieljam," Rainey corrected.

"He shows up," Mirrell continued unabated, "and

goes in the hut at the time he had scheduled. Two bells in the afternoon. An hour later Berubuti or whoever goes to clean up, and finds the guy dead."

Minox took this in. "Who was he meeting? And did they even come?"

Mirrell scowled and looked to Cinellan. "Cap, what's going on? Do we have this, or are you giving it to Jinx and Tricky?"

"It's theirs," Cinellan said. Mirrell and Kellman both looked like they wanted to shout or storm off, and Mirrell shoved his scratch pad into his pocket. "But I need you two on point here as well. There's a lot of questions to ask, a lot of . . ." He gestured at the other Tsouljans working in the gardens. "People. The situation needs delicate handling. I need all my best people on it."

"Fine," Mirrell said. "Bukupi didn't know who he was meeting or if they came." Off a glare from the captain he added, "But Derrick and I will ask some more questions. Not that anyone here speaks much Trade."

"His is perfect," Rainey said, pointing to the young gardener. "You, boy, what's your name?"

"Nuf Rup-Sed," the boy said with a bow.

"Go with these officers, Nuf," Rainey said. "They're going to interview other people in the enclave, and you will translate to the best of your ability."

"That is not my place," Nuf Rup-Sed said. He pointed to his hair, as if that was all the answer needed. "Perhaps Bur Rek-Uti, or one of the other Rek would be more suitable."

"No, no," Mirrell said. "Hearing you talk, Nuffy, you are the man for the job. Come on."

The boy made a face as if he were in physical pain, but he went with them.

Minox looked around the compound again, noting the different Tsouljans with their different dyed hair colors. Reds were at the thresholds, greens were cleaning and working the grounds. Three yellows were in discussion with each other, and a single blue-haired woman sat in quiet solitude next to one of the pools. "A class system of some sort," he said idly.

Rainey nodded. "And we just made a green-haired one do a yellow-haired's job, I think, which is probably against custom."

Minox bristled at that. It was against custom for him, an Uncircled mage, to be serving in the Constabulary. Even if he could join a Circle at this point, no Circle would want to cooperate with Constabulary. The fact that he never chose to be a mage would be irrelevant.

"There is more to the scene, Welling," the captain said, urging them along. "Come take a look."

They were led over to the hut in question, where Leppin was standing at the door. "How'd I beat you two here?"

"We had a thing with a bear," Rainey said. "That was our last killer."

"Bear. Makes sense," Leppin said, chuckling ruefully. "Well, this one is just as fun, I think."

He pushed open the door and let them in.

The interior of the hut was lit with sickly sweet–smelling candles in sconces built into the walls. A low table—not even knee high—dominated the room, and not only because of the dead body on it. There was almost no space to walk around it.

The dead man was definitely Fuergan, with the deep olive skin and long mustache. His ears were richly adorned with interlocking chains of bejeweled gold. He was wearing a long, woven vest that went down to his knees, and tight pants lined with leather, not dissimilar to the kind Constabulary horsepatrol wore. His shirt had been torn open, and a knife was plunged to the hilt into his chest.

Two things drew Minox's gaze, beyond the body. First

were the symbols written on the dead man's arm, as well as the table itself, and on the walls. Twelve symbols, in a box of four across and three down. Second was a cup of some half-drunk liquid.

"We can rule out a robbery," Rainey said. "A thief would have taken those earrings."

"Indeed," Minox said. "There's something almost . . . respectful about this murder."

"Clarify that," Rainey said. She then snapped her fingers. "I see it. Only one blow. No multiple stab wounds."

Minox nodded, crouching down to get a closer look at the symbols. "Whoever did this was not acting out of anger. Or, as you noted, theft or despair."

"So a cold, calculated murder," Rainey said. She glanced around the hut. "That door is the only way in, right?"

"Not exactly," Leppin said. He pointed to the table. "That actually opens, leading to the basements below here."

"Basements?" Minox asked. "So someone could have been down there and snuck up here."

"But not leave that way," Leppin said. "There's no way to open the trapdoor table with his body here." He pointed to the pools of blood. "At least, not without making a smeared mess of that."

"I'll trust your expertise," Minox said. "What about the symbols?"

"It's eastern writing," Rainey said. "But . . . it doesn't look Tsouljan."

"You sure?" Leppin asked.

She shook her head. "I could be wrong, but it doesn't look quite the same as the signs outside. Something else from that part of the world?" She suddenly seemed distracted, like she was lost in a memory for a moment. "Lyranan. I think it's Lyranan."

"Sounds like you know better than most," Leppin said.

"Stranger and stranger, indeed," Minox said. He picked up the cup and sniffed at it. Sweetly floral. There were even the same purple flowers from the trees outside floating in it. "Take this back with you, Leppin, and test it thoroughly."

"You're thinking poison." It wasn't a question, as Rainey nodded and followed the train of thought. "Incapacitate him, move him onto the table, and then finish with the knife."

Minox nodded in agreement. He looked at the knife again, noting something wrong about the hilt. "Leppin, could you remove the knife, please?"

"I'd really prefer to do that in my examinarium."

"I'm certain you would, but it might be crucial. Please?"

Moving like a cat, Leppin climbed up on the table and over the body. He gently wrapped one gloved hand around the hilt, while placing the other on the body's chest, and slowly slid the knife out.

The knife was curved, with the blade split into two parts. Minox had never seen anything like it. "Is that a Tsouljan knife of some sort?"

"Nah," Leppin said, eyeing it with one of the lenses on his cap. "Oh, it's a strange beauty, though. But not Tsouljan. If I were to guess, this here is an Imach blade."

Rainey started to laugh.

"Are you all right, Inspector?" Minox asked. He had noticed she occasionally had these fits of humor in serious moments, especially over a dead body. Reminding her of her rank usually brought her back.

"I'm sorry," she said, though she still laughed. "It's just . . . the whole thing is . . ." She took a deep breath, and composed herself. "My life is ridiculous. We were fighting a bear earlier today."

"I find your sense of humor quite perplexing."

"As do I."

Satrine wasn't sure what had come over her. The entire situation was dire. The Fuergans may well decide to make an incident of this murder—at least the Hieljam family likely would. She shuddered to think what it could lead to.

Blazes, her whole initiation into Druth Intelligence was to cover up the death of a Waish *quia*, and that had been an accident.

This was murder, and the Tsouljans made sure the Constabulary were involved before anyone else was. She imagined that the Sheriffs of the Archduchy, King's Marshals, and Druth Intelligence were all going to drop on their heads any moment now. Especially since it didn't just involve the Fuergan Lavark. The Tsouljans were somehow involved, and possibly Lyranans and Imachs as well.

Something about the Lyranan letters—if it was Lyranan, though she was near certain it was—threw her off balance, and she couldn't place why. Something familiar, on the edge of her memory.

Or maybe just the candles were making her head swim.

"I'll have the blade properly identified," Leppin said. "I'm guessing you want my sketchboy to get the symbols."

"Indeed," Welling said. He glanced around one more time. "I see no reason why you can't take the body to the examinarium at this juncture as well."

"Good," Leppin said.

Welling went to the dome's doorway. "This murder appears intentionally overcomplicated."

Satrine nodded as they went out. "Fuergan victim in a Tsouljan enclave with an Imach weapon and Lyranan writing. My guess is someone wanted to force us to cast a wide net."

"Hide in plain sight amongst many possible suspects.

And given that we don't have any specific suspects at this juncture."

"Save the residents of this enclave, who should all be interviewed."

"Which Inspectors Mirrell and Kellman will be handling. I'll want to review their notes once they've completed it, but I'm confident in their ability to ask the proper preliminary questions. In the meantime, we should probably focus our interviews on those closest to the victim."

"So we're going to see the Hieljam family, while Mirrell and Kellman stay here. They'll be thrilled."

"I really couldn't care about their happiness, as long as they do the work."

They emerged back out into the open-air garden. Satrine looked around, noting several of the Tsouljan residents were still going about their business. They all stayed clear of the crime scene hut, but otherwise appeared to be acting as if nothing had changed. Satrine realized that couldn't continue.

"I'm having a terrible thought," Satrine said. "We're going to have to put this whole place under lockdown."

"I concur, regrettably."

The captain was talking to a yellow-haired Tsouljan—possibly the same Bur Rek-Uti as before. Satrine went over to them both.

"Pardon me, Captain," she said, giving a slight bow of her head to the Tsouljan, which he returned. "We've seen the situation, and for the foreseeable future, we're going to have to secure this facility and all its residents."

"Secure?" the Tsouljan asked haltingly. "Meaning?"

"My apologies, sir," she said. "I'm Inspector Rainey. My partner, Inspector Welling, and I will be handling the investigation of this murder."

"No, sir," the Tsouljan said, though Satrine couldn't quite tell if he was offended. "Bur Rek-Uti."

"Mister Uti—"

"Rek-Uti!"

"Mister Rek-Uti . . ." She paused, awaiting additional correction, but received none. "Right now, we have to treat you and everyone else who is in this enclave . . ."

"Rev Tak Mel," he told her.

"Yes. We have to treat everyone here as a suspect in the murder until we've gathered more information."

Rek-Uti nodded, and spoke again in halting Trade. "You do not know who we are. You must seek answers. You must do as you are guided."

"That means everyone in here has to stay in here," the captain said. "And I can't tell you right now how long that will be."

"Duration will be endured." There was something about Rek-Uti's tone that Satrine couldn't quite figure out; it gave her no read on his emotions. He seemed to be agreeing with them, indicating he understood, but at the same time there was a sense that he was barely tolerating their presence.

The captain continued. "I'm going to put my patrolmen at the entrances to enforce that, sir, while my people continue their investigation."

"As you must. Now I as I must." He started to wander off.

"One more thing," Satrine said. "No one other than Constabulary can enter that hut."

"As it must be," Rek-Uti said. He wandered off.

Welling came over to Satrine and the captain, but his attention was fixed elsewhere as he approached.

"Something wrong, Welling?" Satrine asked.

"That woman," he said, pointing to a blue-haired Tsouljan standing in one of the ponds. She was staring at Welling with fiery intensity. "She's . . . disturbing."

"Leave it," Satrine said. "She's a problem for Kellman and Mirrell. We should get over to the Hieljam household before much longer."

The Tsouljan woman stepped out of the pool and crossed over to them, so quickly that Satrine thought she was about to attack. Satrine went for her handstick, but the woman stopped short, staring at Welling in something resembling disbelief.

"Do you have something to say, miss?" Welling asked. For his part he looked stricken, even pale.

Her head turned to one side, and then she started to speak in Tsouljan, a rapidly paced rant that grew in volume and intensity, until she was all but shouting at Welling. The she held up a hand as if to block him from replying, and stalked off to one of the huts.

"What was that?" Satrine asked him. "I know most people don't like you, Welling, but even that . . ."

"I'm not sure," he said. He stared off at the hut for a moment, and then broke out of his reverie. "You're right. We need to speak to the victim's family. Captain, if you'll excuse us, we'll be off."

Welling had composed himself for the most part, but Satrine noticed that his left hand was twitching rather significantly. Even stranger, Welling himself didn't seem to notice it.

Chapter 4

WELLING CLAIMED SOME FAMILIARITY with the Little East, and took point as he led them up Peston through the Kieran blocks—"Dexilari" on paper, "Pirie City" in practice. They had left their horses with the patrolmen and went on foot.

"So are you familiar with the Hieljam family?" Satrine asked.

"Not specifically," Welling said. "But I do have some contacts here which should help us in locating them."

He brought them to a shop on the far north side of the Little East, the Fuergan enclave called "Srenijam" by the inhabitants and "Feektown" by much of the rest of the city. They went through an open doorway, blocked only by a series of thin ropes hanging like a curtain, where they were assaulted by hazy, sweet-smelling air.

"Your tobacco shop, Welling?" Satrine asked when they entered.

"I'm a regular and well-regarded customer," he said as they approached the counter. "Ushetit sam," he said to the proprietor.

"Ushetit sam," the man replied. "I didn't expect you

today, Inspector. You've gone through your pouch quicker than usual."

"Today I'm here on my business, sadly," Welling said. "My partner, Inspector Rainey."

"Ushetai sam," the man said to her. "I am not facing trouble, Inspector? There are no crimes here."

"Nothing of the sort," Welling said. "There's been—"

Satrine coughed hard to interrupt Welling. There was no need to give this shop proprietor too much information.

Welling looked at her askance.

"My apologies," Satrine said. "We're looking for the household of the Hieljams. Do you know where that is?"

"Hieljam?" the proprietor asked, uncomfortably adjusting his short vest. "Why would you be looking for them?"

"A private matter," Satrine said before Welling could respond. "Concerning their family."

"Of course, of course," the proprietor said. "The address of their home will be one crown three."

"Pardon?" Welling asked. "That's outrageous, sir. You cannot expect us to—"

Satrine cut Welling off before he continued. "You cannot expect us to pay anything more than four ticks for that." She knew Welling was offended on principle, that Constabulary shouldn't have to pay for basic information. But at the same time she wondered how much Welling really understood about Fuergan culture, or if he just liked to smoke their tobacco.

"Let us say I take your offer of four ticks," the proprietor said. "Then it will be known how cheaply my word is for sale."

"Cheaply?" Satrine let just a little bit of her South Maradaine accent come in. "You can't be serious. I could get the address out of five blokes in here for two ticks. I'd be doing you a favor."

"Those folk would have nothing to lose. I run a business. Let us say that giving the address upsets the Hieljams, and it comes back to me."

"It wouldn't," Welling said.

"Wouldn't upset them or wouldn't come back to me?"

"Either."

"You can't guarantee that. But if I could say I was paid a crown, then they would understand why I did it."

He had gone down now. Satrine took that. "So it's less about the money in and of itself, but protecting your reputation as a respectful man of the community."

"Yes," he said, brushing at his vest. "I am Gasta ab Uhren lek Ona. I cannot be bought at the price a Kaln would take."

Satrine leaned in. "What if we give you five ticks, and say it was fifteen?"

"What if you give me fifteen and say it was a crown?"

Welling sighed heavily, reached into his pocket, and pulled out a coin. He held it up in the air and called out, "Half a crown for the address of the Hieljam family home!" Satrine wondered if Welling was aware how much he had just stepped on the toes of his tobacconist. Even if he got a deal now, the cost of his favorite smoke probably just went up.

Several Fuergans throughout the establishment stood up, but no one spoke. Instead they all started making complex hand signals—including and especially the proprietor. This lasted for only a few seconds, and then the proprietor slammed his hand on the counter.

One man stepped forward toward Satrine and Welling. "I am your guide."

Welling started to hand the man the coin, but the proprietor hissed at him. "Inspector. To me."

The guide—who Satrine noticed was wearing a vest that was little more than woven circlets around his arms—gave a signal of agreement. Welling handed the coin over.

"With me, then," the guide said with a thick accent, and he led them out.

As they walked, Welling leaned in and spoke in a low voice, "What was that you were doing?"

"Respecting their custom," Satrine said. "I thought you said you knew these people."

"I expected Gasta to be helpful. I've been a loyal customer for years."

"A customer. You pay for service. He's not your friend."

"Well, no . . ."

"And for Fuergans, every service is paid for."

Welling screwed his face in thought. "Do they have city constabulary, fire brigade, or such things?"

Satrine didn't know. "I'm not sure how things work in their cities. I've never been to Fuerga, I've only dealt with a handful of them before."

"In Intelligence."

She lowered her voice a bit more, hoping their guide wouldn't overhear. "Speaking of, let's not discuss what we're investigating too openly just yet. It could create quite a problem for Intelligence and Druth diplomacy."

"As you wish, but those things are not my problem, Inspector Rainey. My concern is solving this crime."

"Fair enough, but . . . we should strive to be delicate in our dealings, especially with the Hieljams."

"I can handle myself fine, Inspector."

The guide had led them around the corner to a three-story building, almost dead in the center of the Fuergan blocks of the Little East. It was a tall whitestone, the kind that typically held several upscale apartments in the neighborhoods east of Inemar, or on the north side of the city. "This is the home of Family Hieljam."

"They have an apartment in this building?" Welling asked.

"This is the home of the Family Hieljam," the guide

repeated, and he gave them a strange hand signal and walked away.

"This is what I'm talking about, Welling," Satrine said. "These people are, for all purposes, nobility. We have to be respectful."

"I am always respectful, as long as they respect our office."

Satrine put on her best Druth highborn accent, which would be good enough for Fuergans. Someone with a proper ear for Druth accents would spot her as a fraud, most likely. "I'm simply saying, with these people, I should take the point."

Welling made some grumbling noises, but nodded. They went up and knocked on the door. A beefy, squat Fuergan man answered the door.

"This is not a time," he said as he saw them.

"My apologies," Satrine said. "We have urgent business with the household."

The man muttered something in a Fuergan dialect.

Satrine pointed to her vest. "Constabulary. We must speak with the household."

The man frowned and shut the door.

"That didn't go well," Welling said. "Perhaps we're interrupting their evening meal. 'This is not a time.'"

"It's conceivable," Satrine said. It was nearly six bells already. She should be heading home, having dinner with the girls, checking on Loren. "We should be signing out shortly."

"It depends on what this yields. We might need to stay on duty for the duration of investigation."

Missus Abernand would hate that. She groused whenever Satrine returned after sunset. So there was no time to waste. She pounded on the door again.

The squat man opened again. "This is not a time."

Satrine wasn't going to let him hold them off again. Shoving a foot into the doorway—technically a Constabulary violation—she threw some additional haughtiness into her Druth Highborn, channeling the phony princess she had pretended to be for several years. "You will run and fetch your betters, for we must have words unfit for your ears!"

That stopped the little man short, and he stepped back, allowing them entrance into the antechamber. Shutting the door behind them, he scurried off without word.

"That got us in the door," Welling said.

Rich scents hit Satrine's nose, musky and savory. "You may have been right about the evening meal."

"I'm always right about meals."

It had been a bit since he had had those fast wraps, and those were an emergency. Welling might very well need to eat something soon. "Are you all right, as far as that goes?"

"I'm fine for the moment. But perhaps you are right that we should sign out shortly."

"You live just over in Keller Cove, right? You could go straight there from here, make dinner in the Welling home."

"We'll see what occurs, Inspector. But I appreciate the concern."

The stocky man returned and indicated for them to follow. They were led through a wide room, where the floors and walls were done entirely in tile patterns, mostly grays and reds, with designs of interlocking circles. Oil lamps—glass and bronze globes—hung from the ceiling, flickering brightly. Doorways were arches, cordoned with hanging rope curtains. They were brought through one set of ropes to another room, where two youthful Fuergans—a man and woman—were awaiting them at a low table.

"We understand that you have insisted on our hospitality," the woman said in heavily accented Trade. The two of them looked related, with similar dark hair and dusky olive features. They also both wore similar chained earrings in their left ear, matching the one the victim had. They both also wore long, woven vests, much like the victim, but neither as long. The woman's went to her hips; the man's to his waist.

Satrine remembered her training in various etiquettes and put her hand to her chest. "Apologies for intrusion, but our business was urgent."

The man spoke in thicker, broken Trade. "You . . . officials of city. What business?"

Welling stepped forward, mimicking the same action Satrine had done. "We are inspectors with the City Constabulary—Welling and Rainey."

The woman returned the gesture. "Hieljam ab Tishai Anaas mik Nural lek Heina dai Gessaan vil Fiela sim Vojin." She had used the full version of her name, and while Satrine couldn't remember exactly how to interpret the entire thing, she grabbed the crucial parts of information. "Tishai" was this woman's given name, and *heina* was her rank. Essentially a minor baroness, in Druth terms.

"Hieljam ab Orihla lek Veir," the man said, choosing the abbreviated version. He was a *veir*, outranked by the woman.

"You are the ranking members of the Hieljam household?" Satrine asked, directing it at Tishai.

"No," Tishai said, "*Natir* is my *isahresa*, ab Wefi Loriz. He is not present."

"Business wait for return," Orihla said. "Sit." He indicated the fur-lined pillows that were placed around the tables.

"I'm afraid that is why we are here," Satrine said. "Your . . . *isahresa* . . ." She hoped she pronounced that right, even if she didn't know what it meant. Familial terms in Fuergan didn't always translate cleanly. "Hieljam ab Wefi Loriz lek Lavark is dead."

Their faces were unreadable for a moment. Finally, through tight lips, Hieljam ab Tishai spoke. "Accident? Or deliberate?"

"Deliberate," Welling said.

"Then you will sit," she said. She clapped her hands sharply four times, and a servant came through one of the rope curtain archways. She gave stern instructions in Fuergan, and the servant left.

"Sit," she said, taking her place on one of the fur pillows. Orihla did the same. "We must engage in the *hretala*, and you are under our hospitality."

Satrine cautiously took a place at the table, and Welling sat next to her. "Am I incorrect, Inspector," he asked quietly, "or is this about to become some form of initial mourning display that we've been drafted into?"

"No, Welling," she said. "I think you're spot on."

Servants came out with steaming bowls of something unidentifiable, and placed one in front of each of them. If nothing else, Welling wasn't going to have to worry about eating.

◆——◆◆——◆

Minox took his seat on the fur pillow skeptically, but followed Inspector Rainey's lead on dealing with these Fuergan nobles politely. They had suffered a loss and were grieving, in their way.

A bowl of some Fuergan dish was placed in front of Minox and the rest. He didn't recognize anything about it, but it smelled savory and tantalizing.

Hieljam ab Tishai turned her face to the ceiling and began chanting in Fuergan. While she did so, servants continued to place things on the table: eating utensils, cups, and plates of thin bread.

The chant went on for an uncomfortably long time, which Minox presumed was a ritual to honor the dead patriarch rather than something done for every meal. This observation was bolstered by the fact that the various servants all gathered in the room, crowding against the walls, all turning toward the ceiling.

Hieljam ab Tishai finished, and the servants all left. She picked up her utensil and took a bite of the dish. Her male relative did the same, and Minox followed their cue. The utensil was something not entirely unlike a fork, though reminiscent of a post-holer. Minox stabbed it into the dish and took a bite. It was delicious, if odd. The substance of the dish was some form of soft dumpling, stuffed with ground spiced meat, likely chicken. It was bathed in a red cream sauce, with a flavor Minox couldn't identify. In all, it was highly enjoyable.

"If it's all right, Miss Hieljam," he said after a few bites, "we have some questions we need to ask you."

"That is," Rainey said quickly, "Heina-jai Hieljam, we would like to ask you about your *isahresa*'s business, if you can answer it." Minox thought Rainey was being too accommodating to these Fuergans, even if they were nobility or such. There was no need to coddle them.

"Why?"

"Because we're investigating his murder," Minox said simply.

She nodded with understanding. "Yes, I see. But, no, thank you. We will have our own people take care of that."

"I'm afraid it doesn't work that way," Minox said.

"That makes no sense. This is our concern, and we will take care of it."

Rainey spoke up again. "This is not an open market. You cannot hire any investigators you choose."

Hieljam ab Tishai looked utterly perplexed. Hieljam ab Orihla leaned in close to her and there was a brief exchange in their native tongue. There was a moment where her face flashed with anger, but then she cooled and looked back to Minox and Rainey.

"Of course. You are the local officers of justice, and have the exclusive mandate," Hieljam ab Tishai said. "What are we expected to pay for your services?"

"Nothing," Minox said.

"Then you are pledged to poverty?"

Rainey held up a hand to silence Minox. "Our services are not paid for by the families of the victim. Justice is not a merchant."

"Fascinating," Hieljam ab Tishai said. "As to your custom, of course. Ask your questions, I will answer if they are appropriate."

"Your . . ." Minox hesitated, not remembering the Fuergan name for her relation to the victim.

"Isahresa," Rainey provided.

"Yes . . . could you clarify the nature of that relationship?"

"It is . . ." She frowned. "I am sorry, but Druth terms are limiting. Something like 'uncle,' but also 'husband.' "

Minox wasn't entirely sure what to make of that, and turned to Hieljam ab Orihla. "And your relationship to the deceased?"

Hieljam ab Tishai spoke for him. "Ori, like me, is *nokorr* to this household. Also like 'husband,' and ab Wefi Loriz like 'uncle' and 'husband' to him."

Orihla made a hissing noise. "If ab Wefi Loriz died, *natir* is you, Tish."

"Are you saying that she inherits?" Minox asked. Despite the complications of the scene, there was a simple motive. "She becomes the *lavark*?"

"No, no," Hieljam ab Tishai said. *"Natir* is ranking member of household. The holdings of ab Wefi Loriz will be spread to entire *Hieljam* family, here and home. I will not rise to *lavark* from his wealth."

Inspector Rainey took the next question. "Lavark-jan Hieljam was scheduled to meet someone at the Tsouljan enclave. Do you know who he was meeting?"

"He was killed in the enclave?" Hieljam ab Tishai asked. She put down her eating utensil. *"Gacheta enaka Tsoulja!"*

Orihla spoke in calming tone, but she wasn't placated.

"What is it?" Minox asked.

"The *kheshoth* Tsouljans promised their meeting place was safe."

"Who was he meeting?" Rainey asked.

Hieljam ab Tishai took a deep breath and composed herself. "A pair of Kieran merchants. Ravi Kenorax and Estiani Iliari."

"Kenorax?" Minox asked. That was a name he knew. Just about anyone in Maradaine would know it. "KE-NORAX" was liberally branded on crates, bottles, and wagons. You couldn't buy much of anything without seeing the name. "And he was afraid of these Kierans?"

"Why would he be afraid of them?" she asked. Eyes darted to Orihla briefly. The way she held herself shifted.

Rainey took the answer, "Because the Tsouljans promised the meeting place was safe. Why would they do that if he wasn't afraid of something?"

Hieljam ab Tishai picked up her utensil and absently ate her food. Minox took the opportunity to do the same, only to discover he had finished his dish. Rainey deftly slid her own bowl to him, which she had barely touched.

"Heina-jai, what was it?" Rainey pressed. "Heina-jai" must be the appropriate honorific for Hieljam ab Tishai.

After a moment, Hieljam ab Tishai took a sip from her cup and spoke again. "There is a man named Nalas-sein Hajan."

Rainey gave Minox a meaningful glance. That was an Imach name.

"Who is he?" Rainey asked. Minox kept his eye focused on Hieljam ab Tishai and let Rainey ask the questions. The Fuergan woman was performing, it was clear. She wasn't necessarily being dishonest, but she was tightly controlling what she was giving them now.

"He is an importer of goods. We have been having difficulty settling accounts with him."

"He owes you money? Or you to him?" More motives to sort out.

"It is more complicated than that. Do you have time for a lesson in the intricacies of our business?" Deflection to avoid clear answers.

"Humor me."

"We have two primary channels of trade from Fuergan territories to western markets. One is over land, through the highways of the Kieran Empire, which gives us access to them, Waisholm, and northern and interior Druthal. The other is over sea, traveling south along the Imach coast and around the Ihali peninsula, which gives us access to Imach ports, Acseria, and the western coast of Druthal. Both of those paths culminate here, in Maradaine."

"So you have interests in both the empire and Imachan, and Kenorax and Hajan are connected to those interests. Your business is reliant on both."

"Reliant is not the word I would use. Enhanced, perhaps." Now her performance had moved in the direction of deception, but Minox hadn't quite deduced what she was attempting to deceive them about. "Has this been useful?"

"Quite," Rainey said. "Is there anyone else you feel we should be investigating?"

"Not that I can think of." Definite deception.

"Anyone from Lyrana?"

"Lyrana?" The facade dropped for a moment. "We never . . . I can't think of any." That was genuine confusion and surprise.

Orihla tensed slightly, though. So there was a connection.

"Very well," Rainey said, coming to her feet. "I think that's all we have for the moment." She picked up her cup and took a sip. She made a tight, hissing noise. "Is this *Hsiath?*"

Hieljam ab Tishai grinned widely and raised her own cup, swallowing the remaining in one gulp.

Minox lifted his own cup and only smelled. Much stronger than anything he'd want to drink. Putting it down, he added, "One final thing before we go. As the new *natir*, do the debts of Hieljam ab Wefi Loriz fall upon you, and how extensive are they?"

Hieljam ab Tishai's cup slammed onto the table. "I think you can leave now, Inspectors."

"We'll go to the door," Minox said, striding away. Rainey followed in his wake.

"Minox!" she said once they reached the street. Her use of his given name was rare, saved mostly for moments of ire. "What the blazes was that?"

"My apologies," he said, turning back to look at the household. "I do, in fact, have some grasp of Fuergan culture, but it was useful to appear somewhat ignorant to gauge their reactions."

"You let me reel her," Rainey said, clearly slightly annoyed with his tactic. Her face calmed in a moment. "So what are you thinking?"

"Several things, and you were right that we will not be able to continue investigative action tonight." The sky was already quite dark, and under normal circumstances they would have signed out an hour ago. "We must investigate both Kenorax and Hajan tomorrow, as well as examine the discoveries of Kellman and Mirrell from the Tsouljans."

"But the Lyranans are clearly a wash."

"Not hardly. I am not sure why, but Hieljam ab Ofihla was very concerned when you mentioned them."

"So who do we look at with the Lyranans?"

"That may well depend on what the mysterious text says."

"So are we signed out for the night then?"

"Unfortunately, not quite yet. We will have to do one more thing, and it will not be pleasant." On her raised eyebrow, he clarified. "We're going to have to freeze all outbound traffic on the Foreign Interest Docks. But we don't have enough evidence to get the Protector's Office to issue a Writ of Embargo."

"So we're going to have to get River Patrol to do us a favor."

"Exactly."

She furrowed her brow at him. "You're going to take point on that one, then. And tell me what you've been thinking as we walk."

Welling took the lead as they crossed over to Dockview, where the closest River Patrol Stationhouse was. Specifically, it was the stationhouse that managed what was officially called the Foreign Interest Docks. The common local name, of course, was the Pirie Docks, since it was mostly used by Kieran importers.

"Here is the element that stands out to me. Our victim was a *lavark*, the ranking member of the entire Hieljam family. Trade interests throughout Fuerga and the rest of the world. So why was he here in Maradaine?"

"Well, as ab Tishai told us, the two key trade routes the Hieljams use culminate here."

"That's what she said, and it wasn't entirely false. But let me give you a point of comparison. You're familiar with the Caldermane Company?"

The Caldermane Company was the largest wagon-shipping and transport industry in Druthal. It was like asking if she was familiar with roads.

Welling didn't wait for an answer, since it was obvious. "The Caldermane has offices in many cities, key hubs in Fencal and Porvence and Korifina. But where does Marcus Caldermane live? Here in Maradaine. Does he deal directly with every situation in Fencal or Porvence or Korifina?"

"Well, no, he has factors in those cities . . ." The point became clear. "And Hieljam ab Tishai and ab Orihla are the factors in Maradaine. But something had happened — a situation large enough to demand the *lavark* involve himself directly."

"A major agreement, or correcting a major error. We can't say yet."

"Which would explain the Kenorax involvement."

"True. But while I'm not fully versed on the shipping and wagoning business . . ."

"I'm shocked, Inspector," she said teasingly.

"I don't believe that Ravi Kenorax is the top level operative for that industry."

"So the big player was meeting with underlings. That couldn't be sitting well."

"Which leads me to believe that some sort of error — a catastrophic one — on the part of ab Tishai or ab Orihla was being corrected."

Satrine took this all in. Motives for various potential players were taking shape. "Of course, the nature of the murder itself is still very confusing. The theatrical staging, the apparent lack of struggle or argument."

"I'm glad you picked up on that," Welling said. "We'll have to wait for Leppin's report, obviously, but for all it looked . . ."

"It was like Hieljam lay down and accepted the knife in his chest."

"Exactly. And that aspect is troubling as well."

The offices of the River Patrol were little more than a dockhouse with a sign out front. Even upon entering, there was little sense of organization or bureaucracy. A handful of blue-and-white clad men sat around a table playing cards, while a couple more were checking out one of the few boats in dock.

"Pardon," Welling said as they entered, for none of the men took much notice. "Looking for Captain Harker?"

"Cap!" one of them yelled up a rickety wooden staircase to a small office above them. "Got some sticks here for you."

The office door opened up and an older officer, with thick white hair and beard, came down the steps. "Who's coming here at this hour?"

"Captain, sir," Welling said. "Inspector Minox Welling."

"Welling?"

"Lieutenant Thomsen Welling is my cousin. We met at the South City Dinner last year?"

"Right, right. Thomsen isn't here, but I think you know that," Captain Harker said, taking Welling's hand warmly. He gave Satrine a bit of side eye, but said nothing to her. "What's your business here?"

"We're in the process of investigating a murder in the Little East, one which involves people of prominence."

"Oh, really?" the captain asked. "Anyone I might know?"

"Most likely," Welling said. "It's probably best for the sake of discretion that I not divulge."

"Fine, fine," Captain Harker said, though he seemed a bit peeved. "What's that to do with us?"

"We need the Foreign Docks shut down and blockaded. Nobody in or out tonight."

Captain Harker laughed. "Sure, what about the morning? We keep everything locked down until further notice?"

The rest of the River Patrol boys all joined their captain in laughter.

"If you can," Welling said calmly.

"Blazes, Welling, it's already past sundown, you're talking work that would require a triple crew put on for the night. Not to mention, most my boats are already out on the water. Can't be done."

"I'm not talking the whole river, sir. These docks. You could do it with the men in this room."

Captain Harker scowled, but looked around at his men. "Not quite. Need a bit more muscle on ground. You got the authority to pull that?" The man was amenable to the idea, if nothing else.

"Not entirely, sir. This is not something that's been pushed through the Protector's Office. We don't have a Writ of Closure."

"Why the blazes not?"

Satrine stepped forward, putting on the old Inemar accent so thick it could sweeten her tea. "You know why the blazes, Cap. Protector will let these feeks and piries walk all over him. Got to keep it off the books, at least for tonight."

"Really?" Captain Harker raised an eyebrow. "Tell me why?"

"Cuz we got a lead we can't spring on, not yet, hear?" She lowered her voice, like she was letting him in on a secret. "The protector needs proof, hear? Need a bit more time, else these machs will sail off."

"It's machs you wanna stop?" he asked. "Blazes, skirt."

"I ain't saying it is, ain't saying it's not. Just saying we need the night."

"Off the books."

"As a favor," Welling emphasized.

"But don't just hold up machs," Satrine said. "Spread it even, so it seem fair, case it gets back to the Protector's Office."

The captain turned to one of his men. "Hey, Bilky! I think we had somebody come through who might have had Gorree Fever."

Bilky, presumably, and a few other boys stood up. "Sounds like we need a Hot Quarantine."

"I think we just may," Captain Harker said smugly. "Come morning, well, I guess we were wrong. But that'll let us hold up anyone who tries to sneak out at night."

"Obliged, Capper," Satrine said.

Welling shook his hand. "And if you ever need—"

The captain spoke up immediately. "I got a daughter who's a bit sweet on Thomsen."

Welling raised an eyebrow. "And you would like me to . . ."

"Push him in her direction. Hennalia is her name. Maybe the next South City he could take her?"

Satrine almost broke character and laughed, Welling looked so out of his element with that request. "I will endeavor, Captain."

"See that you do, Welling. See that you do."

The blue-and-white went to work on the dock, and Satrine and Welling slipped back out to the street, now relatively quiet for the evening.

"I felt filthy just talking like that," Satrine said.

"An interesting tactic you took," Welling said. "Effective, but I don't know if I fully approve."

"I don't fully approve," Satrine said. "But it's past seven bells, and I should definitely get back home, so effective was necessary."

"I concur," Welling said. He pulled out his whistle and gave a page signal. In a few minutes one of the boys came running.

"Heard a call, specs," he said with a salute. It wasn't one Satrine knew too well, probably because he worked night shift. "What's the word?"

"Run back with sign-out, Welling and Rainey. Return to duty eight bells morning."

"As you will, specs," the page said. He saluted and bolted off.

"The energy of youth," Satrine said wistfully. "It's still quite a slog home."

Welling pulled a coin out of his pocket. "Take a cab, Inspector."

"No, I couldn't." She wasn't about to let him pay for her. He'd already spent a half-crown out of his pocket buying the guide.

"I'm well aware that your salary barely covers your needs," he said. "I can spare it." He pressed the coin into her hand. "I need you rested and alert tomorrow."

"And I you," she said. "Home and sleep. Not back to the stationhouse to dig through files. Promise?"

"Promise." He then said the same phrase he said every night when she went home. "A good night to you, Inspector Rainey, and my best to your husband."

"Give your family mine," she replied, even though she knew at least his cousin Nyla hated her. The rest probably felt no different.

He nodded and turned off to walk north toward home. Satrine whistled for a cab—an extravagance she never allowed herself—and hopped into the seat.

"High River, 14 Beltner." She settled back and let her eyes shut as the cab cantered its way down Dockview to The Lower Bridge.

Chapter 5

THE LAMPLIGHTERS HAD LONG FINISHED their work by the time Minox reached 418 Escaraine, the sizable house in the quainter section of the Keller Cove neighborhood. It, like most houses along this stretch of Escaraine, was over a hundred years old and had been in the same family for its entire existence. Houses like that were uncommon in this part of Maradaine, with high gables and wooden shuttered windows, as well as the carriage stable behind the house. Most of the ones in Keller Cove and surrounding neighborhoods had been razed to build whitestone tenements, or broken down into boarding apartments.

Along this stretch Escaraine was populated by what people called "The Devoted Families," though whether that term was used genuinely or sneeringly depended on the speaker. Those families, like the Wellings, had been fixtures in Maradaine's city services: the Constabulary, the Fire Brigade, the Yellowshields, the River Patrol, the Brick and Pipe Men, and so forth. Most people who lived in these houses still served, including most of the residents of the Welling House.

Minox's brother Oren, a lieutenant in the Constabulary, stationed over in Reining, sat on the front stoop with two of the cousins: Edard, who worked Dentonhill footpatrol, and Davis, who was an examinarium assistant at Keller Cove Stationhouse. All three were drinking beers and chatting loudly as Minox approached.

"Late shift, Minox?" Edard asked.

"Call came in for the afternoon, had to at least lay down the particulars," Minox said.

"You missed dinner," Oren said. "Mother wasn't thrilled. You've eaten?"

"Can always eat more," Davis muttered.

"It's true," Minox said. "And I'm sure Mother kept some aside, right?"

"Yeah, she did," Oren said.

"But your mate came by," Edard said. "So he may have eaten your share."

His mate? "Joshea is here?"

"Chatting up Nyla and Ferah. I think even Alma is being a little moon-eyed at him."

"And the aunts," Davis added.

"Good, good," Minox said. He quickly corrected. "Not the moon-eyed, but that he's here." He hadn't much chance to visit with Joshea in the past few weeks.

Joshea Brondar, like Minox, was an Uncircled mage, though he was far more private about that fact. As far as Minox knew, no one else other than he and Inspector Rainey knew about Joshea's status. Joshea's own family didn't even know, as his father was a superstitious and quick-tempered man. He would not accept his son as a mage.

Minox understood that. His family only accepted it in not actually speaking of it.

"Best get in there," Edard said.

"Right," Minox said, stepping over his cousins. "Is Thomsen in?"

"He's about," Oren said.

"Good," Minox said. "I may have committed him to escort a young lady to the next South City Dinner."

Edard and Davis burst out laughing.

They kept it up as Minox entered the house.

The parlor was filled up, just as Edard had said. Joshea was holding court over Minox's aunts and female cousins, as well as his little sister Alma, telling some salty story of his Army days. One that just skirted the line of inappropriate for mixed company, without quite crossing the line.

"So then the major said, 'I suppose so, she's the one with the boots!'"

Aunts Emma and Beliah howled with laughter, while Aunt Zura blushed furiously and went out toward the kitchen.

"Good evening, all," Minox said as the laughing died down. "Pardon my interruption."

"Minox!" Joshea said, getting to his feet. "Sorry I just dropped in, but . . ."

"Pish, son," Beliah said. "You're always welcome."

"Always," Nyla said with emphasis.

"I'm glad to see you well received, and I'm sorry I was so late."

"You were working," Joshea said. "We made no arrangement." He gave a graceful nod to the aunts and cousins. "Thank you all for entertaining me."

"Is that what you think was happening?" Ferah said. She was still in her Yellowshield shirtsleeves, like she had barely gotten in the door when she spotted Joshea.

"It's been lovely," Joshea said. He closed in on Minox. "Can we speak?"

"Let's go to the kitchen," Minox said. "I could use some supper."

"I can imagine."

Aunt Beliah got in front of Minox before they could leave. "You all right?"

"I'm fine, really."

"Your arm?" His arm had been broken when he had been captured and almost killed in his first case with Inspector Rainey. Beliah—a nurse at Ironheart—had been far too preoccupied with its recovery. Truthfully, it still ached on a daily basis, but he didn't need his aunt to fuss over him.

"It's fine," he said. "Thank you. If you'll excuse me, Aunt."

She gracefully stepped away as he went to the kitchen with Joshea, where Minox's mother had been scrubbing the last of the supper dishes. "You could send a page when you'll be this late," she said.

"That would be a selfish and irresponsible use of Constabulary resources," Minox said. "Father would have said the same."

She kissed him on the forehead and took some bread, cheese, and cold lamb out of the icebox. "You as well, Joshea?"

He was hesitant. "A bit."

"I'm sure," she said, setting up two plates. "I'll leave you two to talk." She went up the back stairs.

"She doesn't know, does she?" Joshea asked.

"I didn't tell her, if that's what you mean. But she isn't a fool."

Joshea picked up a piece of lamb. "I don't think you realize how blessed you have it here, Minox."

"I'm actually quite aware."

Joshea pulled a small glass vial out of his pocket and slid it over to Minox. "I figured you were low on this."

Minox picked it up. "I appreciate it."

He didn't have to inspect it, he knew it was full of *rijetzh*, the Poasian spice that dulled magical ability. He had still been working on the right balance of daily ingestion to give himself control over his ability without sacrificing its use altogether. There was also managing the right amount to minimize its aftereffects: pulses of hot temper, with twinges of almost uncontrollable magic. He was hoping that once he hit the right amount at the correct intervals, he'd have full control over his magic, over himself.

He thought back to the Tsouljan enclave. The place unnerved him, feeling similar to the end stage of a *rijetzh* dose. Especially when that one woman spoke to him.

He opened the lid and put just a pinch over the lamb. Taking a bite, he had to admit, even without the magic-dampening properties, it added a unique and savory flavor.

"How's it been this week for you?"

"I had to use it to hold back a bear," Minox said. "Maybe because it was in a moment of dire need, but it felt . . . focused."

"Hmm," Joshea said. "Necessity does do astounding things. So, just . . . hold it back?"

"Like I was putting my own hands on it—"

"How is your hand?" Joshea interjected.

"I keep having the numbness. Especially today, shortly after this incident."

"We need to find out what that's about, though I'm not sure how." Joshea knew about the spikes, but was similarly at a loss on how to further investigate them. Despite his being acquainted with Nerrish Plum, having served in the same regiment, he had no idea where the bookseller had acquired the spikes in the first place. He had attempted discreet inquiries into their origins, but that had yielded no results.

"And you haven't experienced the same aftereffects of the *rijetzh*?"

"Not to the degree you report." Joshea shook his head. "I'm sorry, continue."

"Like I said, like I was putting my own hands on it, but as if I had extended them. Larger and stronger than my hands could be."

Joshea held up his hands, like he was about to attempt it. "Probably here isn't the best place to try that."

"No."

Joshea looked out the back window to the barn. "It's a shame your cousin has already laid claim out there. That would be a good place to practice."

Minox's cousin Evoy, one of the few in the family not to be in city service, used to report news for the *South Maradaine Gazette*. He was good, with a keener eye for cracking the truth than Minox ever had. He would have made a great inspector, if that had been his path.

Evoy hadn't worked for the *Gazette* in over a year, and hadn't stepped foot in the house for five months. Instead he was in the barn, reading through newsprints, writing his ideas all over the wall. Every time Minox went out to see him, he seemed to have slipped even further into madness. The same madness that had claimed their grandfather years before.

The scariest thing was how much of Evoy's madness, his lunatic leaps of logic to astounding connections, made perfect sense to Minox. He could never see the whole picture that Evoy was painting, but he could get glimpses of the images.

"We should find something, though," Minox said. "I think we've both gotten a strong sense of how to keep control over our . . . abilities. But if we're going to progress, teach ourselves . . ."

"Be as good as any damn Circled mage . . ." Joshea said, glancing around furtively. "I can't ask around too much."

"We'll take our time," Minox said. "We'll find something."

"I know," Joshea said. "Look, I'd stay and talk more, but I have to be up before the sun. Auction at the pighouse, you know . . ."

"I know." Joshea and his family ran a butcher shop in

Inemar, and a damn fine one. As troubling as Minox found the elder Brondars, he had to admit their dedication to their work in meat was equivalent to Wellings in the city service.

Joshea took his hand, and then went to the back door. "See you soon, Minox."

Minox finished the meal and rinsed things off at the kitchen well pump. Blowing out most of the oil lamps in the kitchen, he set off to find his cousin Thomsen. He was probably going to owe him quite a large favor.

<hr />

Satrine had nearly dozed off in the cab. It felt like no time had passed when the driver whistled at her to pay up and shove off. She gave him the coin and stepped down to her home street.

She was almost disoriented for a moment by how normal and plain the streets were. The stores, the people, the clothing—everything was purely Druth again. It was hard to believe that other world existed, tucked away in a few blocks across the river.

She went to her building and down the steps to her door. She had barely started to turn the key when the door flew open to reveal Missus Abernand.

"You're very late!" she snapped. "It's half past eight."

"Very sorry, Missus Abernand. We got a late call, and had to start—"

"I don't want to hear it. Just try to be here. I do have my own concerns beyond taking care of you and yours."

"I know," Satrine said, pressing past Missus Abernand to come into the hallway. "You mention it on a regular basis."

"You seem to forget," Missus Abernand said, taking Satrine's vest and weapon belt from her and hanging them on the wall. She leaned in and whispered, "There is a visitor."

"It's not that boy again?" Poul Tullen had been a source of recurring heartache for Satrine's eldest daughter, constantly trying to come back in her life, and then flitting off again like the spoiled rich boy that he was.

"No, it's . . ."

Satrine had already come out of the hallway into her sitting room to see.

Commissioner Enbrain, the head of the entire Maradaine Constabulary Force, was sitting on her couch, chatting with her daughters.

"Inspector," he said, getting on his feet. "I didn't realize you'd be this late."

She hadn't seen Commissioner Enbrain since he had showed up at the Inemar Stationhouse, furious that she had tricked and forged her way into an inspector position. He hadn't commented or overruled when Captain Cinellan allowed her to continue. He hadn't done anything at all.

And now, here he was, in her sitting room.

"Girls, could you give us the room?" he asked sweetly.

"Of course, Uncle Wendt," Rian said. She and Caribet both gave Satrine a quick kiss hello and slipped off into their quarters. He was still "Uncle Wendt" to them.

"I'll be up there," Missus Abernand said, going up the back stairs to her own apartment. "If you need—"

"Thank you, Missus Abernand," Satrine said. As she vanished upstairs, Satrine took a seat at the table, leaving the couch to Enbrain. He sat down, frowning.

"You've been doing well, Satrine. I've been keeping track."

"I'm not surprised. I'm actually amazed you didn't have me drummed out."

He looked down to the floor, looking somewhat ashamed. "I did initially consider it, but I trusted Brace's opinion. And everything I've seen from the reports I've received indicates he was right."

"That I was right," Satrine said sharply. "I didn't deserve some five-crown clerkship."

"I'm not here to argue with you, Satrine," he said. "I was wrong."

That didn't make Satrine feel any better.

"So why are you here?"

"Your new case. The Fuergan *lavan*."

"*Lavark*," she corrected him.

"As you can imagine, it's been getting some attention. My afternoon was spent with King's Marshals and Druth Intelligence breathing down my neck."

"Really?" Satrine scoffed. "Mine was no better. I killed a bear."

"A what?"

"Long story," Satrine said. She looked around, noting the cleared table and kitchen. "Did the girls have dinner?"

"I believe so," Enbrain said. "Did you eat?"

"The Fuergans fed us," she said absently. "Welling seemed to like it. Well, he ate it, and with him, that says nothing about liking it." She went over to the cupboards and found a half a loaf of bread that hadn't gotten too hard. "What about you?"

"I'm fine. But I did bring you some wine." He picked the bottle up off the couch, which she hadn't noticed before, and put it on the table.

She brought the bread over to the table, grabbing two cups as well. "That's something."

He popped the cork and poured for them both.

She watched him as she picked up her cup. "So is this what you're doing now? You're suddenly a friend of the family again?"

He sat down. "I always was, Satrine. I . . . I had no idea what you were capable of. Who you really were."

"I've maintained a good act," she said. She took a sip. It was a good wine. Probably cost half her weekly salary.

"A man named Major Grieson was in from Intelligence. Did you know him?"

Like blazes she knew him, but she didn't show that on her face. She shook her head and lied. "No. Frankly, I was kept . . . I shouldn't talk too much about what I did or didn't do. But I wasn't exactly walked through the central halls, nor did I have traditional training. It wasn't exactly a boarding school dorm."

"Fair enough," he said. "Well, he knows you. When I said who was handling the case, he backed down."

Satrine didn't know what to make of that. "It's a blazes of a case. No one would want it, frankly. It's a mess, and intentionally so."

"I do believe in you and Welling," Enbrain said. "You enjoy working with him?"

"He's brilliant," she said.

"Good. Because . . . a lot is riding on this case being solved quickly and with minimal embarrassment to the Constabulary, and Druthal as a whole."

"No pressure there," Satrine said, finishing her cup. "Any other miracles you need?"

"Not right now," he said. He voice shifted, becoming warmer. "I took the liberty of checking in on Loren. He's . . . better than I feared he'd be."

There was faint praise. "He's pretty blazing bad."

"I still have hope that someday—"

"He'll never serve again, Wendt. You know that."

"No, of course. But that he could, you know, be a man again. Be a person instead of a burden."

Satrine refilled her wine cup. "May the saints hear you." She raised it to Enbrain, and he returned the gesture.

He put it down and stood back up. "I've been here later that intended. My wife will start to ask questions."

"Good for her," Satrine said.

"Oh," Enbrain said absently, pointing back to the

bedroom door Loren was behind. "Are you going to vote this week?"

"I can't vote," Satrine said. She knew the Parliamentarian elections, as well as ones for the open seats in the city Aldermen, were approaching, but that hardly concerned her. Blazes, there had been a whole business with the Parliament and riots and a few murders just a few weeks ago, and she barely took notice. Not that it was her business. She worked south side. North of the river stuff wasn't her problem. "And I don't have the time to join in with the Suffragists."

"Well, no, of course," Enbrain said. "But Loren is still entitled to his."

"He can't vote either. Not like that."

"No, but his entitlement still holds. A proxy can take claim."

She shook her head. "Now you sound like a Suffragist."

He shrugged. "I'm not insensitive to their point."

"I've got enough problems right now, Commissioner."

"Think about it, Satrine," he said. "Keep the bottle."

"Blazing right I'll keep the bottle," she said.

He gave her a small salute and went to the door. Once he was out, she made sure it was latched and went back to the table. She picked up her cup and finished the wine, and then the wine from Enbrain's cup that he had left.

Then she went into the bedroom.

"Gaa-ee!"

In the past month, Loren had improved, in the sense that he wasn't in a half-dead state anymore. He used to be in bed, eyes open, but never really awake. Never anything but an empty stare.

Now he spoke.

Or more correctly, he made noise. He couldn't stand up or move his arms, for which Satrine was grateful. If he could move his arms like he spoke, he would flail and pummel her when she got close.

Nothing worked except eyes and mouth, and all mouth did was babble nonsense. All the time.

"Hello, love," she said to him.

"Aaa faa a eeempph!"

"I heard you had a visitor," she said. "Hope he didn't bother you too much."

"Aaa ehh baa moh!"

She touched his face. "You're all right," she said. He continued to make noise, while she stared into his eyes. Now it was so much harder than before. Before those eyes may as well have been glass. Now they had life, they had fire. But only in the briefest, most fleeting moments did she see her husband in those eyes.

But those moments let her hope, which was the cruelest thing they could do.

"I'm going to go wash up, and then change you out, all right?" Her evening rituals with him were locked in. Missus Abernand deserved a sainting for all that she did with him during the day, but Satrine was determined to do a small part of taking care of Loren in the few hours she was here and awake.

Every night she'd give him water and medicines, for all the good they'd do. Then she'd strip him down and clean his whole body with a wet cloth. She checked him for sores or injuries, then dusted his skin with the apothecary powder.

Some nights she'd allow herself to lie in the bed, resting on her husband's body, just for a few minutes.

Then she would dress him again, give him more water. During this process, every time, she'd tell him about the day. Today she talked about the bear, about Gregor Henk and his uncle, about the Tsouljan enclave and the Fuergan household.

She prayed that he knew what she was doing, what she was saying. That he understood.

She kissed his forehead, while he continued to babble, and blew out the lamps.

Then she went back into the sitting room to sleep on the couch.

Rian was waiting for her. Satrine noticed the wine had been put away, which had gone against her intended plans for the remainder of the evening.

"Long day?" Rian asked. "Something about a bear?"

"You shouldn't be spying," Satrine said. She sat on the couch and took her boots off. "Why are you out here?"

"Caribet's asleep, and I didn't want to sit in the dark."

"You should be asleep."

Rian raised an eyebrow at her. "You know school is off for the summer, right?"

Satrine had forgotten that. "Of course I know that. But you shouldn't be falling into bad habits."

"Your bad habits."

"Exactly. I'm a terrible role model."

Rian sat down. There were moments when Satrine would look at her oldest daughter and see hints of the girl she had once been. Rian had her coloring, her hair, her eyes . . . but none of her hardness. "Mama, I could be the one here with Pop while you work. You're giving nearly half your salary to Missus Abernand—"

"She earns every tick, too."

"Let me help."

"No, no, you should be . . . doing . . ." Satrine's brain went blank. "Whatever the other girls at the Bridgemont do for the summer."

Rian put on a poor noble accent, probably mimicking her classmates. "Summer on the Lacanjan shore?" She laughed, and then said normally, "I'd love that, but it isn't remotely an option. Girls like me go home, work in shops, and generally be useful. Besides, I've only a year left, anyway. Maybe I should start working."

"No, after you're done at Bridgemont, so help me, you'll go to RCM or the University of Maradaine—"

She did the accent again, "Not the University of Maradaine, Mother. I couldn't bear having to encounter those south side ruffians!" She laughed even harder, then stopped short. "Sorry. I know that . . . that's what you . . ."

"It's fine," Satrine said.

"I want to help, Mama. Either saving money or making money. Please."

Satrine gave her a little smile. "And how would you make money?"

"I heard there's a grand store opening in Gelmin shortly. They'll need shopgirls."

"Really?"

"Especially ones who know how to talk to noble ladies, but will work for shopgirl wages."

Satrine wanted to say no, but practicality won over pride. Plus it would be good to let Rian have a bit of her own pride. "All right, try to apply. We'll see what happens."

Rian wrapped her arms around Satrine's neck. "Thank you, Mama."

"Now go to bed so you can look your best when you go."

"All right," Rian said, getting to her feet. "You too, all right?"

"Yes, ma'am," Satrine said, lying down on the couch. "Blow out the lamp as you go."

Chapter 6

B LAZING DRUNKS AND RUTTING MADMEN, that was what horsepatrol duty meant in the dull dark hours before the sun came up. Even on a quiet night like this one, there were a few who needed to be hauled in. Corrie Welling worked every shift praying to whatever saint would blazing well listen that it would be the last. Some days she even wished she'd just become a clerk or some sewage like that, just so she could work the days.

"They're bringing it!" the drunk shouted from the alley, his pants around his ankles. "No one is even stopping them!"

"Oy!" Corrie called from on top of her horse. "I'm gonna bring it if you don't get those britches up."

"You haven't even seen it, missy!"

"What do we do?" Higgins asked. Higgins was such a tadpole on this job, she was amazed he even knew how to ride his horse. She had no rutting idea whose boots she had pissed on to get saddled with him for tonight's ride. He couldn't be older than her youngest brother Jace, and Jace was still a cadet.

"Butchers! That's what they are!"

"We've warned him," Corrie said, dismounting. "Now we put some irons on the bastard and drag him back to the rutting stationhouse."

"On what charge, though?"

Corrie pulled out her handstick. "You mean besides making me look at his wrinkled pisswhistle?"

"That's a crime?"

"It's blazing well enough of a one for me." She approached the drunk, who really smelled like he had been dead for three days and got back up to start drinking. It may have been dark, but she swore she even saw maggots in his beard. "How hard you gonna make this, buddy?"

"They'll bring blood, they will! Blood and twisted flesh. You will see it!" With that last rant, he punctuated each word with a stern poke on Corrie's chest.

That was rutting well enough of that.

Corrie brought down the handstick on his arm. He cried out and crumpled.

"You can't do that, Miss Welling!" Higgins yelped.

"He put hands on me," Corrie said. She whistled for Higgins to throw his irons over. "You can't do that to a Constabulary officer."

The crazy drunk didn't put up any fight when she ironed him, he just kept babbling about butchers and flesh and horror from below. Once he was ironed, she yanked his pants back up, restraining her urge to knock him about some more.

"So you're gonna call for a lockwagon?" Higgins asked.

"Blazes, no," Corrie said. "This hour, they never respond to a whistlecall. Your first time on the dark?"

"Not the first," Higgins said, in a way that made it sound like it was the second.

She hauled the drunk over, now half limp, as if ironing had drained his spirit. With a heave, she lifted him off the ground and draped him, facedown, over the back half of Higgins's horse.

"Why are you putting him there?"

"Because you're the chum, Higgins," she said. "If you rutting outranked anyone, you could make them do it."

"He better not puke on me."

"Oh, Higgins." She pulled herself back on her horse. "Don't you know? Drunken vomit is the ointment of initiation when you work the dark."

The ride back to the stationhouse was quick, as they were only a couple blocks out, and Higgins groused the whole blasted way.

"Take both horses around to the stables," she told him, pulling the drunk off the back. "I'll take this one into holding."

"Aren't we going back out there?"

"Blazes, no," she told him. The dull gray of sunrise was starting to dust up the eastern sky. "We're just about off shift, ain't no rutting cause."

Higgins frowned, but took hold of her horse's reins and led it off around back.

Corrie dragged the drunk into the holding desk, where Binter was working. Fat bastard was the worst of the desk riders. Far too interested in Corrie's blouse on any given night. She pushed the drunk down on the bench in front of the desk.

"Whatcha got, Corrs?" he asked.

"Drunken mess making a nuisance of himself," she said. "Laid hands on an officer, namely myself, so he can spend a few days here to dry out."

"Can't."

That was new. Binter usually gave Corrie a hard time, but never flat out denied putting an iron in holding. "What do you rutting mean, can't?"

"Well, shouldn't. Apparently there's been scuttle out there, we need to keep the cells clear for the real problems."

"What the blazing sewage is that?" she snapped at him.

"I'm telling you—"

"It's been rutting quiet out there. This bastard was about as exciting as it got."

"Maybe for you—"

"So what the rutting blazes do you need to keep the cells clear for?"

"Would you listen, Corrs?" he snarled. "Down here it may have been quiet, but there was scuttle up in the Little East."

"What kind of scuttle?" In her months riding the dark, she almost never got sent up to the East. Usually they ignored it.

"Blazes if I know. Mostly feeks and machs giving each other some business, based on what got brought in."

"So you can't take this guy?"

"Not for just a dry-out." He shook his head. "If you had a solid knock, I'd find space, but this guy?" He gestured to the drunk, who had slumped down, half asleep. "He ain't worth it, not right now."

"What the blazes you want me to do?" she asked. "Can't exactly put him back in the alley I found him at."

"Maybe I can do you a favor, Corrs . . ." he said softly. Rutting gross.

"Do your blasted job," she said. "I brought him ironed, he's on your bench. Your rutting problem."

She strode off before she heard another word from his disgusting mouth. She figured she'd hit the water closet, slowly work her way back down to the stables, and it would be past six bells and she could sign out.

"Corrie!"

That was a pleasant, familiar voice. Nyla, her cousin, looking fresh and crisp in her clerk uniform. "Aren't you here rutting early?"

Nyla gave a slight blush. "This is about when I always come in."

Corrie hadn't noticed that, but with her working the dark, she didn't see much of the family coming or going at the house. "Thought you came in with Minox most mornings."

Nyla made a disgusted noise.

"Minox do something wrong?"

"You mean besides stand up for that . . . woman?"

For a moment there it sounded like Nyla was going to use a word that was typically only part of Corrie's vocabulary. She didn't like that skirt Minox was partnered with. Most didn't, she was a liar and cheat. Most didn't, except Minox, and most people here didn't like Minox either. They didn't say so around Corrie, of course, because they'd eat their blasted teeth.

But most of the folk here had no qualms talking sewage about the skirt. Corrie didn't like her, either, but she respected Minox's opinion. He said Tricky was worth being his partner, so Corrie believed it. She didn't have to work with the skirt, though. Nyla did.

"You can't be mad at him about that."

"I'm not," Nyla said quietly. "But he gets in when she does. I come in now, I have a couple hours to get things done without having to deal with her. Fortunately she and he will be spending most of the day out in the Little East."

"Something big up there?"

"Something. Turned out most of the specs there yesterday, and they didn't close it up at all." She smiled. "All right, need to work, cousin."

"I feel you, Ny," Corrie said. "I'll leave you to it." She gave her cousin a quick wink and went off.

She eventually made her way down to the stables, where the rest of the boys riding the dark were coming back in to sign out, and the horsepatrol for the day were coming in.

"Listen up," Lieutenant Firren called out to the crowd. "Those of you just coming on, we've got word that we need you making a presence up in the East, and surrounding blocks. They need to see a bit more Green and Red, hopefully that'll calm them down. Those of you who just finished riding the dark, we need some more out there on mount. Anyone want to sign back in to ride out right now, check with me. If you need a few hours in bunk first, and then go out in the afternoon, we need that, too. This ain't an order, just on choice for coin."

Extra shift on choice for coin, and working during the day. Corrie could use a chance like that. Saints knew that she could use the coin, the opportunity for the chiefs on dayside to see her in action.

"Hey, Left," she called to Firren as she moved in. "I could take some bunk right now, work the back half of the day and straight through my dark shift tonight."

"Glad to hear it, Welling," he said. "Head up to the bunks, then. I'll send someone for you around two bells."

"Will do, Left," she said. She took a moment and then added, "So it's bad up in the Little East?"

"Something is brewing, that's for sure," Firren said. "Those folks have got a fire in them right now."

———◆———

The early dawn tickwagon ride into the heart of Inemar was crowded as usual. Most of the same faces Inspector Henfir Mirrell usually saw on this ride. The three ladies who lived on his block and worked at the soapworks. The old codger who seemed to go every day for its own sake. The two blokes who read the newssheet each day and argued about it far too loudly.

"We need more bridges!"

"And who's gonna pay for those bridges, huh? Where they gonna go?"

"You ever try and cross the river? The city is choked up, divided between the two sides."

"Cross the river, certainly. As if I had any cause to go northside."

"Some people . . ."

"And there's the ferryboats. They make a couple ticks for the fare, and everything works. You build another bridge, and the duke's taxes will go up, and no one needs that."

"So then who're you voting for?"

These two had been up and down about elections for the past few days. Mirrell wasn't even sure who was running for Alderman in his district.

Of course, the only man in power who mattered to Mirrell already had his vote, and that was Commissioner Enbrain. Mirrell got his salary, and the peace was kept as best as possible in the city. Those were the things that mattered.

"Hey, specs," one of the blokes called to him, holding up the paper. "Says here there was some business with Constabulary killing a bear. There bears loose in the city?"

"A rutting bear?" Mirrell said. "You know those folks print whatever sewage will sell."

"So you didn't hear about a bear?"

"Ain't no damn bears in the city."

"So you say, spec," the bloke said. "You going to tell me more kids aren't vanishing from the streets either?"

Mirrell had heard enough of this garbage. The kids thing was true—probably another fighting ring had formed after the one he had busted up a few months back—but he didn't need to hear it from this bloke. The tickwagon was close enough to the stationhouse, and he hopped off with a nod to the driver. It kept trundling along as Mirrell walked to the stationhouse.

"Morning, Inspector," Miss Pyle said as he came up the steps. She was her usual bright self. Hard to believe she was blood kin to Jinx. That man could draw the life out of any room he stepped into.

"Any word?" he asked her. "Did Jinx and Tricky solve the feek's death in the middle of the night?"

"Not hardly," she said. "But nothing new on your board yet. Captain wants you to lay out your elements to Minox and . . . her."

His elements consisted of him and Darreck trying to talk to every blue- and green- and red-haired tyzo in that place. Lucky they didn't mind it that they were kept in for the night. Blazes, when the sun set, they all went in their little huts.

"Ain't much to lay out, to be honest. Ain't none copped to it, those that we could talk to."

Miss Pyle shrugged. "Then you and Kellman will be the dancers. Minox will play the beat."

Mirrell grumbled. Captain was clearly putting him and Darreck on second, taking orders from Jinx and Tricky. That was nothing even close to right.

"There tea on my desk at least?"

"As always."

Kellman was thumbing through his notebook as Mirrell approached. "Morning, Hennie. How's the family?"

"Good as can be expected," Mirrell said, picking up the teacup. "You hear we're going to be the dancers?"

"I heard." He gave one of his usual expressions of lack of concern. "Ain't like Jinx and Trick won't need the help. There was a bit of knockaround in the Little East last night. Handful of feeks and machs and I don't know what in the pens below us."

"What, street fights over this stuff?"

"I don't know. Boys on the dark just said knockaround. Nothing big. I think they're restless."

Suddenly Mister Zebram Hilsom, the weasel from the Protector's Office, came striding over to them. "Was it you two? This has your stink all over it."

"Us two stink of what?" Mirrell asked. Hilsom didn't even deserve that much answer, but he didn't even know what to be angry about.

"Apparently the docks over in the Little East had a bit of a Hot Quarantine last night. The River Patrol said it was all in the service of good health, but it sounds exactly like the kind of sewage you two would pull to get a shutdown without a writ."

"We didn't do nothing of the sort," Mirrell said. "Don't you throw that on my desk."

"Throw it on mine," the captain said. "I've told you, Zebram . . ."

"If your inspectors get out of line . . ."

"Did River Patrol say it was my inspectors?"

"Your men are investigating a high-profile murder in the Little East, and then all the Foreign Docks get a quarantine for the night. You're telling me that isn't you?"

"Did the River Patrol say it was my inspectors?"

"There are procedures we follow, through me to the magistration so that—"

"Did the River Patrol say—"

"No," Hilsom finally said. "They said they were legitimately worried. But it stinks—"

"Don't drop this stuff here, Zebram," the captain said. "My inspectors walk outside of the road, then we talk. Besides that, do your job."

"Help me out, Brace."

"What's the problem?"

Tricky had walked up.

Hilsom stared her down. "Seems the River Patrol shut down the Little East docks last night, and quite a few people complained. You know something about that, Inspector Rainey?"

"Me?" she scoffed. "I can barely get a cup of tea here. I'm lucky if my reports get filed."

Hilsom grumbled, and turned back to the cap. "I've got folks down my neck from nine different directions. Let's keep everything on the line, shall we?"

"Always," the captain said.

"Yeah, yeah. I'll send over a couple pages from my office. You need writs—especially over in the East—you get them to run. Hear?"

"We've got pages, Zebram."

"Somehow I'd like my own there." He went off to the stairs.

"Tell me you all have something," the captain asked Tricky.

"We've got a couple names who might have a fire to stoke with the Fuergan. Kieran named Ravi Kenorax, for one."

Kenorax. That was a name Mirrell had heard. "We, uh, grilled some of the tyzos. None of them knew who the Fuergan was supposed to meet with, but one of yellow-hairs spilled that he had taken a few meetings there over past few days."

"So Hieljam was a regular user of the Tsouljan enclave?" Tricky asked. "Who was he meeting?"

"He had met Kenorax before, according to this yellow-hair."

"Did the person who told you this have a name?" This came from Jinx, who had wandered over to the desks. "You did get that, yes?"

"Do you think me stupid, Jinx?" Mirrell asked. He looked to Kellman. "What was his name?"

Kellman consulted his notebook. "Naljil Rek-Yun."

"Right, him. Only one of the tyzos, save that green-haired kid who translated, who told us anything worth a damn."

Kellman laughed. "Right. Most of them talked about cake and the ocean, or something like that. Except the lady who said that we were clarity."

Mirrell remembered that. That blue-haired lady gave him the creeps. Staring at them both with those deep, dark eyes for saints knew how long before she even spoke.

"You were what?" Tricky asked.

"Clarity. That's what the kid said. Didn't make much sense to me."

"Obviously," Jinx said. Mirrell had half a mind to smack him and ask what the blazes that was supposed to mean. "Anyone else?"

"Anyone else what, Jinx?"

"Did Naljil Rek-Yun name anyone else that Hieljam had met with in the past few days?"

"Yeah," Kellman said. "An Imach ... named ..." He flipped through his notebook.

"Hajan?" Tricky asked.

"No. Jabiudal. Assan Jabiudal."

Jinx and Tricky both frowned.

"What, you got a problem?" Mirrell asked.

"No, no, just a different Imach name than we were expecting to hear," Jinx said. "Well done."

"Stay on it, all of you," the captain said. "Minox, Rainey, you're playing the drums on this one. Mirrell and Kellman, dance as they need you to." He went to his office and shut the door.

So that was clearly that.

Jinx rubbed his chin. "We should all head up to the Little East shortly. Inspector Rainey and I will attempt to interview Kenorax. In the meantime, the two of you will endeavor to locate Assan Jabiudal and Nalassein Hajan."

Mirrell had to admit he didn't know how Jinx could keep all these crazy names straight. It was all so many nonsense sounds.

"Sure, sure," Mirrell said. "Is that all you need, since we're the ones dancing to your drums?"

"Yes, actually," Jinx said. "Since we're all going to that

part of town, arrange for one of our wagons to take us up, as well as two or three pages to join us. Twenty minutes?"

Jinx didn't wait for Mirrell to respond, walking off to his desk, Tricky right with him.

Mirrell sighed and looked to Kellman. "Well, let's get down to the stables. Bring your dancing shoes."

——————◆◆■——————

Rainey chuckled as they went over to their own desks. "Those two are going to hate you before the day is out."

"They already do," Minox said. "This will hardly change their opinion."

A file sat on his chair, Leppin's report on Hieljam. Minox picked it up and flipped through, noting the particulars.

"Anything that changes things?" Rainey asked.

"Nothing much," Minox said. "His analysis of the liquid—which he confirms Hieljam drank—says that it was innocuous, at least on its own. But he finds no evidence of a secondary catalyst being used on Hieljam. It's just a floral tea, common in Tsouljan cuisine."

Rainey sat down at her desk and sipped at the tea that was waiting there for her. Nyla's handiwork, serving impeccably despite her dislike of Inspector Rainey. "So that's nothing."

"He confirms the blade is Imach—a *talveca*—so we definitely will want a word with Hajan."

"And Jabiudal."

"Indeed. Presuming they are to be found. Hopefully we won't have to scour the Imach blocks."

"Presuming they even live in the Little East. There're Imach coffeehouses on the north side, a few smaller groups of them way out on the west side of town."

Minox was surprised to hear that. He was under the impression that there were very few people of foreign birth or descent living outside of the Little East, except in the far western slums of the city. He imagined that all the north side neighborhoods would have kept the Imachs out. "We will invite madness if we contemplate all possible places where suspects might be. Though I imagine that we will find fruit in the Little East. The Fuergans and Imachs there were already getting into altercations last night."

"Fallout over Hieljam?"

"Possibly. Or it gave spark to brawls that were imminent anyway."

Rainey reached out for the report, which Minox handed to her. Thumbing through it, she added, "No bruising or other signs of struggle or binding."

"Quite peculiar," Minox said. The evidence so far made little sense, unless Hieljam was a willing participant in his own death.

She gave him a raised eyebrow. "You're not sure the Imachs are really involved."

She had read him well, that had been his very thought. "It feels more like our killer wants us to pay attention to the Imachs."

"Throw suspicion at them?"

"Perhaps not exactly." He had spent half the night thinking about the scene of the murder. "The murder was committed with meticulous precision. Which makes me think no element is there by accident. The tea, the knife, the inscription."

"Someone's sending a message," Rainey said.

"Which means the true key to solving this is determining what that is, and *who* the message is for."

Rainey looked back at the report. "Maybe the Lyranans. Leppin confirms the symbols are Lyranan writing."

Minox had noticed that, also noting that there wasn't a translation. "We'll have to determine their meaning."

"This might help." Nyla approached their desks, carrying a letter.

"What's that?" Minox asked, knowing it was pointless for Rainey to directly address her.

"It arrived for you both, by courier—bald, gray-skinned kid—right at sunrise." Nyla dropped the letter—a heavy stock of paper, sealed with three wax seals—onto the desk. "Maybe it's a confession." She gave him a friendly squeeze on the shoulder and went back to her desk.

Across the top of the letter was written, "To be opened by and only by Inspector Third Class Minox Welling and Inspector Third Class Satrine Carthas Rainey, in conjunction and mutual presence."

"Carthas?" Minox asked.

"It's my unmarried name," Rainey said. "Who even knows that?"

The three seals—as well as Nyla's description of the courier—yielded the answer. Each one was marked with a symbol, similar to the ones found near and on the body.

"We're in conjunction and mutual presence," Minox said. "Shall we? Unless you suspect this is some sort of trap or ruse to hurt us."

"Not Lyranan style." Rainey took the letter and cracked the seals open.

The script of the letter was done by hand, but it was so perfectly executed it could have been printed. It was written in alternating lines, first in Druth Trade, followed by that same foreign script. The letter itself confirmed the identity of the language.

A Missive From Heizhan Taiz, Third Tier Supervisor in Service to the Lyranan Ministry of Foreign Affairs, Bureau of Lyranan Expatriates and Descendants Thereof, Druthalian Division.

To be delivered to, and read by, Inspector Third Class Minox Welling and Inspector Third Class Satrine Carthas Rainey.

Additional Permissions of Reading Granted To: All

relevant superiors in the Maradaine Constabulary Chains of Command, including and especially Captain Brace Cinellan, as well as authorized experts in document authenticity under employ of the Maradaine Constabulary.

With Regards To: The Investigation into the Untimely and Deliberate Death of Hieljam ab Wefi Loriz lek Lavark, etc.

"I'm amazed they didn't write out his full Fuergan name," Rainey said.

"Perhaps they didn't feel the need."

Rainey shook her head. "Given the manner they write everything, I'd say it's some form of intentional slight."

"You may be right," Welling said, reading on.

Point the First: It has come to our attention that you are the officers assigned to the investigation of the untimely and deliberate death of Hieljam ab Wefi Loriz lek Lavark, etc. (Hereafter Lavark Hieljam or "The Lavark") and would seek the hopeful arrest of the interloper responsible for said untimely and deliberate death.

Point the Second: It has also come to our attention that notations written in Lyranan script were found at the scene of the untimely and deliberate death, in a manner that strongly implies they were made by the assailant in question.

Point the Third: Furthermore, we have come to understand that you are interested in interviewing persons with contact or knowledge of the deceased Lavark Hieljam, who could illuminate your investigation concerning his business and acquaintances within the confines of the City of Maradaine, the neighborhood of Inemar, and the collective subdistricts referred to with unofficial colloquialisms as "The Little East."

Rainey stepped away, leaving Minox to read the rest for himself. She sat down at her desk, muttering, "Lyranans."

Proposal: As the above points make it clear that you

would wish to interview an expert in the Lyranan language, as well as those who have had contact with Lavark Hieljam, the optimal solution would be for this meeting to occur today, under proper supervision. It would be ideal if the two of you were to meet with me and Trade Notary First Class Fao Nengtaj, who has had interactions with Lavark Hieljam, as well as my personal adjutant, Specialist First Class Pra Yikenj. If you require the services of your own scribe, analyst, or assistant, they are also welcome to this meeting.

Minox imagined they felt they were being magnanimous in offering such an invitation.

We will meet you at the noon bells (measured by the ringing of Saint Interson's Church), at the Second Auxiliary Public House at 812 Peston Avenue. If you are unable to attend this meeting, please send word for cancellation or rescheduling by means of your dedicated messengers, to my offices at Bureau of Lyranan Expatriates at 830 Dockview Avenue.

With regards,
Heizhan Taiz
Third Tier Supervisor in Service to the Lyranan Ministry of Foreign Affairs
Bureau of Lyranan Expatriates and Descendants Thereof, Druthalian Division

"Fascinating reading," Rainey said.

"Did you finish?"

"I read enough," she said. "Captain!"

Cinellan was passing by the desks and approached. "Something you two need?"

"Not much, we're about to go out to meet with the Kieran merchants, and try to make contact with Nalassein Hajan, if we're lucky."

"All right," Cinellan said. "Good luck with that, and get to it."

"But," she said, getting back up and taking the letter

from Minox, "we've also been invited to meet with Ly-ranan interested parties. And they've been so gracious as to grant you permission to read the letter."

She pointed out the part of the letter that mentioned that.

"Carthas?" Cinellan asked as he read.

"Really?" Rainey asked. "This is what you two latch on to?"

"It's just odd that they know that." Cinellan shrugged and handed it back. "All right, get on it."

"Captain," Rainey said, drawing him back as he stepped away. "I had a visit from Commissioner Enbrain last night."

"In your home?" The captain was clearly shocked.

"He stopped by to talk about this case. It has them buzzing on the north side."

"Blazes," Cinellan whispered. "Their eye is on us."

"We'll serve him and the central office right," Minox said.

"No, it's—I shouldn't talk about this, but . . . did he mention the election?" From the corner of his eye, Mi-nox saw Nyla take note and step forward, and then turn back to her work. She had become passionate about the Suffragist movement in the past month or so. Minox imagined it was only her distaste for engaging with In-spector Rainey that prevented her from starting an argu-ment with Captain Cinellan on the subject.

"Yeah," Rainey said. "Reminded me that I could vote as Loren's proxy."

"He's really looking at us," Cinellan said absently. This time he wasn't annoyed, but somehow intrigued. Even hopeful. After a moment of contemplation, he tapped his fingers on the desk. "Let's get this one put away, quick as you can."

"Will do, Captain," Rainey said. "No matter who we have to deal with today." There her voice soured.

The captain went off to his office.

"Something vexes you about this," Minox said.

"Lyranan Ministry of Foreign Affairs," she said acidly. She took up her belt. "Just another way to say Lyranan Intelligence. These are their spies."

That was definitely of note. "Do you have direct experience with them?"

"Very little," Rainey said. Fixing her belt on, Minox heard her mutter, "But it was enough."

"Then let's be off," Minox said. "We've got a full day."

Chapter 7

SOMETHING ABOUT THE LYRANAN LETTER had made Satrine's meager breakfast of cheese, bread, and tea sit poorly in her stomach. It wasn't just the formal language, or even the fact that it was a Lyranan who—

No, she wasn't even going to think about that. Some of those memories were locked away for a reason.

It was her unmarried name that troubled her. That name was a thing she had hardly ever used. On the streets as a child, she was just Trini or Tricky. The name Satrine was reserved for the most formal occasions— mostly her mother slapping some sense into her the few times she made any attempt at discipline or caring. Even in her time in Intelligence, no one called her Miss Carthas or Agent Carthas or anything of the sort. Rare was the time she'd even been called Satrine in her first years—she got used to the name Quia Alia Rhythyn.

When she had returned to "normal" life, she had even considered going by Satrine Rathan, honoring the name she had lived by. But she had become Satrine Rainey almost right away, so it hardly mattered.

Satrine Carthas wasn't a person who ever really existed.

The Constabulary carriage trundled along, with Satrine riding in the cabin with Welling, Mirrell, and Kellman. Welling and Mirrell were both smoking their pipes, which meant that Satrine and Kellman essentially were as well.

"I never understood that," Kellman said to her jovially. "Lighting something on fire and breathing it in. Where's the joy in that?"

Satrine had to give Kellman some credit—he had been one of the few kind people at the stationhouse after her deceptions were outed. He was the only one besides Welling who truly supported the idea that she should stay on as an inspector.

"It's an acquired taste, I admit," Welling said. "It calms my nerves."

"Same," Mirrell said. "And I'm gonna need that."

"So what are we supposed to do if we find Jaibaba or Hassalla?" Kellman asked. Satrine wondered if he legitimately didn't remember the Imach names, or if he was intentionally mangling them. He didn't throw around words like feek or tyzo with quite the same abandon that Mirrell did, but he didn't seem to mind them much, either.

"Keep eyes on them, send one of the pages for us," Welling said. Four pages, including Phillen Hace, the young man who had been especially loyal to Satrine and Welling over the past months, were riding along on the back rails of the carriage. One of Hilsom's boys was hanging back there as well, looking conspicuously out of place in his gray wool vest and short pants.

"And where are you going to be?"

"There," Welling said, pointing to a series of townhouses that they were approaching. These were all behind a low wall that had taken over the walkways on Peston, like it was no longer a public street. The houses were painted white; not the dirty white of the Maradaine Quarry that the whitestones throughout Inemar were, but a dazzling bright white that almost hurt to look at, with all the roofs and eaves painted a rich purple.

Pirie City—Dexilari—was definitely Kieran Imperial territory, at least in spirit.

"This is where Kenorax lives?" Satrine asked.

"Indeed," he said, knocking on the roof to the driver. He jumped out to the street before it reached a full stop. "Take the carriage over to the Tsouljan compound in Tek Andor. That's going to be our operational center for the time being. One of the pages, stick by Inspector Rainey and me as we're here."

"I'll take that, sir," Phillen said, to no one's surprise.

"Another stay close to Mirrell and Kellman, as they canvas Hesissal." Not only did Welling use the proper names for the enclaves, his pronunciation was excellent. "The rest of you, stick with the carriage, keep your ears out for whistles."

"Should I stay on hand with you, Inspector?" Hilsom's page asked.

"Stick with Phillen for now, kid," Satrine said. She certainly didn't want this one up in their business, but she had to admit he'd be handy if they needed a quick writ of some sort from Hilsom. But she knew damn well he was really here to spy on them, make sure they kept their investigation clean. Hilsom really should know that Welling would be one of the last ones to worry about that with.

"All right," Mirrell said. "Come on, Darreck. Let's go talk to some machs."

They left with one of the pages in tow, and the carriage trundled off.

"So this is where Kenorax lives?"

"According to my sources," Welling said. "And from what I understand of Kieran tradition . . ."

"It's impolite to not take visitors during breakfast," Satrine finished. "Yes, I'm aware."

"How are you aware?"

"Why, Inspector," Satrine said, approaching the low wall. "My stint in Intelligence left me very well educated."

She stepped through the gilded gate—a formality of style, nothing that could actually bar entrance, as one could step over the wall if they wanted to. Welling chose to do just that, possibly out of spite, and went up to the door, pounding it roughly.

A servant—an old Kieran man—opened the door, though he seemed almost too feeble to manage that. "What is about?" he wheezed out.

"Inspectors Welling and Rainey wish an audience with Mister Kenorax."

"Of course," the old man rasped. His voice sounded like a knife had been scraped over his throat. "If you would follow."

He led them through the hallways—polished marble floors and walls, gleaming white. The only color came from the plants that lined the walls, dirt patches built into the floor to hold them.

They were then brought to an open courtyard, where the sun shone brightly over a grand bathing pool, where several people—men and women both—were lounging in the water. The people were all Kierans, by their olive skin and dark, damp-looking hair, and most of them wore flimsy robes that did nothing to cover them. Flower wreathes and petals floated in the water, and several servants stood near each bather, holding trays with food. Surrounding the sun-dappled space were several cages with songbirds.

"We have visitors," the old man rasped. "Two inspectors, by the names Welling and Rainey."

"What a delight!" the man in the center of the bath said. His accent was thick, with an almost musical quality to it. "We never get a visit from the true locals. Please,

Inspectors, sit, sit. Tinari, attend to both of them, with all haste."

"It isn't necessary—" Welling managed to get out.

"But of course it is, do not be absurd."

Four servants came over, and they paired off on both Satrine and Welling. They all attempted to undress the two of them, which Welling was having none of.

"Truly, no, take your hands off our persons!" he snapped.

Satrine pushed one of her servants away gently. "We aren't here for the baths, thank you."

Their host sighed. "Your loss, fellows. But you must take something we offer. We have a paucity of decent fruit, as I'm sure you can imagine, given the season. And the fact that, well, we are in Maradaine. That said, I do have some glorious berries, as well as a few unique treasures from the Napolic Islands. And with those, I must insist—" He raised his voice for the whole room to hear. "Really, friends, the Napolic fruits must be eaten today, or they'll be past their prime."

"We're not here—"

"Tosh, tosh," the Kieran man said. "It's bad enough you refuse to join us properly. Do not come into this household at this hour and tell me you aren't here to eat, because I won't hear of it." He snapped his fingers and a servant held out two plates of diced fruit in front of them—orange in color, with a sticky wetness to it. "Now, most of my guests are afraid to even touch this one, and I confess it has an odor that is reminiscent of vomit . . ."

Satrine had to concur with that.

"But the flavor is truly a unique experience that I'm certain two brave and stalwart members of the City Constabulary would never hide from."

"Mister Kenorax—" Satrine started.

"Ah, no," the man said. "Iliari. Estiani Iliari."

Iliari. The other Kieran man that Hieljam ab Tishai had mentioned.

He snapped his fingers and one of the servants approached him with a sponge and began to scrub his bare chest. Other Kierans were having their bodies massaged, washed, and oiled, all while more servants fed them.

"But this is the Kenorax home, yes?" Welling asked.

"Of course it is. And it's also only nine bells in the morning. Ravi will probably not show his face until after those obnoxious noon bells at Saint whatever-his-name-is ring. However, as I am his primary factor and counselor in all matters, financial and otherwise, you may discuss anything you must with me."

"Mister Iliari—" Satrine started. She was surprised to hear that Iliari was an underling of Kenorax's. She had presumed, by the way that Hieljam ab Tishai had referred to Iliari, that he was a peer to Kenorax.

"Your fruit, Inspector," he said. "Do not offend our generosity."

Welling stabbed his fruit with his utensil and took a bite. His face betrayed no disgust, but as much as Satrine trusted him as her partner, she would never use him as a meter to gauge edibility. He ate that Fuergan slop quite happily, after all.

"Intriguing," he said.

"Thank you, Inspector," Iliari said, turning to Welling. "Now, given your office, I presume that you are here on some form of unpleasant business. Enforcers of law rarely stop by to deliver good news."

"We were hoping to speak with you and Mister Kenorax together," Satrine said.

"And I hope to wake each morning back in Oroba. We live with disappointment."

Welling put his utensil down. "We're here about the death of Hieljam ab Wefi Loriz."

"Ah, yes, the great Lavark," Iliari said. "I should not be surprised that you are here on that matter."

"You were aware of his murder?" Satrine asked.

"Of course we were aware. We were to meet with the man in the afternoon, of course, but we were otherwise engaged in the moment of our appointment."

"Otherwise engaged?" Satrine asked.

A Kieran woman of some years leaned over. "He means that Kenorax was busy here getting everything polished." She made a show of whispering, but without actually lowering her voice. "He likes to take his own damn time with that."

"Hush, Resa," Iliari said, though he sounded like he really didn't care that she was telling them this. He stepped out of the pool, water dripping from his hairy body. "My point is, we arrived at Rev Tak Mel—"

"That's the name of the Tsouljan facility?" Welling confirmed.

"Indeed, and a lovely name, though translated into Trade it becomes something frightfully mundane. 'Place to Sit in Huts,' I think. We arrived sometime and the place was already surrounded by your people. Listening to the murmurings of your common watchmen, we surmised that the Lavark was dead, and therefore the meeting was not to occur, and returned home."

"What was the meeting about?"

"Hardly relevant," Iliari said. "Since it never occurred."

Satrine sighed. "And you can confirm that you, or Mister Kenorax, or any of your people were not in the Tsouljan facility at the time of the Lavark's death?"

"Any of our people?" Iliari laughed, as did many of the folk in the pool. "My dear Inspector, we have quite a few people here, though I would hesitate to call them 'mine.' Friends from the empire, each with a retinue of servants. I could not possibly confirm the whereabouts of each and every one of them." He took up his utensil and stabbed it into the untouched fruit on Satrine's plate. "Nor am I inclined to."

He popped it into his mouth.

"Now," he said as he chewed the fruit, "I have allowed you in here out of courtesy and tradition. I recognize that you are officers with duty, and I will respect that and inform you that we—I speak for Mister Kenorax and his household in using the plural—have very little interest in these matters. We only were even engaged with the matter out of our regard for the Lavark's standing. We wish no further involvement."

"That's hardly something you get to decide, Mister Iliari," Welling said. "This is our investigation, and we will . . ."

"You will politely excuse yourselves and withdraw from these residences. And if you return, I will hope that you have an appropriate Writ of Search. And bear in mind that Mister Kenorax is a close associate of the ambassador when you put in such a request."

Satrine stood up from the table. There was nothing else to be gained here. "Thank you for your time, Mister Iliari."

"Think nothing of it," he said.

Welling stood up. "The fruit was . . . intriguing. But I doubt it is worth the expense of import."

"Likely correct, Inspector," he said. As Satrine and Welling took two steps away, Iliari cleared his throat. "Oh, and one more thing, Inspector? I would appreciate if you made no more attempts to halt or impede activity on our docks. We have business to attend to."

"It shouldn't be a further issue," Welling said. "Good day to you all. Our regards to Mister Kenorax."

They were escorted back out to the street.

"Well, that was useless," Satrine said.

"Not entirely," Welling said. "Now we know that whatever trouble the victim was trying to repair, he was hoping for Kenorax to assist him."

Satrine chuckled. "Where did you get that from?"

"As he said, 'we only were even engaged with the matter out of regard for the Lavark's standing.' Kenorax was also making him wait. That means—"

"Hieljam needed them, not the other way around," Satrine concluded. "So you think they weren't involved in his death."

"I doubt in any direct manner," Welling said. "But they may have had involvement in the reasons behind it."

"So you want to dig a little deeper into what that was."

"Indeed." They approached the two pages, and Welling turned to the page from Hilsom's office. "I'm going to need Mister Hilsom to request documents."

"Sir," the boy said. "What do you need?"

"I'll need records from the customhouses and tariff checks, for at least three months. Preferably six. Anything they have that was brought in by Kenorax or Hieljam. Also make Mister Hilsom aware that I will likely have further requests of a similar nature."

The boy looked like Welling tried to feed him a frog. "As you say, sir."

"Then be about it."

The boy ran off.

"Anything for me, sir?" Phillen asked.

Satrine interrupted. "We should see if Mirrell and Kellman have had any luck finding Hajan or Jabiudal."

"Indeed," Welling said.

Phillen nodded. "I'll run ahead to Machie, see if I can find them. I'll blow a two-squall if I get them."

"Well done," Welling said, and the boy ran off.

Satrine started walking in the same direction at a leisurely pace. "Did we learn anything else?"

"Not sure," Welling said. "Save one fact. That Napolic fruit is horrible."

A quick coordination of whistle bursts between the pages led Minox and Rainey to Kellman and Mirrell, who were waiting on one corner on the edge of Machie.

"You've had luck?" Minox asked.

"Looks like Hajan is in a place called the Alahs Innata," Mirrell said. "At least, he spends a lot of his time there."

"It's a little restaurant or something down that way," Kellman said. "There's a sign with a crane and a fish."

"What about Jabiudal?" Rainey asked.

"Nothing yet," Kellman said. He flexed his fingers a bit as he talked, and Minox noticed scrapes on his knuckles and a few spots of not-quite-dried blood on the cuff of his shirt. So that was how they went about finding Hajan. "We can keep looking."

"Don't bother for now," Minox said. Beating a few Imachs might yield brief results, but in the long term it just hampered their ability to effectively enforce the law in this neighborhood. "Get over to the Kierans. I want good eyes on Ravi Kenorax and a man named Estiani Iliari. Where they go, who they talk to, what they do."

"Just eyes?" Mirrell asked.

"For now," Minox said. He had made a point of saying "good eyes" for the sake of Mirrell's ego. Not that he should have to give the man any butter to do his job, but these two were already troublesome enough. "Keep a subtle distance. They're already a bit sensitive about the dock lockdown."

"They are?" Mirrell said. "Well, we wouldn't want to upset them." His condescension could be spread like jam.

"Eyes open," Kellman said. Then he pointed to Rainey. "Watch your hair in these parts." They both headed off.

"Your hair?" Minox asked. It was an oddly specific warning.

She thought about it for a moment, then chuckled. "It's not a real thing."

"What's not?"

She sighed. "Come on." They walked into the streets, which got decidedly narrower as table-stands and shop carts choked up every spot that they could squeeze into. There was no way to get a wagon, horse, or pedalcart through here. Minox and Rainey couldn't even walk abreast as they worked their way through. He let her take the lead. "Imachs all have black hair, and the women traditionally wear theirs in very tight braids. So a woman with loose red hair—"

"Would be shocking to them?"

"Would be unusual," Rainey corrected. Minox noticed that several people, especially the Imach men, were staring hard at her as they made their way through. "But the presumption—an accepted convention—is that Imach men are enflamed by fair-haired Druth women, and even more so by my coloring."

"Surely they wouldn't attack you."

"Probably not." She held up her wrist, showing her marriage bracelet. "Most know what this means, and tend to accept the idea that I'm a goodly woman rather than a prostitute." Rainey's tone was hard to read, but it seemed equal parts bemused and enraged.

"So Kellman's warning?"

"The belief is, Imach women would see me as a threat, and they would attempt to chop my hair off." She turned back to look at him over her shoulder. "I don't think that's based on anything real, though."

The passage through the street had forced them into tight proximity with several of the locals, and Minox was on alert that none of them touched him or reached in his pockets, or did the same to Rainey.

"Over there," she said, pointing to the crane-and-fish sign. "It's a coffeehouse. Are you familiar with those?"

"I've heard of it," Minox said. Coffee was an Imach drink, he knew, but that was all.

"I strongly recommend that you do not have coffee if offered," she said. "It doesn't sit well with . . . people like you."

Minox raised an eyebrow. "Do you mean that I'm—"

She cut him off, almost putting her hand on his mouth. "Don't even say the word. Not in this patch of streets. They *really* do not care for it."

"I'm used to it." Attitudes toward mages, especially an Uncircled one like him, were far from cordial.

"They will make Druths look downright indulgent."

"As you say, Inspector."

They entered the Alahs Innata—a dim establishment, with almost no windows and a few low-burning oil lamps. There was a smell throughout the air—rich and earthy, and almost intoxicating. Shirtless Imach men—russet-skinned with coarse, thick beards—were grouped at the tables, sipping from small porcelain cups and talking in low voices.

Most of the talking ceased as Minox and Rainey stepped in. With all eyes on them, Minox decided to cut through all pretense.

"We're looking for a man named Nalassein Hajan. We're given to understand he is here."

"I am here," a melodious voice said from the far corner of the room. The men in that area shifted slightly to allow a clear view. Hajan was an elderly man, gray hair and beard, but that didn't stop him from sitting there shirtless like the rest of the men in here. "Why are the Constabulary seeking me?"

"We have some questions for you, sir," Rainey said, lowering her head as she stepped forward. "About your business with Hieljam ab Wefi Loriz."

Hajan let out a large laugh and sipped at his coffee. "Is he in some sort of trouble?"

"He's been murdered, Mister Hajan," Minox said.

"Murder—he—" Hajan put his cup down and put two fingers over his lips, murmuring something. Minox could only presume it was some form of prayer. "Please forgive me. This table is yours."

Rainey gave Minox the slight gesture that he should sit first. He took a seat, and then she maneuvered her chair so she would be behind him. The various Imach men in this place—the ones near the table at least— eased back slightly, but still stood in tense proximity.

"You were not aware he had been murdered?" Minox asked.

"No, I . . . there were whispers amongst my friends here that the Fuergans in the neighborhood were making things difficult." He spoke in rapid Imach dialect to one of the men by the table, who responded in kind. "Yes, two of his brothers were attacked. Most every man in here knows someone who was bothered or fought with last night. Or arrested."

"If someone was—" Minox started, ready to defend the actions of the night shift Constabulary.

Hajan waved a stern finger at Minox. "I am not angry about that. Order must be maintained. Our people, their people, your people start fights, people end up in cells. I would like to help any of my friends, or friends of my friends, who find themselves currently in your custody. Through proper channels, respecting your ways."

"I appreciate that," Minox said. "I'm given to understand most of those detained will be released today, likely with only fines and reports."

"Most," Hajan said. "I imagine there are a few whose infractions were too damning, and true charges must be levied. This occurs. I cannot argue."

Rainey cleared her throat. "Your relationship with Hieljam."

"Yes, of course." He sighed, and signaled to one of his men to bring more coffee. "Do you wish to sip with me?"

"Thank you, no," Rainey said, throwing a warning look at Minox. "We have found it doesn't agree with our systems."

He nodded sagely. "Many Druth have this problem, I understand. If there is nothing I can offer you. . . ."

"We are well, we are well, we are well," Rainey said, as if it were a bit of ritual. Hajan seemed to recognize this and grinned.

"Of course." He folded his hands together. "Wefi Loriz is . . . was . . . a good associate. I would even call him dear to me."

"You were friends?" Minox asked.

"That word is not lightly used. I cannot imagine a foreigner I would use that word for, but perhaps Wefi Loriz would come close. We did business together."

"We've gathered that, Mister Hajan," Rainey said. "Could you be more specific?"

"Of course. I represent a trust in Ghalad that imports products from there to western markets. The Hieljam have several ships that run goods from Fuerga to Druthal, and to accomplish that, they require friendly ports to resupply."

"Ports in Ghalad," Rainey said.

Minox asked the question that was probably foolish. "And Ghalad is?"

"Southern Imachan," Rainey answered. Hajan scoffed at this, but gave no further rebuke.

"My people in Ghalad give the Hieljam the friendly ports, and the Hieljam transport our goods for minimal cost. It has been most equitable for both of us."

"So you've had no complaints?" Minox asked.

"None! And to my knowledge, nor did the Hieljam."

"Hmm," Minox said. That didn't square with Hieljam ab Tishai's claim of "difficulty squaring accounts."

"Would any other associates of yours? Or rivals?"

Hajan peered at Minox with dark, piercing eyes. "You are a very thin man, Inspector. Why have you come to talk to me?"

"The murder weapon," Minox said. "Perhaps you are familiar with it. It's an Imach knife called a *talveca*."

"A *talveca*?" He laughed, and then said something to the rest of his crowd. They all laughed as well. Then his laughter stopped cold. "A *talveca* is not Ghaladi. That is a Kadabali weapon." He spit to the ground when he said it, as did many others.

"Kadabal is . . . another province in Imachan?" Minox asked.

Hajan turned to Rainey. "You seem to be the smarter one here, dear lady. Your associate keeps referring to 'Imachan' like it is a place that means something to me and my friends. *Ghaladina, iat?*" The men around him repeated what he said. "We are all *Ghaladi* here."

"My apologies," Minox said. "I didn't understand."

"Most Druth do not."

Minox hit upon an idea. "Is the name Jabiudal a Kadabali one?"

"Assan Jabiudal?" Hajan said, rising from his chair. "That . . ." Whatever his next thoughts were, they couldn't be expressed in Trade, as he went into a tirade in his native tongue.

"What about Assan Jabiudal?" Minox asked.

"He is piss," Hajan sneered. "He is a stain that deserves to be wiped off my shoe, is what he is."

"So, a business rival," Rainey said dryly.

"A rival? Hardly. I deal in coffee, sandalwoods, spices. Legitimate trade. Jabiudal only uses that as a front for his filth."

That triggered Minox's interest. "What sort of filth? Smuggling? Drugs? Slaves?"

"I will not sully myself with further talk of such things, Inspector. And I do not believe we have more to say. No one in my employ would use a *talveca*, and the death of Wefi Loriz brings me nothing but hardship. So I would hope I am not a suspect."

"We're just gathering information at this juncture, Mister Hajan."

"Then do it elsewhere, I am done." He waved them off, and other men rose up as if they were willing to make the matter more confrontational.

"We'll be in touch," Rainey said, stepping away from the table. "Thank you for your time. *Eht'shahala.*"

"*Eht'shahala,*" he replied with a respectful nod of the head.

Rainey was not the least bit subtle as she pulled Minox back out into the late morning sun.

"That was a waste of time," Minox said. "We may have to get a writ to further interview him."

"Hopefully that won't be necessary," Rainey said. "I think he was telling the truth."

"As do I," Minox said. "And if his opinion of Jabiudal is accurate, then that's the man we should seek out."

"But not right now," Rainey said with an apprehensive sigh. "We have an appointment with the Lyranans."

Chapter 8

"SO, IMACHAN IS NOT actually Imachan," Minox said as they walked to Geinanj Ong—the Lyranan sector of the Little East colloquially referred to in conjunction with the Tsouljan section as Tyzoville. "How did I not know about this?"

"Because you haven't had a traditional education," Rainey said. "Strictly speaking, what we consider to be 'Imachan' is actually—" She paused for a moment. "'The Grand Confederated Nations of the Faithful to his High Holiness the Cehlat of Imachan.'"

"That's a mouthful."

"I'm well aware. But it's essentially ten countries with the same national religion, to varying degrees. Strictly speaking, the Cehlat of Imachan isn't a head of state in the same way the king is here."

"Inspector," Minox said, stopping in their walk. "I know you've been well-trained as part of your earlier career. But how do you know things like this?"

Rainey's face dropped a bit. "I don't always know what I know until I know it, frankly."

"That doesn't make much sense."

"I don't imagine," she said. She stepped off the main

walkway into an unoccupied alley. "When I took the place of the Waish *quia*, I had to have a traditional education to play the role. But there was hardly time to give me one."

Minox nodded, as both those points were reasonable, but he wasn't seeing where she was going with the statement. "So you had to learn enough to fake your way at the beginning, I presume."

"Not even." She hesitated, as if preparing herself for exertion. Her face took on the expression of someone who swallowed vinegar, and when she spoke, she seemed to only be able to manage a whisper. "Do you know what a . . . telepath is?"

That was not a word he was familiar with.

"You can do a lot of things with magic," she said quietly. "But there are limits. Even the most skilled and powerful mages can't get in here." She tapped her forehead.

"I had presumed that to be the case," Minox said. There had been more than one time he had attempted to pull the truth out of a suspect's mind, but he never was able to grab on to anything.

"Telepaths are—blazes, I probably shouldn't even tell you this, but—" She looked back out to the street, checking if anyone was paying them mind. She again spoke haltingly, almost as if she had to force the words to her mouth by sheer will. "They're . . . something else. What they do isn't magic, but they can look at your mind like the threads of a cloth. And in some cases, weave a whole new pattern into it."

Minox had no response for a moment, trying to process this information. Finally he managed to say, "How have I never heard of this?"

"The people who have the capability are rare, far rarer than mages," Rainey said. "And they—as well as Druth Intelligence—do their best to keep their talents generally unknown."

"But Druth Intelligence uses such people."

"Do they ever."

———◆—◆◆—◆———

"We're going to give you a choice, Trini." The man—he wasn't a stick, but he was definitely like a stick, all clean-faced and smooth chin—crouched down in front of her. "There are a few different ways we can do this, but the choice is yours."

"You're a terrible liar," Trini said. "You ain't gonna let me choose nothing."

"We certainly are," he said. "You decide you want nothing to do with this, we'll put you back in the carriage and drive you back to your little corner on Jent and Tannen. You can go back to doing whatever it is you had going on."

Bastard made it sound so appealing. Truth was, she had little going on beyond planning what the blazes she was going to do to keep her throat together when Idre Hoffer got out of the Quarry.

"And let's just say I'm interested," she said. "Then what?"

He gave her a wink. "Then things get really interesting." He pointed to the guy in the corner, with the one twitchy eye and crumbs in his half-grown beard. "That's Oster."

"What's he on? Phat? The White? Or that new stuff from the islands?"

"None of them." He shrugged. "I know, it's hard to believe. Oster's very special, though. He can touch you. Right here." He poked Trini in her forehead.

"Ouch," she said. "So can you."

"He means your mind," Oster said. "Satrine Carthas. Goes by Tricky Trini. You turned another girl over to the Constabulary so you could sleep in peace for a few months. And you're afraid of birds."

"I ain't afraid of them!" Trini snapped. "They're just weird. Beaks and little eyes, it's creepy." She did a double take. "How you know that?"

"Because your mind is a clear tapestry to me," Oster said.

"Here's the way it goes," Smooth Chin said. "You need to learn to be her. The quia."

"What's the blazes is a key-ah?"

"It's like a princess, but in Waisholm."

"Where's Waisholm?"

"North of here," Smooth Chin said. "It's another country."

"Your dad was probably from there, by the looks of you," Oster said. "What was he?"

"Never knew," Trini said. "Can't you see that?"

"I'm trying not to dig around too much. Got to save my strength."

"Why?" Trini asked.

"That's what I'm getting at," Smooth Chin said. "You're going to need to learn all sorts of things. Not just how to read and write . . ."

"I can blazing read," Trini said. She still had the poem book in her coat pocket.

Smooth Chin looked to Oster for some confirmation, and got a lazy-eyed nod.

"Good, that means you're clever. So think hard about this, all right?"

"About what, exactly?"

"Oster doesn't just see what you're thinking, you see. He can touch it."

"You ever see weaving work done?" Oster asked.

"Yeah," Trini said.

"Your mind, it's kind of like a woven tapestry. I can see it, touch it . . . and I can weave new things into it."

"Blazing what?" Trini asked. "Like, change my head?"

"Exactly," Oster said.

"So here's how it can work," Smooth Chin said. "There's three choices here. The first is that Oster can just make you be the qui—the princess."

"Make me . . . the princess."

"You'll be a perfect fake, in that you will completely believe that you are her. You'll know what she needs to, will act like she would."

"But I'll still be me?"

"No," Oster said. "The you that's Trini Carthas will just be gone."

Just be gone. There was a strange appeal to that. Become a princess and never know about the life at the corner of Jent and Tannen. But something didn't smell right.

"So why don't you just do that, huh? Why even ask me?"

"Because that work is delicate," Oster said. "It requires your utter compliance, or else your brain would be hopelessly ruined. Like newsprints in the rain."

She didn't like the sound of that. "What are the other two choices?" she asked.

"First is Oster builds you . . . a mask, as it were. It's sort of like the first choice, except the real you is always inside. The 'princess' will do whatever she needs to do, but you can step in and take the reins whenever you need to."

She looked over to Oster, and could see on his face he didn't like that. "What's the risk on that one?"

"It's tricky work. Do it wrong, and the lines between you and the mask get muddy. The mask—or you—or both, could go mad."

"No to that," Trini said. "Not a chance. What's your third idea?"

"It's the least risk to your mind, but will put you at the most risk when you're out there."

"If I do this."

"If you do this," Smooth Chin said. "You stay yourself, and Oster puts into your head the experience and education she would have had."

"So I'll know fancy learning and how to dance at parties and sewage like that?"

"Exactly."

"But I'll still be me, just knowing more stuff."

"Essentially."

"Well, blazes, that's the way to go."

"Let me remind you that you'll have to fake being the quia by yourself with this method. You won't have that constructed personality to protect you."

"I'm used to not being protected," Trini said. "All right, let's give it a go."

"You're agreeing, then?" Oster asked.

Trini put up her chin, giving her best tough face. "Sure, why not? Got nothing else planned."

"You heard the girl," Smooth Chin said. "Might as well get started. We've got a long boat ride ahead."

"Boat?" Trini asked.

"How else are we gonna get to Waisholm?" he asked. He looked to the rest of the boys in the outer room. "I'm going to make some arrangements, be about an hour. That good for you?" The question was to Oster.

"For the first session," Oster said. "It's going to be quite a few."

"So what do I do?" Trini asked.

"Sit down," Oster said, pointing to the floor. He got down in front of her. "To be honest, I'm glad this was your choice. All three of these options, I need your explicit co-operation, and . . . none of them are easy on you. This one, though, there isn't much risk of it wrecking you."

"I won't be hurt, you're saying?"

"Hurt?" Oster said. "Not exactly. But it's going to be hard on you. I'm sorry."

She shrugged. "I'm used to hard on me."

"Stay still, Satrine." He reached out and put his hands on her temples. Instinctively she flinched away at his touch, but then forced herself to move back, allow him contact.

"Let's do this, boss," she said.

"Again," he said quietly. *"I apologize."*

He took a deep breath, and then a whole year slammed into her skull.

"They did that to you?" Minox asked. "That's a thing that can be done?" The entire concept was boggling, especially the offers that she had passed on.

"It is," Rainey said. "So . . . to be clear, they didn't give me the information of a classical education. They gave me the experience of it. Not a real memory, mind you, there's little confusion in my head about what is really my life and what they gave me. But if you were to ask me about, say . . ."

Realizing she was fishing for an example, Minox offered, "The lineage of Kieran dynasties in the High Imperial era?"

"Then I would realize that I know them to be, in order: Kieran, First Luciex, Tanaphus, First Gelmin, Pomorious . . . see? I didn't know that I knew that. But I know it. I could continue."

"Not necessary."

"Then let's move on."

They pushed their way out of the Imach-occupied streets and worked their way over to the unimaginatively named Second Auxiliary Public House in Geinanj Ong. This part of the Little East was completely unrecognizable in comparison to the Imach sector. The streets were not only open and easily accessible, they were completely clean. Minox was used to seeing some degree of filth and rubbish scattered on the streets and gathered in the drainage ditches. There was none of that. The cobblestones almost shone.

Here the buildings were painted shades of gray, and there was copious signage in multiple languages identifying streets, offices, and the Second Auxiliary Public House. Minox noted that they also passed the Primary Public House and the First Auxiliary Public House, which both looked exactly the same as the Second Auxiliary.

Each Lyranan public house had a wide doorframe, though Minox noted no door actually hung in the frame. Instead there was a canvas sheet that could be lowered and tied off at the floor to prevent entry. Minox also noticed that the public house windows—indeed all the windows—had no glass. Instead they were filled with a thin cloth, drawn tight, allowing a diffuse light into the building. At the far end of the building, there was an empty stage, and between the stage and the entrance there were several long tables laid out in neat rows.

Closest to the entrance was the kitchen line. A handful of Lyranans were queued up to receive their midday meal, all looking strangely similar. They all had the grayish skin pallor, and heads shaved bald, and wore coats that were either dark gray, dark blue, or dark brown. The only differentiation between any of them were the flairs of colored braiding at the collars and cuffs of the coats.

No food was being served yet; the Lyranans were just queued up.

"Is the heraldry of Lyranan clothing something you have in your brain?" he asked Inspector Rainey.

"That is not something I know," she said, sounding almost surprised. "I'm sure the people we're meeting will recognize us, however. And we actually are a few minutes early."

Five Lyranans emerged from some unseen back room and took to the stage, each carrying musical instruments: two long-necked stringed instruments, similar in concept if not in appearance to the Druth guitar; another grand string instrument that needed to be rolled out; one that was flute-like, except much larger; finally something not quite unlike a drum. They took places on the stage, but stood in silence.

Waiting like the queue for the kitchen.

Rainey was about to say something when the church bells of Saint Interson rang noon. Then many things suddenly occurred. The players on the stage immediately began playing, slow and atonal, with an odd haunting quality to it. Someone behind the kitchen counter whistled, and the people at the front of the queue began giving orders, which the cooks behind the counter responded to with absurd rapidity. And there was a tap on Minox's shoulder.

"Punctuality is an admirable trait, Inspector Third Class Welling. We are gratified to find you in possession of it."

Minox turned to see three Lyranans standing before him. Like the rest of the line, they were gray-pallored, dark-eyed, and bald-headed. Their uniform jackets were blue, with the one in the center sporting significantly more braiding on his collar and cuffs. It took a moment for Minox to even realize that one of the three was a woman—the lack of hair and similar cut of their clothes threw off his usual signifiers of gender.

"You must be Third Tier Supervisor Heizhan Taiz," Minox said. He held out his hand. "Inspector Welling, as you have surmised."

Taiz took his hand after a moment of hesitation, as if he were conforming to Druth custom out of obligation.

"Well placed, Inspector. It is also gratifying to see you, Inspector Third Class Rainey. My associates, Trade Notary First Class Fao Nengtaj—" He indicated the man to his left, and then the woman. "—Specialist First Class Pra Yikenj." The two other Lyranans just bowed their heads. Taiz's Trade was excellent, though he clearly spoke with a Lyranan accent, which gave his voice a strange tonal quality, like he was singing his words with a single note.

"Glad to . . . meet you," Rainey said haltingly, her attention on Yikenj.

"Let us not dally," Taiz said. He stepped over to the kitchen line, and when he made a sharp whistling sound, the rest of the people in line immediately deferred to him. He made whispered comments to the kitchen staff, and then returned. "We will take our meal at the table farthest from the entertainment, so it will not distract us from our business."

As Minox followed the Lyranans to the table, he asked, "Is there always a band playing at lunch?"

Taiz looked over to the musicians, and back to Minox, giving something almost resembling a smile. "In your country, we have made alterations to fit your clock schedule. Our day is broken into several sections, keyed to their purpose. In Lyrana, right now would be *te-ungzhai*. A rough translation would be 'the hour of easement.' It is when we eat, enjoy the artistic merits of music, and converse with our peers. Right now we are making an exception, honoring a Druth tradition of combining vocation with our meal."

"It's less a tradition and more a habit," Minox said.

"Perhaps a poor one," Taiz said. He sat down and indicated for the rest to do the same. "But there must be room for proper exceptions in order to achieve mutual goals. For example, the musicians and kitchen staff must work at this time so that others may have their *ungzhai*. But that is the nature of their position."

"This is fascinating," Rainey said. "Should we discuss why you've invited us here?"

"In due moment, Inspector Rainey," Taiz said. He glanced over, noting the waitperson who came over with wooden bowls of food, all identical. The waitron silently placed a bowl in front of each of them and slipped off.

"No one else is getting served to the table," Minox noted.

"There are privileges attached to rank," Taiz said. He leaned in. "It actually has been years since I've come to a public house for *ungzhai*." The look on his face was almost wicked, as if he had confessed a great transgression.

"Sir," Nengtaj said firmly.

Taiz leaned back. "Please, Inspectors."

The dish was like nothing Minox had seen before. It was primarily a mass of transparent strips that he could not identify on sight—looking almost like worms, were they made of glass. The strips rested in a broth, but not quite enough broth that it could properly be called a soup, with chunks of mushrooms, root vegetables, and a meat that Minox's nose told him was fish.

Minox picked up the eating utensil—which was neither spoon nor winescrew, but made Minox think of both—and prodded at the strips. They felt tender, easy enough to eat. Even still, despite his usual lack of discerning palate, he paused.

"Is this a traditional dish in Lyrana?"

Taiz held his utensil just away from his mouth—Minox noticed he was able to scoop up broth and fish while wrapping the strips around it—and thought for a moment. "It is a close approximation. The fish of your river and the fish of our ocean are not the same, but we adapt." He then took the bite. The other two waited for him to eat before starting.

Watching the three Lyranans carefully, Minox was disturbed by how hard it was to read them. They spoke in similar ways, with that tonal quality, and their faces had nearly no expression, at least none that Minox could properly understand. The only thing he could get out of it was haughtiness, but that might just be his own biases. Even the graceful, fluid way they moved their hands was odd, almost inhuman. More disturbing was the difficulty he had in identifying their differences. There was no sense of age he could place on any of them—the universal hairlessness was throwing off his skill at determining that. He wanted to say that Nengtaj was the youngest, but even that was based only instinct. Little more than random guess.

He was understanding why Rainey had been annoyed with the Lyranans from the moment they received the letter.

Rainey started on her own food, and knowing that she was far more unwilling to eat something she found distasteful, he went in. He was unable to get everything onto the utensil with the same deftness as the Lyranans, but he believed he managed to not embarrass himself.

The flavor was unique. Fishy, certainly, with a rich earthy sense, complimented by the tender slickness of the strips—the texture of which was not unlike the outer layer of the Fuergan dumplings. Minox idly wondered if they were made with a similar process.

He continued to eat at the pace the Lyranans set, and when Taiz had several bites, he put his utensil down.

"Specialist, proceed with the briefing."

Yikenj put her own utensil down, in a sharp manner that demonstrated a certain degree of precision was second nature to her. "We are aware that the Fuergan man, Hieljam ab Wefi Loriz, has been murdered at the Rev Tak Mel, and that he was to meet two Kierans to discuss business, and that the weapon used to kill him is indigenous to one of the Imach countries."

"You're very well informed," Rainey said.

"We are aware that there was writing in a script that you believe to be Lyranan. Logically this would lead you to see the connections that our people may have with the deceased and the crime. To facilitate your investigation, we are prepared to disclose this information."

"That would be very helpful," Minox said. Though the straightforward nature of their offer made him immediately suspect they were using their openness as a cover for something else they wished to hide.

Yikenj gave a nod to Nengtaj. "How familiar are you with the Eastern waters?" he asked.

"It's not something I'm versed in," Minox said. He looked to Rainey.

"Not particularly," she said, though he wasn't sure if she was telling the truth. Something in her had turned hard and unreadable.

"It is an area overwhelmed with chaos," Nengtaj said. "Piracy, smuggling, slave raids on the Xonocan or Ch'omik coasts, petty wars that spread to the seas. The turmoil caused by the fall of the empire never ceased."

"The empire?" Minox asked.

Rainey supplied the answer, though Minox wondered if she did not realize she knew it until this moment. Her revelations had disturbed him, and it made it hard for him to fully focus on the current task. "The Tyzanian Empire, which collapsed four hundred years ago."

"Most of what you think of as 'the East' was controlled or touched by the empire," Yikenj said.

"The Lyranan government is the only power in the region attempting to assert the authority of order on the seas. Which is where my department is involved."

"Trade Notary," Minox said.

"We are designing a system for ships of legitimate purpose—cargo trade, naval defense, and so forth—to be registered and easily acknowledged. Lyranan ships patrol those waters that, for example, Fuergan ships, such as the Hieljam family's ships, pass through on their way south around the Imach cape."

"And so you had dealings with Hieljam." Minox led Nengtaj.

"Permits were to be issued to the Hieljam, pending certain details that the factors in Maradaine were unable to provide. We were awaiting a meeting with Hieljam ab Wefi Loriz, but it never came."

"He refused to take a meeting with you?" Minox asked.

"Refuse is a strong word," Yikenj said coolly.

Taiz spoke up. "We left word that we were open to a meeting and could schedule one at his convenience. We never received a response."

"Why do you suppose that is?" Rainey asked. Her question seemed almost aimed at Yikenj, who answered directly.

"There are several potential reasons. He may have had more pressing business while here, for one. While we take this registration matter seriously, for Hieljam and the other Fuergans, it would simply be a minor bit of administrative duty. The sort of thing I would imagine many people commonly put off until it is absolutely necessary."

"I would imagine," Rainey said.

Taiz finished the last bite of his dish and pushed the bowl to his left. "If there is nothing else, Inspectors, I would be gratified if we could take our leave."

"There is the matter of the text," Minox said. "Text written at the crime scene, which we've identified as Lyranan."

"So we've heard," Yikenj said.

Minox pulled the piece of paper that Leppin had copied the text on out of his coat pocket. "Given that it may provide key information about the murderer, or at least their motivation, we would like to know what it says."

"Of course you would," Taiz said.

Yikenj also added, "Though it is likely another, how do you say, 'dead end'?"

Rainey drew a sharp breath, as did Taiz. Taiz looked at his aide and made a strange whistling sound. She bowed her head to him and focused on the last bites of her meal.

Taiz turned again to Minox. "If I may see it?"

"Of course." Minox slid the paper over to Taiz.

Taiz glanced at the sheet, his face first maintaining its haughty expression, as if the mere act of translation was well beneath him. Then that expression melted away. He turned the sheet upside down.

"Is it relevant?" Minox asked.

"No," Taiz said quietly. He turned the paper again, and then once more. Tears started to well in his eyes. "I'm sorry, it's . . ." He slid the sheet over to Yikenj, who reacted in the same way, and then passed it to Nengtaj. While their reactions were highly emotional, Minox still couldn't read if they were overcome with grief, joy, or horror.

"What?" Inspector Rainey asked, though she kept her focus trained on the woman. "Is it a confession?"

"It is . . ." Nengtaj said, his own voice trembling. He took a moment to compose himself, as he was also overcome with emotion. "Let me explain. Our language is written with several symbols, but each symbol takes a different meaning depending on its orientation." He slid the sheet back over to Minox, pointing to one of the symbols. "Ejai." He turned the sheet on its side, and pointed to the same symbol. "Heza."

"I think I understand," Minox said. "How does that mean anything?"

Taiz spoke up again. "There is an art form, called *eizhein*. A kind of poetry, done in a block of twelve symbols arranged like this. To be a 'perfect' *eizhein*, it must make sense when viewed in all four directions, and the symbols themselves must retain a certain aesthetic balance."

"And this is an *eizhein*?" Rainey asked. "A perfect one?"

"This . . . this is possibly one of the most elegant examples of the form I've ever seen."

"So is it a famous *eizhein*? One of the great masterworks?"

"Not at all," Yikenj said. "I've never read it before."

"But it could stand with them," Taiz said.

"So what does it say?" Minox asked, looking to any of them.

"You have to understand it will lose its poetry in translation."

"Granted," Rainey said.

"In this orientation, it says, 'Vines choke the earth, and nothing blooms.'"

Taiz turned it on its side. "The fires must be deprived of fuel, or we burn."

Another turn. "The air cries with smoke, no breath."

Last turn. "Hold it under the water while it can still drown."

Pra Yikenj raised an eyebrow. "Yes, it was quite lacking in Trade. It should not be repeated."

"I don't think that will be a problem." Rainey took the sheet away from Taiz, her eyes still locked on Pra Yikenj. "It's poetic nonsense in any language."

"I presume that it means very little in terms of your investigation," Taiz said to Minox.

Minox definitely couldn't draw sense out of it. Not yet. But that didn't mean it was meaningless; it just meant nothing to him, yet. For all he knew, translating it into Trade ruined its purpose as a message. Perhaps it gave a direct clue being translated into Fuergan or Tsouljan.

"There is still much to contemplate." He got to his feet. "If there's nothing else?"

The Lyranans all rose. "I believe that is all for the moment," Taiz said. "If you need further consultation, you are aware where my offices are. Specialist Yikenj can make arrangements if you need."

Rainey stood up. "I'm sure she can."

The Lyranans bowed, and stepped away from the table, as if they expected Minox and Rainey to be the ones to actually leave first. Minox returned the bow and walked out. Rainey was with him, but walked with one eye on the Lyranans until they reached the door.

"Blazes," she said once they were in the street. Her hands started trembling. "It's clear now who the real suspect here is."

Minox was surprised. "Did we just come from the same meeting?"

Rainey stopped, glanced back to the public house, and after a moment, grabbed Minox by his vest and pulled him into the alley. "I'm talking about Pra Yikenj."

"You were oddly fixated on her during the entire exchange."

"Fixated, right." She looked back out the alleyway, and even glanced up to the sky. "That woman is a spy and an assassin."

"You know this, Inspector?" Minox asked.

"I know it. Fifteen years ago she nearly killed me."

Chapter 9

"**Y**OU'RE CERTAIN?" Welling asked. He must have noticed the change on her face that came with him questioning her word. She thought they were past him doubting her. "I'm simply saying, frankly, I found telling the Lyranans apart challenging at best. Add in fifteen years of memory . . ."

Satrine shook her head. She knew all too well. "It was Yikenj. I wasn't entirely sure on her face, but I *knew* her voice."

"And she tried to kill you?" He glanced about behind him. "This is when you were in Intelligence?"

"The end of my time in Intelligence, shortly after I left Waisholm."

Welling looked at her as if he expected a further story to unfold.

"The details aren't relevant, Welling."

"You say that, but I've already learned many disturbing things that have altered my worldview."

There was just a hint to his voice that made her think he was joking. It wasn't something he did very often.

"My point is, as an agent, I had a run-in with her in which I barely escaped with my life. And shortly after that I was cashiered out, met my husband . . . and thanked the saints that I survived."

"So you think she may be involved."

"Since we're apparently looking for someone who could get in and out of the compound without being noticed, and kill Hieljam without leaving another mark on him. A known spy and assassin is a good place to be looking."

"Your argument is quite valid, but it's on a shaky firmament."

Satrine felt her blood boil. "I know it's the same woman."

"I'm not doubting you, Inspector. But the same woman is fifteen years older. Are you as physically capable as you were back then?"

"No," she said.

"Let alone motivation. We're completely lacking for that on all fronts."

Satrine had to agree to that. "Everyone we've looked at seems unhappy that he's dead."

"Precisely." Welling took out his pipe and lit it up. He was now in serious thinking mode. "We've been led around by the nose to visit various parties, none of whom benefit from the victim's death. We know more about his business, but little meaningful toward solving his murder. We've heard contradictory stories from several parties, and, I must confess, I'm at a loss to determine who, specifically, is being dishonest."

That was unusual for Welling. Most of the time he could spot a liar before ten words got out of their mouth. "What's messing you up?"

"Body language isn't the same for any of these people. The cues I usually notice are all wrong."

"We'll have to just figure it out the normal way," Satrine said. "So who benefits from his death?"

"At this point, I might think Assan Jabiudal, but I

have absolutely no basis for that." He took a few more puffs of the pipe. Satrine glanced around at the business in the streets. They were in the part of the Little East where Lyranan holdings—gray with elegant squares—abutted with the Tsouljan ones—golden colors and curves. The street was crowded, but there was a visible gap—just wide enough for a pedalcart—between the two peoples. They didn't look at each other, they didn't acknowledge or shout. The only ones who crossed the street were from other countries. Druth, Kieran, Fuergan mostly.

"I think we should go back to the Tsouljan compound," Satrine said. "I think there's more there than Mirrell and Kellman shook up."

"That is quite likely," Welling said. He glanced back and forth and at the separation between the Lyranans and the Tsouljans. "There is something to this neighborhood, a pattern I haven't quite put my finger on."

He was twitching and talking about patterns. Satrine had learned that was when he was starting to get too deep into the waters of his thoughts. Time to pull his nets in. "Is it within the scope of this investigation?"

He shook his head. "Most likely not. I just. . . ." He snuffed out his pipe. "Let's go to the compound."

They made their way around the block to the compound entrance, where the two footpatrolmen stationed at the gates were being screamed at by Hieljam ab Tishai, who was dressed entirely in white furs. Satrine couldn't quite make out what she was saying, as her accent seemed magnified by her shouting.

At least four other Fuergans were at Hieljam ab Tishai's side, large men who looked like they might be carrying weapons. They also wore white fur, but only as bands around their heads. They also looked like they were willing to engage the footpatrol officers at a moment's notice.

One of the two footpatrol glanced in their direction as Satrine and Welling approached. "Ma'am, here they are. I'm sure they can help you."

Hieljam ab Tishai responded in a string of Fuergan words that sounded like insults to Satrine's ear.

"Heina-jai Hieljam," Satrine said, putting herself in between the Fuergan woman and the duty officers. A respectful use of formal title should help bring this woman back to the ground. "Is there something we can help you with?"

She narrowed her dark, angular eyes at Satrine. "Yes, Inspector, there is something you can help me with. The two of you *people* are exactly who I was looking for. Your underlings were utterly useless in locating you."

One of the footpatrol cleared his throat cautiously. "Inspector, ma'am, I was trying to . . ."

Hieljam ab Tishai launched into further expletives at him.

"Heina-jai," Satrine said firmly. "Let my officer speak."

Hieljam ab Tishai pursed her lips, like she was physically holding back a further torrent of Fuergan profanities.

"What is it?" Satrine asked the footpatrol.

"She was trying to bribe us, ma'am," he said.

"What is this word you keep using?" Hieljam ab Tishai asked.

"We really could put charges, Inspector," the footpatrol said. "I was trying to be reasonable, but she was . . . insistent."

Satrine understood what the difficulty was. "Heina-jai Hieljam, you don't need to hire our footpatrol. They aren't—they cannot be—paid directly by you."

Hieljam ab Tishai scowled. "That is a terrible way to ensure proper service."

"Perhaps so, Heina-jai. You were looking for us? We're here now."

"Indeed I was. I require the body of my *isahresa*."

"His body? It's at our stationhouse, in the examinarium."

"In the what?"

Welling stepped in. "In murder cases it is necessary for our experts to examine the body in detail, with specialized tools, in order to determine as much possible information that could yield resolution."

Hieljam ab Tishai's face turned crimson. "You took his body and desecrated it?"

"We examined it, ma'am," Welling said, holding his ground. The four Fuergan attendants all stepped a bit closer. "I apologize if our actions caused offense, but it was necessary."

"I will decide what is necessary for my *isahresa*'s body," she said. "And it is time for his *srehtai*."

Satrine presumed that was a mourning or funeral rite. "It may be our people have concluded their examination and can release the body to you. Would that be all right?"

"Perhaps. Take me to him now, Inspectors."

"We're still in the midst of investigating . . ." Welling started.

"I do not care," Hieljam ab Tishai said. "Do not ignore me, or pass me on to your menials." The four attendants all tensed their bodies, like they were about to spring on Welling. Welling didn't budge, but there was a shift to his demeanor, including gripping his handstick.

"Fine," Satrine said. She might as well get on top of this, and try to get some further information out of Hieljam ab Tishai. "Welling, I'll escort the *heina* back to the stationhouse, while you continue the investigation here." Welling seemed to pick up on her cue, using the woman's rank: this was part of treading carefully. The Hieljam were for all intents Fuergan nobility, and they needed to treat the woman like they would a countess in the same situation.

Welling relaxed. "If you think that's best, Inspector. Return here as quickly as possible. I think we'll need several hours here."

Satrine gave him a quick nod, which he returned, and then he went inside the Tsouljan enclave.

"Heina-jai, if you'll come with me?"

"Hardly, Inspector," Hieljam ab Tishai said. "My sled is over there. You will come with me."

———◆◆———

As Inspector Rainey went off with Hieljam ab Tishai, it occurred to Minox how strongly he had misjudged his understanding of the Fuergan people. What he had taken for cultural appreciation and mutual respect was merely his own affinity for tobacco and a shopkeep's politeness with a valued customer.

He passed through the portal into the Tsouljan gardens, again greeted by the red-haired guardians. "Qhat nek dav."

The Tsouljans seemed to be about their business, much the same as they were yesterday. There appeared to be no real reaction to a man's death in their space; there was still no apparent reaction to their imprisonment within their compound.

The place was the very picture of peacefulness. Which was why Minox couldn't understand why it made him feel so restless. Just from crossing the threshold, he was already unnerved.

Minox spotted the green-haired Tsouljan who had helped Mirrell and Kellman. "You there, boy. You speak excellent Trade, yes?"

"Yes, sir," the boy said, jumping to his feet from the pruning work he was doing at the walkway.

"I may have further need of your services, if you'll come with me."

"Sir, it is . . . I should not have . . ." the boy faltered.

Someone else—a yellow-haired Tsouljan—snapped some harsh invective syllables from across the garden. The green-haired boy scurried away.

Minox marched over to the yellow-haired Tsouljan— was it the same one who they dealt with yesterday? He quickly determined it was not. This man was much older. "Why did you chase him away?"

The old Tsouljan raised up two fingers. "Calm."

"Pardon?" Minox asked, not sure if the man was threatening him in some way.

"No shout. Speak calm." His Trade was heavily accented, probably limited in vocabulary.

Minox lowered his tone, relaxed his shoulders. "You shouted at the boy."

"Boy out of place."

"Yes, but . . ." Minox struggled for a moment to find a way to express what he wanted to say in the simplest manner. "I need to ask questions, I need to understand answers. He speaks Trade and Tsouljan well."

"Out of place."

"But I need him."

"Not what you need."

This was not going anywhere Minox was interested in. "Where is Bur Rek-Uti? Is he in charge here?"

"Bur Rek-Uti. Not what you need."

"I need . . ." Minox started sharply. He felt his temper rising, and with that a slight buzz in the tips of his fingers in his left hand. If history was any indication, that buzz would quickly evolve into prickly sensation up his arm; an unscratchable itch. This—the intense emotions and feeling of magic building within his extremities—must be tied to the use of the *rijetzh*. Sometimes, when the magic-dulling effect faded, the aftereffects were unpleasant. It typically didn't last very long, and he was still working on mastering that aspect of its use. He hated the brief loss of his own person that it caused, even as the price for hours of control. He had no idea why it was affecting him so strongly now, though. "Do you know who I am?"

"Druth man. Officer of law."

"Inspector Welling," Minox said, indicating himself. Minox presumed that, unlike the Lyranans, this Tsouljan man didn't care about the particulars of his Inspector Third Class status. "You are?"

"Naljil Rek-Yun."

This was the one who had answered Mirrell and Kellman's questions.

"Yes, you are the one I'm looking for. Yesterday you—"

Rek-Yun held up a hand. "I . . . center this place. You. . . . You do not yet know."

Minox took a deep breath. "I need to . . . investigate. Someone was killed here yesterday."

The old man looked pained. "I am . . . aware. But it is done."

"No!" Pure anger surged through Minox, including a wave of magical energy rippling up his arm to the center of his body.

"Center!" the old Tsouljan said sternly. "Calm!"

"Do not tell me my business, sir," Minox said. This post-*rijetzh* fit was the worst ever, which made no logical sense. He pointed a finger at Rek-Yun, but he could see how much his hand was shaking. His left hand—numb and trembling. "I am here . . ." His knees buckled.

The old man grabbed him firmly and pulled him to his feet, showing a surprising degree of strength. "You need Sevqir Fel-Sed."

"Who . . . or what . . . is that?"

"This way," Rek-Yun said, leading him to one of the huts. He called out to someone else in Tsouljan. Minox let himself be led, tamping down the urge to throw the old man off, trying to keep the magic from bursting out of his arms.

Satrine was not prepared for riding in what Hieljam ab Tishai referred to as a "sled." She had been on Waish dogsleds, built to run on the snow and ice. That was not what this was, though the design had a vague similarity.

The vehicle was low to the ground, much like those dogsleds, and its lush cushioned seats were open to the air. Where the dogsleds would have had wooden runners or metal blades, this contraption had a series of small wheels. And it was yoked to a team of four Fuergan horses.

Satrine would never consider herself an expert on horses—she rarely considered them anything other than functional beasts that people who were not her would tend to. But even she could recognize the magnificence of these particular animals, with musculature, power, and beauty that Druth horses couldn't match.

The creatures looked like they could run like thunder, and Satrine couldn't imagine being on the sled when they did that could be pleasant.

"Sit," Hieljam ab Tishai said, taking her place in one of the seats. Only one of her attendants was taking a place on the sled, standing on the front to drive the horses. The rest stood at the ready on the sides, like they intended to run along.

Satrine took her place in the offered seat, gripping onto it as tightly as she could. Instinct told her she might easily fly off this thing as soon as it started moving. The cobblestone streets of Maradaine would not be friendly to those wheels.

Once Satrine was in place, Hieljam ab Tishai whistled to her driver, and he snapped the horses forward. The sled surged forward, rumbling and bumping over the stones as the whole contraption sped off, like on a whistle gallop.

Satrine gripped onto the seat tighter, noticing the

guards running alongside, shouting at anyone else in the street to clear the way.

Hieljam ab Tishai was oddly sedate, maintaining a poised position in her seat as the sled bumped and caromed down the street.

"You can't go this fast," Satrine shouted, feeling like there was no way Hieljam ab Tishai could hear her otherwise. The sled pounding on the stones made a horrible noise.

"So it would seem," Hieljam ab Tishai said, her voice raised but perfectly calm. "Your streets are in horrible state."

Shouts and whistles ahead, followed by the sled slamming to a stop, indicated they had reached the intersection at Upper Bridge. That was absurdly fast. Hieljam ab Tishai had a heated exchange with her driver, and then she sighed and turned to Satrine. "One of yours is blocking the road."

"He's directing traffic," Satrine said. "It keeps carriages and carts from bashing into each other. He'll let you pass in a moment."

"Would one of your Parliament members be subjected to this? Or nobles?"

"Actually, yes," Satrine said. "Unless they had arranged to clear the streets."

"That is what we should have done. What does that cost?"

"It's more complicated than that. Permits and arrangements."

"Complicated, yes. Most things are with you people."

"Well, we do like our paperwork," Satrine said ruefully. "I suppose we're not unlike the Lyranans like that."

Hieljam ab Tishai sighed in a noncommittal way. So that wasn't going to give Satrine any ground.

"We've translated the message that appeared with your *isahresa*'s body. It was Lyranan."

"Lyranan message and Imach weapon," Hieljam ab Tishai said. "So you've said."

"It's apparently a form of Lyranan poetry," Satrine said, and told her the poem, as best she could recall it. Hieljam ab Tishai frowned slightly when she finished. "Mean something?"

"It's odd. A Lyranan poem?"

"Written in Lyranan, at least."

"The fire, air, earth, and water are Fuergan spiritual totems. The imagery—choking, burning, drowning. It matches our own imagery for a life out of balance." She offered this as if it were a mere academic curiosity, nothing more.

"I was wondering if, given that you've had time to consider it, there's anything new you might want to tell us."

If Hieljam ab Tishai was about to say anything more about that, she was interrupted by the sled driving forward again. The rumbles of the wheels on the stone made further conversation impossible until they reached the stationhouse.

Satrine directed them around to the back stable doors, which Hieljam ab Tishai did not care for. "We are to skulk in the rear, like some shameful *va* begging for mercy?"

"I'm not sure what that means," Satrine said, even though her memory lit up with the full list of Fuergan caste-rank *krais*. "*Va*" was the lowest rank of all, so destitute and indebted that many high-ranked Fuergans didn't feel it worth the effort to feed or clothe them. "If you wish, we can enter in the front gates, but the sled would have to use the stable doors. And I presume we'll be loading your . . . uncle's body from here." It appeared her telepathic education did not include the details of Fuergan familial relations.

Hieljam ab Tishai scoffed. "We are bringing my

isarehsa, the *natir* of my family, on his *srehtai.* It is appalling enough that it must be done here, through Druth streets. It will not begin from any back doors, or with anything less than the full dignity of his station."

That was an overload of Fuergan terms. "All right, but then your retinue will have to wait out here with the sled and the horses." She whistled a couple of pages over—fortunately, they were milling about outside the stationhouse. "Lads, get some space open by the main gates for the—lady's horses and sled."

She led Hieljam ab Tishai and the retinue through the main station floor, stares burning from every direction, and down two levels to the examinarium. The cold room was filled with macabre equipment, charts and diagrams of human bodies, and desks covered with stray paperwork. "Leppin? You down here, man?"

The squirrelly little man came out from some hidden corner, his lensed skullcap askew on his head. "Something I can help you with, specs?" he asked.

Satrine cleared her throat, "I'm here with the closest relative of a victim. The Fuergan man?"

"Oh, right," Leppin said. He gave a slight tick of his head to Hieljam ab Tishai. "May your road find your way back to him, ma'am."

Hieljam ab Tishai gave a slow nod in return. "May we all walk our own way."

Leppin scratched at his teeth. "So I figure you're here for his body. Procession back to the house and all."

"That's correct," Hieljam ab Tishai said.

Leppin nodded. "If you go around that corner, through the wooden doors, you'll find him there. I've left a bowl of water and a candle there for you."

"Most kind," Hieljam ab Tishai said. She issued a few orders to her people, and they all went into the back.

"You were expecting that," Satrine said to Leppin.

"Yeah, well, I've made a study of death and burial

customs of different peoples. A few years back, when Gorky was in charge of the examinarium, we had a real mess when he didn't know he had 'violated' an Imach holy man's body in an investigation. A little knowledge saves some trouble."

Captain Cinellan came into the examinarium. "Rainey," he said, glancing around uncomfortably. "I heard you had come through with some suspects."

"Mourning family, not suspects," Rainey said. "We're releasing the body to them."

"That wise?" he asked, partly at Leppin.

"I'm finished, and it's the appropriate thing for them. Ain't no harm."

"And it'll help keep us from having some sort of diplomatic incident that'll cause Marshals or Intelligence to sweep in," Satrine added.

Cinellan nodded. "Incidents are happening, diplomatic or not. Last night we had a few arrests up in the Little East. Most were nothing bits, cool off in the walls, but some real cases."

"We're doing as much as we can," Satrine said. "But people aren't exactly forthcoming up there."

"Like they are down here."

"Fair enough," Satrine said. "But we've got a long list of suspects, yet no one pops as obvious. Not to mention we're kind of at a loss how it was done, let alone who did it."

"Keep on it," Cinellan said. "I presume you're heading back up there."

"Of course," Satrine said. "Welling is still there, can't leave him unsupervised."

Cinellan gave her a hint of a smile. "We're sending in additional support up there—double the foot and horse-patrol, until things cool off a bit."

"Might be best to send those folks up soon," Leppin said. "Because the Fuergans will be walking up the body

in a bit. Wouldn't be a bad thing if we sent an escort with
it."

"What's this 'walking up the body'?" Cinellan asked.

"She called it '*srehtai,*'" Satrine added.

"It's a ritual of bringing the body through the community and back home. So they'll be going up the street—
slowly—and chanting and calling out. They'll get strange
looks, probably some jeers—"

"And if there's trouble, it'll be harsh," Satrine said.
"How many foot and horse are ready to go? Wouldn't
hurt to make a procession of it."

"You don't think that's a bit of a hard hammer?" Cinellan asked.

"Of course it is, but we're going to bring the hard hammer regardless, sir," Satrine said. "If we're sending extra
patrol up there for tonight, might as well put some show
into it."

Leppin leaned back, listening down the hallway
where the Fuergans were collecting the body. "If you
want my advice, Cap, you should get that moving pretty
quick. They'll be coming up in just a few clicks."

"Just what I need, advice from my bodyman." Cinel-
lan muttered something unintelligible for a moment.
"Stay on them, Satrine. I'll get the lieutenants in gear.
Looks like we're going to have a parade."

<hr />

Minox was brought inside the hut, virtually identical to
the one that Hieljam's body had been in. He couldn't
help but think that this might have been the same thing
that happened to the man. Something in the air, in the
garden, that he reacted to? Something that Leppin
wouldn't notice? Something that Minox, as a mage, was
sensitive to?

Rek-Yun laid Minox down on the table, not unlike the

very position the body had been in. Was this how Hiel-jam died? Were they about to do the same to him?

"No, no, wait. . . ." Minox said, but he found it challenging to even get words out. This was far beyond the usual aftereffects of the *rijetzh*. He could barely see anything, but he couldn't tell if that was the dim lamplight or whatever was affecting him. He tried to get back on his feet. His legs barely held him up, but his arms still worked. He grabbed Rek-Yun by the front of his robe and dragged the man closer, magic crackling in his hands.

"Please, sir . . ." the old Tsouljan said. He tried to pry Minox's fingers off his robe. He got the right one off, but Minox's left hand was clenched like iron.

"You will not . . ." Minox wheezed out.

Another hand grabbed Minox's wrist, and all that magical energy was sapped. Minox's hand spasmed open, releasing the old man's robe, and a harsh female voice snarled in Tsouljan.

Minox's eyes focused on the new person—he hadn't even seen her come in. A Tsouljan woman with blue hair. This face he had seen before—she had snapped at him the day before.

"If you . . . if you . . ." he said. This woman had to know that if he died here, the Constabulary would swarm upon the compound, if not burn it to the ground.

She ignored him, leaning in and pulling his eyes open wide, looking deep at them. She muttered in Tsouljan. Then she slapped at his face.

"Stop it!" he shouted, his voice suddenly coming back in full. That came with a fire of anger, which came surging out of his hands and lit up the entire hut.

The fire flew out at the woman, but icy clouds surrounded her, which then ran up Minox's arms. The clouds pinned him back down to the table. She spoke, more in the creaky tones of the Tsouljan language.

"What are you saying?"

"She said, 'Hold still, fool,'" Rek-Yun said.

"Who is she?" Minox shouted. "What is she doing to me?"

"Sevqir Fel-Sed," Rek-Yun said calmly. She then spoke, and Rek-Yun continued to translate. "All she's doing to you is keeping you still. The rest of what is happening is your own doing."

"This isn't me," Minox said. The burning anger was now hot in his chest, like it had nowhere else to go. "It's this place."

"It is you." She tapped him on the chest as she spoke, Rek-Yun's translation right on top of her. "You have the gift of *ge-tan*. But you are a child with that gift."

"*Ge-tan?* Do you mean magic?"

She scoffed, stepping out of his line of sight. He noticed that Rek-Yun wasn't translating back to her. She understood Druth Trade, but didn't—or wouldn't—speak it. "That is what the Druth call it. And this is how the Druth teach themselves how to use it. Terrible."

"No one taught me."

"That is obvious."

"Is this what happened to Hieljam ab Wefi?"

"Who?"

"The man who was killed here?" He snapped his words. Rage coming again. It ebbed and flowed now, almost like it was coming from outside of him.

Fel-Sed came back into his line of sight. "I don't know anything about that. You are unbalanced. Why is that?"

"I don't know!"

"You don't know. How is that?" She placed something on his chest. Minox couldn't see what it was, but as soon as it touched him, the anger melted away.

"Do you know?" he asked.

"It is that you do not know." She shook her head, now

placing other things on his forehead and stomach. "How is it you Druth are so ignorant of the *ge-tan*?"

"Plenty aren't."

She leaned in close, her eyes piercing. "So why are you ignorant?"

"Circumstance."

She placed two more of whatever she was putting on him on his hips. "Explain."

He really felt like he should be asking her the questions. "Education in magic only comes through being in a Circle. Which I'm not. I can't be."

"Circle? Explain."

Minox thought about it for a moment, as he realized all the pulses of errant magic in his body were dropping down. Whatever Fel-Sed did had worked. "Circles are organizations of mages, for mutual legal protection and . . ."

"No, no. Why does that affect you?"

"No Circle would allow its members to be in the Constabulary."

"Ah!" She grinned maniacally, allowing Minox to see that several of her back teeth had symbols carved into them. "That is the imbalance. Who you are here." She tapped in the center of his chest. "Very strange people, you Druth are."

"I don't know if we have a monopoly on strangeness," Minox said. "Can I . . . stand up now?"

"You are fine for now." She scooped up the things she had placed on his body; they seemed to be pebbles of some sort. "I cannot guarantee that you will stay that way. You are out of balance, and you seem to be insistent on unbalancing yourself further."

Minox sat up. "So, you are a mage? You . . . have the *ge-tan*?"

"I have it and harness it."

He pointed to her blue hair. "Is that what that means? Your hair color seems to indicate different roles."

She turned to Rek-Yun, and the two had a brief exchange in their native tongue. Finally Rek-Yun responded.

"Very strange, you Druth are. You see the mark of our *linsol* here, she tells you she is Fel, and yet you seem confused."

Blue is Fel. Which means the yellow is Rek, and the green is Rup. What those meant, though, Minox was still confused about.

"So is your *linsol*, being Fel . . . that's like your Circle?"

She made a strange noise with her tongue. Then more Tsouljan, translated by Rek-Yun. "Attempt to maintain some balance. Especially here." She held up his left arm, which was now completely limp. Minox could barely feel her hand against his. "Once you have proper questions, then return to me."

She left the hut.

Rek-Yun then gave him a slight bow. "I apologize for your discomfort. I will allow you rest and take my leave." He backed out of the hut.

Minox stayed sitting on the table for some time, his thoughts far from the murder of Hieljam ab Wefi. What had happened to him just now? Was it tied to the *rijetzh*, the problems with his hand, or both? He flexed the fingers in his left hand. Now it felt almost normal again, just the slight tingle in his fingertips as the numbness faded. But he couldn't ignore that something was definitely wrong with it.

He would need to think of proper questions for Sevqir Fel-Sed, because it was clear that she might actually have something to teach him.

Chapter 10

"BLAZES, KELLMAN, what are you eating?" Mirrell couldn't believe that his partner was actually eating that Imach junk.

"I ain't sure," Kellman said, holding it up. It was in flatbread, like those wraps Jinx was always eating, but it definitely wasn't meat in there. Mirrell couldn't identify it at all, but it smelled like his son's school shorts after a sweltering day like today. This whole part of town stank in ways Mirrell couldn't even put words to.

Kellman took another bite of the sewage. "Not too bad, actually."

"Not too bad, bah," Mirrell said.

"Hey, I'm hungry, and this is where we are," Kellman said.

"What are you, Jinx?" Mirrell asked. "Did that sewage-seller at least know anything?"

"Beats me," Kellman asked. "He knew about five words in Trade, mostly 'crowns' and 'pay.'"

"Not surprised." Imachs were grubbers, that was for sure. Between grilling these bastards for any scrap of info, following around the blasted piries, and the infuriating tyzos yesterday, Mirrell had had his fill of the Little

East for the rest of the blazing year. All these foreign tossers could drown in each other's blood, as far as Mirrell cared.

At least the machs stayed in their blasted blocks most of the time.

Not these bloody piries, though. Once they came out of their fancy house, they were all over the area. Over to the docks, talking with folks in the Hodge, buying a few strange fruits, and now in a trinket shop in Machie.

"They're mucking with us, you know," he said to Kellman. "Even if we weren't in our vests, the two of us stand out like a fly in the soup around here. They know we're trailing them, so they're giving us a guided tour of nothing."

"Yeah," Kellman said with his mouth half-filled with the junk. "I got a feeling, though."

"You got a feeling. Saints, you are turning into Jinx."

"Nah, listen," Kellman said. "Like you said, they know we're on their heels. So here's what I think—there's someplace that they want to go, but don't want us to know about. So they do all sorts of wandering, figuring we'd get bored and leave them be, or if it's one stop out of a dozen, think nothing of it when they go there."

"You may have something there," Mirrell admitted. He glanced over to the trinket shop. The two of them were still clearly visible in the window. So they weren't trying to ditch out the back or anything like that. "And they might win this because I've got a mind to head back to the stationhouse and see if a real case popped up. Must have been something in the regular blocks that needs an inspector—"

"Constables!" a heavily accented voice shouted. The throng of people suddenly opened up on the street, and nearly a dozen machs came through. Men and women combined, though the men were striding through in loose open shirts, long thick hair flowing, while the women had their hair and bodies covered in brightly colored cloth. Mirrell found the women far more disturbing, showing little more than their dark eyes, heavily accented with colored lining and shading. Those eyes looked angry as blazes.

One man stood at the forefront of the group, eyes bright with almost maniacal glee, his shirt brighter and bluer than anyone else's. "You have been searching for Assan Jabiudal. Here he is before you! What quarrel do you have with me?"

A quarrel was definitely in the cards here. Each one of them had a knife prominently displayed on their belts. The same kind of crazy Imach knife that the Fuergan swell was killed with.

A glance from Kellman, still with that sewage in his mouth, showed Mirrell this was his show. "You're Jabiudal?"

"I said as such."

"You can prove that?" Mirrell asked. "Papers of Transit, something like that?"

Jabiudal cackled and said something Imach to his acolytes, who also laughed. "You ask for proof? I stand before you the man that God has made. The name Assan Jabiudal has been given, and you ask for proof. God's fire does not burn me away, so I am clearly truthful."

"That's hardly proof," Mirrell said. "People lie all the blasted time."

"Yes. This is a city of lies, I know. Lies and filth."

"Hey, pal, you want to talk filth, Machie is the filthiest part," Mirrell said.

"And that is where you keep us, Constable. In the filth like the swine."

"That's how you all live," Mirrell said. This tosser was already on his nerve.

"A reckoning is coming. Enlighten him, Dahar!"

The man to his left, who was carrying a book, started to read from it in Imach.

"What is that, some kind of threat?" Mirrell asked. He moved in closer to Dahar. "You threatening me, mach?"

"Those are the holy words, *nassat*. Fire is coming, from God and his hosts."

Mirrell turned to Kellman, who had had the sense to get rid of his food by now. "This sounds like these boys are threatening me, don't you think?" He turned back to Jabiudal, getting nose to nose with the man, despite the fact that he smelled like the worst parts of this street. "Are you and yours threatening officers of the law, Jabi?"

Jabiudal grinned, wide with great, blackened teeth. "This is not for me to say, Constable. This is the word of God, which we must all submit to."

"You want to tell me—"

Jabiudal raised his voice over Mirrell's. "You tell me, Constable, why the faithful are locked in your cells in your stationhouse, why you and your friend are content to beat and harass anyone who might know who I am?"

"Look, mach, we've got a dead body with one of your crazy knives in his chest, and are told that you had business with him. So you're a fella we need to talk to."

"And here I appear."

"We got to bring him to Jinx," Kellman said. "Or maybe the stationhouse."

"Are you arresting me?" Jabiudal asked. "You will refrain from sullying my person with your profane touch."

"We ain't arresting you, but you've got to answer some questions. So come with us—just you, Jabby." Mirrell waved at the clade of zealots surrounding Jabiudal. "And come easily, or there may have to be some sullying going on."

"I do not wish to come with you. The public will hear me when I speak."

"Blessed be the holy words!" Dahar shouted, holding his book up high. The crowd of Jabiudal's followers all dropped to their knees, as did several others in the square.

"Enough of that," Mirrell said, grabbing Jabiudal's arm. "Come along with us now."

Jabiudal started to release a shriek that was almost inhuman, but it was drowned out by several Constabulary whistles blaring through the air.

"Good, backup," Kellman said.

Mirrell looked to the source of the whistles, but what he saw wasn't going to relieve matters here. If anything, it would light up the oil jar.

———————◆◆———————

"Boots on, Welling!"

Corrie popped up, completely confused for a moment. Once her eyes adjusted, she realized she wasn't in her own bed, but one of the racks in the stationhouse bunkroom. Memory returned next: she stayed to work the double, get some daylight time in.

"I'm up, tosser," she said, though she wasn't sure who she was talking to. It wasn't the captain, so it didn't matter. Even if it was her left or the sergeant, they wouldn't give her any guff for that. She pulled herself onto her feet and stepped into the boots she had left next to the bunk. "Already time for saddle?"

"Yeah." It was Gassle, another one of the horsepatrol on the dark with her. "Something is going on, they want a cadre on horse to run escort."

"I thought we were patrolling in the East," Corrie said, pushing past him to get to the water closet.

"We are," he said, raising his voice so she could still hear him. "The escort is going up to the East."

"You know what it's about?"

"Something fancy, I don't know. That skirt spec told us we need to saddle up."

"Did she?" What the blazes was going on that Tricky

was giving out orders to horsepatrol? "We don't have to wear dress coats or some sewage like that?"

"Not that I heard," Gassle said.

"All right," Corrie said, coming out of the water closet and buckling her belt as she walked. "Let's see what the noise is."

The noise had Tricky in the stables, lecturing some sewage to the rest of double-shifters.

"I'm gathering they're going to go at a deliberate pace, but we need to let them do that unmolested. That means you're going to have to clear the path ahead of them so they never have to stop. You know how to do that, right?"

"It's called a rutting Cascade Ride, Trick," Corrie said, strutting over to her brother's partner. "How many of us are doing this blasted sewage?"

"You can count, Corrie," Trick said. "How many you got?"

As much as Tricky set Corrie's teeth on edge—she knew damn well why Nyla and most of the other skirts working the desks hated the woman—she had to admire that she didn't give a goddamn inch of ground. Most of the stationhouse would just as well see her trampled in the streets, and she didn't give one blazing rut about what they thought.

Corrie glanced back at the double-shift volunteers. Ten of them, including herself. Mostly tadpoles, fresh out of cadet coats. The only one who had any real miles in the saddle besides her was Gassle, and she had several months on him. "Oh, rutting blazes, am I the ranking for this ride?"

"No, I am," Tricky said. "But it looks like you'll be playing sergeant."

"Ter-rutting-riffic," Corrie said. "All right, kids, you've all done a Cascade before, right?"

They nodded half-heartedly.

"All right, then. Saddle up and let's get a move on. Where's our package, Trick?"

"Is that the term for who you're escorting?"

"Rutting yes, where are they?"

"They're getting ready in front of the main gates."

"So who are these swells?"

"The niece of the Fuergan lord who was murdered. She's . . . bringing his body home, and it's some kind of specific rite for them."

A feek funeral, all the way back to the Little East. Just what Corrie needed.

"All right, boys," Corrie snapped at her crew of volunteers, "you heard the skirt. Mount up, get up to the main gates."

She got on her horse—not one of her usual steeds, but an underfed chestnut. It was poor pickings right now, the increased patrols emptying the stables to the dregs. This nag was well past its best days, but it would do for a slow-paced Cascade, though.

Corrie led the boys around to the front, where the feeks were already gathered. They had four glorious horses yoked to some vehicle that looked kind of like a wagon, but low to the ground with tiny wheels. The dead old man was laid out on the floor of the wagon, his body draped in furs. Four feeks—real sides of beef, these four—stood in pairs on each side of the vehicle. Each of them held a small bowl. One more stood at the front of the vehicle—clearly the driver. Finally the last feek—a lady, real regal type by the stuck up way she held her head—stood behind the contraption. She was a haughty skirt, no doubt, wrapped up in white furs.

"Is this what we need to clear his way home?" she asked Tricky.

"I believe so," Tricky said. "Welling, make it happen."

With a few hand signals, Corrie let them know that

she and Gassle would stay at pace with the procession, and the other eight would run the Cascade itself. Two of them raced up ahead, whistles on alert, opening up the path and blocking the upcoming intersection.

"When you're ready," Corrie told them.

The feek driver whistled, and the vehicle creeped forward. The horses were going at a very deliberate pace— at this rate it would take them an hour to reach the Little East.

Corrie sighed. She got paid the same either way. The rest of the escort rode along at the same pace.

Then the feek lady started to sing. Or wail. Or make some sort of racket.

Corrie did not get paid enough for this.

They slowly worked their way upstreet, and at each intersection the front pair of riders would race up and secure the next intersection, while the former lead pair fell to the back as they passed.

The crowd in front of them was ugly. Disgusted looks, sneers, spitting on the ground. More than a few shouting that the Fuergans should get the blazes out of their city.

Corrie didn't exactly disagree.

As soon as the procession passed, the crowd on the street swooped in behind them, almost like mad animals. Corrie knew folk were in plenty of a hurry and this deal was clogging up their day, but there was no rutting need for that.

Then she saw why. Every so often when the feek lady reached the height of her wailing noise, she threw a handful of coins behind her.

"Trick," Corrie whispered, since the skirt was walking along near them, "we gonna do something about that stupidity?"

"They're her coins to throw away," Trick said.

"Yeah, but—" Corrie glanced back. She didn't see any fights breaking out behind them, not yet, but she imagined it was only a matter of rutting time. "That's trouble brewing."

"This all is trouble brewing," Trick said. "Let's just get them rutting home, all right?"

"You're the specs here," Corrie said.

The ride to the East took them the better part of an hour, and they were rutting up the traffic for all of Inemar in the process. Crossing Upper Bridge probably fouled things all the way across the river.

When they reached the East proper, though, things shifted. Now other feeks were approaching, and these folks were wailing and throwing coins in the air. More than one landed on Corrie. Then these new feeks joined in the procession.

"How much more of this, Trick?"

"To their home, I presume. Only a few more blocks."

Suddenly there were shouts and cries up ahead. The front riders of the Cascade came charging back.

"We got a problem," one said. "They ain't moving."

"Threw a rock at my horse!" the other said.

"I got this," Corrie said. She spurred her horse forward to the intersection, where a group of eastern folk were gathered up.

"Clear off," she shouted. "We've got a procession coming through."

The mass of them shouted at her in their gibberish, and then shouted at the procession.

Corrie drew her crossbow. "Rutting well clear off, tossers!"

That only enraged them, and more of their type ran over. Imachs, Corrie thought.

"She told you to clear off!" Two more specs were on the scene—she recognized them, Kellman and Mirrell. Kellman was shouting at a specific one of the machs.

"This is our place!" the one Imach shouted back. "We will not suffer the indignity of their profane ritual!"

The procession had reached the intersection and halted. Feeks were now shouting at the machs, and the machs threw it right back.

"Form a wall!" Corrie shouted, putting her horse between the two groups. Several of the other riders took formation with her.

"Get your people to disperse!" Mirrell yelled.

The Imach leader pointed an accusing finger at the feeks. "Tell them to do that."

The feek lady strode to the front of her people. She saw the Imach leader and shrieked in her own tongue. *"Hrenssesa!"*

The feeks all shouted and pressed forward.

Tricky tried to force her way to the front, but couldn't make any progress in the angry throng.

"Hrenssesa!" the feek lady shouted again. "Murderer!"

<hr />

Minox came out of the compound more troubled than when he went in. He knew nothing more about the case, had very few theories—beyond a wild speculation that some mystical element had an effect on Hieljam ab Wefi, and was now having a residual effect on him. But that was hardly something he could prove. Protector Hilsom would laugh it away.

"Inspector?" One of the red-haired Tsouljans was addressing him from the entranceway.

"Yes?" Minox asked. "Is there something you need to ask?"

"Will you be continuing the embargo of this facility?" His Tsouljan accent was strong, but he spoke Trade with confidence.

Minox's own patrol people looked to him, their expressions indicating they wanted the answer to that as well. "I'm afraid it will need to continue. The entire compound is still an active crime scene, and everyone who is engaged here under suspicion."

"Understandable," the Tsouljan said. "This place must return to being a sanctuary of peace. We will enforce that."

So the red-haired caste were peace officers. Green were laborers. Minox still hadn't quite discerned the difference between the yellow and the blue, but they seemed to represent mental and spiritual disciplines.

"Specs!" Phillen Hace came running over, the page from the Protector's Office right behind him. "You gotta come!"

"What's going on, Hace?"

"A group of Imachs are up in Mirrell and Kellman's faces. And there's the Fuergan . . . something, like a parade, and we've got a Cascade Ride around it, but they're gonna bump right into each other!"

Trouble indeed. "You, page, what's your name again?"

"Torvie," the Protector's page said. "Torvie Belt."

"Belt, I'm going to need Writs of House Binding. Possibly a lot of them."

"All right," Belt said. "I'll need names to bring to Mister Hilsom."

"That's the problem. I don't have them yet." He turned to the two regulars guarding the Tsouljan compound. "I'll put out a whistle call in just a bit. You two need to ignore it and stay here. No matter what. Even a Riot Call. Hear?"

"Heard," said one of the regulars.

"Boys, with me," Minox said, pulling his whistle out of his coat pocket. This one wasn't going to be solved with his crossbow.

"Sir," Belt said. "I'm serious, I can't go to the Protector with a request for an open House Binding. Certainly not several."

"I understand, Belt," Minox said.

"What do you need from me, sir?" Hace asked.

"You've got a pad and charcoal, Hace?"

"Always, sir," Hace said.

"Good. When we get there, you'll be taking names."

"There" was only two blocks away, where a clowder of Imachs were riled up in the center of an intersection, screaming and jeering at the procession of Fuergans. Hieljam ab Tishai was at the forefront of the Fuergans, screaming right back at the Imachs. Inspector Rainey was at the woman's side, trying to restrain her without actually putting hands on the woman. On the Imach side, Kellman and Mirrell were not showing as much restraint. They were trying to grab the man leading the Imachs, but the rest of his crowd were blocking them.

A few horsepatrol had interceded in between the groups, but their presence didn't look like it would hold either side off for long. One small bit of comfort was that Corrie was one of the horsepatrol here. The rest of the horsepatrol looked far too inexperienced. Minox wasn't sure if any of them would hold up once the dam broke here.

"It's gotten worse," Hace muttered.

Minox nodded and blew a call for regulars to come. Hopefully the show of color would prevent any violence, but there was already a fair amount of color present, and that wasn't dissuading them.

"All of you, disperse!" Minox shouted to no one in particular, approaching the horse line that Corrie's squad had formed.

"We will not!" Hieljam ab Tishai shouted. "We will finish our *srehtai,* and we will not be impeded by these animals!"

"Animals!" the man in the center of the Imach group snarled. "How dare a *hesesaan* like yourself—"

"Enough, you!" Mirrell shouted. He pushed past the two that were blocking him and grabbed the Imach leader.

"You dare put hands?" One of the other Imachs, on the edge of that group, grew incensed. He grabbed a stone off the ground and hurled it at Mirrell.

Minox reacted, channeling magic to block the stone before it struck Inspector Mirrell.

Nothing was there. The magic didn't flow, nothing happened.

Kellman, however, was on point. He lurched in front of his partner and caught the stone, sending it right back to the head of the man who threw it. That man howled and dropped to the ground, blood flowing from his head.

Now footmen were swarming onto the scene. They took position on all sides, boxing the Imachs and Fuergans into their positions.

Minox stood still, shocked at what just happened. The magical energy was around him, he could feel it coursing through his bones, but . . . nothing. He tried to bring a flame to his fingertips, an ability he had long since mastered.

Nothing. The magic coursed through his body, to his hands, and went nowhere.

"Everyone just stay calm!" Inspector Rainey was yelling. Her eyes darted to Minox, clearly showing concern. Probably wondering why he was so inactive in this moment. "Next person to move on anyone else will be ironed and put in the wagon!"

Minox pulled himself out of his reverie. The mystery of his inability would have to wait.

"Officers!" he shouted. "Question every person here—Imach, Fuergan, Kieran, whatever." He added the Kierans, when he saw a couple looking on from the outskirts. One of them was Iliari, and he would bet his next meal the other was Kenorax. "I want names, I want home addresses, or the closest equivalent. I want you to check papers. Then each and every person here will be escorted to their residence for Home Binding."

"For what?" This came from Hieljam ab Tishai.

Belt nudged him on the hip. "Yeah, specs, for what?"

Rainey took a cue from this. "You mean besides public danger? You're all persons of suspicion in the death of Hieljam ab Wefi Loriz."

"You can't possibly think that," Hieljam ab Tishai said. "The man who would want him dead is right there." She pointed her accusing finger at the Imach leader.

Mirrell had the man in an armlock, and looked like he wanted nothing more than to shove his face into the cobblestone. "You know this one, Tricky. He's Assan Jabiudal."

"Oh, he is?" Rainey came up close. "We've been looking to talk to you."

"Yes, talk," Jabiudal said. "While Dahar bleeds to death in the street."

Minox noticed the man, now inert on the ground, blood coming from the wound on his head. "Call for Yellowshields," he told Hace. The page blew his whistle, while Minox closed in on the injured man.

"He threw a rock at city constables," Kellman said, coming over. "I didn't do anything wrong."

"You responded with equal force," Minox said. "Or at least equivalent." Kellman was a good deal more muscular than Dahar was. Minox turned the man onto his back. The gash on his head was bleeding quite heavily. Minox pulled a handkerchief out of his pocket and pressed it against the wound.

"He's going to have to go to Ironheart," Kellman said. "I just . . . snapped back."

"Hold it there," Minox said, taking Kellman's hand and pressing it on the wound. He didn't have time to assuage Kellman's guilt.

"Can you just, you know?" Kellman made a vague gesture over the bleeding man. The meaning was quite clear: Kellman wanted Minox to magically heal the man. Minox didn't have any idea how to do that.

"No, I can't," Minox said, and left it at that. He went to Rainey, noting out of the corner of his eye that Yellowshields were approaching. The footpatrol regulars were following their orders, taking names and checking papers. Hace and Belt were hard at work gathering the information from the regulars.

"We must finish the *srehtai*," Hieljam ab Tishai said. "It is unjust that my *isahresa*'s honor and peace is disrupted, especially by that man."

"We'll get you home," Rainey told her. "You and your *isahresa*."

"I have a crucial query," Minox said. "When we asked you yesterday, your concern was about Nalassein Hajan. So why do you now call Mister Jabiudal a murderer?"

"Hajan came to show his respects midday," Hieljam said. "He told me that the weapon that killed my *isahresa* was a Kadabali one. He told me about Hajan."

"What, exactly, did he tell you?"

"That Hajan was making threats to people who wouldn't deal with him. My *isahresa* was not going to do that, which surely enraged Hajan."

"What sort of deal?" Now this was necessary information.

"We have many arrangements all over the world, Inspector. I cannot speak in great detail of my *isahresa*'s long-term agendas. I was not privy to them."

Footpatrol were clearing people out, one at a time. The immediate crisis seemed to be defused.

"Let me know when I can finish," Hieljam ab Tishai said.

"Soon," Rainey said. She stepped to the side with Minox. "What do you think? Is Jabiudal our man?"

"I think Miss Hieljam believes it. But that is hardly evidence."

"What's our play now? Besides Home Binding."

"We talk to Hajan."

"Hey, Mine," Corrie said from her horse. "What's our play, now that we're here?"

Minox looked up at his sister. "I presume you're on extra patrol, to counter the unrest from last night?"

"Presume rutting right."

"For now, take Missus Hieljam and her people to their residence, and put them in under Home Binding."

"Without a rolling writ?"

Minox pointed to Belt. "He's your man."

Corrie leaned down and lowered her voice. "You're talking, like, thirty Writs of Binding. Won't the Protector's Office piss their shoes over that?"

"Likely," Minox said. He pulled out his notepad from his pocket and his charcoal stylus. "Who is the command officer with feet on stone for tonight?"

"Beats the sewage out of me," Corrie said.

"What are you thinking?" Rainey asked.

"I'm thinking I'd love to impose a curfew on the whole area," Minox said, writing a quick note for the unknown night commander. "But I think that would put Hilsom into new levels of fit."

"To say the least," Rainey said.

Corrie guessed the instructions. "So you want a soft curfew. Strongly encourage folk to stay inside."

"Exactly," Minox said, tearing out the sheet and handing it to his sister. "I have a feeling tonight is going to be very challenging for you."

A funeral rite nearly turned into a brawl. This was far away from the "minimal embarrassment" that Enbrain had asked for. And more fight than Satrine was in the mood for this late in the afternoon. The heat was oppressive, sticky, and threatening a rain that wouldn't come.

Now the regulars and horsepatrol were rounding folk up. The Fuergans went quietly to their own blocks once the Imachs were cleared out of the way. The Imachs were hardly being quiet, especially Jabiudal. Most of them had to be searched for their papers, and hauled off by at least two or three footpatrol. Yellowshields came for the injured one—not Satrine's problem. It was Kellman's, though—the man looked devastated.

And Welling looked . . . spooked. Satrine suspected it had nothing to do with the incident.

"Unhand us!" This came from the Kierans who had come a bit too close to the proceedings. "Do you know who we are?"

Welling stepped forward, ready for response, though his face still betrayed that his attention was elsewhere. "You are Ravi Kenorax and Estiani Iliari. We met this morning, Mister Iliari."

"Indeed, Inspector," Iliari said. "I thought I made it clear you were to leave us alone."

"Oh, is that how you think it works, Mister Iliari?" Satrine said. "I'd remind you that you are on Druth soil. Neither this neighborhood, nor your home, are an embassy. You are still subject to the law."

"Then my lawyers will hear of this," said Kenorax. Despite his Kieran appearance—the olive complexion and dark, almost wet hair—he had an accent indistinguishable from an educated South Maradaine resident. Which, Satrine reminded herself, was exactly what he was. Somehow she had expected Kenorax to be a pure Kieran in every aspect.

"In the meantime, we are issuing a Writ of Home Binding upon you. I don't recommend you break it."

"We'll have to see it."

"Belt!" Welling shouted out. "Make sure that Mister Ravi Kenorax and Estiani Iliari are the first to receive their Writs of Home Binding. And you should remember that address from this morning."

"Aye, sir, on it," the Protector's page said.

"Good lad," Welling said to no one in particular. "Footmen, stay with our friends here. If they try to escape, you are authorized to use force and bring them to the station."

"You wouldn't dare!" Iliari's eyes went wide.

"Oh, Mister Iliari," Satrine said. "We would love to have the opportunity to question you in our house."

Satrine walked away, with Welling beside her. "Mister Jabiudal now?" she asked him.

"Indeed," Welling said.

"Something wrong, besides the obvious?" she asked him.

"Nothing directly relevant to the case." She had learned well enough this was Minox Welling's way of saying that something magical was bothering him and she should mind her own damn business. Which she did.

"You imprison my people?" Jabiudal snapped at them as they approached. He was staring down two regulars who were trying to get identification papers from a pair of Imach women. "And for what?"

"We're sending them home with orders to stay there," Welling said. "That's very different from imprisoning."

"It is unacceptable," Jabiudal said.

"So is starting a brawl in the streets."

"We started nothing," Jabiudal said. "You on your horse tried to shove us away, then the Fuergan woman screamed at us."

"Yes, she called you a murderer," Welling said. "We find that interesting, as the murder weapon in our case is a Kadabali one. You are Kadabali, aren't you, Mister Jabiudal?"

"I was born there, but my path led me here," he said. "The weapon was a *talveca*? Then you know that I am innocent, for mine is at my hip. As are all my people's here."

Satrine noticed that each and every Imach man and

woman were armed with the weapon. This riot could have gotten very ugly.

"Why are you all carrying those?" Welling asked.

"It is our right, and it is our duty to God."

God of the Imach faith. Not the same one invoked at Saint Limarre's. And Jabiudal's friends were clearly among the deeply faithful.

"And there's no chance you could have gotten another person's *talveca*, right?" Satrine asked. "Or gotten a new one after leaving one in Hieljam ab Wefi's chest?"

"You speak profanely," Jabiudal said. "I will not be having it from you."

"Won't be having it?" This came from Mirrell, who had stepped back over to them. "Maybe he's wanting to start something. Looking to get ironed and brought in."

"You would like that, wouldn't you?" Jabiudal said. "Bring me in, question me in your stationhouse, and God be praised! You have a confession to present to your magistrates."

"It doesn't work like that," Welling said.

"I know well how it works," Jabiudal said. "I will go to my home." He glanced around at his followers and gave them instructions in his native tongue. They went off, with a dozen footpatrol following them.

"Don't suppose either of you understood what he said there?" Mirrell asked.

"Something about prayers," Satrine said. That was one of the few words she was able to pick out. Apparently her telepathic education contained a small sample of Imach dialects. So small she couldn't help but think it was a useless thing to include.

"Maybe he told them all to go home and pray." A new voice from behind Satrine. She turned, as did Welling and Mirrell, to see Mister Rencir of the *South Maradaine Gazette* standing there.

"You all are off your usual beats, aren't you?" he said.

"It's an unusual situation, Mister Rencir," Welling said. His attention was still elsewhere, not paying attention to Rencir. Satrine knew well enough that they were usually on friendly terms.

"Death of a Fuergan *lavark*, a funeral ceremony throwing money through Inemar, a near rumble in the streets here."

"What's your interest in it?" Satrine asked. Something about Rencir rubbed her the wrong way, but she couldn't put her finger on it. Still, she wasn't interested in developing much of a professional relationship with him.

"Well, it's the sort of thing that sells the newssheets. Salacious-sounding stuff, and with it all leading here, well . . ." He shrugged. "It has the allure of the exotic."

"Very little allure, Mister Rencir," she said. "Right, Welling?"

"Yes," he said, still not paying full attention. He snapped out of his reverie again. "I'm sorry, Mister Rencir, we have no further comment at this time, as we are still proceeding with our investigation."

Satrine wasn't sure what was distracting him. Maybe it was hunger—they hadn't eaten since the Lyranan public house. However, this wasn't how he usually behaved when hungry.

"Beyond the salacious element," Rencir added, stepping closer, "I would be negligent if I didn't point out how unusual handing out so many Home Bindings at once is. I don't think you could get away with it in a more . . . traditional sector of Inemar."

Now the man was goading them. Satrine was going to be annoyed, but Mirrell was already stepping forward. "We said, no further comment. Unless you want to test who else we'd give a Home Binding to?"

Rencir stepped away from them all, hands up. "I'll find you again when you aren't so busy," he said. With a small lift of his page cap, he strolled off around the corner.

"Welling," Satrine said in a low voice, "What's going on with you?"

"It's nearly five bells," Welling said. "We should return to the stationhouse."

"Right," Satrine said. "We've done enough damage around here today."

Chapter 11

"PLEASE TELL ME you have a key suspect."

Captain Cinellan looked harried, even more than usual. His gray-salted hair was a tangled mess, and his desk had seven teacups scattered around it.

"Perhaps," Satrine said. "We have a few good prospects."

"Tell me," he said, gesturing for her and Welling to sit down. "And I really hope those prospects are among the ones you ordered the Home Binding for."

"Some of them," Welling said. "We've identified the key players in this tangle, for what that's worth. First there are the immediate relatives of the deceased, Hieljam ab Tishai and ab Orihla."

"I don't think either of them are responsible," Satrine said.

"No? Could be a simple inheritance thing, right?" Cinellan fumbled through his desk for his pipe.

"Inheritance is a very complicated thing in Fuergan society, and I think they've lost more prestige and influence—at least here in Maradaine—than they would gain."

"They aren't being entirely forthright, though," Welling said. "But I'm not sure if the secrets they are keeping are relevant to the investigation."

"Fine, those two aren't suspects," Cinellan said.

"Aren't key suspects," Welling said. "I wouldn't rule them out entirely."

"Who are key suspects?"

"First, for me, would be Assan Jabiudal," Welling said. "Though I admit that is mostly due to Miss Hieljam's reaction to him."

"Hajan implied that Jabiudal might have something to gain from it," Satrine added.

"Hajan is?" Cinellan asked.

"Nalassein Hajan. Imach importer. He seemed genuinely broken up over Hieljam's death."

"So, you're thinking the killer was Imach?"

Satrine really didn't. "The weapon was Imach, and even if neither Jabiudal nor Hajan personally committed the murder, they both seem to have a decent entourage of loyal followers."

"Zealots, you mean." This was Kellman, standing in the doorframe.

"People who would kill for their leaders, either way," Cinellan said.

Kellman nodded. "I'd bet a week's pay that if we came close to pinning it on Jabiudal, one of his folks would confess to keep him free."

"Who else are you looking at?" Cinellan tapped on his desk. "Welling?"

Welling was again staring into the distance, his thoughts clearly not on the conversation in the room right now. He popped back. "I'm still seriously considering that someone at the Tsouljan compound is responsible. One of them has easiest opportunity. And I'm . . . I'm certain they have magical means at their disposal. A factor we should consider."

"There's a Tsouljan mage in there?" Satrine asked.

"A member of the blue-haired caste, Sevqir Fel-Sed. She's . . . I'm not sure."

"Three words I rarely hear from you, Minox." Cinellan looked concerned.

Welling brushed past that. "In addition, while I don't have significant suspicions of Kenorax or his people, but again, there are things they are hiding from us."

Satrine agreed with that. "If we crack the stone of why Hieljam was murdered, I'd bet the reasons tie back to the Kierans."

"Are those all your suspects?"

Satrine hesitated. "I have one more. Among the Lyranans we met with, there was a woman named Pra Yikenj."

"I'm not convinced the Lyranans had any meaningful connection," Welling said. "The poem was there to deliberately mislead us in some way."

"I don't know about connection, but Pra Yikenj has the skillset to sneak into the enclave, quickly kill a man, and slip away."

"You know this how?" Kellman asked.

Kellman didn't know about her time in Intelligence, let alone the things she did there. "I met her once before, long ago." She gave Cinellan a meaningful glance, so he could glean her meaning. He seemed to understand.

"Worth paying attention to. In the meantime . . ."

"I put in a request for documents from the Protector's Office," Welling said. "Records regarding imports, exports, and assets connected to Hieljam, Kenorax, Hasan, and so forth. I'll start combing through those—"

"Not tonight," Cinellan said. "Both of you, sign out and go home."

"That seems premature," Welling said. "We haven't made significant headway in today's investigation."

"I know, and the two of you look like you're ready to collapse. Blazes, Minox, I've seen healthier-looking men laid out in the examinarium."

"I'm fine, sir," Welling protested, though now Satrine realized he looked far more pale and drawn than usual. "I think it's crucial—"

"I think it's crucial that you both go home, have a proper meal and a decent night's sleep. I don't want to hear any word that either of you were in here before eight bells tomorrow morning. Understood?"

"Yes, sir," Satrine said, getting to her feet.

"Welling?"

"Understood, Captain. Not back in here before eight bells." He got out of his chair and left the office.

Satrine gave a last salute to the captain and went after him.

"Welling," she called out as she caught up to him on the stairwell. "What's going on?"

"We're following orders and signing out," he said flatly.

"I mean with you. Did something happen to you in the Tsouljan compound?" She lowered her voice a bit. "Something magical?"

He looked down to the floor, unable to meet her gaze. "I experienced a disturbing loss of control. Fel-Sed, she . . . stopped it. I found it very troubling."

Satrine decided not to press. He was clearly embarrassed by the whole thing. "I understand. We'll tackle this all tomorrow, then."

"Until tomorrow," Welling said. "A good night to you, Inspector Rainey, and my best to your husband." He turned back down the stairs. He was already gone before Satrine made it to the ground floor.

◆—◄◆►—◆

Minox stopped at the fast wrap shop for two wraps as he left the stationhouse. The day had left him spent and famished, even though he was feeling little connection to his power at the moment. Ever since the Tsouljan enclave, it was almost like the magic had been turned off altogether, and not in the same way as with the *rijetzh*. So now he was having the negative effects of the magic with none of the benefits. That was even more annoying.

Inspector Rainey was clearly aware of something being wrong with him. Not that she could help.

Swallowing down the wraps as he walked—wasting little time with any banter with Missus Wolman—he went over to the Brondar butcher shop on Jent and Tannen. The situation was unique and distressing, and he needed to speak to someone about it, and that meant Joshea. He didn't typically just stop at Joshea's home without warning, due to the Brondar family's attitude toward magic. The father, especially, had a near apoplectic reaction to the mere mention of magic, and thus Joshea's ability and that being the reason their interaction was kept secret from the family.

But today's events warranted immediate discussion.

The father wasn't in the front of the butcher shop when he arrived. The elder brother, Gunther, was cleaning up the cutting block when Minox came in.

"Eh, we're shut for the—oh, hey there, stick. You crawling around for business?"

"No, not tonight," Minox said. "Would Joshea be around, by any chance?"

"Ayuh," Gunther said. "Now, look, stick. I know he feels terrible that he sent you to get your arm broke by that crazy fellow. But you can't be holding a debt over him too long over that."

"You're right," Minox said. This must tie into whatever elaborate excuse Joshea had given his family for being in Minox's company at all.

Gunther laughed and clapped Minox on the shoulder. "But milk him a bit longer. Does him good, eh?"

Minox nodded. The blend of affection and aggression the Brondar family showed each other was harsher than in the Welling house, but it had a familiar air for Minox. Army or Constabulary, there was always a degree of grit found between members of a service family.

"Eh, Josh! Your stick buddy is here for a lesson!"

Joshea came out from the back. "Inspector," he said calmly. "Wasn't expecting you tonight."

"I had an early sign-off," Minox said.

"Right," Joshea said, wiping off his hands on his apron. He untied it and threw it to his brother. "Finish up, Gunth."

"Finish up, yourself," Gunther said, tossing the apron back in Joshea's face.

Joshea threw it back, and then knocked his brother on the arm. "Just rutting do it, I'll take opening tomorrow."

"Tomorrow and next."

Joshea sighed. "Fine. Tosser."

Minox stepped out of the shop with Joshea right with him. "There some sort of emergency?"

"Rather," Minox said. "What are you supposedly teaching me?"

"Army fighting, so you don't get jacked again," Joshea said with a chuckle. "So what's the story?"

"Let's get farther away before I explain," Minox said. "It is rather involved, and I need to eat something as well." Those fast wraps had done nothing to quell the hunger.

They headed five blocks away before ducking into a corner pub, one which Minox had never frequented and was far enough from the Brondar shop to risk bumping into one of Joshea's family. They ordered food and drinks and took a back corner table, away from most prying eyes.

"You look spooked, Minox," Joshea said. "What happened to you?"

Minox laid out the entire escapade involving the Tsouljan compound and the strange effect the place had

had on him, as well as the actions of Sevqir Fel-Sed. That right now his magic appeared to be blocked.

"Blocked?" Joshea asked. "They can do that to you?" It was hard to tell if he was concerned or excited. "How did they . . ."

"She did something with stones on my body," Minox said. "But it's like the magic is still affecting me. I'm ravenous right now."

"I noticed," Joshea said. Minox looked down at the table. Somehow over the course of the story he had eaten five lamb sausages and two heckie pies.

"And I'm still hungry," Minox said. "What can we do? This is horrifying."

"I can imagine," Joshea said. "All right, then, I don't like this, but I can only think of one thing. You and I need to go see that Tsouljan lady."

As they reached the Little East Minox wasn't sure what Joshea's intentions were. He was excited, and Minox's first thought was the idea of learning something about magic outside of Druth Circle politics had invigorated him. But the more they walked, the more Joshea's energy seemed primal, aggressive. Minox wondered if Joshea was planning on starting a fight with Sevqir Fel-Sed.

"Never come up this way," Joshea said, his eyes darting about. "I mean, even when I go to your house, I usually take Promenade to head north until I hit Oscana. You?"

"I'll admit, save my tobacconist, the past two days are the most time I've spent in the Little East."

"Your boys are out tonight, eh?" Joshea said. "Green and Red on every corner." He was right, the presence of the footpatrol and horsepatrol was verging on oppressive.

"And not much else," Minox added. "Which is good, given the tensions."

"You can't talk about the case itself, I imagine," Joshea said.

"You would find it tedious and confusing. Far too many moving parts, almost by design."

"By design?" Joshea asked, his interest clearly sparked.

Minox was probably saying too much, but it distracted him from what was going on in his body. Everything inside him felt out of sorts. Disconnected. Like his body was a puppet he controlled from a distance. "Without delving into details, it seems the murder scene was staged to explicitly draw attention to a number of parties, none of whom are necessarily guilty."

"I get it," Joshea said. "Instead of giving you no clues, the killer gives you many different ones, in order to spread you thin."

"Spread thin is how I feel right now."

"All right," Joshea said. "So there's not usually this many sticks walking in the East at night?"

"Not at all. Even when I worked foot and horse, we almost never came up around here without a specific call. Which were rare."

"Makes sense, really," Joshea said. "Let these people deal with each other their own way, and only clean up the big messes."

"Which we're in," Minox said. They were now crossing through the Kellirac and Racquin blocks of the Little East. This was where Minox's mother grew up, when she was Amalia D'Fen. She rarely ever spoke of her childhood, and never with anything resembling wistful fondness. The buildings were especially shabby—it seemed all the doors had been pulled off their frames. There were only a few locals in the streets, a group of old Racquin men in big floppy hats like Minox remembered his maternal grandfather—his namesake—always wearing. These men sat around a makeshift firepit made from an empty metal barrel. Exactly the sort of thing that would get someone cited, if not ironed, in any other part of the city.

Two of those old men looked up at Minox as he passed, and openly snarled.

"Looks like your colors aren't too popular here," Joshea said. "I imagine it'd be a lot worse if I were wearing my army colors."

"I suppose we let it be," Minox said absently. "It's just another block this way."

Two patrolmen—no one Minox recognized, but they looked like fresh-out-of-cadet types—were at the gates to the Tsouljan enclave. "Inspector," they both said, saluting him as he approached.

"Gentlemen," Minox said, noting they were both looking at Joshea in confusion. "This is a special consultant I'm bringing to observe the scene."

"All right," one of them said, though he seemed more compliant than convinced.

"You are the inspector of record, right?" the other asked.

"Yes, Inspector Third Class Minox Welling."

"As you say, sir," the second guard said. "Whistle if you need anything."

They went inside the enclave, the two red-haired Tsouljans greeting them upon their entrance. "Consultant?" Joshea asked.

"It's hardly inaccurate," Minox said. "Something magical is occurring here, and it may well be related to the crime. You are the closest thing I have to an expert at my disposal."

"All right, let's find that old woman."

Finding her proved no challenge at all. They had barely begun to walk through the compound when three blue-haired Tsouljans came up on them, with Rek-Yun in tow behind them. Sevqir Fel-Sed stood in the center, clucking her tongue in disapproval.

"You have returned, Inspector," Rek-Yun said from his anterior position. "But not on Constabulary business."

"How do you know that?" Minox said.

Fel-Sed replied, all in Tsouljan, pointing to Joshea. Rek-Yun didn't get much opportunity to respond.

"What did you do to him?" Joshea snapped at Fel-Sed. "What gives you the right?" He moved in on her, towering over her slight frame.

Fel-Sed didn't seem cowed at his advance, instead she gently placed a hand on his chest. Again she spoke softly. Rek-Yun translated.

"Wisdom gives her the right. Wisdom you seek."

"I'm only seeking—" Minox started.

"Control." Fel-Sed responded on her own this time, in heavily accented Trade.

"You've left him without any," Joshea said. "How dare you?"

She again answered in pure Tsouljan.

"The best of bad choices," Rek-Yun offered. "Until he could learn."

"Learn what?"

Fel-Sed launched into a long monologue in Tsouljan, pointing at Minox's chest, his head, his bad arm, and occasionally at Joshea. She concluded with a gesture to their surroundings, and finally to one of the huts.

Rek-Yun stepped out from his position behind the group of Fel. "My apologies, Inspector. Much of what was said is beyond my capacity of understanding."

Joshea turned on Rek-Yun, who did startle back in response to his soldierly bearing. "Meaning you don't know how to say it in Trade, or you don't understand what she's talking about."

"Both, in honesty, good sir," Rek-Yun said. "I will attempt. There is something wrong with your . . . river. And your arm is poison. You must learn to dam your rivers so your arm doesn't kill you, but the trees are the flood."

"Well, that makes perfect sense," Joshea said. He turned back on Fel-Sed. "You need to undo what you did to him." She clucked her tongue again and spoke at length.

"If she merely opened his skies, there would be a great storm," Rek-Yun offered, though it seemed like he thought he was saying utter nonsense as well. "You could be . . . washed away?"

Minox already felt like he was drowning. The magic was churning in him now, leeching strength right from the pit of his stomach, and going nowhere. He was already famished again. "I need to do something. Can you help me?"

Fel-Sed spoke, Rek-Yun again interpreting. "We can teach, but only you can help you."

She pointed again to the hut, and started to walk.

"Is this a good idea?" Joshea asked.

"Probably not," Minox said. "But I believe I'm looking at the least bad option right now." No Druth Circle would help him, for certain. The only chance he had to understand what was going on was the Tsouljan way.

"I won't let you do it alone." He gestured to the hut where the Tsouljans were leading them.

"I appreciate that, Joshea."

Saint Limarre's Church was not, strictly speaking, on Satrine's route home from the stationhouse. More often than not, though, she found herself walking past there at the end of her shift, just as evening services were about to start.

Sometimes she allowed herself the luxury of taking a moment for herself in the pews in the back. Small acts of selfishness were a ministration her closest spiritual advisor had recommended, and a few minutes in the church, listening to the sermon without any specific responsibility of work or family served that purpose, if just for a few moments.

This night her usual spiritual advisor was on the front steps of the church, but Sister Alana was not welcoming people to come in for evening services as she typically did. Tonight she was sternly admonishing a young novice—blonde girl with an angry face. The girl seemed to be taking her rebuke with silent furor. Satrine couldn't hear the details but recognized the tone of voice Sister Alana was using. She hung back at a respectable distance until Alana dismissed the girl.

"I'm not the only one having a bad day," she said once Alana noticed her.

"I am being tested," Alana said, her voice straining. She approached Satrine warmly. "The saints are testing my faith with that one."

After a quick embrace Satrine laughed. "I'm guessing she's much like we were at that age."

"She would have owned Jent and Tannen in our day," Alana said. "That girl has fire that would put ours to shame at any point."

"But she isn't going to work out?"

"Are you perceptive or just prying?"

"Bit of both, comes with the vest," Satrine said.

Alana smiled ruefully. "I'm not sure. For all her temper, she has faith like nothing I've seen. She puts some of the eldest cloistresses to shame. And me, especially as I was when I was nineteen."

Memory washed over Satrine at that. "I was just thinking about myself at nineteen early today."

"In what way?"

"In how I got handily slapped around by a Lyranan spy back then."

Sister Alana's face lit up. "This sounds like a worthy story to tell your absolution confessor."

"It probably is, but this isn't the time."

Alana sat down on the church steps, inviting Satrine to do the same. "Is there something you need to talk about?"

Satrine sat down. "I thought by now it would have gotten easier."

"The work?"

"No, that's going to be a horror, just by its nature. Yesterday had a mauled body and a dead bear—"

"I heard about the bear."

"Old Giles Henk, running a bear fight out of that basement? Can you imagine?"

"I've tried to forget about that basement," Alana said with a shudder.

"I've given up on forgetting," Satrine said. "Blazes, that's the one thing about this job that's been . . . I wouldn't go so far to say a blessing, but—" She let the thought hang. She wasn't sure how to say what she was feeling.

"You're finding the person you are at the center of your spirit." Alana shrugged. "This place forged that spirit."

"I'm not so sure that's what I mean," Satrine said. "I've been so many people. My memory is a jumble of truth and fabrication, and . . . this job, this place . . . it reminds me who I actually am."

"So what isn't easier yet?"

"The people in the stationhouse, mostly."

"That's not going to get any better, Satrine. I don't know why you thought it might."

"I've been proving myself—"

"You lied and tricked your way into a position and stepped on a lot of necks. Saints may forgive that sort of thing, but most people don't."

"It sounds like you don't either."

"You didn't wrong me, so my forgiveness is irrelevant." She glanced back at the church doors. "And whatever arrangement you make with God and the saints that intercede for you is your business."

"Aren't you praying for me?" Satrine asked.

"Every damn day," Alana said. "Blazes, I did that before I even knew you were still alive."

"Does the reverend know you talk that way, Sister?" Satrine teased.

"Unless he's gone deaf."

That made Satrine laugh, which was what she really needed. "I don't know what I'm supposed to find here, Alana, but I'm glad I found you again."

Sister Alana glanced up at the clock tower above the church. "I would think you need to get home."

"I should," Satrine agreed, coming to her feet and dusting off her pants. "At some point I'd like to have you come to the house, meet my girls."

"And your husband."

Satrine winced. There wasn't much of Loren to meet. "He's not really there, you know."

"The most important part still is, Satrine." Alana must have sensed she was making Satrine uncomfortable, as she waved it off. "But you should be off, and I should make sure Sister Myriem hasn't broken anything in a rage."

"Good luck with that," Satrine said, taking her old friend in an embrace. She watched Sister Alana go into the church, and after taking another moment for herself, headed over to the Upper Bridge.

The sky still had the warm haze of the lazy summer evenings, the setting sun dappling the water downriver on the Maradaine as Satrine made her way across the bridge. Plenty of the folk seemed to be taking their time, strolling across the bridge. Satrine matched their pace, but more out of exhaustion rather than the idle fancy the rest seemed to be in. She wondered what their days consisted of that they could be so carefree. It wasn't as if they didn't all also have money problems, illness, and saints knew what other maladies in their lives.

But Satrine was reasonably certain they didn't have dead bodies, foreign nobilities, and old spies in their lives.

The lamps were finally being lit on the street as she approached her home. She had barely gotten her key in the lock when the door flew open from inside, and she was confronted with the face of Missus Abernand.

"There's a visitor here for you."

This was not Missus Abernand's usual face or tone. There was none of her usual put-upon air, her presumptive wisdom of her elder years, or disdainful sighs.

The look on her face was one of terror.

Satrine drew out her crossbow and signaled for Missus Abernand to step aside. The woman did without hesitation, her hands trembling.

Satrine raised up her weapon and strode down the short hallway to the main room.

"Put that away, Inspector."

The voice, the accent, the face were all unmistakable, there at Satrine's table, seated in between Rian and Caribet.

Pra Yikenj.

Chapter 12

"**W**HAT THE BLAZES are you doing here?"

Yikenj smiled, like a hairless cat might. "Now, now, Inspector, there's no need for that."

"I'll decide what there's a need for in my home." This woman, this nightmare from years ago was at her table, right between her daughters. To their credit, neither of them looked as frightened as Missus Abernand, or as terrified as Satrine was. Rian was on her nerves, more caution than fear. Caribet looked scared, but a child's fear of a stranger. There was a bald, gray-skinned woman in her home, and she didn't know why. "So why are you here?"

"Inspector, you'll frighten the children." She reached out and stroked Caribet's hair.

Satrine fired her crossbow right at Yikenj's heart.

It didn't land, as Yikenj's hand snapped in front of her faster than the blink of an eye. She had caught the crossbow bolt.

"Now, Inspector. Be so kind as to sit down," she said, placing the bolt on the table calmly. "There's no need for further theatrics."

Satrine sat down across from Yikenj. "Girls, go upstairs with Missus Abernand. Right away."

Rian moved like an arrow, on her feet and grabbing her sister, pulling her away from the Lyranan woman.

"They really are lovely girls," Yikenj said. She gave a glance at Caribet. "I imagine you are the very picture of your father, aren't you?"

Caribet gasped and pulled back, Rian holding her protectively. For the first time Satrine saw real fierceness in her eldest daughter's eyes.

"Let them be," Satrine said.

"But she," Yikenj said, pointing at Rian, "in this house, she is all yours."

"Go," she said to her daughters, and they scurried off to the back stairs with Missus Abernand.

The remnants of Yikenj's smile vanished. "You remembered."

"Clearly you did as well."

"Who do you think wrote the letter addressed to Satrine Carthas Rainey?"

"Did you come here to reminisce, Yikenj?"

She got to her feet. Sitting at the table no longer suited her without the dramatic image of being flanked by Satrine's children. "Your daughter, the one who favors you, she doesn't know?"

"No," Satrine hissed. "It will stay that way."

"That is not my business here," Yikenj said. "But you should thank her, Inspector. It's thanks to her that you are still alive."

Satrine had expected Imachan to be hot—a sweltering, deathly heat where she would desperately claw for a drop of water to sate her thirst.

It certainly was warm, but it was nothing like that. Though any place would feel warm after Waisholm. Not two weeks since her mission was declared finished—the Rainstorm clan securely on the Waish throne—that she was returned to Maradaine, only to be shoved back into a boat for a new mission.

"Short term," she had been told. "Nothing like the last one, Agent Carthas. Go in, gather information, and get the blazes out."

There had been something somewhat thrilling about being called "Agent Carthas." Despite years of being "Quia" or "Her Grace" she never let herself grow accustomed to that. "Tricky Trini" was a girl she hadn't been in a while. Agent Satrine Carthas had a lovely sound to it.

This mission, though, consisted of little more than a rough map, a contact in Kiad, and the instructions, "Scout where that map leads you, report what you find."

Her contact had been an old man on the outskirts of the city who gave her a basement to sleep in, a hot meal, a change of clothes, and a lot of weapons. The basement was actually an obscene arsenal, and he just shrugged and said, "Take what you need." His only other advice was to approach her destination at nightfall, which was what she had intended.

Armed with a crossbow, a bandolier of darts, and as many knives as she could strap onto herself without making noise when she walked, she slipped out into the twilight. The map led her to a farmstead, and she began her investigation.

She didn't know a damn thing about farms. There seemed to be only one crop growing, a tall grass shoot. Nothing odd about that. She crept her way to the buildings, figuring whatever she should be looking for was there.

Most of the buildings seemed to be barracks of some sort, likely for whoever worked this place. She didn't bother with those. The building that stood out was much larger, and as she approached, gave off a distinct hot, sweet smell. Not quite like honey—but heavier, more oppressive.

She drew out her crossbow and slipped into that building. Inside the heat was intense, scorching. This was the sort of heat she expected from Imachan. But it came from massive metal vats—nothing was boiling in them right now, but they still had heat pouring off of them.

Satrine took two steps closer when her feet were swept out from under her.

She rolled to one side and fired at her attacker before she even had her footing. The shadowy figure—a woman—moved like lightning, grabbing the bolt midair.

This was trouble.

Satrine threw two of her darts at the woman, half wild. That was only a feint as she dove in with her fists.

Nothing connected as the woman fluidly dodged and blocked everything Satrine gave her. Satrine couldn't say the same, as three punches landed on her chin and sternum before she was even clear where they were coming from.

She didn't let herself get dazed by that. She'd been hit harder plenty of times. This woman had finesse, Satrine had street-sense. Satrine wasn't about to give her a proper fight, but a brawl.

She dove at the woman, grabbing hold of her outfit, and tried to pull her down with her weight. This seemed to confuse the woman long enough for Satrine to grapple one arm.

Satrine had every intention of twisting that arm behind the woman's back, but the woman flipped her body over in a seemingly impossible way, wrenching Satrine's arm up. Suddenly she found herself in the position she had planned for her attacker.

The woman shoved her against one of the vats—hot metal snapped Satrine into the severity of the moment. She pulled a knife with her left arm and drove it backward, getting a piece of the woman. That gave her enough latitude to push away from the vat and turn back around.

The woman still had a grip on her arm, and Satrine brought down the knife on her. That forced her to let go, and allowed Satrine to get a few steps away.

"Not bad," Satrine said, knife held up defensively.

The woman gave no rejoinder. Instead she closed the distance, grabbing Satrine's knife hand and slamming her against a wall. One hand was firmly around Satrine's neck. It was only now, helpless, that she got a good look at the woman. Grayish skin, bald head. Lyranan. Her eyes took in Satrine.

"Druth? Waish?"

"Piss yourself," *Satrine responded, dropping into her native Inemar street accent.*

"Druth," *the woman confirmed. A slight smile played over her lips.* "Foolish."

She squeezed, and Satrine flailed impotently with her free arm, a vain attempt to get free. The woman's eyes were locked onto Satrine's as her vision started to cloud. Satrine struggled for air, struggled with the woman's hand, kicked lamely at her feet. Just as she was about to slip into blackness, something changed in the woman's face.

She let go and looked Satrine up and down with discernment. Then her hand shot to Satrine's abdomen.

She didn't strike this time. Instead, reached under Satrine's shirt and placed her palm on her belly. After a moment of groping—which Satrine was far too weak to resist—she let go completely and stepped back.

Satrine collapsed to the floor.

She lost time in a haze of confusion—next thing she knew she was lying in the dirt back in the crop field. Something was burning. As she struggled to find her feet, she saw in the distance the boilhouse on fire.

"This is done," *a harsh accented voice said next to her.* "Neither of our governments need worry about it."

Satrine couldn't quite get herself upright, but she turned to this woman—the Lyranan who had just beat her senseless. "What the blazes did you do?"

"What was necessary. The masters are dead, the place is destroyed, and the western children who had been stolen and enslaved have been given mercy."

"Mercy?" Satrine managed to say. Western children enslaved? Was that what she was sent to discover? "Did you kill them?"

"Painlessly," the Lyranan woman said. "They had no chance of rescue or escape. Certainly not from you."

"Who are you to—"

The woman crouched in front of her. "You will go back to Kiad now. In the northern wharf there's a Fuergan ship leaving for Druthal at dawn. Be on it. Go home."

Satrine pulled herself to her feet. "Why the blazes do you think I'm doing that?"

"Because, foolish girl," the Lyranan woman said, "the only reason I am not killing you is the innocent life that grows inside you. Go home, and cherish the gift the child has given you."

Before Satrine could protest anymore, she was grabbed by the scruff of her neck and thrown back down to the ground. Lying in the dirt, panting for breath, the Lyranan woman's words hit her harder than any of her blows.

The innocent life inside her.

Once she could get on her feet, she wasted no time getting to the northern wharf.

The tunnels underneath the Tsouljan compound were astounding. It wasn't just some sort of interconnected root cellar, which was what he was expecting, but an elaborate network of hallways and chambers. It wasn't just elaborate, but elegant: ceramic tiles along the floor, painted frescoes on the walls, lamps in engraved sconces, detailed woodwork in the support arches. The air even felt fresh, like a breeze flowed through the whole place.

It was also far more populated than he had thought the entire compound was.

The hallway they were led through opened up to some form of community kitchen, where several green-haired Tsouljans were cooking and serving, food that at the same time smelled sweet and rancid. Minox wasn't sure what to make of the assault on his nostrils, but he was sure that there were several dozen Tsouljans seated at the circular tables. Men, women, old, young, with blue, red, yellow, and green hair.

It immediately struck Minox that this could represent almost a hundred potential suspects.

It was also now clear why they had no argument to being confined to their compound. They had everything they needed here.

"Who knew this was hiding under the city?" Minox said out loud.

"It is impressive," Joshea said.

"They must have utilized old sewers and catacombs and built this up." Minox thought to the last time he had been underground, when Nerrish Plum had assaulted him and brought him to hidden mausoleum tunnels under his shop. There was almost an entire second city hiding underneath Maradaine.

He wondered who, if anyone, was in charge of that secret city.

"Mister Rek-Yun," he called out, "do these passages lead outside the compound? Or connect to the city's own tunnelwork?"

"I am told they do not," Rek-Yun responded. Minox noted that he did not answer definitively in the negative.

"But why do this?" Joshea asked.

They were being led down a set of stairs into a deeper chamber, and Minox could hear something echoing in the distance.

"Why build high towers, great walls?" Rek-Yun asked. "This is what we do."

Fel-Sed added her own thoughts, though in her native tongue.

"What did she say?" Joshea asked.

Rek-Yun sighed, like he was having to correct a slow child. "She said it comes from our ancient history, when our ancestors were set upon by aggressive neighbors. Due to their own faith, the idea of going underground was terrifying to them."

"So you build down, and they don't bother you."

"That is the legend," Rek-Yun said with a strange shrug. "I do not know how much I would draw from it."

"You don't believe it?" Joshea asked.

"There are sources of lore, and sources of research. I am not of the Fel, I do not read the former."

The stairway opened up to a chamber, this one just carved right out of the white limestone. There was also an underwater stream running through it, flowing in from a hole in the rock on one side, and out through the other, presumably to the river.

Minox immediately considered the idea that a capable swimmer might be able to penetrate the compound by this stream, and then escape the same way. Of course such a person would clearly be seen in the hallway. The hallways were like busy streets.

"That was not what I was expecting," Joshea said.

The two blue-hairs with Fel-Sed started placing candles along the side of the stream, lighting each one of them as they were placed.

"This is where you'll teach us?" Minox asked.

Fel-Sed gave him a slight nod, and then proceeded to remove her robes. Once she was undressed, she stepped into the stream.

"Do as she does," Rek-Yun said.

"This is really what we're doing?" Joshea pressed.

"I think we must trust this process," Minox said. Everything about this went against his instincts of what was appropriate, but something about Fel-Sed's manner struck him as utterly genuine. He began undressing.

With a chuckle, Joshea started to do the same. "This better be useful, that's all I have to say."

Minox stepped into the water—far warmer than he expected it to be. Almost hot, even. A few steps in and he was already up to his chest. The current was far stronger and more turbulent than he was expecting. It took a fair amount of concentration and strength to simply stand still.

"Saints," Joshea said, taking his place next to Minox. He seemed to be struggling to keep his footing just as much as Minox was.

"The *ge-tan* flows around you and through you." This seemed to be the voice of Fel-Sed, who stood serenely in the stream facing the two of them, now speaking in Trade. But she didn't speak. The words both echoed around the cavern and whispered right in Minox's ear. Was this the telepathy that Rainey had spoken of? Was Fel-Sed a master of both arts? "You stand in the current, and you cannot let it control you, or you will be swept away."

"That's what this is," Joshea muttered.

Ignoring his interjection, Fel-Sed cupped her hand in the water, allowing it to flow over and through her fingers. "Hold it, but let it flow."

Minox mimicked her action, though he needed to use his left hand, as it was the downstream one. It still felt odd, stranger than the rest of his body.

"Feel where the *ge-tan* is in your body. Be as aware of it as the water."

The magic was always in the pit of Minox's stomach, like a churning fire. When he needed it, he pulled it out of there and sent it to his hands. But that was what wasn't working right now. He closed his eyes, holding his arms out to keep his balance in the rushing water. The fire was there, as always, but as an angry ember.

"Find it in every part of you. Know those parts, and let the *ge-tan* flow through it."

Water buffeted his body, flowing over his hands and fingers.

Minox reached for the magic, trying to pull it to his hands, where he could shape it. Again, just like in the street earlier, it went nowhere.

"Slowly," Fel-Sed's voice soothed. "It is not just a fire."

Did she know his thoughts here? How he saw the magic? "Then what is it?" he asked.

"It is water and breath and fire."

That wasn't helpful.

"Breathe and flow."

That definitely wasn't helpful.

He looked back at the fire in his stomach. He tried pushing it, like air in his lungs, out from his center into his arms.

That time there was something. It didn't quite go to his hands, but now he had a sense of where it was stopping, how it stopped.

"Now bring the flames of the candle to you."

"How are we supposed to do that?" Joshea asked. He looked about the room like he was expecting a group of Tsouljans to leap out of the shadows at any moment. Minox understood that—he certainly felt ridiculous.

"The *ge-tan* flows. The water flows, the air in the chamber. The flame of the candle. Feel each of those things, and how each is part of the room, part of you, part of your balance."

Minox didn't quite understand, but an idea in what she was saying clicked with him. Magic wasn't something he could just do, it was something he could sense. He could feel it in himself, in the world around him, just as he could feel the water rush past him, the air he breathed, the heat of the candle.

He had trained his other senses to be aware of fine

details around him, in order to be the best inspector he could be. Notice everything.

This was a sense he had never trained.

He tried to tune out everything but the magic, find where that sense was located. He remembered the tether he traced that led him after Jaelia Tomar. That was this sense. He knew it was there, he just needed to focus.

The magic was there, in his stomach.

It flowed in the water; it swelled around him, Joshea, and Fel-Sed. It danced around the flames of the candles.

He opened his eyes, and for a brief moment, he saw it, as light that moved like smoke. Fel-Sed pulsed with the light. Joshea was surrounded in a nimbus of it. His own body was infused, save his left arm. There it was—right above his wrist, a blur of purple and blue.

On instinct he pushed light into that blur.

In an instant there was no flow of magic. Instead it burst, so bright it deafened him.

Then heat, flame, a rush, and water. No air. Darkness. Pulling. No air. Water.

Hands on his leg, arm, body.

Pulled back, he was back in the air. On the stone. Couldn't breathe. Hands on his face.

"Minox! Minox!"

Blurs of light became Joshea's face. Minox found himself being handled, turned onto his stomach. Struck on his back, water came out of his mouth and nose. He gasped, thirsty for air. He couldn't get enough, coughing out more water.

"Sweet saints, woman!" Joshea was shouting. "This is craziness! You could have killed him."

Fel-Sed responded in Tsouljan nonsense, real words from her mouth. Minox realized he was out of the water, on the stone floor, Joshea crouched next to him. Whatever method she was using to speak to them before must have ended when they left the stream.

"What happened?" he asked, his voice more of a hoarse whisper than he expected.

"You tell me," Joshea said. "She said the magic was part of our balance, and then you went under. I barely got you before the current swept you down that tunnel."

"That quickly?" Minox asked.

"More or less. I wasn't counting the clicks of the clock. But it was barely a moment."

That didn't track for Minox. It felt like it had been several minutes of trying to sense the magic. Had that affected his perspective of time?

He flexed his left hand. It felt different now. Almost hot.

Fel-Sed emerged from the water, snapping at them in Tsouljan.

"What is she saying?" Minox asked. Was Rek-Yun still present?

"Nonsense, I'm sure," Joshea said, pulling his pants back on. "Let's get dressed and get out of here." He tossed Minox his own clothing.

"She said you have shattered the dam. She must re-build it or you will be in great danger." Rek-Yun still stood at the bottom of the stairwell.

"A dam?" Joshea snarled. "You hear that? She blocked your magic. She did it to you. There's your mystery."

"Why?" Minox asked, first looking at Rek-Yun and then Fel-Sed. "Why do this to me?"

"Because you are out of balance," Rek-Yun interpreted her words as she spoke. "You will activate horrible things."

Joshea was fully dressed now, his hair still dripping. "If you don't let us out of here, back up to the open sky, I will show you terrible things."

Minox pulled his pants on. "There is no need for threats. I'm sure they'll let you leave."

"Threats?" Joshea asked. "Minox, they almost killed you, and for what? Come on."

Minox hesitated. As unorthodox as this process was, it hadn't been useless. For a moment he felt like he almost understood how his own magic and body worked. He wasn't sure he could find it again on his own.

"Maybe we should . . ."

There was a commotion above them, someone shouting. Druth Trade.

"Inspector! Are you all right?"

Minox pulled on his shirt and vest. "Everything's fine, Patrolman," he called back.

"No, it isn't!"

Minox came up the stairs to the kitchen chamber, Joshea charging with him. One of the patrolmen from the gate was in a frantic state, two of the red-haired Tsouljans holding him back.

"Report, Patrolman."

"We're hearing trouble in the streets, sir. Shouts, cries, and then whistle calls soon after, of all sorts. There's definitely a brawl going on, sir. Maybe even a riot."

—◆—◆—◆—

Satrine stared down Pra Yikenj, as the smug Lyranan woman smirked at her. The same damn expression she made fifteen years ago in that burning field outside of Kiad. "So tell me your business here, or get out."

"You suspect I am your murderer, and with good cause."

"Because you're quite capable of committing it."

"I have the skills and the will, yes. As you know."

Satrine resisted the urge to reload her crossbow and take another shot.

Yikenj continued. "But I am, like you, an officer of order. I was true to my word fifteen years ago, and I am now. So I'm telling you that I am not your killer. I do not know who your killer is, and I am not interested in putting my considerable skills to work in determining it for you."

"And here I thought we were going to be friends," Satrine said. "How surprising."

"I am telling this to you out of ... is 'kindness' the word?"

"Probably not."

"No, I have done you one kindness already in this lifetime. The word I want is 'warning.'"

"I presumed you being here was a warning of some sort."

Yikenj scoffed. "Not from my government. I have taken this initiative out of professional courtesy to you. I recognize you have a job that you must do, and it is a worthy and important one."

Satrine took this as her cue to scoff. "As we say here, I don't need all this butter. Tell me what you have to say."

"It is this, Inspector Rainey: despite the remarkable poem at the scene, this murder has nothing to do with Lyrana."

"That's for me to determine," Satrine said.

"We have extended you two courtesies today to assist your investigation. That is more than any other party, no matter how tangential they are to this case, has been willing to do." Yikenj was now standing like a cat getting ready to pounce.

"Fine," Satrine said, getting on her feet. If this was going to be a scrap, she'd not be found wanting. "So what is it you want, Yikenj? I presume you're not here for dinner."

"Am I not being clear, Inspector? Very well. This murder does not involve Lyranans. Therefore *you* and the rest of your Constabulary will not involve yourself in Lyranan affairs. Myself, my superiors, or any other Lyranan in Maradaine. Even the band that plays at the public house. No one."

Satrine stepped forward, getting in Yikenj's gray, hairless face. "Am I not being clear, Miss Yikenj? That's not yours to say."

Unsurprisingly Yikenj was not cowed by Satrine's bravado. She gave no ground, simply flashing that disturbing smile of hers. "Ignore my warning if you wish, Inspector. It is ironic, if you'll allow me. Two days ago your Constabulary gave little thought to what occurred in the Little East. Two days from now some shiny object will capture your attention, and you'll stop thinking of it. That is why we've had to act."

"Act how?"

The question wasn't answered. A sound from the kitchen drew Satrine's eye for a moment, and in that brief instant of distraction, Yikenj moved. Not a blow was thrown, though. Instead, she was just gone. The front door slammed shut before Satrine was even sure what had just happened.

She went to the door and threw the double latch closed. She doubted that would keep Pra Yikenj out if she intended to get in, of course, but it made her feel a little safer.

Then she went to the kitchen. The source of the distracting noise was easy enough to find. A *henzh*—a Lyranan dart—was imbedded in one of the cabinet doors. Yikenj grandstanding even as she left, showing that she could throw her weapon with just as much silent grace as she caught the crossbow bolt.

Yikenj was in all likelihood being honest—neither she nor any other Lyranan was the killer here. But that didn't make Satrine feel any better. Once again that woman had violated her, and then let her go just to show she could. Just to be magnanimous.

Satrine would be damned before she gave Pra Yikenj a third chance to do that.

Chapter 13

THERE WASN'T A DECENT PLACE to get a bite in this blazing part of town. Certainly not now, after dark with a soft curfew. Corrie hadn't had anything significant to eat since—blazes, when? Last she remembered was before she went to shift the night before. All day without eating, that was rutting stupid of her.

She had done three circles around the Machie part of the East. Quite a few of them had been in the street, and she stopped a few who looked up to no damn good. She hadn't caught anyone under Home Binding out of doors, and it seemed most of them were going to the same place: a public house or community center of some sort. Maybe a church for them, Corrie had no blazing idea. She didn't care, all she knew was her stomach was screaming at her.

"Any luck?" she called out to two other horsepatrol as they approached. Just about everyone on horse tonight was dealing with the same problem she was, and everyone was trying to find something to eat in the Little East that didn't make them want to puke it right back up.

"Not really," one of them said back to her. Venkins, who had been riding the night shift for almost a year now. "We heard that there's a Lyranan public house still serving food, but we haven't heard much about what they eat."

"Have you been patrolling bleeding Tyzoville?"

"A bit," Venkins said. "That part of the East is still pretty crowded, stuff happening."

"Should we crack down on that?" Terrick, the guy riding with Venkins, seemed a little too eager to have something to crack down on. He'd been talking like that all night.

"Ain't no Lyranans on those writs," Corrie said. "Can't bleeding well chase them off for doing nothing wrong."

"Smells like trouble," Terrick said.

"Then do a rutting ride-through," she snarled. "Show the color, and maybe there's some tyzo who'll give you some food."

"And what are you bleeding doing, Cor?" Venkins asked.

An idea sizzled in her head. "I'm going to head up to Feektown, circle around it for a bit. You all keep an eye out."

"You too," Venkins said, and Corrie spurred her horse forward.

Of course she wasn't going to Feektown. She'd go through it, and then only two blocks away from that was home. There she could pop in, get some decent food, and pop back over with no damn problem.

Corrie spurred her horse, heading over to Peston. She wasn't riding Hosker or Brane, her two usual mounts—blazes, she didn't even know this one's name—so she'd actually have to guide it home. If it was Brane, she could doze off and it would take her there. But this one she wasn't fond of. It was a bit sluggish and stubborn. Easy to see why it was one the day shift had left in the stables. So she had to focus on making sure it went where it should and stayed on the right side of the road, instead of daydreaming of the food that she would find at home. Dinner was already over, of course, but Mother would have squirreled a few things away in the larder.

It was hardly the first time Corrie would pop to the house for a bite of something mid-shift.

She was letting herself think about spiced cured lamb, soft cheese, and mustard when she heard voices on one of the side streets. Not speaking Trade, and certainly more than one or two folks.

Gritting her teeth, she turned the sluggish horse up that street. Eating would have to wait.

Five feeks—big bruisers, even the two ladies—were striding down the walkway. They were going somewhere with a plan, and from the looks of them that plan would involve some broken teeth.

"Hey," Corrie called out, moving the horse up on the walkway to block their path. "Where you all headed?"

The one in the center said something in Fuergan to her. She didn't know a word, but she could imagine he suggested shoving her handstick somewhere.

So she pulled her handstick out. "Let me rephrase. Show me some papers and explain why you're out of doors."

The group stopped. They all stood still for a moment, staring down Corrie.

Her blasted horse took a step forward.

The leader yelled something in Fuergan, and the five feeks all ran in different directions.

Corrie spurred the stupid damn horse and pulled out her whistle, giving out a quick Runner Call.

She charged after the leader, figuring that was the best one to iron. He ducked into one alley, which she tried to turn into. The stupid rutting horse balked, giving the guy a blazes of a lead.

Return Call whistled through the night. She spotted two footpatrol coming down toward her. "Five feeks out of doors, ran every which way! Run them down!"

She dropped to her boots, leaving this rutting horse behind. It was worse than useless.

The feek was nearly through to the other end of the alley, but she tore down after him, pulling her crossbow out as she closed. He turned to the left, into the open street, but there was only so far he could go before she caught up.

She came out of the far end of the alley, turning to see him duck into one of the households. "Stand and be held!" she shouted, though she didn't expect him to listen. Blazes, the feek might not even understand Trade. Certainly the bastard wouldn't care about arrest rules.

Corrie bounded up the steps of the household, to find a stout feek woman blocking the door. She shouted in feek sewage, with a few "No!" in there for good measure.

"Stand aside, I have just cause," Corrie snarled.

The woman responded by pushing Corrie in the chest, knocking her down the steps. She managed to keep her feet as she went down, but she fumbled her crossbow. It fired wildly into the street.

Her lieutenants were always chiding her for keeping her blasted finger on the trigger.

"You rutting slan!" Corrie shouted. She swapped the crossbow for the handstick, intent of giving the feek skirt a few bruises.

"Welling!" One of the other horsepatrol came thundering up. Kenty. Good stick, if a bit of a priss. "Where's your mount?"

"Left that nag behind," she said. "We got a runner hiding in this household. Just cause for entry."

"No time," Kenty said. "A whole mess of the Fuergans went into Machie. Kicked in the doors of their church."

Corrie pointed her handstick at the feek matron. "I'm gonna remember you, skirt."

The feek shut her door.

"Get your horse and get over there," Kenty said. Did

he outrank her? Corrie couldn't even remember. Maybe. "We're looking at a Riot Call."

And as soon as he said it, the piercing whistle cut through the air.

"No time for my rutting mount," Corrie said, and pounded her boots back to Imachtown.

She barely made it half a block when a horde of those bearded freaks came flooding toward the Fuergan houses.

———— ◆◆▶ ————

Even from the serenity of the Tsouljan gardens, it was clear there was chaos in the streets of the Little East. Shouts, screams, and whistles pierced through the air. Minox quickened his pace while making sure his crossbow was loaded and he had his handstick. The fact that his vest probably wasn't buttoned would have to wait.

"Patrolman, I appreciate your diligence. But no matter the call, you and your partner keep your stand on the gates to this place."

"Really, sir?" the patrolman asked. "You might need . . ."

They pushed past the blooming trees and reached the gate. "What I'll need is irrelevant. If this unrest is tied to the murder, this place and the people inside might be targets. I am not assigning you a meaningless task."

"Aye, Inspector," the patrolman said.

He was out in the street and heading toward the sounds of the disturbance—somewhere where the Imach and Fuergan districts met, likely—when he realized Joshea was at his elbow.

"This is no place for civilians," he said.

"Good thing I'm not one," Joshea said. Minox glanced back and noticed Joshea had grabbed a Tsouljan gardening tool on their way out.

"Joshea," he said firmly, "you could be charged for assault, or possibly murder. Not to mention theft." He glanced at the tool in Joshea's hand. "You have no authority to take action here."

"I have a right to be armed and protect my person," Joshea said. He placed a hand on Minox's shoulder. "And I think the law even provides for protecting a fellow person."

"Within reason," Minox said. The hostilities he was hearing were growing increasingly violent in tenor. There was no time to waste. "Do nothing that could be considered actively aggressive."

"Aye, sir," Joshea said with military crispness, the sort of tone he reserved for his father. Minox couldn't read if that was sincere or some sort of jibe, but he didn't have time to think about it. Trouble was afoot.

They approached the market square at the corner of Peston and Necker, which had erupted in a full brawl between Fuergans and Imachs. The riot between them had spread out in almost every direction. A handful of regulars were in the thick of it, but they looked like they were in danger of being overrun by the fighting. Footpatrol were coming in from all over, most of them too stunned to take action.

Understandable. They had never seen anything like this. Minox certainly hadn't.

"Trouble," Joshea said, pointing out one thing in particular. Minox saw, and was impressed with Joshea's eye, picking out a particular piece of this chaos that was worse than the rest.

Two footpatrol had their crossbows drawn, screaming at the Imachs around them to back away, their orders laced with obscenities. These two were spinning around wildly, no discipline with their weapons. There was already enough danger and destruction going on; the worst thing would be for the Constabulary to add to it.

"Sir?" one of the footpatrol asked. "What's the word?" A good dozen of them had gathered by him.

Minox was the ranking on scene. Of course they looked to him.

"I need those two pulled out now," Minox said, pointing to the regulars who had nearly lost their minds. "We need horsepatrol to form a perimeter. Call for lockwagons and Yellowshields. Gather a line of footpatrol and prepare to sweep in."

"Aye, sir," the footpatrol said. Two of them ran back out down Necker and blew out the calls needed. A couple more charged in toward the two wild regulars and dragged them out.

"Joshea," Minox said. "I have a job for you."

"Name it," Joshea said.

"Yellowshields aren't going to have an easy time getting into here. Once we sweep through, you see anyone in critical need of care—"

"Pull them out of field, aye," Joshea said. "I can do that."

"Sir?" one the footpatrol asked. "Do we wait for the lockwagons to sweep?"

"I don't think we can, son," Minox said. "On my mark, we go."

He drew out his handstick.

Before he could give the order, there was a different cry from the east side of Peston. A couple dozen men and women came pouring in, armed with truncheons, clubbing down Fuergan and Imach alike.

Lyranans.

———◆———

Ferah went around the sitting rooms of the Welling household, putting out oil lamps. Usually Aunt Amalia did this, but between Corrie staying on for a double and Minox not coming home at all from his shift, she was a mess. Jace and Alma got her to bed, and Emma and Nyla helped clean the kitchen instead of going to their Suffragist meeting. Despite her feet aching from running her Yellowshield shift, Ferah stayed up to shut down the house for the night.

At least as much as it should be shut down. Corrie and Minox were still on the job. Mother was working a night shift at Ironheart, and Pop . . . Pop and Colm had both been working doubles and sleeping at the Brigade house after the big fire in North Seleth. Pop blamed himself that the Brigade hadn't been there.

Ferah worked her way over to the kitchen. She checked the oil lamp in the window by the back door. It was burning low. She went into one of the cabinets to find the oil jar. Ferah had little hope that her brother would come out of the stable and back into the house during the night, but if he did, she would make sure there was a light there for him.

"Why ain't you asleep yet?"

Edard had come down the back stairs, out of his foot-patrol uniform, but otherwise fully dressed.

"Why aren't you?" Ferah asked. "You heading out right after midnight?"

"Things need doing," Edard said. He let that hang there.

Of all her cousins, Edard was the one Ferah was closest to. They both worked Dentonhill, they both had seen things. Ferah knew damn well that a few of her fellow Yellowshields did sew-up work for Fenmere's thugs. Edard never spoke about it, but she was worried he was taking some look-the-other-way money. Maybe even doing a favor or two, if not for Fenmere's people, then for another stick in Denton who was deep in Fenmere's pocket.

She didn't say anything either. Unlike anyone else in this house, she knew what working Dentonhill was like. She'd patched up enough sticks and doxies and 'fitte-heads to know. She also knew Edard was trying to get

shifted to any other part of town. He'd even work deep
west side, even in the landfill in Old Quarry. But his lieutenant wasn't letting go of him.

"Can't keep the left waiting," Edard said after the
long moment, heading to the front door. "Really wish
you'd been asleep."

"Well, I'm not," Ferah said, following after him.
"Damn it, Eddie, don't do anything—"

"I ain't talking about it," he said. He reached the door,
his hand resting on the handle. "Look, it's all right. It's
just this guy, he's a real—he ought to be ironed and in
Quarrygate. We're going to take care of it."

"For who?" Ferah pressed.

"Just doing what I'm told."

He opened the door and went out. She wanted to
shout after him, but at the same time, she didn't want to
make a scene, wake up his father and brothers. They
wouldn't understand at all.

Not that she understood either.

Before she could say anything else, he was in the dark
of the night.

She was about to go back in, latch the door, when a
whistle cut through the air. Two short and one long.

A call for a Yellowshield. Somewhere east, probably
Inemar. It'd have to be the Little East to hear it from here.

Then there was another Yellowshield call. Then another. Five. Seven. All east of here, and they kept repeating. Then other calls. Riot Call. Panic Call.

Her coat and her kit were hanging on a peg by the
door. She grabbed both and ran out into the night.

———◆◆◆———

Satrine startled. She had dozed off. The oil lamp was still
burning low, and she could see Missus Abernand asleep
on the couch. Her joints aching, Satrine picked up the
crossbow in her lap and stood up from the rocking chair.

As soon as Yikenj had left, Satrine had brought Rian and Caribet down to their room, and made Missus Abernand sleep on the couch. The old woman had gotten significantly spooked, so it wasn't hard to convince her.

Once they were secure, she double-checked the latch on her door, and then wedged a broomhandle in place to keep it jammed shut. Brute force would still knock it down, but that's what it would take to pull it off.

Then she went up to Missus Abernand's apartment, checking every point of entry and sealing it off best she could. She hoped it would make a difference, though for all she knew, Pra Yikenj had long since snuck back into the house and was just biding her time.

Of course, that was paranoid. Absurdly so. If for no other reason than if Pra Yikenj wanted to kill her and her family, she could have easily done so.

Yikenj wanted her scared, and she certainly was.

She double-checked the door, the windows, and the girls' room. No sign of trouble. She checked the threads she put over the door to the upstairs. Still in place. Not that Yikenj couldn't work around such a basic trick.

It was still dark out. Probably around four bells.

She went to the bedroom. Loren was asleep, quietly so.

Back over to the kitchen. Looking through the cupboards, she found the bottle of wine that Enbrain had brought the night before. She briefly considered forgoing the cup, but decided she wasn't that deep in yet.

After all, on some level, she was still a noble lady.

Pouring herself a cup, she went back to the rocking chair and lay the crossbow back in her lap.

Pra Yikenj might scare her, but she'd face all damnation before she let that Lyranan woman hurt anyone she cared about.

Corrie had given up trying to quell or even control this rutting riot. These blasted feeks and machs had swarmed around her, mostly intent on beating on each other. All she could manage was to push her way out of this mess.

"Welling!"

Corrie turned to see Kenty pulled off his horse by a group of feeks. As he went down, one of them got on the mount and charged at the machs.

Corrie swore even more profusely than usual and dove into the crowd, handstick swinging liberally. Feek and mach alike, she knocked them down, not caring about anything other than carving a straight line to Kenty.

Three feeks were kicking and stomping on him when she got to him. No time or blazing desire to use "appropriate force." She cracked the handstick across the jaw of the closest one, and then spun it to knock him over his thick skull. As he went down, she stomped on the knee of the next one. His leg made a satisfying snap and he dropped. For good measure she smashed the butt of her handstick into his nose.

The third one—a feek skirt—punched Corrie in the chest, and then a cross to her chin. Corrie stumbled a bit, but wasn't dazed, and she wailed back on the damned skirt with her handstick, over and over again.

"Messed with the wrong rutting sinner, you did!" she snapped at the feek, hitting her until the girl dropped in a bloody mess.

"Welling," Kenty muttered. He was a fright, blood gushing from his mouth and eye. Teeth were gone. The right eye was probably gone as well. One of his legs was broken in two places, bone sticking through his slacks.

"Blazes, Kenty," she said, bending down to scoop him up. She managed to get him over her left shoulder in a rescue carry, keeping her right arm free to beat down whoever got in her blasted way. She made for the closest alley, away from much of the chaos. Was this the one she came through earlier, with her useless nag at the other end? She couldn't even remember. A few blows to the head had gotten her all turned around.

"I heard them whistle the Yellowshields, Kenty," she said. "We're gonna get you to them, hear? You'll be rutting fine."

She ran down the alley, which was blessedly clear. She was terrified that she'd be set upon by a nest of hiding machs or feeks, or that the blasted thing would be blocked off by a gate.

Instead, she came straight out the other side to an even larger riot. This was a scrum the likes of which she had never seen. Not only feeks and machs, but a whole mess of gray-skinned tyzos truncheoning anyone they came across. She couldn't even make out who was fighting who, and only a handful of sticks were around, vainly trying to hold something resembling a line.

"I need some rutting help!" she screamed. No one marked her. There was no way she could get through this to the line, not with Kenty on her shoulder. But she'd be damned if she'd leave him here.

She'd have to make a run for it.

Two of the tyzos knocked down a big mach bruiser, giving an opening. She'd just have to dash about twenty yards, with a couple mach skirts far too interested in beating some feek to pay her much mind.

She charged out, handstick at the ready to clobber anyone who got in her way. Five yards out, that mach bruiser slammed the tyzos, forcing her to jump around them. She almost lost her footing, almost dropped Kenty. She lurched to the left to regain her balance, maintain her momentum.

"Help!" she shouted again, hoping someone from the line would hear her.

She collided into one of the Imach skirts. The woman growled—she rutting well *growled*—and turned on Corrie. Corrie clubbed her with the handstick before she could get a shot in.

Ten more yards to the line.

The other mach skirt tackled Corrie, shouting in crazy gibberish. With Kenty on her shoulder, Corrie couldn't stay up, and they all went tumbling to the ground. Corrie's head cracked on the cobblestone as she dropped.

Her left arm was pinned under Kenty, and before she could get her right arm up, the Imach skirt was on top of her. Two more punches to the head. Everything went fuzzy.

As Corrie's head swam and plunged into blackness, she felt the woman grab a swath of her hair and pull it taut. Then she heard the metallic swipe of a knife being drawn from its sheath.

<hr />

"Minox!" Joshea was at his arm, pointing into the fray. But there was too much, too many things happening. Minox couldn't possibly see all the details. There were no options here but bad ones. They were going to have to sweep through with handsticks, clubbing and ironing every person here, aggressor and victim alike.

The Lyranan incursion didn't change that. It just meant more people in the wagons.

"Get in line!" Minox called out to the regulars who were here. Nearly three dozen, and while they were still outnumbered, it would have to do. He could hear the lockwagons coming up. Waiting any longer would just cost lives. "Sweep through on my mark!" He brought up his whistle to signal them.

Joshea grabbed his shoulder. "Corrie!"

This time Minox saw it. Corrie, pushing through the fight, another officer on her shoulder, and then pulled down by an Imach woman.

Instinct fired up the magic in his belly. He barely even

thought about what he was doing. The power welled and then shot out with a wave of his hand. A thunderous crack echoed through the square, and Imachs, Fuergans, and Lyranans in his line of sight were bowled down like they were Eight Pins.

They weren't the only thing bowled over. Minox felt something snap in himself as soon as he did that, starting from his left hand. It was like he was hit with a hammer.

He would have dropped to his knees if it wasn't for Joshea.

"What did you—"

"Corrie, go," Minox wheezed out. Joshea let him go and dashed in. Minox forced himself to stay on his feet, despite every muscle screaming. He fought to take breath and blew the signal for the sweep.

The footpatrol charged in as two waves, the first line pounding through and tearing the rioters from each other and beating them down with their handsticks. The second line grabbed those people once they were beaten down and put them in irons. From other sides of the square, the horsepatrol, running off of Minox's signal, pressed in.

Minox turned to wave in the lockwagons and Yellow-shields. His hands were shaking now, legs like Mother's apple preserves.

He looked back toward Joshea. He was over Corrie, but was embroiled in a fight with a large Imach man. Joshea was holding his own, using the Tsouljan farming tool like the Druth Pikemen of legend, despite a deep bloody gash across his head. He fought with clarity and control, doing nothing but defending Corrie's limp form.

Minox couldn't tell what condition Corrie was in. He took a step toward her; maybe he could get her out while Joshea kept the Imach goliath at bay.

His knees gave out completely, and he dropped to the ground, vomiting as he fell.

Hands were on him. He tried in vain to bring up his handstick, knock off his attacker, but they pushed it aside with ease.

"Hey, hey, Minox. What happened?"

Ferah, in her Yellowshield coat.

In his daze he said the first thing that came to mind, despite it being largely irrelevant. "You don't work this neighborhood."

"I don't ignore whistles when I hear them," she said, cupping his face and looking in his eyes. "Were you hit in the head? I don't see a wound but you show signs of—"

"Not hit," he managed to say. "Magic. Something wrong."

"Blazes," Ferah said uncharacteristically. "We need to get you—"

"No, I need to help—"

"Your folk have things contained," she said. "Let me do my job."

"Indeed," he said, words coming like he was forcing them through cloth. "For Corrie."

He managed to point weakly in her direction. Ferah turned.

"Oh sweet saints and sinners," she muttered. On her feet she shouted, "I need wheels! I need wheels to Iron-heart now!"

Minox tried to argue further with her, but he found himself unable to use his mouth or hands anymore. His vision was a blur, and he was only vaguely aware of being lifted into a wagon before he became completely insensate.

Chapter 14

MINOX WASN'T ENTIRELY SURE how or when he was brought to Ironheart Ward. He was aware of the sounds of doctors, nurses, and Yellowshields tending to more patients than they were prepared for. Screams of agony, moans and cries, tears of frustration, all that also found his ears.

He was on a cot in a far corner of one of the ward rooms, no one paying much mind to him. Some strength had returned, but whatever magical ailment struck him hadn't gone away. Sitting up in the cot, he looked at his left hand, which was now turning gray and black. He could barely move his fingers.

What was this? Did the Tsouljans do this to him?

Or did he do it to himself, and he prevented them from stopping it?

He managed to get onto his feet. The room he was in had several injured people, some Constabulary, as well as civilians of every stripe. Fuergans, Lyranans, and Imachs, as well as a few of Druth stock. Minox noted one resting on a cot, with his head bandaged up.

"Joshea," Minox said, stumbling over to the cot. "Are you all right?"

"Let him rest," a ward nurse said, gently drawing Minox away. "He's one of the ones we don't need to worry about."

"There are ones to worry about?" Minox asked. "Pardon me, ma'am, it's just ..."

"We'll attend to you shortly, Officer," she said calmly. She pushed past him to rejoin the doctor. She then glanced back at him, and after a moment scurried off somewhere else.

"Inspector?" A man with a notably young face came over, his Constabulary uniform in shambles, though his collar showed lieutenant's marks. "Lieutenant Bretton, street commander from last night."

"Bretton?" Minox struggled to think if his face or name was familiar. All thought was cloudy. "Forgive me, Lieutenant, if I acted out of place during the incidents. I presumed I was ranking on scene."

"For all intents you were, sir," Bretton said, though he sounded like he was trying to be political rather than complimentary. "Once I arrived, the riot had been nearly broken up. I had the injured brought here, the rest brought to the stationhouse. I'll gather information on everyone involved and make sure proper charges are filed upon them all once they are treated."

"Good, good," Minox said. "There is an ongoing investigation, and I fear that some of my suspects were embroiled in all this."

"I was told as much by the captain, sir. I'll cooperate with the coordination on this end until all the suspects are cleared."

"Good," Minox said. He pointed to Joshea. "Do you know about his condition?"

"Blow to the head, some bleeding. Nurses say he should be fine, though, once he sleeps through the *doph* they gave him." Strong pain medication. "He's an odd case, sir."

"No charges on him," Minox said. "He was in the neighborhood on my request, and he risked his life to save a fellow constable."

Bretton nodded. "I'll make a note of that."

"Do we have a casualty count?" Minox asked.

"Still too early, Inspector. Same with arrest numbers, charges. There's a lot to sort through."

"Of course," Minox said. Despite still feeling weak and woozy, he pushed himself on toward the exit. He noticed he was just in slacks and shirtsleeves. "Would you know where my vest and belt are?"

"They're up at my desk." Aunt Beliah stood in the exit doorway. "Didn't want you trying to slip off without me knowing."

"Thank you, Lieutenant, that will be all," Minox said. Bretton nodded and stepped away, tipping his hat to Aunt Beliah as he passed.

Minox approached Beliah so he could speak in a low voice. "I wouldn't slip away. I have duties to attend to."

"Yes, I know," she said, narrowing her eyes at him. "You think I don't know you? Your father would likely get on a horse and ride his shift even if he were on fire."

"As would any other officer in our family," Minox said.

"Ferah told me you couldn't even stand or speak when she found you."

"My point exactly," Minox said. "Ferah ran out in the middle of the night, off shift and outside of her beat, because she felt an obligation to her duties."

"Minox! That isn't even the issue. Something is wrong with you. We weren't sure what, so we left you on the cot—"

"I wasn't injured in the riot, Aunt," Minox said. "My condition was caused by other factors, but I believe I will recover."

"Other factors?" she asked. An understanding dawned over her face. "And it's passed? You're certain?"

"I feel better," he said. It wasn't a lie, though it over-stated his condition. He needed to change the subject before she inquired further, especially about his hand. "Is Corrie all right?"

"She'll survive," Beliah said ruefully. "But we need to wait to see how bad her eye was damaged."

"Her eye?" Minox faltered. Perhaps if he hadn't failed, hadn't allowed his magic problems to distract him, he could have been there to help her.

"It looks bad, but . . . we'll just have to wait and see."

"Should I see her? Does Mother know?"

"No and yes. Corrie's sleeping off the *doph* after the doctors worked on her. Everyone at home knows, but I told them all to stay put. Enough trouble in here without them all underfoot. Poor Jace has been running back and forth all night, giving them reports, though."

"Very well," Minox said. "Then I should report for duty."

Beliah sighed and led him to her desk. His vest, belt, and weapons were lying neatly on it, next to her impec-cably organized paperwork. "Two promises, Minox."

She always liked to extract promises from him. "Go on."

"If you worsen at all, I want you to seek help. Imme-diately."

"I will," Minox said, noting that "help" was an open-ended promise. "The second?"

"When you go home—and you better go home to-night—spend some time with Evoy. He's not even letting anyone in to bring him food now. No one but you."

Evoy's condition in the barn was deteriorating. It was clearly only a matter of time before he would have to go to the asylum with Grandfather.

"As you wish," Minox said. He strapped on his belt and weapons, taking care not to draw too much attention to his discolored hand. He gave her a quick embrace and left her company before she could extract any more half-truths out of him.

Nyla stood waiting in the entrance lobby of Ironheart. "Are you waiting for me?" Minox asked her.

"I was only going to wait another few minutes," she said with a smile. "If whatever happened to you made you late for duty, I would know it was very serious."

"I will make it to duty," Minox said, forcing himself to stand straight and strong. "Let's be off."

He maintained the posture as they left the building, in case Beliah or any of the doctors was watching. Once they were outside, he nearly collapsed on Nyla.

"Minox!"

"Just help me," he said, as she took his weight, cradling his bad arm.

"What is happening to you?"

"I don't know . . . I'm sure if I eat something, I'll recover." He wasn't sure at all, but it made some sense. He hadn't eaten anything since early last night. Perhaps that was the source of the trouble. "Just get me to a vendor, Nyla."

"We need to get you back in there, they can—"

"Do you think the doctors understand this better than me?"

"Maybe this isn't . . ." She lowered her voice. "Maybe this isn't magic. Maybe it's some plague or such. You've been in . . . that part of town the past two days. Who knows what you could have caught."

Minox briefly considered this, but quickly dismissed it. The magickness of what was happening to him was evident, and if it were plague, then Rainey or Kellman or the host of other Constabulary would be showing signs. "Impossible. Help me get some food and get to the stationhouse."

"You have a fever as well," she said. "I should get you home if not back in there."

"Nothing of the sort, Nyla," he said. "Please, I need . . ." He paused, unsure how to articulate what he was feeling. "I have a responsibility."

"So do I," Nyla said, pulling him along to a fry-up stand. "Saints help me, Minox, if anything happens to you today, it'll be my fault right now."

"I won't hold you accountable."

"Good for you," Nyla said, putting him on a stool in front of the fry-up. "I doubt our mothers—or the saints—will feel the same."

Satrine woke to commotion. Her hand went to the crossbow before her eyes opened, but when she saw through the bleary haze of sleepy eyes, she saw only Missus Abernand and her daughters preparing themselves for the morning.

"What time is it?" Satrine asked as she got to her feet. Her neck and back were very unhappy with her. Her shirt was stuck to her skin with sweat; the oppressive summer heat had already fully invaded her home.

"A breath after seven bells," Missus Abernand said from the kitchen. "You eating?"

"I've got a moment to, I suppose," Satrine said. She went off to the water closet to prepare herself for the day.

When she came out, Rian was right in the doorway, holding the empty wine bottle. "Really, Mother?"

"It's too early for this, Ri," Satrine said.

"But not too late for this," she said, shaking the bottle at Satrine. "Don't say 'for your nerves.'"

"I'm allowed a bit of nerves, given everything," Satrine said. She did not want to get angry at her daughter, especially since the girl had a blasted point. She was even proud of her for being brave enough to get in her face.

"Fine, what's 'everything'?" She lowered her voice, supposedly so Caribet and Missus Abernand wouldn't hear. "That foreign woman, who was she, and what did she want?"

"She wanted to scare me, and it worked," Satrine said. "Though not how she wanted."

"What are you going to do about her?" Rian asked. There was a hint of steel and defiance in there, even though Satrine couldn't believe that Rian could back it up with anything. All bravado.

Satrine wondered if this was how she sounded to Grieson back in the day.

"I'm going to solve this case, and if that leads back to her, put her in irons," Satrine said. She looked again at her eldest daughter, thinking of what Yikenj had said. Carrying this girl had literally saved her life, and now she stood tall and strong, looking her mother right in the eye. "When did you get so tall?"

"I'm wearing heeled boots," Rian said, sounding like she was trying to be sophisticated, but also seeking approval.

"Where did you get heeled boots?"

"From the back of Missus Abernand's closet."

"And they fit you?"

"My feet were much smaller when I was a young woman," Missus Abernand called out. "Are you two done muttering? There's porridge and tea."

"Why are you wearing heeled boots, though?" Satrine asked as they went to the table.

"Because—" Rian faltered. "Right, I didn't get a chance to tell you. I'm meeting with the managers in the shop."

The job. She actually was trying to get it.

"You're interviewing for a shopgirl?" Satrine still wasn't convinced it was a good idea.

Missus Abernand interrupted, probably following Rian's instructions to help her case. "By the way, the ice bill is due today, as is the milk bill. And I'm going to need to order dry goods."

"Point taken," Satrine said. She looked back at Rian. "Make sure they're having you work the counter. Do not accept any of that window model sewage."

"Window model," Missus Abernand with a scoff. "A step above a primped-up doxy, saints forgive me!"

"Ugh!" Caribet said.

"I won't, Mother," Rian said.

Satrine took a few more bites of porridge and got up from the table. "Be brilliant, then," she said, kissing her daughter on the forehead. She then did the same for Caribet. She crossed into the kitchen to Missus Abernand. "About last night . . ."

"Don't think on it," Missus Abernand said. "My Royce used to say, 'When they come to scare you is when you're doing the right thing.'"

"He was a wise man," Satrine said. "I'll try to live up to that."

"Six bells," Missus Abernand said as Satrine went to the door. "I'm holding you to that!"

"I'll do my best," Satrine said, putting on her belt and vest. She was going to forgo the coat today, with this heat. "Be safe, all of you."

She opened the door, and the muggy heat of the day assaulted her.

This day was going to be unpleasant, for certain.

✦━━━◆━━━✦

The tickwagon crowd was in a state, and all of them were carrying newssheets. And they had opinions they wanted to share with Mirrell.

"Look, you're an inspector, so what are they doing about this?" was the first thing said to him as soon as he hopped on, by one of the usual newssheet readers. The rest all shouted demands and shook their newssheets at him in empty fury.

"Morning to you all," Mirrell snapped. "The blazes are you on about?"

One of the newssheet pair—the younger one who complained about inaction in the Parliament—shoved his sheet at Mirrell. "Riots in the Little East! Apparently those blighters knocked each other all around!"

"Sticks and decent folk got knocked by them, too!" the old codger said.

"First I'm hearing of it," Mirrell said.

"They're all savages over there," a woman said. "I don't know why you don't just pound them into the river."

"That's not fair," the young one of the newssheet pair said. "We bottle them up within five feet of each other, of course they're going to explode."

The codger snapped at him. "You would have those tyzos and machs and who even knows live in our neighborhood? I bet there's even ghosts in there. We were killing those pale bastards in the Islands when I was your age, and now they live here."

"There isn't a Poasian district in the Little East," the young man said. "Blazes, Poasia is west of us."

"Don't you tell me where Poasia is! I was at Khol Taia, boy! I saw things—"

"Hey, hey, enough!" Mirrell shouted. He snatched a newssheet out of someone's hand. "This is a mess, but we've got people working on it. Just mind your own damn business."

"Is that an official statement, Inspector?" Familiar voice next to him. Sitting right there on his usual tickwagon, that rat Rencir from the *Gazette*.

"Blazes you want?"

"Question," Rencir said. "Inemar Constabulary, over the course of investigating a single death, somehow decided to House Bind half the Fuergan and Imach population in the Little East, based on little more than the fact they don't care for each other. You have no evidence, no real suspects. And now your holding cells are filled with people of foreign birth. The rest frightened out of their minds, holed up in their homes. Not to mention the illegal blockade of their ships."

"There wasn't a question there, rat."

"Was the death of a Fuergan dignitary a convenient excuse to dredge the Little East of 'undesirables'? After all, Inspector, they're just feeks and tyzos to you."

Mirrell wanted nothing more than to grab Rencir by his stupid rat face and throw him under the wheels of the tickwagon.

"We had a murder, we're working to solve it. Anything else those people do is their own problem, and they'll face the same law as anyone else."

He didn't need this headache. He jumped off the tickwagon. The walk would do him good.

Plus, if things were as bad as they all were saying, being late would be the least of the problems.

◆━━◆■◆━━◆

Kellman was lurking around the square outside the Constabulary House when Satrine approached for morning shift. There was something oddly listless about his demeanor. If he had been a pipe smoker like Welling or Mirrell, she'd have believed he was desperate for a smoke.

Maybe there was some other fix he needed.

"You waiting on something, Inspector?" she asked, coming up to him.

He startled, then eased when he saw her. "Not exactly, Trick. Just not too eager to be the first one to report for duty today."

"I always thought you were eager to catch new cases, Kellman."

"Nah, nah, it's not that." His west side accent was really coming through, thicker than usual. "You hear about what happened last night?"

Satrine knew what happened to her at home, but she was certain that wasn't what Kellman referred to. "News doesn't reach me at night unless a page comes pounding on my door."

"Has that happened?" Kellman asked with a smirk.

"Whenever Welling gets so wound up in a case that he doesn't go home," she said. "It's not uncommon."

"I don't know, Trick. It's a lot of noise, and it's gonna be on all our ears. Probably you and Jinx most."

"With the Fuergan case?"

He nodded. "There are some night side blokes who live in the same boarding as me, and it was a scene up in the East."

"Worse than the night before?"

"Full-on riot, I hear. Ironed a whole passel of those people—fee . . . Fuergans, Lyranans, Imachs, the whole lot."

"Lyranans?" Why were they involved in it?

Kellman continued unabated. "And Ironheart has half of them, as well as quite a few of our folks."

"Blazes."

"That ain't the worst," Kellman said. "My blokes told me that Hilsom's been in there since before dawn even cracked. Breathing fire about every single inspector-grade officer."

"Lovely," Satrine said. "Well, do we face the noise, or you want to wait until Welling and Mirrell get here as well?"

"I'm wondering if a stick sick is in order," he said in a tone that made it seem like he was probably joking, but with a hint that he was being serious. A stick sick was an all too common way for officers to skirt some noise, especially from the Protector's Office or the Council of Aldermen. Inspectors and patrolmen report that they're too ill to work and stay home until the trouble blows over — sometimes nearly a whole stationhouse's worth at once.

Loren hated stick sicks with a passion, and loathed any officer who pulled one. Satrine felt about the same.

"That's not even funny, Kellman," she told him. "Let's get in there. Odds are there's a blazes of a lot of things to handle today."

The main stationhouse floor was a madhouse. The holding cells must have been filled to capacity, as there were people ironed up in almost every spare space around the desks and benches where the patrolmen and floor clerks usually worked. It was as Kellman had said: Fuergans, Imachs, and Lyranans mostly, with a smattering of just about every other skin hue imaginable. There were a few Fuergans and Imachs shackled to the front benches — screaming at each other while officers did their best to break them up.

Satrine noticed there were very few faces that didn't have a bruise or a gash, anywhere on the floor.

The Lyranans all looked calm, though. Like they were waiting. That made Satrine more nervous than anything.

"Inspectors!" Zebram Hilsom, somehow still looking impeccably groomed and pressed, worked his way through the madness. "This is quite a mess we have on our hands. Do you have any idea what the Archduchy Court, not to mention the King's Marshals, is trying to do to us here? I've even received notice from the Office of the High Lord of Diplomacy himself!"

"Morning to you too, Protector," Satrine said. "Why don't we go up to the inspectors' floor, and talk about this calmly over some tea?"

"Talk calmly, Rainey?" Hilsom scoffed. "Would you look at this place? Let alone the property damage we have through several blocks on Peston Avenue. And the injured in Ironheart?"

"You saying this is our fault?" Kellman asked. "Blazes, Zebe, we weren't working the dark."

"You all started—"

"We were doing our jobs," Satrine hissed. "You can't—" She cut herself off, spotting one familiar face among the arrested. A beefy Fuergan—the same one who answered the door at the Hieljam household. "Just a moment."

She ignored Hilsom's protests as she went to the desk clerk.

"Hey," she said, "that one right there, the Fuergan."

"There's a lot of Fuergans, Tricky," the clerk said without looking up.

Satrine banged on the desk. "Listen, you horse's ass, look at that man on that bench over there. Who the blazes is he, or do I have to get Captain Cinellan down here to ask you?"

"Hey, hey," he said, throwing his hands up. "I ain't got no idea. We're still getting all these bastards noted and filed before they go into holding. We're up to our ears if you ain't noticed!"

"I noticed." She pointed at the beefy Fuergan and turned the clerk's head so he had to see. "You note and file him next, and then get him to a questioning room before Welling and I have tea in our hand upstairs. You have that clear?"

"Clear," the clerk grumbled.

Satrine turned off and brushed past Hilsom. "You want to talk, come upstairs," she said, heading to the inspectors' floor. She knew Hilsom would be hot on her heels, regardless.

"You knew this would explode on us, Inspectors!" Hilsom shouted as they reached the inspectors' floor. "Do you have any idea—"

"We did have an idea," Satrine snapped back at him. "Which was the whole point behind the Home Binding, the curfew, and the extra patrol. So what the blazes happened out there?"

"They didn't give a damn about Binding or curfew, and when that many people start a blazing riot, your extra patrol was mowed down!"

"Zebram!" Captain Cinellan's voice echoed through the floor. "You do not lean on my inspectors over this."

"Someone has to answer for this!"

"And you're afraid it's going to be you," Satrine said. "It was your name on those Binding orders."

"Yes, it is." Hilsom pulled out a handful of papers from his bag. "And it's your names on the action placed against this Constabulary House."

"What rutting action?" Cinellan asked.

"Two businessmen, Ravi Kenorax and Estiani Iliari, filed complaint—through the Kieran embassy, even—with you. Namely Inspectors Minox Welling, Satrine Rainey, Henfir Mirrell, and Darreck Kellman. It's all right here."

"That's sewage," Kellman said. "What're they complaining about . . ."

"Don't worry about it," Cinellan said. "I'll take care of this."

"Take care of what?" Welling came onto the floor, Nyla right at his side. He looked like sewage—pale skin, dark circles under his eyes, and his left arm curled against his body. His hand trembled noticeably.

"Blazes, Jinx, what happened to you?" Kellman asked.

"I'm fine," Welling clearly lied. "What are Kenorax and Iliari claiming?"

"That you are harassing them and obstructing their business."

"We've done nothing of the sort."

"Except for that stunt you pulled on the docks the other night, Welling."

"Even . . . even . . ." Welling faltered for a moment,

and then went over to the closest desk. "Nyla, if you could bring me some tea?"

"Of course." She dashed off once he was in his chair.

"Saint Ferrin, Minox," Kellman said. "You sure you ain't sick?"

"I just need some tea, and I'll be fine."

"Have you eaten?" Satrine asked. Welling nodded his head. She lowered her voice. "Do we need to get you to Ironheart?"

Welling chuckled. "I just came from there."

"You should have stayed."

"Am I interrupting?" Hilsom asked, wedging himself in with the two of them. "There are grave concerns . . ."

Satrine had heard enough. "Mister Hilsom, the grave concern I have is that you seem ready to allow potential suspects in an extremely sensitive murder case to walk all over you."

"They have filed complaints—"

"Then challenge them, Mister Hilsom. Or are you doing the Justice Advocate's job instead of your own?"

"Help my challenges, Inspector. Get me some evidence I can use in court, and make an actual arrest!"

"We're working on it!" Welling snapped. "In the meantime . . ."

"In the meantime, the results of your fishing expedition are on your desk. Are you going to dig through those records, or was that just to waste my damn time?"

He stormed off.

Captain Cinellan stayed by his office door. "Not to add to Hilsom's sewage, but we're on thin butter today. We've got several folks in Ironheart, and you've all seen what downstairs looks like."

"I take it this case can't go to unresolved, then?" Welling asked.

"We can't handle any more trouble, is what I'm telling you," Cinellan said. "If there's much more trouble in the

Little East like last night, or problems like Hilsom's dealing with, then King's Marshals are going to step in. The commissioner—"

"I've heard," Satrine said. "I take it there aren't still any riots happening in the East?"

Cinellan frowned at her—she shouldn't have stepped on him. "Not right now, but about a quarter of the residents are either downstairs or in Ironheart. But patrols have been suffering in the rest of Inemar. Already this morning there's been an unusual amount of petty thuggery."

"So we need to make a show of color and leave the East to itself?" Welling asked acidly.

"We can't devote everything we've got to a few blocks in the tip of the neighborhood, and let the rest go to sewage," Cinellan snapped. "I've got no muscle to hold back King's Marshals or anyone else if they come snatching."

"Understood," Satrine said. She grabbed Welling by his good arm and dragged him over to their desks. "So you came from Ironheart. Were you caught in the riot?"

"I was, to a degree."

"You look like sewage, really," she said. "Did you hurt your arm?"

"My arm is not relevant to our investigation, Inspector Rainey."

She let it drop, even though it was clearly a significant problem beyond mere injury. "Fine. Given that you were in the thick of it last night after our sign-out, did you learn anything that would help us close this case?"

They reached their desks, half hidden behind the slateboards. Several leather-bound folios were piled on top of the usual clutter.

"Not in the slightest," he said, slumping down into his chair. He eyed the pile of folders wearily. "This situation has far too many moving parts to see clearly."

Miss Pyle came with two cups of tea, which she put on

the desk without looking at Satrine. She crouched down
and fussed over Welling. "Drink this, and stay put for a
bit. You hear?"

"I'll do what my duties demand," Welling said sternly.
Despite that, it seemed like even picking up the teacup
was a strain.

Miss Pyle stood up, and despite keeping her back to
Satrine, she clearly addressed her. "Don't let him push
himself. Am I clear?"

"As the window, Miss Pyle."

She went off to her desk.

"I don't suppose you've had any revelations," Welling
said, drinking the tea.

"Oh, I have, not that they clear anything up," Satrine
said. She quickly told him about the encounter with Pra
Yikenj at her home.

He chuckled as she finished. "If Miss Yikenj's intention was to remove herself from suspicion, it's failed sub-
stantially. Which only further muddles the situation."

"Well, there's one thing that could help," Satrine said.
"One of the Fuergans arrested in the riot was the Hieljam's manservant."

"We should question him immediately."

"I'm already working on that," Satrine said. "Downstairs has their hands full, so it'll be a moment." She sat
on the desk in front of him. He really did look like he
was about to fall over. "This isn't from the riot."

"You needn't concern yourself—"

"Sewage," she said, putting her hand on his forehead.
He was burning up. "With a fever like that I'm amazed
you're able to talk coherently."

"My reasoning faculties are fine. My condition is not
relevant to the case."

She lowered her voice again. "You only shut your trap
like this when it's about magic. I want to respect your
privacy about that—"

"Then do so."

"But in your condition you could put my life and yours at risk on the streets, not to mention jeopardize this case. So don't sell me any bunk that you're fine."

He glowered at her for a moment, and then put his left arm on the table, pulling up his coat sleeve. The hand had turned an unnatural shade of blackish purple, and was starting to wither.

Satrine was almost afraid to touch it, but she forced herself to. It was nearly cold. "When did this start happening?"

"Last night," he said quietly. "But it's been causing me difficulty ever since Plum."

"But this is new. What changed?"

Now Welling looked down at the ground. This was something she had never seen in him before: shame. "The Tsouljan enclave."

"What about it? Were you investigating there last night?"

"I was, but not the case." He pulled himself to his feet and moved himself over to the other desk, so he would be hidden from the rest of the inspectors' floor by his slateboards. "The Tsouljans understand magic, and are not bound by Circle doctrines or other Druth superstitions."

"Oh, blazes, Minox," she said. "They did this to you, can't you see?"

"I don't . . . I just . . ." He stammered. "I'm just trying to be a whole person, in command of my own self."

"I get that, I really do," she said. Tapping on her forehead, she added, "Blazes, it took me a long time to figure out who I am out of all the things in this skull."

"I don't know what to do," Welling whispered.

"Let me ask you something, and tell me plain. When this arm was broken, did you use magic to heal it, or help it along?"

He shook his head. "I wouldn't even know how to do that."

"And you didn't try?"

"No."

"Good," she said. "Since no one would have told you this, you need to know: never do that. I don't know a lot about magic, but I do know that. You can't use it to heal injuries."

"It can cause something like this?"

"Maybe, I don't know." Her mind was racing, trying to bring up any other bit of psychically jammed knowledge that could help. "Listen—"

"Hey, Tricky," Kellman called. "That feek you wanted to talk to is now in interrogation."

"Thanks," she shouted back. "You and I will drill into him in a minute."

"Me?"

"Him?" Welling echoed.

"You're in no shape to," she said. "If you refuse to go home or to the ward, then just . . . stay here. Go through these records. I'll question the servant, follow up on that, and . . . I don't know. Maybe we can go to Major Dresser—"

"He would not help me."

"I'll make damn sure he will," she said. "We'll get this sorted, hear?"

"Understood," he said. "You deserve a partner at his best."

"Damn right I do," she said. She finished the rest of her tea and called out, "Kellman! Let's do this."

Chapter 15

THE INTERROGATION ROOMS were down in the
basement levels of the stationhouse, near the holding
cells. As Satrine came down with Kellman, she saw one
of Hilsom's scribes waiting for them, as well as a young
man in an ill-fitting suit.

"Miss Trennar," Kellman said to the scribe, his voice
filled with cream and honey. "Glad to see you on duty
today."

"Are you?" she asked coolly, not even looking up
from her notebook. "I would think a person glad to see
me would come to the social he was informed about."

"That's not fair, Miss Trennar," he said.

"Save it for off-duty, Kellman," Satrine said.

Miss Trennar glanced up, throwing darts over her
spectacles at Satrine. "We're here to work, after all," she
said.

The young man shoved his hand in between Satrine and
Miss Trennar. "Inspectors," he said, taking Satrine's hand
with an overeager grasp. "Cheed Cheever, Justice Advocate Office. I'll be watching for Mister . . ." He let go and
looked at his own notebook. "Oo-eetay. His interests."

Kellman voiced what Satrine was thinking. "Saints, kid, when did you get your Letters? Last month?"

"I did, indeed, receive my Letters of Mastery just a month ago, from Delikan Public, which is as noble an education as any of the Elevens or the University of Maradaine."

"Don't have to prove it to me, kid," Kellman said. "I'm just a grammar book rat they gave a vest to."

"He really is," Miss Trennar said. "He could stand some education of manners."

"Hey, now, I never said—"

"Please," Satrine snapped. "Can we move along to the interrogation? Thank you."

"Right," Cheever said, glancing at his own book again. "Now, according to my understanding, Mister Oo-eetay has been detained out of a general roundup during a moment of disorder. Accordingly, I will have to insist you produce a witness—"

Satrine snatched the book out Cheever's hands. The Fuergan man's name was listed as Uite lek Ni, and that came from his documents of residency, so it was probably a reasonable transcription of his given name. "You came here for this interrogation, Mister Cheever?"

"Well, no. Justice Advocate sent several of us when we got word of the general roundup. We're here to make sure—"

"Yes, that proper arrest procedure and application of rights is observed," Kellman said. "You know that these are all feeks and tyzos—"

Miss Trennar gave an audible gasp.

"That is, many of these folks ain't Druth citizens. So the application of rights—"

"Still applies, Inspector," Cheever said. "They are called the Rights of Man for a reason. They are universal truths which we—"

"Save me the speech," Satrine said. "Let's be along. I presume you don't want to watch from the booth."

"I cannot properly administer to the interests of Mister Oo-eetay—"

"Uite," Satrine said, correcting his pronunciation.

"Without being present," he finished.

"As you wish."

Satrine went into the interrogation room, where the beefy Fuergan man sat with his head down on the table, wrists ironed to it. A footpatrolman stepped out as they came in, giving a small nod to Kellman.

"Are those necessary?" Cheever asked, pointing to the irons.

"We'll see," Kellman said. He sat down opposite Uite, while Miss Trennar took a seat at a small desk in the corner. "Morning, Mister Ute."

"Uite," Satrine corrected again, sitting next to Kellman. Cheever sat opposite, next to Uite. The Fuergan man ignored all of them.

Kellman knocked on the table in front of Uite. "I'm talking to you."

"Not necessary, Inspector." Cheever's voice cracked with nerves.

Uite looked up and mumbled a few Fuergan words.

"What was that?" Kellman asked.

Uite repeated himself, louder, and with more spittle.

Kellman wiped off his face. "Think you're funny?"

"You speak Trade," Satrine said. "I know you do."

Uite squinted at her. He shot a bit of Fuergan invective, but it was clear he understood what she said.

"Let's not harass the man," Cheever said.

"Fine," Satrine said. "You do understand you're in trouble here, don't you, Mister Uite? Uite lek Ni. How in debt are you?"

That made him blink.

"Let me tell you something, Mister Uite," Satrine

continued. "This man next to you is from Justice Advocate. His job is to make sure you are well treated, your rights are observed, and make sure that your trial is conducted fairly."

"Or that there isn't even a trial if there's no just cause," Cheever said. "Which I'm finding hard to justify."

"He was in a riot where Constabulary officers were attacked," Satrine said. "I imagine finding a witness who will testify that Mister Uite attacked them won't be hard."

"Not at all," Kellman said. "Blazes, I can go find a few right now."

"That's spurious," Cheever said.

"Maybe," Satrine said. She focused her attention on Uite. "But it'll mean legal fees, fines, who knows what else. And who is going to pay those, Mister Uite? You, a 'lek Ni'?"

"Hieljam," he said quietly.

"Right, because that's what they need. To throw more money at you, deepen your debt, drop your status further."

"They'll probably let him hang," Kellman said.

"Oh, they can afford it," Satrine said. "They're a *lavark* family, after all. Deepening Uite's indebtment would put more of his family in their permanent employ."

Uite scoffed.

"Something funny?" Kellman asked.

"She said." Uite's accent was thick and halting.

"What did I say? That your family would be indebted? For generations, even."

"My family is and always will be," Uite said. "These fees? Nothing."

"So the Hieljam will take care of you," Satrine said. "Good."

"Hieljam will do what they can."

What they can. Was that just Uite's poor Trade, or did it mean something more. "Why 'what they can'? They've got the money. Blazes, they threw enough money in the street yesterday."

"Had to. Appearances."

"Are you going to ask him about the riot and his part in it?" Cheever asked.

"A little latitude, Mister Cheever," Satrine said. "What was that about appearances?"

Uite now looked quite nervous. "I don't know what you mean."

Appearances. What they can. Satrine thought back to his scoff. It wasn't about his indebtment. It was about the Hieljam.

She leaned in. "Are the Hieljam out of money, Mister Uite?"

Nerves shifted into cold sweat.

"It is not mine to say," Uite said.

"What does this have to do with him being in the riot?" Cheever asked. "I'm afraid your questions are exceeding scope."

"We'll decide what our scope is here, Cheever," Kellman said.

Miss Trennar offered her own opinion. "The inspectors are investigating a murder of a man that this man worked for. In light of that, there is some interrogative latitude that they must be granted."

"I should have been informed," Cheever said. "This is quite improper, Inspectors. You cannot question a man—"

"The Hieljam are out of money, yes," Satrine pressed. "Or at least their money is tied up in goods and trade, something going wrong?"

"There is concern," Uite said quietly. "It is not my place to know details."

"But their position is at stake now, isn't it?" Cheever

was sputtering something and Kellman was snapping back at him, but Satrine focused entirely on Uite. "That's what you scoffed at, yes, when I said they were *lavark* and could afford your fees?"

"I should not speak of such things." Uite pressed his hands against his forehead. "I am but to serve."

"The Hieljam aren't *lavark* anymore, especially with Wefi Loriz dead." She barked this at Uite. He nodded pathetically.

"*Lavark* should be gone. Empty claim."

"Why?"

"It is not my place to know."

"Don't give me that sewage." Kellman said this, pointing a beefy finger in Uite's face. "You work the household, you hear things."

"You have to stop badgering him," Cheever said.

"So what do you know?" Kellman shouted.

"It's very complicated," Uite said quietly. "I say it is not my place, I mean I do not understand. I serve the house, I don't know about business or schedules or deliveries."

That was something. "Did something go wrong with the schedules?" Satrine asked. "Were deliveries missed?"

Uite nodded.

"You're leading him," Cheever said.

"For who?" She almost offered the Kenorax name, but that would be too much of a lead. Even a tadpole like Cheever would catch that and spoil the arrest.

"I don't know," Uite said.

"Then we can't help you," Kellman said. "Maybe he should join the rest going to Quarrygate."

"That hasn't been established," Cheever said.

"Oh, but use your head, Cheevs," Kellman said. "We've got cells out there packed beyond capacity, right? It's damn near inhumane, wouldn't you agree?"

"Of course it is!"

"And we're going to have to feed them, and this house doesn't have the resources to do that for that many people. We can't let them go hungry."

"No, you mustn't."

"So we've got to be efficient about this, Cheever," Kellman continued, his West Maradaine accent making him sound like a streetcart shuckster. But a damn good one. "Folks in the riot get charged with Disruption of the Peace and Ignoring a Whistle Call. Harsher charges for those we can pin them on."

"You can't just charge everyone with that!"

"But then we can wagon them to Quarrygate for trial, and those who can afford Collateral will be released until their day in court. Beats them being crammed and starving in here while we sort it out."

Kellman's twisted logic seemed to have confused Cheever for a moment. He stammered, thinking about how to respond.

"Now, you can't afford Collateral for release, can you, Uite?" Kellman asked.

"No."

"If we had a good reason to not lump you in with the rest of those poor sods, then maybe we don't need to send you over to Quarrygate to wait trial. Because Cheever is right, in the end you might not even *need* a trial. But why spend a week in the Quarry waiting to find that out?"

Cheever was still in a fugue of deep thought. Uite looked like he was about to crack. And a glance at Miss Trennar showed that she had stopped writing to gaze starry-eyed at Kellman.

For half a second, Satrine could understand that.

"Give us something," Satrine said, giving as much South Maradaine honey as she could to her voice. "It doesn't need to be much."

"There ... there's a warehouse," Uite said. "Goods

are waiting there for something. I don't know more than that, but I know whatever is in there was very important to the *lavark*. Much of his fortune — as well as the rest of the family — centered on those goods."

"See?" Kellman said. "Now, if we get an address and it checks out, I think we can overlook your role in this riot. He'd be free to go, Mister Cheever. Is that all right with you?"

"Yes, I think so," Cheever said.

Uite gave the specifics of a warehouse near the Little East docks, which Miss Trennar dutifully transcribed. That finished, they all left the interrogation room, giving the patrolman on duty instructions to let Uite stay there, and maybe even bring him something to eat. Cheever mumbled something about the rest of the mob and wandered off, while Miss Trennar lingered for a moment, tapping her fingers on her notepad.

"I'll bring this straight to Mister Hilsom, so you can get a Writ of Search," she said warmly, eyes on Kellman. "There's another social at the Halliday House in three days, you know."

"I'll see what I can do, Miss Trennar," Kellman said as she left.

"See what you can do?" Satrine echoed back at him. "You're terrible, you know this?"

"Nah, I'll be there," he said with a grin. "But I can't seem too eager, you know?"

"Come on, Prince Fulton," she said, referencing the classic romance *Demea*. "Let's bring this to the captain."

Muted clattering and conversation pulled Corrie back into consciousness, which she regretted as soon as it happened.

"Rutting blazes," she said, not even opening her eyes. Her voice creaked out dryly. Several places on her body hurt, especially her head. Wet and soft on her head. Bandaging. Left leg hurt like blazes as well.

She pulled herself up from whatever she was lying down on, fighting through the fog in her head the whole time. Opening her eye she saw only light filtered through white gauze. They had bandaged over her eyes.

And she could only get the left one open. The right eye, she could only feel pain.

"Where the rutting blazes am I?" she shouted, but her voice didn't give her much more than a hoarse whisper. "Any of you bastards there?"

"Language," a familiar voice said to her, soft hands on her face.

"Beliah?" she asked. "I'm at Ironheart?" Either she was at the ward her aunt nursed at, or somehow she had been taken home.

"You and several score more, dear," Aunt Beliah said. A cup of water touched Corrie's lips, which she took in greedily.

Having taken enough to drink, Corrie pawed at the bandages on her face. "Do I need this? Is something rutting wrong with my eyes?" She couldn't remember what had happened last in that scrum with all those foreign folks. There had been that one Imach lady with the knife who had jumped her, but past that, nothing.

Imach lady jumped her and grabbed her hair.

Corrie's hands shot to the back of her head. Bandages covered everything, and she started clawing at them.

"Corrie, Corrie, easy, easy." Beliah's hands took a firm grip on Corrie's. "Just stay calm."

"Did that crazy Machie slan chop off my hair?"

"Shush now, child," Beliah said fiercely. "No need for talk like that."

"Auntie," Corrie said, reverting to a term she hadn't used since she was a child. "I need this off my head. Please."

"Let me get one of the doctors, all right? Just be calm for a few minutes." Her hard shoes snapped away in a hurry.

"Is that what my sisters are to you, constable woman?" a harshly accented voice hissed. "You call them 'Machie slans'?"

"Who the blazes are you?" Corrie snarled back. "You one of those who tasted my boot out there?"

The voice came closer; Corrie could feel his presence as he approached, the earthy sweat wafting off of him. "I felt the constable boot, as did my brothers and sisters. Now we are here, those who are not jailed at your house."

"Animals, the lot of you," Corrie said. "You think because I can't rutting see you, I won't knock your teeth out?"

"I know you would try."

"Back the blazes off, bilge." Corrie shoved at him, forcing herself off the cot despite the pain. She could make out a vague shape in the light coming through the gauze. Tall and dark.

"Always ready to fight us!" he shouted.

Another mach voice called out, this one harsh and strained, but still able to wail in despair.

"Dahar?" the mach confronting her said. He shouted in his language, and then charged away. Other Imach voices—at least three—started calling, feet pounding.

This was no rutting good. Corrie wasn't going to wait for Beliah or a doctor, tearing the bandage off her good eye and head. That confirmed it—her hair had been cut off, leaving her with just a savage inch on the top.

The machs were converging around one of the beds in the ward room—one in the back behind a curtain. Corrie knew enough to know the curtain meant whoever was in that bed wasn't going to make it.

Shouts, cries, and laments in Imach. Corrie limped her way over there, fearing that some form of authority was going to be necessary shortly. There were other sticks in beds in this ward room, but from the looks of things, most of them were worse off than her.

Blazes, there was Kenty. They had already taken one of his legs.

Corrie pulled the curtain aside. Four Imachs—three blokes and a skirt—were surrounding a bed where a fifth Imach was at the end. His skull was half caved in, and he was wailing nonsense. Corrie figured even if she understood the balalalas of the Imach language, it would still be rutting nonsense.

And then it stopped.

"You all get back in your beds before I give you better reason to be in this place," she said.

One of the Imachs turned to her. He was the one who had confronted her before, from his voice and smell, and the same one who was the leader in the trouble at the procession—Jabiudal, was that his name? He wept and pointed at the dying man. "This man, my friend, was killed by your people, and yet we are to be beaten and locked away?"

"You're to step the blazes away," Corrie said.

"Corrianna!" Beliah came running over. "You need to—"

That was all she managed to say. Jabiudal, despite having one arm in a sling, struck like a snake, grabbing Beliah by the throat. Corrie couldn't do anything before he had her aunt in a lock, his hand pressing against her head.

"What are you—" Beliah wailed.

"You let her rutting go, or saints help me—"

"I will kill her!" Jabiudal said. He hissed at his people, who leaped onto the beds of other infirm patients—all injured sticks—grabbing whatever makeshift weapon they could. "I will kill her, and all of them, and everyone I see, unless all of my people are freed from this place and your jails."

"You just—"

"All my people, Constable! I do not have much patience. Go tell your superiors."

There was no rutting chance Corrie was walking out of that room without Aunt Beliah.

She glanced over to the beds by the entrance to the ward room. There was a kid—maybe a cadet or a brand-new regular, who looked like he was just a little banged up. "You," she snapped. "Beat your feet and tell the news." The kid pulled himself out of bed and ran.

When she looked back at Jabiudal and Beliah, he had managed to get a razor in his hand, now pressed against Beliah's cheek.

"Do not doubt my commitment, Constable," he said. "A dear friend of mine has gone to God. Take care, or he will not be alone."

If he was stuck working the paperwork, he'd do it properly. Minox wouldn't let himself do anything less than that. He cleared off one portion of the slateboard and went to work.

The documents were the usual minutiae of shipping and import business. Inflow, schedules, inventories, tariffs, customs. Nothing that, individually, stood out as unusual or suspicious, from Kenorax, Hieljam, Hajan, or Jabiudal.

Of course, Minox didn't care about things that stood out individually. It was a matter of patterns. Patterns were the secret. Find what the connections were. Five separate innocuous purchases months apart added to a greater whole. Recurring shipments of usual weight. Imach goods coming into Maradaine via Fuergan ships, other goods leaving in Kenorax caravans to the northeast, toward Kieran.

A perfect image formed on the edge on Minox's

mind, like a church's colored glass fresco. It was almost clear. Everything fit. Dates lined up, weights matched, and of course it tied back to all those—

"Minox?"

A hand on his shoulder broke the reverie, the image shattered. Minox found himself in front of the slateboard, chalk in his hand—his bad hand—tapping at the board in rapid staccato.

Nyla was at his side, terror in her eyes. "What are you doing?"

"I'm—" He paused. Everything that was just in his thoughts had floated off like so much tobacco smoke. He still had a vague sense of the idea of what he was just thinking ... but that was all. "I was going over the records Hilsom procured."

"You were—" She gasped, tears forming. Then she swallowed. "No, Minox, that's not what you were doing. You ... just look."

Minox glanced around. The desks were a disaster— more so than usual. The pile of records was now strewn around the entire area. Some pages ripped up, some blotched with ink, everything in complete disorder. What was now on the slateboard was even stranger. Half of it was just dots and squiggles, nothing even remotely resembling cohesive thoughts. The rest were random words: "sweet tar," "what provides?" "Shaleton purchase," and so forth.

He had no memory of any of this.

"For how long, Nyla?" Minox asked, not even bothering to hide the fear in his voice. "I don't ... I couldn't have done this in just a few minutes. ..."

"I don't know," she said.

This was how it started with Grandfather. This was how it started with Evoy.

His hand—the good one—was trembling.

"No more of this," she said. "We need to get you home, now."

"Home?" Minox asked. "I can't go home. Work to do."

"Something is wrong with you," she said quietly. "Your hand, the trembles, the fever? And now this? You have to rest. See a doctor."

"Doctor can't help me," he said. "Does this look like something—"

"I don't know!" Nyla shouted. "God damn it, Minox, how can you be so smart and so rutting stupid?"

That was surprising. Minox could not recall any time when Nyla spoke profanely.

"I just . . ." He was too shocked to even properly respond. He looked back at the board. "I think I almost solved this."

"What?"

"I was . . . Just on the edge of something . . ."

"Minox," she said firmly, grabbing both shoulders and pulling him down to force him to look her in the eyes. "Do *not* fall into madness. No. No."

"I don't think I get to decide that, Nyla."

That earned him a slap.

"You are not going to do this to me," Nyla said.

Any vestiges of the ideas his mind had been touching at were gone now. "You may be right," he said. "But . . . I can't leave this mess. I promised Inspector Rainey—"

"I don't care," she said. "Look at me. You go home. I'm going to call on Ferah . . ."

"I don't need Ferah to—"

"And she is going to make sure you are taken care of."

Minox gestured to the desk. "My work . . . I can't . . ."

"You will. Now. I'll tell the captain. I'll clean this mess, and saints preserve me, I will let Inspector Rainey know that you left."

Minox sighed. "As you wish, Nyla."

He took up his coat, laying it over his bad arm. Now it felt strange in an entirely new way. Numb and cold, but yet like something hot was being flushed through it. He couldn't quite describe it any other way.

Nyla hovered over him until he got to the stairs, and watched him as he made his way down. He had no doubt she would keep an eye on him until he was in the street, and did not dally further.

As he stepped out into the sweltering sunlight, he realized that he hadn't been hungry, not for the entire morning. That felt significant. He couldn't remember a time — even since he started using the *rijetzh* — when he hadn't felt hunger for so long. Was this his hand, the sickness, or something else? He really had no idea.

He flexed the hand under the coat. Now, despite everything, it still functioned. He hadn't lost strength or motion.

Whistle calls pierced the air, and several uniformed footpatrol went running out of the stationhouse. A page came running toward the station, whistle in his mouth blowing wildly. Minox moved to intercept him.

"What's the ruckus?" he asked.

"Ironheart!" the page shouted. "Four Imachs have taken hostages on one of the ward floors. Patients and nurses!"

Corrie was a patient at Ironheart right now, and Beliah was working.

Promises to Nyla would have to wait.

Minox drew out his handstick and ran to Ironheart Ward.

Chapter 16

"**R**EPORT!" Minox shouted at the first group of Constabulary he came across when he entered Ironheart. "What are we dealing with?"

"Inspector?" the sergeant at the center of the group asked. "Are you taking situation command?"

"For the moment," Minox said. "Until we receive further support from the stationhouse. What's happening?"

"Third floor west ward, several of the injured from the riot were placed there. A mix of our folks and civilians. Some of the Imach patients have taken control of the room, holding the rest at knifepoint."

"Were they all patients in the same ward room?" Minox asked.

"Apparently so."

"Why?"

"That was our decision." One of the doctors came over, wearing the traditional heavy gray apron over his suit. "We were organizing the patients to their medical needs first, and we were overwhelmed. We couldn't even think of other potential considerations."

"Fair enough," Minox said. "I presume they've secured the room, and there's no obvious way to storm them."

"Not without injuring the hostages."

"Which we don't want." Minox was putting up a strong front, but his head was swimming, his bad hand felt like it was both numb and on fire. He wasn't sure how long he could maintain the pretense of being capable of leading this situation. "Do we have a list of the hostages?"

The doctor passed a notebook with a list of names. "These are the patients who were housed in there. And we know one doctor—Doctor Ilton—and two nurses—Serrick and Frain—were in there as well."

"Serrick?" Minox confirmed. "That would be Beliah Serrick?"

"Yes, do you—"

"My aunt," Minox said. He glanced at the names of the patients. Two jumped out immediately. One, Assan Jabiudal. Most likely the one who started this, and was in charge now.

The other was Corrie.

"Blast and blazes," he muttered. With the count of doctors and nurses, minus the five Imach names on the list, that meant seventeen hostages. "Let's to the third floor, then."

He charged up the stairs—truly punishing his weak body, but he was being fueled by rage and fear, pushing through the pain over everything else.

"Have they made any demands?" Minox asked as he reached the designated floor. More Constabulary were gathered in the hallway, some ready with crossbows. Certainly no one would get out of the ward room without being shot. Minox also noted half the Constabulary were bandaged and wounded. They probably were patients and went right to their duty when called.

"You in command, Inspector?" someone asked.

"So it would seem," Minox said. Surely someone else would arrive to take proper charge in a matter of minutes. "Have we heard from them?"

"They said they wanted all their 'brothers and sisters' released from holding at the stationhouse. And 'blood for their dead.'"

"Is that all?" Minox asked.

"And food."

"Of course," Minox said. He approached the ward room door. "This is Inspector Minox Welling! May I presume that Assan Jabiudal is in charge in there?"

After a moment an accented voice called back. "God and justice are in charge in here, Inspector. But I am the voice of both."

"I understand you have some demands, Mister Jabiudal," Minox said. "Can we discuss them?"

"Stand in the doorway. Unarmed, hands raised."

Minox passed his crossbow and handstick to one of the regulars. "I don't suppose anyone has a heavy vest?"

"They don't have crossbows, sir," the regular said. "Though maybe they can throw their knives well."

Minox took no comfort in that. Raising his hands up, crossing them behind his head to hide the way his left hand was looking sickly, he stepped into the doorframe.

Jabiudal was standing twenty paces away, Beliah held in front of him, knife at her throat. She looked terrified. The rest of the patients had been gathered in a far corner, well away from the door, and the three other Imach brandished makeshift weapons at them all. Corrie was sitting at the foot of one of the beds, her face horribly bruised. Minox wasn't sure if that was from last night, or fresh injuries from Jabiudal and his people.

Rage was now roiling the magic in Minox's stomach.

"Mister Jabiudal," he said calmly, forcing himself to maintain the face he needed. "I want these people set free, unharmed."

"Very good, Inspector," Jabiudal said coolly. "I respect that you make your needs clear and plain. I have things I want as well. If I receive them, then yours will be granted."

"Tell me," Minox said. "But I make no promises."

"I need all the faithful sons and daughters of God released from your holding cells. One of them will come here and tell me that they were the last to leave."

"That can't be easily done," Minox said.

"I need the killer of my dear friend Dahar brought before us, so we can have blood for his death."

"Who is Dahar, and how can we bring his killer here?" Minox asked. "We hardly know who did what last night."

"His killer is that giant brute of an inspector. Your friend. He struck Dahar with a stone."

They meant Kellman. "When Mister Dahar threw a stone at him."

"There will be blood for the dead," Jabiudal said. "If not the killer, then another."

"If you hurt the people in here—"

"We are at an impasse, Inspector," Jabiudal said. "But I am the water, not the stone. I can be reasonable. As this will take some time, we will need food. We will need chamber pots cleared. I will give you . . . five of the innocents in here, in exchange for those things."

"I can arrange that," Minox said. Five released was a start.

"It will not be a member of your Constabulary to deliver the food and take the pots," Jabiudal said. "Try to trick me, and there will be a death. Likely this nurse, who you clearly care deeply about."

Beliah whimpered.

"No tricks," Minox said. Raising up his hands, he stepped backward out of the room.

"We'll bring food in," Minox told the regulars around him. "Arrange with the ward commissary."

"You want a couple of us to remove their coats, dress like ward workers?" a sergeant asked.

That was Minox's first thought, but he feared that Jabiudal would see right through that. The man was perceptive. "That might be dangerous."

"Sir, we can't ask the actual ward staff to go in there!"

"No, we can't," Minox said. His gut churned, his head swam. He shouldn't be the one doing this, he was in no condition . . . but he also couldn't walk away while Corrie and Beliah were in danger.

"Sounds like you need a volunteer, then."

Minox turned to see who had spoken, though he knew the voice perfectly well.

"After all, I'm not Constabulary," Joshea said.

———————◆◆◆———————

Satrine and Kellman found Cinellan in the middle of the inspectors' floor, surrounded by a dozen people, each of them shouting at him, and him giving as much in return. Hilsom was among the group, as were a few of the stationhouse lieutenants. The rest were civilians, in suits ranging from cheap and threadbare to resplendent.

"You know them?" Kellman asked.

She didn't, but she could guess. "Representatives of the Council of Aldermen and Justice Advocate, most likely."

"We've got people taking care of Ironheart," Cinellan said, his powerful voice drowning out the others. "Please let me focus on the other priorities here."

"I've got actual miscreants I need cell space for," one of the lieutenants said. "Regular footpatrol and horsepatrol duty in Inemar needs to continue. It's become chaos!"

"You can't be putting all your resources on the Little East," one of the fancier suits said. "Ordinary citizens need to—"

"We'll go to the *Gazette*," one of the worn suits said.

"Enough!" Cinellan shouted. "Rainey, what do you have?"

"What's going on at Ironheart?" Satrine asked.

Captain Cinellan hesitated, and one of the other lieutenants—a real straight-nose named Bretton—spoke up. "A group of Imach dissidents managed to seize control of one of the ward rooms. They have several patients and ward staff hostage. Some of which are injured Constabulary."

"What do you need us to do?" Kellman asked.

"You two, nothing. As far as that's concerned," Cinellan said. "I've got enough folks, with Mirrell in charge, over there. Is there anything on the Hieljam case? That's the crack we need to seal up."

"We have a lead on a warehouse that might provide us with the key to the motive," Satrine said. "The scribe from the Protector's Office was supposed to find Hilsom here so we can get a Writ of Search."

"Zebram?" He looked to the Protector.

"I'll go find her," Hilsom said. "Though I don't know how much help that will be. The city is on fire and you ask for a bucket." He stalked off.

"Once we have that, Welling and I—"

"Welling is gone," Cinellan said. "And I'm glad, because he looked like he was about to fall into his grave. Miss Pyle made him go home."

"All right," Satrine said. "Then I'll go up there—"

"Like blazes you will," Cinellan said. "Kellman's your partner for now."

"But shouldn't we be—" Kellman started.

"Unless the next words out of your mouth are 'solving this murder,' Darreck, I don't want to hear it!"

Kellman gave a casual salute. "Like you say, sir."

Satrine hid her desire to sigh. Not that Kellman was bad—he was sharper than Welling gave him credit for, but he was crass and more interested in locking someone up than actually solving the crime. His little speech about sending them all to Quarrygate and let the trial sort out fit his method. She was going to need to take charge to bend him to her needs.

"All right," Satrine said. "We'll head up there in ten minutes. If Hilsom doesn't have the writ ready in time, he can have one of his pages run after us. If you need to grab something to eat or hit the closet, now's your moment."

Kellman looked bewildered for a moment, and then shrugged. "See you in ten."

Satrine went back to her desk, hoping Welling had left a note behind, having found something in the pile of documents he had requested.

Instead there was madness. The slateboard was a mess of scrawled notes and lines and arrows, several of the records affixed to it. She had learned, in the last two months, how to read his scratch handwriting, but figuring out this message was a puzzle that made the murder look like a child's riddle.

"Oh, Welling," she muttered to herself. "You've really gone in deep this time."

Cinellan came over to the desks, having seemed to have lost his entourage for the moment. "Is Assan Jabi-udal one of your possible suspects?"

"He's on the list," Satrine said. "But I think he's more growl than teeth. All performance for his zealots."

"I hope you're right about that," Cinellan said. "He's the one who took the hostages."

◆━━◆▶━━◆

"Specs, is this a good idea?"

Minox was relatively sure it wasn't, but fear, anger, and magic were clouding his thoughts. He had to fight his way to approaching the situation rationally. The perverse urge to resolve it with violence coursed through him. His arm was trembling, and Minox wasn't sure if it was his emotions or the magical ailment.

One thing was clear, though—Joshea was an anchor

in this moment. He shouldn't let the man get involved, but he desperately wanted his help.

"It's what we're doing," Minox said. "It may not be a good idea, but there isn't a better one."

A cart loaded with bread and soup had been brought up from the kitchens, ready to be wheeled into the ward room. Minox was impressed with how quickly it had been provided. Perhaps they had been preparing to serve it now, regardless.

"Ready?" Joshea asked.

Minox nodded, moving closer. "We may have to take . . . extraordinary measures. I know you're not comfortable with the idea, but . . ."

"I understand. Let's go," Joshea said. He wheeled the cart into the room, Minox following behind and staying in the doorway.

"No farther, Constable," Jabiudal said. He was still holding Beliah, who was now looking back and forth between him and Joshea. "Who is this man?"

Joshea stood tall. "Joshea Brondar. I was a patient in the ward, and volunteered to help when the Constabulary needed it."

"You have the bearing of a soldier, Mister Brondar."

"Former," Joshea said. "I won't lie to you about that, sir. But that's why I'm bringing your food instead of ward staff. None of them should be put in danger."

"We brought you food, Mister Jabiudal," Minox said. Another wave of weakness pulsed through his body, starting with his hand and then running through his whole body. Minox almost collapsed, leaning on the doorframe to hide it. "Make good with your end."

"I offered you five," Jabiudal said. "First—you, the profane one." He pointed at Corrie.

"What do you blazing want?" Corrie asked.

"Come here and taste the food," Jabiudal said. "Make sure they did nothing foolish."

Corrie walked over to the cart. "Hey, specs?" she asked Minox, feigning ignorance. "You do anything foolish?"

"Not to the food," Minox said. It was growing harder to draw breath. Minox wasn't sure how much longer he could maintain.

Corrie shrugged, picked up a bowl of soup, and started eating it. "Good enough?"

"Sufficient," Jabiudal said. "Bring my people their meals first."

"Release five, Jabiudal," Minox said.

"I am true to my pledges," Jabiudal said. He pointed to three patients—all Constabulary officers, all of them with relatively minor injuries. Exactly the sort who could give a good fight back. "You three will leave now with no trouble."

"Go on," Minox said to them. They shuffled out. "That's three."

"True," Jabiudal said. "The doctor and the other nurse will also go. We will need one nurse with us, in case of emergencies, and this one is the best to keep close." He pulled Beliah tight to him.

Corrie and Joshea both bristled.

"Come along," Minox said to the other two released hostages. As they left, Joshea and Corrie distributed the soup to the rest of the hostages. Minox barely noticed the moment when Joshea passed a knife to Corrie—the man had quick and quiet hands.

"So what next?" Minox asked Jabiudal. His legs were numb, his left hand full of needles. "Are we at an impasse?"

"There is no such thing. There is only patience, as we await the wisdom of God."

"What the blazes is going on?" a voice shouted from the hallway. Mirrell. "Who is in there, and who authorized this?"

Jabiudal grinned. "And the wisdom arrives."

Minox was about to speak, but then all the strength in his legs left him. He collapsed in a heap on the floor.

"Minox!" Beliah shouted.

"Confirmed," Jabiudal said.

Minox tried to force himself to stand up, but he had nothing in his legs. Only in the center of his gut, a black fire burned, a great forge of churning magic.

One of the other Imachs stepped forward, and shouted something in his native tongue. He pointed at Minox.

Jabiudal snarled, and pointed his weapon at Minox. He said something, which Minox presumed was an accusation of him being a mage.

Which made perfect sense, and a blackened cloudy glow was coming from his hand.

In that moment Joshea and Corrie both struck. Joshea leaped on one of the Imachs, while Corrie wrenched Beliah from Jabiudal's grasp. Beliah fell to the ground, screaming in panic. Corrie and Jabiudal both had knives out, grappling to overpower the other.

Joshea had his man by the skull, thumbs pressing into his eyes. The man screamed, and the other two Imachs came to his defense, slashing at Joshea with their knives.

Jabiudal's knife was about to find Corrie's throat.

The fire within Minox's stomach could no longer be contained. His arm was engulfed in the black glow.

And then it filled the room completely.

Chapter 17

THE WARRANT THAT HILSOM WROTE OUT for them was extremely limited, only giving Satrine and Kellman access to the one dockside hold that Uite lek Ni named. "No latitude here, not an inch," he had said. "If there's nothing there, too rutting bad."

This had to be a problem if he was resorting to profanity.

"Blazes, Trick, what do you think we'll even find here? A signed confession?" Kellman asked as they approached the building, which was nearly indistinguishable from every other one on this strip. "This is a waste of time."

"Evidence is a waste of time?"

"Blazes, it probably was Jabiudal or one of his zealots. Why do you think they've taken hostages now?"

"Humor me, Kellman," Satrine said. "Besides, they've got all the hands they need at Ironheart. We might as well be useful now."

She was starting to think that Kellman coming with her was also a waste of time, but even she admitted she needed another pair of hands, especially using the doorcracker. That was a two-person tool; even Kellman couldn't use it alone. "This is the one."

Kellman had the doorcracker slung over his shoulder, and he put it on the ground. "All right, but we got to do this clean down the line, or Hilsom will have our heads. And I mean yours, Trick."

"Glad you're looking out for me."

If clean down the line was what they'd need, then that's how it would go.

Satrine went up to the metal door, dingy and poorly painted. She would have thought the Hieljams would have kept their property in better state, but maybe that was another sign of their finances being in trouble.

She gave three hard pounds. "City Constabulary," she announced. "We have a Writ of Search issued from the Office of the Protector and signed by a justice. You are required to open this door."

She counted to ten awaiting a response. When no response came, she repeated the pounding and the speech.

"Have I satisfied the requirement of announcement?" she asked Kellman.

"Yeah, all right," he said. "Try the door."

She pulled at the door, but it didn't move. "It's latched. Is the use of the cracker warranted?"

He picked it up off the ground. "You're a little too excited about this thing."

"It's my first time, Kellman," she said, taking hold of one of the handles as he wedged the blades of the device inside the gap of the door. "Be gentle with me."

He chuckled as he braced himself. "Do it."

She pushed her handle toward Kellman as he held his side in place, and the blades of the device pried open, forcing the door open with a very satisfying crack.

"Did you like that?" he asked.

She realized she was grinning. "There really are few simple pleasures on this job."

He set the doorcracker down. "Constabulary! We have a Writ of Search. Resistance will result in ironing!"

He gave her a nod, and she drew her crossbow, stepping across the threshold. The place was dim—only a row of small windows near the roof providing any illumination. "Might need a lamp," she said.

He came in behind her, crossbow up. "I left it in the wagon."

"We'll go back for it once we're secure here," she said. "Though I think that's not an issue."

If anyone was in here, they were making a point of staying hidden. Satrine didn't drop her guard, but shifted her focus to looking for whatever might be in the warehouse. The place was filled with barrels, hundreds of them, marked with both Imach and Fuergan writing. The thing that stood out was the smell. Sickly sweet, and oddly familiar.

"So what do we have in here?" Kellman asked. "You smell that, right?"

"I do," Satrine said. "You ever smell that before?"

"No," he said, moving closer to a barrel. "Think it might be *effitte*? Or some other junk we haven't heard of?"

"Maybe," Satrine said.

"What do the squiggles say?"

She couldn't read the Imach or Fuergan words. She knew the letters, the symbols, and could pronounce them, but the words didn't meant a damn thing to her.

"*Sukkar* in Imach, *Hsugir* in Fuergan," she said.

"Shu-gar?" Kellman said. "So what is it?"

"I don't know," she said, though her nose told her different. "I know this smell."

"Well, you've got that," he said. "From where?"

Satrine found a prybar on the wall and took it to the lid of one of the barrels. "That's what I'm trying to remember."

"Were you ever in Imachan?" he asked, clearly joking.

She had been. That was the smell.

"I was once," she said. "Many years ago." The lid popped off, revealing a thick brown liquid. "A farm with a boilhouse of some sort."

"Boilhouse?"

Cautiously she dipped her finger in the liquid. "You ever go to Waisholm, Kellman? Or one of the northern archduchies when they tap the maples?"

"That's not maple syrup, or honey," he said.

"No," she said. "This might be very stupid, so be alert." She dared to allow a drop of it on her tongue.

A burst of sweetness.

"You all right?"

She had made a face. "I'm fine. It's much sweeter than maple or honey."

"Fine," Kellman said. "So why was this so important?"

"I'm not entirely sure," Satrine said. This was the same scent from that Imach farm. From the boilhouse. Where Pra Yikenj had nearly killed her. "This barrel is, what, thirty gallons?"

"About," he said. "And we're looking at at least a hundred barrels. And we don't know what it is, exactly."

"Let's keep looking around. There's not an obvious office in here, but there's probably paperwork, a manifest, something. Even if it's in Imach or Fuergan. We need to figure out what this is and where it's going."

"Why do you think it's going somewhere?"

"Besides the fact that there isn't a market for it here?" Satrine asked. "At least, not yet, but . . ." That was the thing missing. Why was this stuff here, in Maradaine? "That's part of what we need to figure out. If Uite is telling us the truth—"

"That's a big if."

"If he was, then the Hieljam are fully invested in this stuff, this *sukkar*. Why, unless they thought they could turn a profit?"

"So where's the profit?" Kellman asked, though he was clearly on board. "Figure out the money, we figure out who benefits from Hieljam's death. So who's tied to this stuff? Kenorax, Hajan, Jabiudal?"

"Everyone and all?" she said.

There was a desk in the corner of the warehouse, and stacks of neatly organized papers. Some of them were in Fuergan, others were in Imach, and a few with notations in Trade, including the Kenorax name on several of them.

"What do you have?"

"Timetables, I think," she said. "It's in multiple languages, but it looks like this stuff is supposed to go to one of the Imach groups, but after Kenorax was supposed to take it and bring it back three weeks later."

"Kenorax is in shipping and cargo," Kellman said. "If his company is taking it, why are they bringing it back? Or are they bringing it somewhere that it takes three weeks there and back?"

"No clue, especially since it seems they never did any of it." She flipped through the paperwork, which was mostly in Fuergan and Imach, but from the Trade she could read it seemed like the Kierans were supposed to pick up barrels of this stuff weeks ago, but never did.

"I'm at a loss here, Trick," Kellman said. "Saints know I can't make sense of this foreign nonsense. Anyone could be the person gaining from this."

Satrine had to agree with that. She dug through the sheets, not that she could read any of it either, until she spotted a crucial piece of information—a stamp in neither Fuergan or Imach symbols.

A Lyranan stamp.

"I've got a hunch who that might be, Kellman. Whistle some footboys and pages over. We need to lock this whole place down."

Just as Mirrell reached the room were those blasted machs had taken their hostages, the whole place became a thunderstorm.

That was the only way he could describe what was happening. Black clouds, flashes of lightning, a great clamor of thunder. The last thing blew out his ears, and he was knocked off his feet, as were most of the rest of the men in the hallway.

"Blazes was that?" he said, but he could barely hear his own voice.

The sergeant closest to him seemed to say something, but Mirrell couldn't hear a bit of it.

"No good," Mirrell said, raising his voice.

The sergeant made a sign like he couldn't hear either.

Mirrell got back on his feet and made hand signals to the men around him. He raised up his crossbow, and let them know to fall in on him.

He took a few steps toward the ward room. Whatever had happened, now there was just a thick haze. No more flashes or thunder.

In the back of his mind, he threw out a prayer to Saint Alexis, and moved in.

"Everyone on the ground now!" he shouted. Still couldn't hear his own voice, and anyone who had been in here wouldn't be able to either. There didn't seem to be any immediate argument or attack, though.

The haze was dissipating. There was a row of high windows along the top of the walls, and the glass had been shattered. Now Mirrell could see what was happening.

Everyone was on the ground—Imachs, patients, a nurse. They weren't out cold, but they all looked dazed and stunned.

"The blazes happened in here?" he asked. He could hear himself now—but the ringing in his ears was murder.

"Inspector Welling was in here!" the sergeant shouted. No one's ears were any good. But that explained a lot— if Jinx was in here, he must have done some magical whatever to send everyone down. And blown out the windows and saints knew what else.

"Iron every one of the Machies before they get up!" Mirrell said. "I don't care about if they're injured or not. We'll sort that out later."

One of the others stirred—a young woman in patient robes, but Mirrell knew who she was. Corrie Welling, night shift horse. Jinx's sister. "Minox?" she muttered. She looked horrible—her right eye a swollen mass of blackened blood and pus, her hair chopped to shreds.

"You all right, Welling?" Mirrell asked. "Can you hear me?"

"Rutting barely. Blazes going on?" She pulled herself up onto her elbows, looking around.

"Hoping you could tell me."

"I was tussling with this bastard," she said, giving a hard kick to Jabiudal's inert form. "Minox had just fallen over, and . . . where is he?"

Mirrell looked around. "Jinx! Where are you?"

Now Corrie was on her feet, looking around frantically. She pointed to the nurse, lying on the ground. "That's my aunt. She . . . rutting take care of her, someone." The room secure, Mirrell waved in the Ironheart staff to bring the patients out, including Corrie's aunt.

"Welling!" Mirrell called out. "Did someone already pull him out or something?" Several of the regulars shook their heads.

"He was in a bad way," Corrie said.

"Yeah, I know," Mirrell said. He was in a state in the stationhouse; everyone saw it. Captain said he went home, and that was for the best. What did he even come here for?

Stupid question. Jinx was annoying as all blazes, but

he was a dog with a bone when it came to his cases, and this mess was tied right to his case. Add in his own sister and aunt in the mix, Mirrell doubted if any power in the city could have kept him away.

"Saints," Mirrell muttered. "Where the blazes did he go?"

"Joshea is gone too," Corrie said.

"Who the blazes is Joshea?"

One of the sergeants offered the answer, as the regulars hauled off the Machies. "When the perpetrators insisted that the food be delivered by someone who wasn't a constable, we had a volunteer. Patient, former soldier."

"He's Minox's friend," Corrie said.

"Specs!" a regular shouted. "You got to see this!"

By one of the ward cots, there was a hole in the floor—a rutting stone floor. The hole was a perfect circle, clean all the way through to the floor below. There was no way this was cut by Imachs with a few weapons. "Where the blazes did this come from?"

"Rutting saints and sinners," Corrie said, looking down the hole. The ward room below it had a matching hole in the floor straight beneath it, and beyond that, darkness.

"You got that right," Mirrell said. This had to be more rutting magic. "Must be where Jinx went."

"Where he went?" Corrie snarled at him. "What the blazes do you rutting mean by that?"

"Mind your tongue, Officer," Mirrell snapped back. "You want to be slapped back to lamplighting?"

"No, sir," Corrie said. "But my brother—"

"Is sick," Mirrell said. "Tell me I'm wrong."

"I don't know," Corrie said.

"I do. Don't think I don't know all about your family. I know what happened to Fenner Welling. And your cousin."

"Don't you rutting dare—"

"And did you see what he did in here? We all saw it, Welling. Magic, exploding through the room, nearly killing everyone in here."

Corrie went quiet. Clearly didn't have a response to that.

"Then he blasted a hole through the floor, all the way to the sewers, by the looks of it, and ran away!"

"He wasn't in a state to—"

"Then maybe his 'friend' got him out. Who is this guy?" He shouted to all the regulars. "Did anyone get a blasted name off the guy who Jinx let dance into this?"

"It's Joshea Brondar," Corrie said. "Served in army. Family runs a butcher shop in the neighborhood."

"All right," Mirrell said, coming back out into the hallway. The Machies were ironed and taken off. The patients were getting help. Time to move forward. "We've got a new situation. Two men are missing; we don't know what their state or frame of mind is." The assembled regulars and sergeants all looked a mess—injuries, covered in soot and dirt, saints even knew what else. But they also looked like none of them were ready to sign out at this point.

"Maybe they need help, maybe we need to iron them and bring them down, we don't know. I need two footpatrol."

Hands went up. Good lads, all of these.

He pointed out two. "Run to this Brondar butcher shop. Find out who this Joshea fellow is. Maybe they went to hide there."

Those two ran off.

"The rest of you, get out there and spread the word. I'm putting an All-Eyes out for Inspector Minox Welling."

"Specs!" Corrie shouted. "That ain't—"

"You want to sign out for the day, Welling, feel free. You've done your duty."

"No, sir," Corrie said. "You're calling an All-Eyes? I still got one good one." She strode off. The rest of the regulars dispersed.

Mirrell fumbled in his coat pocket for his pipe. This blasted day was already one of the worst he had seen in twenty years in the Green and Red, and it wasn't even twelve bells yet.

And it was likely to get a lot blazing worse.

———— ◆━◆ ————

"It didn't make any sense, the Lyranans in the station," Satrine said as she hurried back to the stationhouse with Kellman. A wagon crew were already at the warehouse, fully cataloging and impounding its contents. It all was evidence, as far as Satrine was concerned.

"They got in the scrum last night, got pinched as well. We probably have folks from every corner of the East in there."

"Maybe, but I mostly saw Fuergans, Imachs, and Lyranans. Quite a few. Why?"

"I can't even tell the different tyzos apart," Kellman said.

"Saints, Kellman, I know you're smarter than this."

"Nah, I really ain't." He thickened up his West Maradaine with that.

"Tsouljans and Lyranans look completely different from each other, and that's not even taking into account the hair coloring or dress."

"If you say so."

"Regardless, Kellman—what time is it?"

"Noon bells went a few minutes ago."

"I just realized we hadn't stopped for food today."

"I could eat," Kellman said. "Though I figured we were in a hurry. And I wasn't too keen on eating in the East again."

"I hear that," Satrine said. "We had lunch with the

Lyranans. Do not recommend." That reminded her of her point. "But the Lyranans in the riot, why were they there?"

"Got in the mix because why not? Some people want a fight sometimes. Or they just were in the wrong place."

"Doesn't make sense, though. Lyranan enclave of the Little East isn't close. Fuergans went after the Imachs, and the Imachs hit back. Lyranans would have to go through Kieran and Tsouljan districts to get there."

Kellman seemed to get it. "So they made a point of getting involved. Fine, so then what?"

"Why? And did they have a stake in the goods being held by the Fuergans?"

"Still think this is an empty hunt."

"Humor me, for the rest of the day."

"Yes, ma'am," he said.

The stationhouse didn't have the usual group of patrolmen out front, though between the prisoner duty and the situation at Ironheart, the force was pretty thinly spread.

"So what's the plan?" Kellman said as they went in.

"Lyranans are obsessed with status and rank. Of all the people we're holding, someone is the queen of the cats. I'm going to find me the ranking Lyranan and have some words with them."

The main station floor was abandoned when they came in. Not only were the detainees from the riot gone, but so was the usual bustle of clerks and desk officers.

"Blazes is this?" Kellman asked.

Satrine jumped over the front desk. On the floor, several of the clerks were laid out, maybe dead.

"Call for . . . blazes, anyone," Satrine said.

Kellman went for one of the many ropes on the wall to ring the house alarm. "How the blazes could this happen?" he asked as he rang it out.

Satrine turned over one of the clerks, noting a dart in

her neck, with black-and-purple-colored veins surrounding the wound. She pulled it out, her brain firing up with recognition. A *henzh*. "Lyranan," she said. "Still think this is an empty hunt?"

"Holding cells," Kellman said, drawing his handstick out. "Probably a breakout of some sort."

"I'm on it," Satrine said. "Get to the stable doors, secure that exit."

A few pages came running in, looking shocked and confused. "Latch down the main doors," Satrine ordered them. "Find the captain, and anyone else who's still standing."

She dashed through the desk floor, down the back hallway to the drop pole leading to the holding cells. She leaped onto the pole, her knee protesting as she wrapped her legs around it. She slid down, taking her crossbow out as she dropped.

The guards at the holding cells were all down, the same darts having felled them. The main door into the cells was ajar. Satrine didn't waste a moment going through, weapon high, finger on the trigger.

Someone was in the hallway, unlocking one of the cell doors—a Lyranan woman covered in gray from head to toe, including a hood and mask. Not that Satrine had any doubt who this was: Pra Yikenj.

She took the shot.

The bolt struck true, hitting the Lyranan woman in the head. Of course, Satrine was only loaded with blunt tips, so she didn't have the pleasure of burying a bolt into her brain. Yikenj didn't even flinch, but pulled two darts off her bandolier and threw them at Satrine, her movements so fast they were almost invisible.

Satrine flattened against the wall, feeling the darts brush past. She raced down the hall as soon as they cleared, closing the distance between her and Yikenj, drawing out her handstick. The woman was still working on opening the cell door—thank the saints for old rusty locks—and Satrine brought the stick down on her arm.

Yikenj went for another dart, but Satrine jammed the end of the handstick under the bandolier and tore it off before she could get one.

"I wanted to talk to the ranking Lyranan," Satrine said, feeling a wicked grin pull on her lips. "Looks like I found her."

Chapter 18

SATRINE IMMEDIATELY REGRETTED THAT grin, as it was greeted by Pra Yikenj's fist. A hard shot, drawing blood on her lip, though her teeth stayed intact. She stumbled back, forced to release any hold she had on Yikenj.

Yikenj launched a flurry of attacks, hands and feet, but Satrine was ready for them, using the handstick to block. No fancy attempts to grapple her this time. She didn't need to win, she just needed to buy time until backup came.

"You're not as fast as I remember," Satrine said, striking back with the stick.

"You should have let this be," Yikenj said. "We are not your concern."

Satrine took an opening for a jab, feinting toward Yikenj's chin. She dodged, and then effortlessly blocked the real blow aimed at her chest.

"This is my stationhouse," Satrine said. She couldn't land another hit now that Yikenj was fully engaged. She was managing to keep Yikenj's attacks from being devastating, but a few blows were getting through.

Fifteen years later, she was still incredibly outmatched.

The fact that she was still on her feet was pure luck. Satrine needed to change tactics. Yikenj might be faster and more skilled, but that didn't mean her bones weren't breakable. Especially at her age.

Satrine let herself take a punch that gave her a bit of purchase on Yikenj's arm. Taking the opportunity, despite the pulsing pain in her chest from the blow, she hammered the handstick on Yikenj's arm; three hits as hard as she could until she heard a snap.

Yikenj was not impeded. Her other hand shot out at Satrine's neck. "There is little reason to show you mercy now."

Then she cried out, a cry so savage it surprised Satrine. She was certain Yikenj was about to kill her, but instead she bashed Satrine against the wall and let her drop to the ground. She strode toward the door, pulling a pointed crossbow bolt out of her broken arm.

"On your knees, hands behind your head," Kellman said, his huge frame filling the doorway. He was reloading his weapon, while Satrine struggled to find her feet. Yikenj charged at him.

"Don't speak Trade, tyzo?" he said, raising up his loaded weapon. He fired again, and his shot would have been true, but Yikenj plucked the bolt out of the air, throwing it right back at Kellman. He was struck in the chest.

Satrine gasped, surprised to see Kellman wasn't felled by the shot. "She's dangerous!" she shouted to Kellman.

"And I ain't?" he said with a smirk, pulling the bolt out of his chest. He swung a meaty fist at Yikenj, but she dodged and grabbed his arm. She used the force of his punch to flip him onto his back.

Kellman coughed sharply as he hit the ground, and then had her foot come down on his chest, then his stomach, then his groin. He groaned in pain as she spun around and delivered another kick to his head.

Satrine was finally up as Yikenj walked back toward her, calm as anything, despite the fact that one arm was twisted at an impossible angle. Satrine raised up her handstick, ready for another bout with the Lyranan woman.

Without missing a step, Yikenj kicked up her bandolier from the floor, caught it over her broken arm, and drew two darts out, swift as a hummingbird.

Satrine didn't even have time to realize that the darts had hit her square in the chest before she dropped back down to the ground, unable to move a muscle.

As she drifted into a gray haze, she heard Yikenj whisper in her ear, "You are fortunate I was instructed not to kill any constables. You have earned no mercy from me today."

<hr />

Clouded fire. Falling, burning. Words whispered in his ear.

Walking.

Minox realized he was walking, but he didn't know where. Or for how long. Or why.

"Jabi—" he said. He wasn't sure why. Words—thoughts—didn't hold in his brain. Some went to his mouth. Everything was so hot.

Burning.

Minox tried to lift his hands in front of his face, so he could see them on fire. Eyes couldn't focus. Hands and feet didn't obey.

But he was walking.

"The purchase," he said. It made sense a moment ago, but then it was gone.

"Shush," a voice said. "Let's just—" The voice continued, but it sounded so far away. Minox couldn't hear the words. Or he heard them but they didn't make sense as words.

"Wait," Minox said. He was walking, but he could decide not to. Or his legs decided not to. He wasn't in his body. He was a passenger.

He was on the stone. Wet. Cool on his burning flesh. He was sitting now. When had he sat down? He remembered walking. He remembered a room, an Imach man.

Corrie.

"Where's Corrie?" he said. Words lost their purpose from mind to mouth. But he knew that he said things for a reason, and that reason mattered. He held on to that like an anchor. "Corrie?"

"I think she's fine."

The voice was familiar. Minox couldn't figure out why, but it was known. Trusted. Moving in and out of hearing.

Hands were on his face. "You're burning up."

"Put it out," Minox said. He was clearly on fire. Why didn't this friendly voice with cool hands understand that? Why didn't Joshea do something?

Joshea. That was who it was.

"Josh," Minox said. "I . . . I . . ." Thoughts to words still were hard.

"I got you, Brother," Joshea said. "What do you remember?"

Minox wasn't sure what he even knew right now. "Where? Where are we?" Through the haze of fire and darkness, his friend's face came into focus. No, there was light, light from Joshea's hand. Bright and soft magic, Joshea in command of it, illuminating the brickface tunnel they were in.

"Sewer tunnels," Joshea said. "Or something like that. I thought it would be worse."

"How?"

Joshea's cool hands on his head. "Really, tell me what you remember last."

Minox forced his thoughts to find order, even though they wanted to spill in every direction. Think through the fire. "Jabiudal trying to kill Corrie."

"You did something . . . astounding."

"Magical?"

"Exactly. It was like you released a thunderstorm in the middle of the room. Lightning and fire blasted out of you."

Minox tried to understand that. It made no sense. "Did I hurt anyone?"

"A lot of people, I think," Joshea said. "I had a sense something was about to come out of you, and I managed to protect myself and Beliah. I don't know about anyone else."

"But how?" Minox asked. That was all he could get out; further thoughts clouded around his brain, unable to find a path.

"How did we get down here?" Joshea asked him. Minox managed to nod—Joshea understood. "You—once everyone was dropped you were in a state. You were on the floor, clawing at it. Then you pounded on it, and suddenly magic burst out of you again. Next thing I knew there was a hole, and before I could stop you, you dropped down."

"And you?"

"I jumped in after you, did my best to catch us—you know, magically—before we both cracked our necks."

"I—thank you. But where?" Minox hoped Joshea would understand.

"You don't—I'm sorry. You've been delirious for the past half hour."

"I still am." Minox tried to pull himself to his feet. Nothing obeyed.

"You said the Tsouljans were the only ones who could help you."

"And that's where you're taking me?"

"I was at a loss for a better idea. I mean . . . no offense to the sew-ups in Ironheart, but they wouldn't be able to do anything for you."

"Can anyone?" Minox said. In the pale glow of Joshea's magic light, Minox lifted up his left arm. Now he felt almost nothing but heat and magic in it. The rest of his body was burning up, but it ached and protested. Not this ruined hand—pitch-black, almost shining like glass. "Did I do this to myself?"

"I don't know," Joshea said, looking around. "This is just dead reckoning, but I think we're just about to the Little East. Another couple blocks this way, I figure."

"But—" Minox was finding it hard to keep his thoughts clear. They wanted to run away from him. "Why are we in the sewers? Why not take the street?" That's what he wanted to say, but he only heard his mouth say "Why . . . sewer . . . street . . ."

"Not until we're closer," Joshea said. "You do understand you filled a hospital ward room with lightning, yes? And you're not right in your skull."

"No," Minox said. He wasn't sure if he was agreeing or arguing with Joshea.

"I don't trust your fellow sticks not to fill you with crossbow shots right now." Joshea pulled Minox up onto his feet. "Let's get you to the Tsouljans. It's probably the best plan we have."

Minox wasn't able to do anything except allow Joshea to carry him along.

The Tsouljans could help. If they wanted to. There was something about them he had realized, he thought, but he couldn't remember what it was.

———◆———

Corrie went in the front door of the Welling house at full stride. She didn't have a whole lot of time. The whole neighborhood was hip-deep in bilge and sewage, and Minox was on the verge of drowning.

"Oy," she shouted out to the household in general. "Who's about?"

"Corrie?" Mama and Aunt Zura came out through the dining room. "Are you all—oh my saints!"

Her eyes filled with tears as soon as she saw Corrie. Zura immediately kissed her knuckle and began mutter Acserian prayers.

"It looks worse than it is," Corrie said. "Who else is home?"

"Just us and Mother Jillian," Mama said. "And Evoy in the barn, of course."

"Right," Corrie said, peeling off her clothes and dropping them on the sitting room floor. "I need to clean up, get a bite and a fresh uniform, and get back out there."

"Corrianna, are you mad?" Mama said. "I'm astounded you—you were in Ironheart, and you look like you should have stayed. Where is Beliah? Does she know—"

"No, she—" So much to say, and Mama wouldn't want to take it. "Look, both of you, better sit."

Zura took one of the chairs, still praying quietly. Mama took another. "Don't you dare tell me Beliah is. . . . She . . ."

"No, she's not dead, Mother," Corrie said. Though she might have gotten a lot rutting closer than Corrie would want to admit. "A real mess went down at Ironheart. Beliah was in the middle of it, but they're taking good care of her. She's going to be fine."

"And you?" Mama asked.

"What happened to your hair?" Zura finally asked.

"A crazy mach lady chopped it off," Corrie said.

Zura muttered something about Imachs that made even Corrie's ears burn.

Mama took Corrie's hand. "Your hair, your eye—Corrie, I know your dedication to the Constabulary, same as anyone else in this family, but . . . for today you've done enough. Saints, dear, this is the first you've been home in two days."

"Minox—" Corrie started to say. Mama needed to hear this.

"If Minox were here, I'd say the same thing."

"Minox is in trouble out there, Mama." She lowered her voice a bit. "You know how he—you know. Something went mighty wrong with him and he nearly destroyed Ironheart."

"Wrong?" Mama flushed. "You mean like Fenner and Evoy?"

"No, I mean with—" Corrie shook her head. Mama was going to make her say it. "I mean the rutting magic."

"Corrianna!"

"It's the truth, Mama. He was a mess, shaking. One hand has turned black as pitch. He let loose a rutting thunderstorm in the middle of the ward."

"He can do that?" Zura whispered. She got up from her chair and went into the kitchen.

Mama sat quietly for a moment. "So where is he now?"

"We don't know," Corrie said. "Somehow in the madness of it all he just . . . ran off. That's why I've got to go back out there."

"Why you, Corrie?"

"Because he's a mess, and the other inspector put out an All-Eyes for him."

"The woman Nyla hates?"

"Nah, not Tricky. She's . . . I don't even know. She wasn't there. One of the other ones. An All-Eyes with every steve and bastard on the force with a finger on their crossbow. Most of them never liked Minox. Something goes wrong, they could—"

"Enough!" Mama shouted. "You think you can find him first?"

"I have to try, Mama. And we need more family on the street. Every bloody one of them if we have to."

"How are we supposed to do that?"

Corrie stepped away. "Put out a call. Get Jace home and have him run to everyone else. I need to get back out there."

She went up the stairs to the water closet, cleaning herself off as best she could once she was in there. For the first time she got a good look in the mirror at her face. Her eye really was a mess. Now she could sort of see out of it, all blurry and red. Her hair was a choppy mess of stubble. She grabbed some bandages from Beliah's supply and wrapped it over the eye. Better to keep it covered, let it heal. Maybe it would be right again in a few days.

She went to her room—the one she shared with Nyla and Ferah, though she almost never saw them in it—and changed into a fresh uniform. She rebelted her weapons and went back out into the hallway.

"I heard," Granny Jillian said, standing in the hallway. She looked like such a frail thing, though she still held herself like the street tough scrapper she had been back in the day. "You're sure Minox isn't . . . he's so like Fenner was at his age. He might be going on us."

"Nah, Granny," Corrie said. She didn't think about that. She didn't want to. "It's the . . . it's the magic, pure and simple."

"Ain't nothing simple about rutting magic, child," Granny said. "I could tell you a few things."

"When I have the rutting time," Corrie said, embracing her grandmother. "I need to go look for him."

"You do. Keep a good eye out for him."

"It's all I got left," Corrie said.

"Corrie," Granny called as Corrie got to the top of the stairs. "It could be both things at once. And there may be nothing we can do for him."

That was so rutting horrible Corrie didn't even want to think about it.

"I'll get him home," Corrie said.

When she reached the front door, Mama had her own coat on. "Zura is completely useless right now. She's gone to her shrine in the cellar and won't speak to me." She handed Corrie a cold pork and flatbread wrap, with Zura's pickled onions—Corrie's favorite whenever she stopped in the middle of the night.

"What are you going to do?" Corrie asked before she took a bite.

"First I'll find Timmothen. He should be at the Keller Cove Stationhouse, and he can get the kind of rally we need." Uncle Timm was a captain; he had the muscle. Corrie kicked herself that she hadn't thought of that. "What are you waiting for, girl? Go find your brother."

Chapter 19

SATRINE SAT UP WITH A START, gasping, eyes wide. Involuntarily her hand lashed out and grabbed hold of whatever was in front of her and yanked it toward her.

"Oy, let go!"

Satrine realized she had Leppin by his smock. She looked around and confirmed what she feared. She was in the examinarium. And something smelled horrific.

"Leppin," she said, barely able to manage more than a whisper. "What's happening?"

"A right blazing mess, that's what," he said, prying her clamped fingers free from his apron. "Ain't nothing right in this house."

"Did you think I was dead?" she asked. That smell was pounding in through her nose up to the top of her skull.

"No, no," he said. He held up the Lyranan dart. "Pretty vile stuff this thing is tipped with, but it doesn't kill. At least not with the amount you got in your system."

Satrine looked down at her open blouse and the two bandaged wounds. Thick purple veins surrounded them. Despite that she felt energized, even jittery. She actually wanted a rematch with Pra Yikenj right away. If it wasn't for that horrid scent giving her a headache, she'd be perfect. "What is that scent, Leppin?"

"Ah," he said, pulling a handkerchief from his pocket. "A bit of 'wake-up paste.'" He wiped away some gunk from her upper lip, and that took away most of the trouble. "Countered the toxin, but you don't want to get too much of that in you, either. You'd end up—I won't dwell on it, just . . ." He opened up a jar, scraped the stuff off the handkerchief into it, and closed it back up.

"Fine," Satrine said, rubbing any remaining residue off with the back of her hand. She hopped off his table. "Why are you tending to me instead of the house doctors?"

"First off, they got their hands full up there. But also because the captain wanted you on your feet, and they didn't know how to go about it."

She laced her shirt back up, and looked around for her weapons. Her belt was on the floor, in a pile with her vest. "And you did?"

"I do deal with toxins," he said with a shrug.

"Half the station floor had darts in them. You going to give that paste to them now?"

"No, I ain't," he said. "Let's go upstairs, all right?" He made his way to the doors of the examinarium.

"What aren't you saying, Leppin?"

"A lot of things, Inspector," he mumbled. He hedged for a moment, his hand on the door. "Like I said, the paste countered the toxin. Not cured or neutralized, hear? So you've got two different things swirling and fighting in your system. You're on your feet, but it probably ain't that good for you. Be better if you could just sleep it off."

"But the captain needed me on my feet." She nodded. "Anything I should know? I'm not going to drop dead by six bells, am I?"

"Not if everything goes fine," Leppin said, though he didn't sound completely certain. "Don't push yourself. And I'd lay off any wine or hard cider over the next night or two, though."

"Sure," Satrine said, all her gear back on. "Are we going?"

They went up the stairs to the main station floor, where several pages and cadets were cleaning up the place, and Captain Cinellan was talking to a group of regulars, passing sealed notes to each of them.

"East Maradaine, Dentonhill, Aventil, Colton—anywhere we can get boots and sticks from. Every captain out there has leaned on Inemar House; let them know I'm calling those markers."

"Captain?" Satrine said, crossing over to him. "What's our status?"

"How do you feel?" he asked, looking her up and down. "You took a real hammer."

"Ready to fight another bear, frankly," she said. And she really felt like that was the case, but it was probably Leppin's wake-up paste.

"How about Lyranans?" he said. "Since the assailants only busted them out, I presume they're at the center."

"The assailants?" Satrine said. "It was just one Lyranan woman."

"One Lyranan woman did all this?"

"Her name is Pra Yikenj, and she's a member of Lyranan Intelligence. A very dangerous woman indeed."

The captain raised an eyebrow. "Prior engagement?"

"Another life," Satrine said. "But, yes. I'm two bouts in with her, losses both."

"You, Kellman, and half the station floor."

"How is Kellman?" She looked to both the captain and Leppin, but the answer came from elsewhere.

"He'll live, the big ox." Mirrell came over to them. "I imagine he won't be on cases for a few days."

"Tricky shouldn't be, either," Leppin said. "I really think she needs to rest."

"I'm fine," she said.

"You *feel* fine. That'll pass."

Leppin was actually frightening her right now.

"I don't have time to rest, though," Satrine said. "Am I right, Captain? Kellman injured, Welling gone home, it's on Mirrell and me . . ."

"Jinx didn't go home," Mirrell said, his voice acid.

"What are you talking about?"

Captain Cinellan cleared his throat awkwardly. "It seems that Minox took it upon himself to engage the situation at Ironheart."

"He was in no shape to do that," Satrine said.

"No state for what?" Leppin asked, but Mirrell talked over him.

"Like blazes he wasn't," Mirrell said. "Do you know what he did?"

"He resolved the situation, Hennie, let's keep that in mind," Cinellan said.

"I don't blazing care, Cap! He dropped criminal and victim alike."

"Wait, what happened?" Satrine asked.

Captain Cinellan looked down at the floor. "In his . . . state, he unleashed magic. And incapacitated everyone else in the room. Including his sister and aunt."

"He's out of control!" Mirrell shouted. "It's time we said it, Cap. He's a blasted mage—Uncircled—and he needs to be brought in and charged!"

"Hold on, did he kill anyone in there?" Rainey asked.

"No," Cinellan said. "Everyone is recovered, and—"

"And nothing!" Mirrell was on a tear. "Not killing people ain't a standard—"

"Watch yourself, Inspector," Cinellan snapped. "None of us really understand what Minox did or his state of mind. Unless you have some insight, Rainey."

"I really don't," Satrine said. "I have some people I could contact, but I don't know if they'd be—" She stopped herself. "Available to be useful." She couldn't say what she was thinking. If Welling really was a menace, if he had lost control of himself and his magic, then her old contacts in Druth Intelligence were likely to either kill him or lock him away in a deep hole. And there was no Circle that would protect him from that.

"Let me lead the All-Eyes, Cap," Mirrell said. "In his state, if nothing else, he's a danger to public safety. We can't have him out of control out there. Wearing an inspector's vest, I might add."

"He's right," Satrine said.

"I know I am."

"Fine," Cinellan said. "Hennie, you find Minox, and get him safe. You hear? That's all. This is not a manhunt, clear?"

"With Tricky?" he asked.

"No, with whoever you can pull together. I'm bringing in more regulars from neighboring houses, saints help me. Grab a few cadets and pages; use them to coordinate your efforts."

Mirrell nodded and stalked off.

"So what do you need from me, Captain? Besides finding who killed Hieljam?"

"We've got Jabiudal and his cronies ironed up. That's done."

Satrine's gut churned. It might just be her reaction to Leppin's paste and Yikenj's toxin, but she didn't think so. This was the sort of thing Welling always fought against. But he wasn't here.

"I don't think Jabiudal is our man on this. Or his people."

"So who did it? This Lyranan woman?"

"I'd love to say it was her, Captain. Not that we don't have a solid case to lock her in a room and bury the room."

"So go get her."

"There's something far more complex at play, and the Lyranans are just a piece of it. What Kellman and I found in the warehouse . . . it raises a lot of questions. I need to be able to put the screws on the people I need to ask those questions to."

"Saints and sinners," Cinellan muttered. "No, you're right. The commissioner is going to want to have this closed properly, given everything we have going on. What do you need?"

"Let me draw up a list of names and addresses. We're going to need Writs of Search and Orders to Compel."

"For how many people?"

"Eight, nine. Maybe more. Do we still have the men stationed at the Tsouljan compound?"

"Yeah, but I was going to pull them off."

"No, I'll need them there." Ideas were cementing in her head. "Is Hilsom around?"

"He went back to his office."

"I'll send the list to him, and he and his scribes can meet me there. We should have someone from Justice come over as well for good measure."

"You'll compel questioning *there*?" Cinellan asked.

"We're in no state to do it here, and I can't be running back and forth," Satrine said.

"She really can't," Leppin said. "Not in her condition. She shouldn't even be left alone." Satrine had forgotten the bodyman was still there.

She looked around the room, until she spotted the very person she hoped was still around. "Hace!"

Phillen Hace looked up and ran over to them. "Inspector?"

"Leppin here says I can't be left alone, so you're my shadow for the rest of the day."

"All right," Phillen said, looking at Leppin and the captain. "Why can't she be left alone?"

"Because she's been poisoned and has a powerful stimulant in her system," Leppin said. "Things might turn left on her." Leppin dropped one of the lenses on his skullcap over his eye and leaned in to Satrine. "You shouldn't do anything that gets your blood excited. Running, shouting, fighting?"

"Those are my favorite things, Leppin," Satrine said dryly.

He turned to Phillen. "Keep an eye out for sweating or giddiness. If she starts laughing, something's probably wrong."

"I'd presume that anyway," Satrine said.

"What do I do if that happens?" Phillen asked.

"Throw her over your shoulder and run like blazes to a hospital ward or another doctor."

"You're saying that's gonna happen?" Satrine asked.

"It might. Or you might just black out and collapse in a heap. You feel dizzy or disoriented, you sit the blazes down, hear? Else you really will be on my table."

"Get me that list, Rainey," Cinellan said. "I need to get my house in order."

"Come on, Hace," she said. She ran up the stairs to her desk on the inspectors' floor. Leppin must be out of his skull—she felt better than she had for months.

Hace was right with her. "Should you be running, ma'am?"

"No time to lose, especially if I might drop dead," Satrine said back.

"Inspector, I don't think you should joke about that."

"If I'm laughing, you know what to do."

The desk was a mess, still. Of course it was, since she hadn't sorted it since Welling exploded all over it. His notes and pinned papers were damn near madness, that was all there was to it.

"Just let me get this all down, Hace. Then we'll be off to the East." She found a blank sheet of paper and wrote out the names and addresses. She knew who she was dealing with—the parties were painfully clear. The Hieljam family; the Kierans, Kenorax, and Iliari; the Lyranans, Taiz, Nengtaj, and of course Pra Yikenj; the Imachs, Hajan, and Jabiudal. Getting Writs of Search and Orders to compel was a pure fishing expedition, but between the riots and the breakout, there was no way Hilsom could object.

There were still missing pieces to it all. Fuergans bringing Imach goods—*sukkar*—into Maradaine for the Kierans. Lyranan stamps all over it. Satrine pulled the sheets she had taken from the warehouse out of her pocket. She still couldn't make sense of it all—the goods were to leave the warehouse—via Kenorax—and come back three weeks later, and then be put on an Imach ship. Hajan's name was on that part.

But the goods were coming from Kadabal in the first place, which meant Jabiudal, not Hajan.

That made no blasted sense. All the players were in the mix, but she couldn't see the why behind it.

Still she copied the addresses.

"Why bring it here at all?" she muttered.

"Ma'am?" Hace asked.

"How well you know geography, Phillen?"

"I can get to any street in Inemar with a blindfold on."

"World geography. You ever look at a map of the world?"

"Ain't never seen such a thing."

"All right," she said, realizing she needed to talk this out, and Phillen was all she had. "Fuerga, Imachan, Lyrana, the Kieran Empire—all to the east of us. Thousands of miles."

"If you say so."

"So why would the Fuergans bring in stuff from one part of Imachan, have the Kierans take it, just to send it back with different Imachs. Why would they do that?"

"They make their money being in the middle of it, right?" Hace asked.

"They could do that and never take the goods out of the east. Why ship them all the way to Maradaine?"

"I guess to do something to it," he said with a shrug. "I mean, this is a real city, not like they have in Fuerga or Imachan."

"You'd be surprised." She glanced back up at Welling's scrawlings. Two things suddenly jumped out. "Sweet tar." "Shaleton purchase."

She grabbed the sheets Welling had affixed to his slateboard under those words. Records relating to Kenorax. Mostly import and export forms, and a few real estate purchases. Specifically, Iliari had purchased land out in Shaleton. Way out in West Maradaine, where they were building more gearhouses and factories. "Minox Welling, you magnificent bastard," she muttered as she wrote down the address.

"What is it?" Hace asked.

"Let's get this list to the captain and head out to the East," she said. "I think I've got an idea what's going on here. We're going to have to bring up some lockwagons."

"Some?" Hace asked. "How many do you think?"

"How many do we have?"

◆━━◆◆━━◆

Fever and confusion had taken Minox's senses again— he had lost track of where Joshea had brought him. More than once he had forgotten where he was or why, and only knew that he was hurting and didn't know why he couldn't go home.

"Why can't I go home, Joshea?" he found himself saying.

"We can go there," Joshea said, sounding a world away. "Is that where you want to go?"

"I don't, I—where are we?"

"Near the Tsouljan compound. You don't want to go there anymore?"

Minox let that sink into his mind. It was what he needed. Balance. Restoration. Fel-Sed could help him. She would. Unless she was the killer and wanted him dead.

"Does she want to what?" Joshea's voice again.

"No, that's not it," Minox said. "I'm . . . I can't think straight and—"

"I know, Minox." Joshea placed Minox on something. A seat or a crate. "Do you want to go in there?"

"Yes. I think. Yes." Everything was just so much haze and fire.

"All right. Just stay put for a few clicks."

"I can't . . . I'll just . . ."

"Right back."

Joshea's hands let go of Minox's shoulders—he had barely realized they were there. Minox slumped back against a wall. There was a breeze on his face. Where was he? Why couldn't he go home?

He looked around. Alleyway. Why was he in an alley? Where was Inspector Rainey? Why had she left him here, when they needed to arrest—

The thought went away in a puff of smoke.

He tried to grab at it. But the thought wasn't actually smoke in front of him, and his hand grasped at nothing at all. His right hand. His left hand wasn't doing anything. He snatched at empty air again, until he lost his balance and fell forward.

His face was pressed against cool cobblestone. It felt oddly comforting.

Inspector Rainey really should be here. He needed her help. They had to get to—

Where was he?

Hands pulled him back up. Pulled his vest off.

"It really is quite inappropriate," he said to no one in particular. "I should remind you . . ."

"Minox."

"Yes, Inspector Rainey? Why haven't we gone to—"

"The Tsouljan compound?" It wasn't Inspector Rainey. It was . . . his friend. His magical fellow. The name had escaped him.

"Yes, exactly," Minox said. That was where they needed to go. He needed Fel-Sed to help him.

"All right, here's the challenge. The compound is still being watched by Constabulary. Two men at the door."

"I'll order them off."

"Yeah, that won't work," Joshea said. That was his name! Joshea Brondar, Uncircled mage. Three years in the army. Works in the butcher shop.

"Many of my cousins fancy you, you know," Minox said.

"Saints, you're bad off. Look, I heard some talk. There's a search for you—what do you call it? All-Eyes."

"Nyla is always threatening to call one on me." Minox felt that made perfect sense.

"Yeah, I think this one is because you aren't in your right head and blasted magic all over Ironheart."

"I did that?" Minox had a vague memory of something like that happening. Lightning and storm clouds from his hands. Hands. Hands on his face. "What are you doing?"

"I'm going to make you look a bit more Racquin. And hopefully with some quick talking and your vest, I can get us past those sticks at the door."

"Impersonating an inspector is a serious offense, Joshea." Somehow clarity floated in for a moment, long enough to say that, and then wisped away into nothingness.

"Then I'm doing you a big favor." Something went over Minox's head. Woolen and heavy.

"Too hot for this."

"Just for a few clicks."

Joshea had him on his feet; they were walking. Bodies brushed past him, Minox unable to see more than a few feet in front of him. His vision faded with everything else.

"What's this, specs?" a voice said. Minox focused on the green-and-red uniform in front of him. A regular of some sort.

"We got a Quin here, got a snootful of some tyzo poison. He's in a bad way." Joshea was speaking with glass clear confidence, talking exactly like Mirrell or Kellman would.

"Right, he looks it. So why you got him here?"

"Well, it made sense. Ironheart is a mess, and if anyone knows how to deal with some tyzo poison, it be more tyzos, eh?"

"Fair point, sir," the regular said. "He a witness or something?"

"Something like that," Joshea said.

"You ain't from the Inemar House," the regular said.

"No, I'm not," Joshea said without a blink. One hand came off Minox's shoulder and reached out to the regular. "Inspector Cal Eaton, from East Maradaine. A bunch of us from the East House were called in to help fill out the ranks. This fellow knows something about the feek case you all are working on — I don't know the details. I'm just trying to help."

"Makes sense," the regular said. "That why the tyzos tried to kill him?"

"I think so," Joshea said. "Forgive me, footman, but time is crucial here."

"Of course, Inspector Eaton," the footman said. "Head on in; hope they can do him some good."

Minox was brought across the threshold, and as soon as they were in the Tsouljan enclave, his whole body shuddered. The tremor in his hand became a frenzied shake.

"Saints, Minox," Joshea said. "Maybe this—"

"No, here," Minox said. "Fel-Sed . . ."

Minox felt himself being hauled up on Joshea's shoulders. "Where is Fel-Sed?" Joshea shouted. "Where is she?"

They went into one of the huts. Joshea put Minox down on the table. Hands on either side of Minox's head. "Stay with me, Minox. You hear me?"

"Hear you," Minox said. Magic was building up as a fire in his gut. "Something is happening."

"That's the truth," Joshea said. He opened up the trapdoor.

"This place . . . something . . . the Tsouljans are doing."

"I don't know," Joshea said. He looked about the room, like he was trying to see the magic. "But we'll figure it out, get you right."

Joshea dropped out of sight, down the trapdoor. Minox could still hear him shouting for Fel-Sed, screaming for someone to come help them.

Then there were more hands on Minox, hands on his face, chest, and arms. His eyes were pried open wide, and his vision focused on a face.

The face of Sevqir Fel-Sed.

She muttered for a bit in Tsouljan, and then looked right at him. "You've made yourself into a mess," she said in heavily accented Trade. "You Druth treat your bodies like the trash in your streets."

Then she pressed a finger against his head, and again he burst into lightning.

Chapter 20

"**I**NSPECTOR RAINEY!"

Hilsom came running up to Satrine as she was about to hop onto the runner of one of the three lock-wagons they were bringing up toward the Little East. Those and a handful of the freshest regulars were all that she could be spared. A crusty sergeant assured her that there were plenty of horse and foot in the area she could whistle for if she needed.

"You get my note, Hilsom?" she asked. Based off her own instincts and Minox's scrawls, she had come up with a list of names and addresses for Hilsom, as well as additional tasks for Leppin.

"I did and it's absurd. Writs of Arrest and Compulsion on this many people? And given how Mister Kenorax has already leveled a complaint—"

"I really couldn't care less about that, and neither should you." She stepped up onto the runner, where Hace was already waiting. "If you want to continue this conversation, hop on. I need you up in the Little East."

Hilsom looked hesitant, but gingerly stepped onto the runner and held on to the outer bar. "Is there a reason we don't ride inside?"

"Because it's a lockwagon, man," Hace said lightly. "You don't ride in it unless you're locked up."

Satrine whistled to the driver, and it trundled into the street, making its way in the procession of lockwagons to the Little East.

Hilsom sighed, then gave his attention to Satrine. "I wasn't intending to come up to that part of town just yet, Inspector, but you aren't giving me many options."

"My day hasn't exactly been filled with the things I intended," Satrine said.

Hilsom gave her a conciliatory nod. "I heard you were injured in the attack here."

"Not as bad as most."

"You'll tell me—" Hace started.

"Yes, Phillen," she said. Back to Hilsom, "I have a saint watching over me now."

"I'm still not clear on what you intend to achieve, Inspector. We have Assan Jabiudal. He will go to Quarrygate, unless the Imach government makes some sort of extradition request. That would be out of my hands, but—"

"Jabiudal didn't kill Hieljam," Satrine said. She hadn't quite figured out everything she was thinking, but that part was clear. "But whoever did wanted Jabiudal to be considered. Not suspected, considered."

"I see working with Welling has had an effect on you."

"Quite possibly," Satrine said. "We're going to need to know the official status of these people, Hilsom. I presume not everyone in the Little East is a proper Druth citizen."

"Hardly," Hilsom said.

"Starting with the Lyranans. Not just the ones who escaped, but the ones I named to you: Taiz, Nengtaj, Yikenj."

"That's hard to say," he said, scratching his head.

Heavy panting proceeded a young man dashing after the wagon and jumping on the runner, his sweating body interceding between Satrine and Hilsom.

"Cheed Cheever, Justice Advocate," he said between wheezes.

"I know who you are," Satrine said. "We met this morning."

"Lovely," Cheever said. "Then you know why I'm here now. You're intending to issue Writs of Compulsion."

"All within scope, Cheever," Hilsom said drolly. "Your office shouldn't worry—"

"We don't worry," Cheever said brightly. "Because I'm going to be observing your practices. It should be quite enlightening."

———— ◆◆ ————

Corrie knew that the All-Eyes for Minox was a real blazing search, not just some rutting alert to keep a lookout. She knew a sweep of the roads in the making when she saw one. Just outside the stationhouse that specs Mirrell was giving all sorts of orders to his small army of regulars. Corrie didn't have a clue who half of them were, probably borrowed from East Maradaine and Denton-hill. Maybe Eddie was around.

She didn't check in with Mirrell, though. He could roll himself for all she cared. She gave a nod to the sergeant on duty and made straight for the stables. The station-house was in a state, that was clear—she half listened as some horsepatrol on day shift nattered to her about the place getting attacked, a jailbreak of the tyzos. Today was a blazing bad day for everyone, but that wasn't her problem. But it meant no one called her out when she saddled up and rode out like she was on patrol. Probably they wanted whatever boots on the streets they could get right now.

Corrie needed to find Minox, and he was probably with Joshea. Even though she knew Mirrell had sent a couple boys to check on his family, giving it a second go around wouldn't hurt. They might take kinder to her than they would any old stick regular.

So she led her horse to Jent and Tannen, and the Brondar family butcher shop. The place was pretty quiet when she came in—two men who made Joshea look like a kid were sweeping up. The both of them were, like Josh, something of a cool drink—but she got the sense that they were in a dumb, beefy way, as opposed to Joshea's cracky charm. They didn't dissuade her of this opinion when they opened their mouths.

"Hey, stick lady, you need something?" one said with a mouth that never closed all the way.

"She needs some beef," the other said. "Or a good portion of hard sausage?"

"I don't need any of your lip, steve," she said. "You're both Brondar boys?"

"Name on the sign, stick lady."

"What happened to your eye, stick? You got a tony who likes to pop you?"

"We could have a word with him."

"He wouldn't give you no trouble if we had a word."

Saints, these two rutters. How the blazes was Joshea kin to them?

"Is Joshea around?" she asked sharply.

They both cooled in tone real smart. "He ain't done nothing."

"You all need to stop hassling Joshie."

"He didn't do it."

"Do what?" Corrie asked.

"Whatever it is you're thinking he did." The taller one was agitated, turning to his brother. "Go tell Pop there's another stick."

"On it," the other said, and he bolted off.

"I ain't looking to iron or hassle Josh," she said. "That ain't it."

"What is it? Is he the tony who's popping you?"

"No, and if he tried he'd eat the rutting floor," she said. She needed to stop being stupid with this one. "Look, I'm Corrie Welling. Minox is my brother."

"Oh!" he said. "Well, saints, girl, you should have said that."

The younger brother came back in with an old man who looked like a salted side of beef with a mustache. "What do these sticks want now?" he asked in a strong East Druthal accent.

"She ain't a stick, she's Minox's sister! She's looking for Joshie!"

"What do you know of Joshea?" the old man asked. "Do you know my son?"

"Yeah, I know him," Corrie said, biting her lip on the "rutting well" that was about to come out with that. Something about Joshea's pop inspired clean talk.

"And why are you people looking for him? He left here with your brother last night, and never came home!" The man closed the distance to Corrie, and he had a good foot of height over her, and his arm must have weighed as much as she did. Still she wasn't going to let a steve like this push her around, even if he was Joshea's pop.

"Right," Corrie said. "I don't know everything, Mister Brondar. That's why I'm here. Last night there were riots up in the East. You hear about them?"

Mister Brondar only grunted in reply.

"Joshea and Minox got caught up in that."

"How you know that?" a Brondar brother asked.

"Because I was rutting caught up in it," she said. Off of Mister Brondar's glare, she added, "That's how my eye got messed up. Some Imach slan was pounding on my face; Joshea pulled me out of there. But he got knocked about."

"What?" the father boomed. "How badly?"

"Pop, let her talk."

Corrie wasn't going to mince the truth. "He spent the night in Ironheart. But he was on his feet this morning."

"So where is he?"

"I had hoped he was here, frankly." Here she probably should tamp down on all the truth. The Brondars didn't need to know all the particulars about Minox. Corrie's gut told her this old man didn't have a very keen opinion of magic or mages. "More trouble happened at the ward, and . . . my brother, he's sick. Not thinking straight."

"What do you mean?"

"Like he ran off from the rest of the Constabulary."

"Sounds sensible to me," a brother joked.

"Yeah, sure," Corrie said. "Last I saw, Joshea had gone after him. Or with him. I hoped maybe he talked some sense into Minox, or managed to get him somewhere to cool off."

"So this is why the other sticks came asking? They were really looking for your brother."

"That's right. Are they—"

"Not here," the old man said. "We have not seen him or your brother."

"Fine," Corrie said. "If you do—"

"I'll leave your brother lying in the gutter outside the shop." The old man returned to the back of the shop.

"Pop's just upset," one of the brothers said.

"I hardly rutting blame him," Corrie said. "Look, if somehow you do see my brother, then—" She thought for a bit. There was no way they could get word to her, or anyone else in the family. What would be the safest thing they could rutting do for Minox? Especially in his condition. "Try to bring him to the stationhouse."

The brothers looked at each other and shrugged. The taller one spoke. "Do what we can, depending on what's going on with Joshea. If your brother's hurt him, I ain't gonna protect him, hear?"

Corrie didn't have time to deal with this sort of sewage.

If the Brondars hurt Minox, they'd get the full boot of every stick named Welling on their throats. But she bit her tongue again. No need to throw the color around right now.

"I've got more places to look," she said, heading out the door.

"Hey, Welling!" the younger, dumber one said, coming up to her. "If you ever want to come back around, I wouldn't complain."

"You got a thing for girls with their eyes all rutted up and their hair carved off?" she asked. "You poor steve." She didn't give him time to answer before she went back out and onto her horse.

There was still one place he might be, though that was right in the thick of the East.

<hr />

Golden-skinned, blue-haired sinners and malefactors, that was what he was surrounded by. Minox felt all their hands pawing at him, words from their mouths that made no sense. He was fire and lightning, and they were killing him.

How did he get here? Where was Joshea?

"Joshea!" he screamed out. "Where are you?"

"I'm here." Minox craned his neck back to see, amid the Tsouljans surrounding him, Joshea was standing in the back of the room. Not just standing—two of the red-haired Tsouljans were holding him back. Not too forcefully, just enough to make it clear that more force could easily be applied if he made them.

The Tsouljans around him spoke, all the while touching him with metal-pointed fingers, or placing stones on his body. Every time they did, lightning and fire leaped from his body.

"You're killing me!" he shouted. "Joshea, they're—"

Hands pinned him down. Hands pressed against his chest.

Is this what happened to Hieljam ab Wefi Loriz? Is this what was done? Were they doing it to him now? Because they feared he would discover the truth?

The truth—that was his mission.

"Tell me what you're doing!" Joshea yelled.

"First the hand," one of the blue-hairs said. Was it Fel-Sed? Minox couldn't tell, couldn't see clearly. "It is *jenval*."

"What does that mean?"

Minox tried to center his thoughts. The truth, justice, that was his mission. He had a murder to solve. Nothing else mattered.

Hieljam ab Wefi Loriz was killed in a room just like this. Lying on a table like this. Perhaps surrounded by a ground of Tsouljans engaging in a mystical ritual.

He needed to find the truth. He had found it. It was somewhere in the back of his brain. He just had to get it out.

Sharp, piercing pain shot up his left arm. Were they doing something to his hand? The arm was afire with pain, but the hand was dead numb. Nothing.

"What are you doing?" he snarled.

"Stillness," a Tsouljan said to him, like it was a command.

Minox would have none of that. One of them pressed a sharp metal finger to his temple, and the lightning and fire came again. This time he grabbed at it. He clutched that magic leaping out of him and sent it all over the room.

All those hands fell away from him.

"Minox!" Joshea rushed toward him, but the red-hairs grabbed him hard and threw him back.

Minox was on his feet, and a red-haired Tsouljan grabbed at him. Minox, summoning strength he didn't know he still had, pummeled the man in the chest and arm until he let go.

"No more!" Minox said, and ran for the door.

He sprinted across the garden through the Tsouljan enclave, toward the exit. A green-haired boy tried to get in his way.

"Please, we did not mean—" he started, but Minox bowled over him. The two red-hairs at the entranceway did not get a chance to grab him as he ran out, nor did the regulars assigned to the gate.

"Was that the Quin?" one of them asked as he ran into one of the alleys. If they said anything further, he didn't hear.

He careened down the alley, and fell into a rubbish bin.

Where was he going?

Where was he now?

The Little East. He had escaped the Tsouljans. They were trying to kill him. So he wouldn't learn the truth.

But the truth was his mission. He would root it out.

And he knew where he needed to go to find it.

———◆———

There were barricades where the Little East met the rest of Inemar, with regulars at attention. Satrine figured she should have expected that, given what'd been going on. What was strange was, it was impossible to tell what their objective was. There were small, riled crowds on both sides of the barricade. On one side, Imachs, Fuergans, Lyranans, Tsouljans, and who knew what else were united in shouting at the crowd on the other side.

On the other side, "normal" Druth folk, ready with rocks and sticks, looking to start a fight, if only the constables would let them.

Satrine couldn't figure out if the barricades were to keep the Little East in, or keep everyone else out.

"Should those folks be ironed up or something?" Hace asked as the lockwagon rolled to a stop.

"Like we've got a place to put more lock-ups," Satrine said.

"Who would you iron?" Cheever asked. "None of these people are doing anything except assembling and expressing their voice."

"Are you kidding me?" Hilsom asked. "What sort of voice do you think they're going to express with sticks and rocks?"

Satrine hopped off the lockwagon runner and shot a few whistle blasts. "Clear it out, people. You've got better places to be."

"You gonna lock those booners up?" someone shouted. "Do your blasted job for once?"

"Clear away!" Satrine shouted again. "We've got to get these wagons through!"

This was met with shouts in two or three languages on the other side.

"What're you going to do?" Hace asked, now right at Satrine's side.

"I really did not want to have to knock any more skulls around today," Satrine said. She called over to the driver. "Just push forward."

"Can't do that," the driver balked.

"Just go," she said. She gave a few more sharp trills of her whistle. "Clear a path!" she shouted.

A few people started moving out of the way as the wagons rolled forward. "Hace, get the regulars to open the barricade for us."

"I'm not supposed to—"

"Saints, Phillen," Satrine said. "I'm still right here and I feel fine. I'll be in your sight."

"All right, Inspector."

She did feel fine. But Leppin had spoken of the coming crash like it was inevitable. Back in the day when the kids on her block would dose out on *effitte* or *hassper* or *phat*, they would always feel great until the wall hit them.

The main thing Satrine remembered from the one time she dropped a vial of 'fitte as a kid was the wall hitting her. She couldn't even move for the whole night, soiling herself on the cold floor in the back of Henk's cursed flop. It was the blessings of the saints that she didn't end up dead or tranced.

The regulars pulled the barricades open, all the while holding up their handsticks. Those boys looked like they expected the crowd—on either side—to rush them at any moment.

"Bring it through!" she shouted to the wagon drivers, hopping back on to the runner with Hilsom and Cheever. Hard eyes met hers as they trundled along, from all parts of the road, but if any of the citizens or foreigners had any intention beyond glaring, none of them acted on it. The train of lockwagons passed through the blockade, and the regulars quickly closed it up behind them. Hace ran along and joined them on the runner.

"What's our first stop?" Hilsom asked. "This is your show, Inspector."

"Lyranans," she said. "830 Dockview."

"Jolly good," Hilsom said. "These are writs I've no issue with serving. I should go in with you."

"If you wish," Satrine said.

"Oh, I wish," he said with a heated rumble in his throat. "Trust me, Inspector Rainey. You will need me."

The streets of the Lyranan sector were quiet, almost eerily empty, as they approached their destination. Engraved on a brass plaque it read clearly, "Bureau of Lyranan Expatriates and Descendants Thereof, Druthalian Division." Satrine waited until the rest of the wagons were stopped and she had her regulars assembled. Hilsom was rifling through his valise, pulling out the relevant paperwork, while Cheever glanced about nervously.

"Joining us, Mister Cheever?"

"No," he said, his voice almost cracking. "I think I will observe the activity from a distance."

"As you wish. Gentlemen."

Satrine strode into the office door with her small army at her back. Fresh youths, the lot of them, but a show of color nonetheless.

A young, bald Lyranan woman stood at a rostrum in the antechamber, not showing an ounce of concern that a Constabulary force had descended upon the office. "May I be of assistance?" she asked in only slightly accented Trade.

Satrine reached out to Hilsom, who took his cue with an actor's timing, depositing the writs in her hand with a satisfying snap. "I have Writs of Search for these offices, Writs of Arrest for twenty folk known to these offices, including and especially Specialist First Class Pra Yikenj. We also have Writs of Compulsion for Third Tier Supervisor Heizhan Taiz and Trade Notary First Class Fao Nengtaj."

She nodded and took the papers from Satrine. "Excellent. I will have to confirm the validity of these writs before I can allow access—"

"Zebram Hilsom, City Protector's Office," Hilsom said, dropping another document on her rostrum. "You will find everything is in order in terms of the validity of these writs, as they are signed by me."

"Excellent," she said, glancing at the document he had given her. "However, I will need to—"

"Confirm my credentials, of course," Hilsom said, dropping another document in front of her. "You will find that is the seal of the Council of Alderman and the Duke of Maradaine."

"Excellent," she said, though she had the slightest waver in her voice. "I must of course confirm the status—"

"This office has a Level Four Status with the Lyranan Ministry of Foreign Affairs, thus it and its officers do not hold protected status in regard to local laws and statutes. Per Diplomatic Agreement 47-B between the Nation of Druthal and the Lyranan Ministry of Foreign Affairs, all city level statutes apply to each member of this bureau, though appeals for retroactive dismissal may be filed to the Lyranan Ministry within forty-five days of their being served. Until I receive said dismissal request from the Lyranan Ministry you and your superiors in this bureau are obliged to comply. The Inspector Third Class and her officers here are authorized to use whatever force they deem appropriate to gain your compliance."

The Lyranan woman blinked, and for a moment her face was blank. Then she returned the papers to Hilsom. "Excellent. If you will follow me."

Satrine let out a low whistle while Hilsom regrouped his papers.

"Like I would be out-lawyered by a doorkeeping functionary," Hilsom muttered.

She led them through a hallway—all gray walls, with gray-on-muslin paintings hanging at even intervals—to a large office. As they walked, Satrine signaled to her regulars to check each door along their route.

"Make sure everyone gets a list of the escaped Lyranans' names," Hilsom said to Hace. "And anyone who doesn't identify themselves can be ironed."

Heizhan Taiz sat at a desk that was grand in scope but utterly lacking in adornment or aesthetics, with Fao Nengtaj at his right arm. The two of them looked like they had been waiting patiently for Satrine this whole time.

"Inspector Third Class Rainey," Taiz said. "We are gratified to have you visit us. How may the bureau aid you today?" While he said all this, the functionary from the door whispered in his ear.

"First off, you can tell me where Pra Yikenj is," Satrine said. "She is officially wanted for—how many charges, Mister Hilsom?"

"Seventy-nine, Inspector," Hilsom said. "Zebram Hilsom, City Protector." He presented a handful of documents to Taiz.

"Interesting," Taiz said, dismissing the functionary with a wave of his hand. He glanced at the documents and passed them to Nengtaj. "I am afraid that you cannot charge Specialist Yikenj. While this office and my people here may not enjoy a protected status of diplomacy, Specialist Yikenj has dispensation that can be detailed for you at length. She cannot be charged by the City Protector's Office."

"I thought that might be the case," Hilsom said. "That's why I included High Crimes of Espionage and Sabotage charges as well. That will go to the Grand Royal Court if needs be."

Satrine, begrudgingly, had to admire Hilsom here. He had done the work.

"Nonetheless, I cannot tell you where to find her," Taiz said. He glanced at the list of names. "Or any of these individuals."

"You're rather quick to determine that," Satrine said.

"Grant me some credit, Inspector. I know that the people listed are the ones of Lyranan nationality and descent who were arrested last night and freed by Specialist Yikenj. I know that they are not functionaries in my employ, and they are not people I am responsible for. I cannot be held to account for individuals who are outside of my domain."

"Then let's talk about your domain," Satrine said.

He held up a condescending finger to silence her. "I understand that you have Writs of Compulsion for myself and Trade Notary Nengtaj. Forgive me if I am unversed in the minutiae of your crude laws. What does this mean?"

"It means you are both compelled to come with us for questioning," Satrine said.

"You are free to ask me whatever question you wish," he said.

"A formal questioning is a different matter," Hilsom said. "The questioning is a matter of record, and you are obliged to answer."

"Under threat of incarceration?" he asked.

"Indeed," Hilsom said.

"Interesting. Now I believe—if I understand your custom—this is where I am granted challenge of said writ. What is the phrase I must say, Trade Notary Nengtaj?"

Nengtaj stepped forward. "Demonstrate your burden!"

"Yes. Demonstrate your burden."

This, Satrine was expecting. She had been composing her own speech in the back of her mind, really since leaving the Hieljam warehouse. "I have, at the moment, a warehouse of seized goods, just a few blocks from here. Said goods are material evidence in the investigation of the murder of Hieljam ab Wefi Loriz. Said goods have been inspected and stamped with a seal from Trade Notary Nengtaj. A seal issued by this office. Therefore both of you are persons of interest, determined to have information of critical value to the investigation."

"I'm satisfied that burden has been demonstrated," Hilsom said dryly.

"I am not surprised by that," Taiz said. He stood up, straightening out his coat as he got to his feet. "Very well. I presume that we are spared the indignity of being shackled as we are escorted to this questioning?"

Chapter 21

SATRINE HAD SEPARATED from Hilsom and Cheever, as well as one of the wagons, as they went off to the Tsouljan compound. Hilsom didn't give her too much guff over using that place for the questioning. Luckily he didn't actually question her reason for wanting it. She had given one that suited him—it was easier than hauling everyone all the way back to the station-house—but her real reason was far less logical.

The truth was, while she had visualized the various pieces of this puzzle, she didn't quite know how to make it fit. She couldn't think in spirals like Welling did. Her gut told her that if she could see the whole picture at once—the people in the place—it would all fall together.

Her lockwagon train—now three wagons—moved on to the Imach streets. She noticed that Hace, clutching onto the wagon runner, was sweating profusely. Far more than he should just because of the heat.

"Don't care for Machie, Hace?" she asked. The wagons barely had space to push through, as carts and vendors clogged up every part of the causeway. The drivers had to make liberal use of their whistles to push along.

"Sorry, ma'am," he said. He moved a bit closer on the runner. "I feel like they're glaring at us."

She looked about at the Imachs in the street. It was true, they were the center of attention, and unlike the Lyranan quarter, there was no shortage of people here. "Well, we are not popular here. We're going to be a whole lot less so in a few moments."

"Why is that?" Hace asked.

"Because we've already locked up one of the community leaders for these people, and we're about to grab another." She signaled to the driver. "Over there's our place."

She hopped down off the runner and walked the rest of the way while the wagon made its way through. Looking back to Hace, she found he was ever so slightly hesitant in his shadow duties. If he was scared of the Imachs, then the Alahs Innata—the coffee den—must have looked terrifying. A few swarthy, shirtless, thick-bearded Imachs milled about the front door to the dark-looking place.

"We're going in there?" he asked.

"We are," she said, walking up to the door. The Imachs moved slightly—not enough to truly block her, but enough to force her to brush past them to get in.

One of them said something in an Imach dialect.

"Afraid I didn't get that." Satrine looked up at the three of them—all of them a good half a head taller than her.

"He said," another offered, his accent thicker than tar, "that you have no business here."

"That's where you're wrong, and I have writs backing up that point. So either you let me pass or I'll have you ironed for interference."

The first one said something again in Imach, and then added in Trade, "Unclean." Now she understood their tactics—trying to shame her on their terms. For her to touch them on their bare skin and not be family or in one of the official stages of courtship would be the equivalent of declaring herself a prostitute.

She didn't have time for this, and pushed her way through. Hace was right on her heels.

Nalassein Hajan sat at the same table he was at the other day, discussing something with a larger group of his people. He didn't even look up as she came over.

"I have a Writ of Compulsion for you, Mister Hajan," she said, "regarding the death of Hieljam ab Wefi Loriz."

He glanced up, and muttered something to the rest of his people.

She dropped the writ on the table. "I am within my legal right to take you in irons if you do not comply, as well as anyone who interferes."

One of the men at the table shouted to the men by the door, who had followed her in, and they responded back. Then he looked up at her. "Are all women in the constables wanton, or just you?"

Satrine was about to respond with a backhanded slap, when Hace got over whatever fear of the Imachs he might have. The man found himself facedown on the floor, with Hace on his back, putting his hands in irons.

"That's interference, by the saints," Hace said. "I believe you were warned."

The other men started out of their chairs, but Hajan waved them down. "I have been congenial and helpful, Inspector. Why are you here to harass me?"

"Because you're involved, Mister Hajan," Satrine said. "And I need everyone involved to cooperate."

"But I have cooperated. I told you the murder weapon was Kadabali. I pointed you in the direction of Assan Jabiudal. Hasn't he proven to be the very man you seek in this crime?"

"He has not, not to my satisfaction."

"Hmm," Hajan said. "And yet I am told he and his followers are, how do you say, 'ironed,' and likely destined to spend a fair amount of time in your charming prison by the old quarry hole."

"That would be a convenient way to close this all up," Satrine said, taking the seat vacated by the man Hace had bound up. "Jabiudal locked away, as well as his followers, and with him, any competition or complications you have importing—what do you called it? *Sukkar?* Those disappear."

"I do not understand what you are insinuating."

"Hieljam is dead, and if Jabiudal is blamed and jailed, then who benefits the most? I think it's you, Mister Hajan, in that you can bring in the *sukkar* and sell it directly to the Kierans."

"The Kierans?" Hajan looked genuinely confused. Either he was a great performer, or Satrine had just opened a new vein of information.

"You see, there's so much for us—all the involved parties—to go over together, Mister Hajan. Thus I need you to come with me."

Hajan waved at her dismissively. "You will go alone. I am not interested." The men at the table all shifted their bodies toward Satrine, as if they were now ready to enforce his will.

"I was certain your interest alone wouldn't hook you, Mister Hajan. That's why this is best done with a legal writ." She held up the paperwork. "You are compelled."

"I confess, I am not sure how I can be compelled, Inspector. Unlike many of the men in this part of Maradaine, I make no claim to being a Druth citizen, or even aspire to reside. I came here to conduct business, but I am a Ghaladi, and a *kezah* at that." *Kezah*—a sort of holy noble rank in southern Imachan. "Arresting me would create a challenging incident, especially without good cause."

"Writs of Compulsion are funny things, Mister Hajan," Satrine said. "I'll confess, I am not a lawyer, but I understand their authority is not limited to the city. For example, one couldn't just run to Monim or Scaloi or any other archduchy in Druthal and avoid its consequences."

"I would return to Ghalad—"

"And one consequence is forfeit and seizure of assets," Satrine continued. "So were you to attempt to avoid this Writ of Compulsion by returning to Ghalad, every ship registered to you, Mister Hajan, would be seized at any Druth port."

"You couldn't—"

"I, personally, could not, but—" She tapped on the papers. "But there're the offices of the City Protector, the sheriffs of the Archduchies, and the King's Marshals. They do not take avoidance of writs lightly. Not at all. Without respect to the law *here*, Mister Hajan, the entire structure of authority breaks down."

"You would threaten—"

"I'm simply saying, Mister Hajan, that it's worth the hour or so of your time it would take to accede to the authority of this writ."

Hajan scowled and drank his coffee. "Release my friend there and I will come without further difficulties."

"Hace?" she asked.

"He was very rude to you, Inspector."

"We'll let it pass," she said. "This time. After all, we're very grateful for Mister Hajan's willing cooperation." She let that drop sweeter than the *sukkar* this whole trouble seemed to be over. She only hoped it was worth the trouble.

Mirrell didn't have much of a plan to find Jinx, but he didn't want to admit that to any of these regulars. He had given instructions to call for backup if Welling was spotted, and then approach with caution. He phrased it delicately enough: "Inspector Welling is unwell and in need of medical attention to avoid further harm to himself." That was true, but it tamped down the fact that Jinx was a rutting mage who was out of his skull.

And that terrified Mirrell beyond his ability to think straight.

The three blocks surrounding Ironheart hadn't yielded a damn thing, either.

"Really?" he asked the handful of regulars he had about him. "We've got a chance for people to turn in a crazy stick, and no one has seen anything?"

"Oh, a few people said they saw something," said Iorrett, one of the more experienced sergeants on the hunt, "but most of it was bunk."

"You're sure?"

"Yeah," Iorrett said. "Believe me, if someone had something real . . ."

"Fine, fine," Mirrell said. He didn't like this business they had to do, going after Jinx, but it was necessary. It was already becoming clear some of the regulars relished it. "We ain't got the manpower to spread beyond three blocks. Anyone got a plan?"

"Northwest," someone said—a sergeant he didn't recognize, walking over to his group of regulars. The man came over and extended his hand. "Cole Pyle, Horsepatrol in Keller Cove."

"You come off your beat to bail us?" Mirrell asked.

"Something like that," Pyle said. He pointed to a handful of sticks standing a bit away—from officers to cadets—as well as a couple River Patrol, Fire Brigade, and even a Bodyman. "You're looking for Minox Welling, we got a few people to help you out."

"Right," Mirrell said. "Pyle? We've got a—"

"That's my daughter, Inspector."

"Right." So Jinx's family came out for the hunt. Made

sense. Deep roots in the Green and Red meant something, even for Jinx. "Don't see your niece about. How's her eye?"

sense. Deep roots in the Green and Red meant something, even for Jinx. "Don't see your niece about. How's her eye?"

sense. Deep roots in the Green and Red meant something, even for Jinx. "Don't see your niece about. How's her eye?"

"She's on her own hunt for Minox. In the meantime—"

"You said northwest."

"Two things in that direction. The house—"

"I presume you've checked there."

"He hadn't come home, but he might head that way."

"And we—"

"We've got that handled, Inspector."

Wellings and their kin were going to put up a wall. Fair enough. But he was also remembering who this Pyle fellow was, besides Miss Nyla's pop. He was a tough old stick, who ran horse in Keller Cove, Seleth, and parts of town farther west that most Inemar regulars wouldn't go near.

He partnered with Jinx's pop back then, from what Mirrell had heard, until they got jumped by a Seleth gang. That had been Jinx's pop's last ride.

"What else is northwest of here?" Mirrell asked.

"The Little East," Pyle said. "And with it, Minox's case."

"I don't think—"

"Look"—Pyle shifted his tone a bit—"I know that something with—you know—has driven Minox off the saddle right now. But you can count on one thing about that boy. If he's got a case to solve, no matter what else is going on in his head, he's going to solve it."

Mirrell had to admit, that sounded like Jinx.

"All right," he said, calling out to the regulars he had. "Whistle out and regroup. Push in teams of eight, from here through the Little East, up to Keller Cove. Scour and sweep each damn street." Glancing at the collection of Wellings, he added, "Don't forget, we got one of ours that needs our help."

That was the truth. Because the saints only knew what sort of state Jinx was in right now.

———————◆◆◆———————

"How are you feeling, Inspector?" Phillen was looking at her a little too deeply for Satrine's comfort as they rode on to the Kenorax household.

"How'm I looking, Hace?" she shot back.

"Like you could use a week on the Yinaran coast," he said.

She turned to him, raising her eyebrow. That was a strange response. "What do you know of the Yinaran coast?"

"Nothing," he said sheepishly. "It's just a thing people say."

That was probably true. It was a thing her mother used to say when she was deep in her jug. As far as Satrine knew, her mother had never been to the Yinaran coast. Maybe that was where she had run off to.

"Well, it's a nice idea. I'll settle for a day off once this is solved."

He nodded, smiling. "If you can untie all this mess, that'll be earned."

"Tell me something I don't know, Phillen."

He actually gave that some thought. "Did you know the Firewings abandoned their chapterhouse in town a few weeks ago?"

"I did not know that, no." It was surprising, but maybe with two members ritually murdered and narrowly avoiding a war with one of their rival Circles, they figured a change of scene was for the best. Of course, the killer was caught, the case was closed, but that was one of the ones Welling considered "unresolved," in that strange way of his. Did he know they had moved out? Did that give the case a sense of resolution he had lacked, or did that only add to it being "unresolved"?

At some point, Satrine knew, she and Welling should have a long talk about the "unresolved" pile. If they ever got the chance.

As they approached the Kieran household, Satrine found herself sending a prayer up to Saint Jesslyn for Minox's health and safety.

She only had a small group of regulars with her now, and most of them looked like it was their first month on the job. She had them follow behind her as she crossed the gate and pounded on the bright white door.

The old servant opened up. "May I help you?" he croaked out.

Satrine held up her writ. "We'll be seeing Misters Kenorax and Iliari now."

The old man didn't argue, he simply opened up and led them to an antechamber filled with exotic flowers and far more caged birds than Satrine had ever seen at once. The regulars and Hace all stood around uncomfortably amid the tweeting and cooing.

"Is this normal?" Hace asked.

"The waiting or the birds?"

"I thought it was the Acserians who worshipped birds," one of the regulars said.

"No, they just won't eat them. Kierans will. Maybe this is for dinner."

"And maybe we simply appreciate beauty in all its forms." Two men came into the room—Iliari was standing in the back, while the man Satrine presumed to be Ravi Kenorax stood sternly in the entranceway. Wearing little more than a sheer robe, he stared hard at Satrine, trying to look imposing, despite being a few inches shorter.

"Mister Kenorax, I presume."

"I thought I had you people dealt with."

"We aren't so easily dismissed, Mister Kenorax," Satrine said. "You might have filed a complaint, but I've got Writs of Compulsion for you and your man back there."

"Compulsion? You think you can come in here and compel me—"

"I can and I will, sir. I have the authority—"

"Do you know who I am?" Kenorax sneered. "I'm one of the richest men in Maradaine. One of the richest *Druth* men, period—I was born in this city, just as the two of you were. But I'm just another greasy pirie to you, aren't I?"

That was unexpected. "I never said—" Satrine started. Kenorax already had a full sail in his speech, though. He got closer to her as he railed, his breath heavy with wine.

"My grandfather was born in a Kieran Debt Camp— born a slave, in debt with the interest for a fine levied on *his* grandfather's grandfather for a crime no one could even remember. He escaped to Druthal, a land of 'free' men, without so much as shoes on his feet. And he was forced to wander until he reached Maradaine, where his prison camp was the three square blocks of Kieran ghetto in the Little East. The only place he was allowed to live."

"That was never true," Phillen snapped back at him. Satrine gave the boy enough of a glare to silence him. She admired his moxie—it would serve him well if he ever became a regular.

Kenorax picked up on where Phillen led him. "Of course, boy, there were the slums on the west side of the city, around the prison and the old quarry pits. Anyone could live there. But even now, with Druth birth and a business and fortune built from nothing—"

"Mister Kenorax ..." Satrine started.

"Even now could I buy a home in Callon Hills? Or Fenton? Sun and moons, even in High River? Could I be your neighbor, Inspector?"

"Mister Kenorax, your railing doesn't change the fact that a man is dead," Satrine said. "And your ties to his business are far more intricate than you let on."

"Intricate, yes," Kenorax said. "Meaning I stand to lose money from his death. Remember that, would you?"

"Would you?" Satrine shot back. "That's the part I'm having a hard time sussing out. Which is why we want to question you."

"I am here, Inspector! Ask me your questions!"

"No, I don't think so," Satrine said. "You see, between you, the Hieljams, Hajan, and the Lyranans, I'm hearing a lot of different stories. So you and your man there will come with us, so all of us can talk this out together."

"I will do no such thing," Kenorax said. "Eject these people."

Satrine wasn't sure who this directive was aimed at, as there was no one in the room for him to order beyond Iliari and the old servant. How they intended to eject a half dozen constables was beyond her.

"Take them both if they don't comply," she ordered. "Misters Ravi Kenorax and Estiani Iliari, by lawful order of the City Protector's Office, you are hereby compelled to be escorted to a session of questioning with the lead inspector regarding the murder of Hieljam ab Wefi Loriz."

Kenorax looked stunned, and then dashed down the hall. The regulars didn't need any further cue—they went after him. Two of them tackled Iliari straightaway, as he moved like he was trying to block them. The other four regulars gave chase, with shouts and cries of a fight. Satrine was about to run after them all when Hace put his hand on her shoulder.

"No running, no fighting," he said firmly.

"Damn it, Hace, I should—"

"They got it."

The sounds of the struggle reached a peak, and then dulled down. The four regulars came back, dragging Kenorax with them. He was still struggling despite the four of them holding on to him and irons on his wrist.

A few other people came into the room—clearly to

see what the fuss was. Kierans all, much like the other morning, all dressed similarly in gauzy, flimsy robes. Satrine didn't have to wonder what kind of event they had interrupted.

"Go back to your business, folks," Satrine said. "We're just taking these gentlemen in for some questions. Unless you would like to interfere?"

The Kieran hangers-on all scattered.

"Cowards!" Kenorax shouted. "I'll have you all put out of doors before long!"

"Good loyal friends you have here," Satrine said. "Let's move along, we're losing the day."

Kenorax and Iliari were brought out into the lockwagon, and it took all six of her regulars to stuff them into the back and lock them in.

"We're running out of manpower, and we're going to need all we can get on the last stop," Satrine said.

"Right," Hace said, pulling out his whistle. He blasted out an escort call. "Let's bring someone in to take these brawlers over to the Tsouljans."

"Is there anyone?" Satrine asked.

"I bet there's a few of us working the All-Eyes for Inspector Welling." Hace blew the call again. "Which is a waste of people, you ask me. Inspector Welling surely can take care of himself."

<hr />

No one looked at him, at least right at him. They all looked around him. It made sense. He looked like a sick Racquin after all, and they probably feared that he would beg for money if they made eye contact.

He even looked right at a few of them, and they turned away in fear.

He saw them for what they were. Not just the fear. Their crimes and sins were written all over their faces now. Plain as writing on a slateboard.

The slateboard. He had written something there. There were answers.

More answers in the barn. There he could escape it all, especially the burning heat of the summer evening.

He had to move quickly down Escaraine. The average folk might fear a mad Racquin beggar, but they also wouldn't stand it in their street for too long before they brought a constable. He didn't need that trouble. He needed to solve this situation.

He just needed to find the answers.

The house was just ahead, a few lamps burning in the windows. No one on the front stoop. No one visible in the sitting room, at least from the street. None of the family looking out the window, either.

This was his house, he remembered. But he didn't want to go inside. He had a purpose. He fought through the fog and fire to remember that. He was Inspector Minox Welling, and he had a purpose in coming here.

Minox went up the darkened walkway, now confident with each step. No one had thwarted him on his way to the barn.

He went inside to find a few candles burning, and Evoy poring over newssheets. Evoy, with his overgrown, disheveled beard and long, black fingernails. "Leave the tray," he muttered.

"I don't have a tray," Minox said, closing the door behind him.

"Minox!" Evoy's eyes went wide, and showed as much joy as those sunken, dark-circled eyes could. "It's been a few days, yes?"

"I think it has," Minox said. He looked up at the wall, where Evoy's true work was spread out. Newssheets, slateboards, names, places, and dates, a wide web patterned out. "This is it, isn't it? All the secrets in the city?"

"I don't know about all of them, but quite a few,"

Evoy said, looking quite proud. "But there's something more I'm still grasping at the edge of."

"Yes, I understand," Minox said. "It's why I'm here."

Evoy nodded. "The Fuergan *lavark*, and the riots, right? It's all connected."

"More than you know," Minox said. Finally, he could talk to someone who understood. "I had it, Evoy." He tapped at his temple. "I had it all worked out, but then it faded away."

"Yes!" Evoy shouted. "You have it, but you don't get it written down, and then someone speaks or there's a dog barking and then it's gone in smoke."

"We need silence, focus," Minox said. He pulled off the Racquin pullover and tore strips off the edge. He was far too hot to be wearing such a thing.

"Why are you dressed like a Racquin beggar?" Evoy asked. "And your face is colored."

"Needed to sneak past the regulars, and then get to the house," Minox said. It should have been obvious, especially to Evoy.

"Why would you sneak past regulars?"

What was with these questions? "Are you writing for the *Gazette* again? Are you doing a story on me?"

"I can't—"

"Then why are you wasting my time?" Minox snapped. "We have work to do."

He wadded the strips into balls and shoved them into his ears. It was a bit challenging—left hand wasn't properly obeying him at all. It was just flexed in a claw, black as pitch.

"What happened to your hand?" Evoy asked, though it was hard to hear him through the wadded strips. As it should be.

"Nothing that matters," Minox said. He looked up at the wall, finding the first name he needed to craft a path, spin the web to the answers. Kenorax.

He grabbed a piece of chalk and went to write a connection. But he couldn't quite grab hold of it. The answer was clear, but yet he didn't have the word in the front of his mind. His hand wouldn't write it. Maybe because it was too hot. He was burning up again, inside and out.

"Minox, maybe you should—"

"Quiet!" Minox snapped. "I'm going to figure all of this out. All of it." He pointed to a part of the wall. "There was an agenda behind the Haltom's Patriots and their murderous attacks. Is it connected to this? Fuergan trade deals were at the center, tied to the Kierans, but does it touch the Parliament? Do you know?"

Evoy stammered, and stepped back.

"Good," Minox said. "Let me work this out, then."

Still the answers weren't coming. Something wasn't right.

Minox placed the chalk in his withered, black hand. It gripped onto it, but not of his own will. He wasn't moving his hand; his hand understood what he wanted.

It started to write. He let it take him into the fire.

Chapter 22

ANOTHER BLAZING WHISTLE CALL pierced the air, this one for a horserider. Escort call. Corrie knew she'd have to answer it; it was just a block away. One part of her hoped that maybe someone had found Minox and needed help, but she couldn't believe that was the case. He had gone into the wind. No sign of him at the tobacco shop, and every damn feek in the place yelled at her when she asked about him. She didn't need that sewage.

The call brought her around to the Kieran blocks of the East, where a couple of lockwagons were parked in front of one of the swell houses—bright white walls with the purple roofs.

Tricky was standing outside one of the wagons, with a page standing at her elbow, six other regulars standing around. Blazes, were they doing calling for her?

"You called a rutting escort?" Corrie asked, sliding off her horse. "Looks like you got some here already."

"I still have another pickup, and I'll need them on hand," Tricky said, coming up to her. "Saints, your eye."

"It'll heal," Corrie said.

"Surprised you're on duty," Tricky said.

"Well, yeah, your buddy Mirrell called an All-Eyes for Minox, so I still got one that works."

"There's no word, nothing?" she asked. Skirt did sound concerned.

"Nah," Corrie said. "So what did you whistle for?"

"We've got a wagon with two unruly Kierans, taking them over to the Tsouljan enclave."

"Why the blazes over there?"

"It—it's complicated. But I need someone who can keep them in line." She moved closer. "There are a lot of moving parts here, and I'm trying to solve this case. I could use someone to show the color until I get over there."

"And you're asking me, a night-horse slan?"

"I thought I was asking a Welling."

Saints, Nyla was right about her. Pretended to be an inspector, and pretending to know who she's talking to.

"Don't try that sewage with me, Tricky," Corrie said. "My brother says you deserve that vest, so I won't make you eat the road and tear it off you. But don't act like you know me."

"Fine," Tricky said. "Officer, escort this wagon over to the Tsouljan compound, make sure the men inside are brought in, and deliver them to Mister Hilsom inside. Stay there and report to him until I relieve you. Are we clear?"

"Yes, ma'am," Corrie said, pulling herself back up on the horse. "Always a pleasure to serve."

She whistled to the lockwagon driver and led him along over to the Tsouljan enclave.

The place was a strange batch of some crazy tyzo rubbish, that was for sure. Like they had built their own little park with fancy trees and ponds and sewage like that. She spotted a few normal folks, standing around on one of the bridges, as well as some regulars keeping an eye on the other tyzos and machs.

"Oy!" she shouted. "Tricky sent me with a couple of piries, said they were for you."

One of the steves in a suit came over—this guy, she had seen him around the station plenty. "You're saying Inspector Rainey sent you?"

"You're Hilsom, right? Yeah, I got some piries, she said to bring them over, keep an eye on them, and report to you."

"Yes," he said dryly. "I suppose that's good. She's almost done collecting the people for the compulsion."

A few of the regulars came over when he waved, and they brought the two piries out of the lockwagon, who were kicking and cursing the whole way.

"Where do we put these two, sir?" one of them asked.

"This is very unseemly behavior on your part, Mister Kenorax," Hilsom said. "For now ... first, um, Miss—" He bent down close and peered at her name badge. "Ah, Welling. Related to the inspector?"

"Sister."

"Never would have guessed." He glanced around, and pointed across the garden. "Check out those huts over there to make sure they're clear. If one is, we'll put them in it until Rainey comes to get the show started."

Corrie gave the tosser a salute and went over to the huts. The first hut she checked out had a bunch of blue-haired tyzos humming and rubbing stones together. They didn't even seem to note her when she came in, and ignored her as she looked around. She was tempted to push one of them over just to see what they would do, but decided to listen to the saint on her shoulder.

The next hut was also occupied, by two red-haired tyzos and a familiar face.

"Corrie!" Joshea Brondar was sitting at the table, the two tyzos hovering over him like they would wallop him if he got up. He even started to stand when he saw her, but then sat back down as the two men edged over him.

He didn't look bound or hurt. And he was wearing a Constabulary inspector's vest.

"Joshea, what the blazes are you doing here? Where's Minox? Is he here?"

"I don't know where he is, not anymore," Joshea said. He glanced awkwardly at the tyzo guards. "He was in a bad way, and . . . I brought him here. It was probably a stupid idea, but it was what he wanted."

"Why the rutting blazes would he want to come here?"

Joshea hedged for a moment. Did he not want to say things in front of these tyzos?

She reached out to take Joshea's hand, pull him up out of his chair. One of the tyzos moved like lightning, somehow moving Joshea and keeping her from touching him without laying a hand on her. Which was smart, because that tyzo would get a new elbow if he touched her.

"Excuse me, pal, but I'm going to get my friend out of here." She reached out again.

The tyzo held up a hand, and that seemed to stop her as she stepped closer, despite never making contact. It was almost as if he made her want to stop walking. "When the damaged mage returns."

"When the what?" Corrie asked. "You know I'm a rutting stick, don't you? I could arrest the two of you and drop you into the cages at the stationhouse."

"You will not. He needs to stay until the damaged mage returns."

"What the blazes is going on, Joshea?" she snarled.

"Minox—in his state, he thought . . . he thought the Tsouljans here could help him. I don't know, I was scared, I didn't know what was going on with him. It was something magic, right? They're calling him the damaged mage."

"Where is he? Returns from where?"

"From where he went," the tyzo said cryptically. "He was not in balance, according to the fel."

Corrie didn't know what to make of that sewage. "Josh, can you translate that rubbish?"

"They were doing something to him. Healing him, fixing him, I don't know. And he . . . he exploded, like he did in the hospital ward. And then he ran out of the compound. And they haven't let me leave since."

"Yeah, I ain't having that," Corrie said. "You listen to me, tyzo. My brother is in trouble out there, and when I find him and find out what your folk did to him, I'm going to take it out of your skin."

"You will not," the tyzo said.

That tore it. She drew out her handstick and brought it down on his arm, and followed that with slamming it into his chest, and drove the palm of her left hand into his chin.

At least she would have, but each swing and strike hit nothing but empty air. She threw a few more blows at him, but each time he was gone by the time her fist reached where he had been.

"Continue if you wish," he said calmly. "We will wait until the damaged mage returns."

"Fine," Corrie said, trying to hide how winded she was. "Sit tight, Josh. We'll sort this out."

She left the hut to see Hilsom staring at her. "Is it empty?"

"No, sir," she said.

"Well, then find me one," he said. "Stop wasting time."

Corrie went into the next hut, all the while forming a short list of who she would punch in the face before the day was over.

Tricky was at the top.

———◆——◆———

The sun was almost down as Satrine led the final lock-wagon over to the Hieljam household. She hadn't yet felt any of the horrid effects that Leppin had warned her about. Maybe she would be just fine.

And maybe this case would come together, Welling would be fine, and they would both sign in tomorrow morning with some perfectly ordinary murder to solve.

A few people stood on the stoop of the Hieljam house as they approached. Not muscle or bodyguards, though. These were respectable folk, and two of them were in Druth attire. Fancy suits, northtown types. The rest were Fuergan, but their clothes also gave a sense of refinement. Longer vests than the rest of the Fuergan folk on the street, for one.

"Inspector Rainey?" one of them called out as the wagon slowed down.

"That's me," Satrine said. "I take it we're expected?"

"You've been very efficient this afternoon, Inspector. So your arrival was anticipated."

Satrine cautiously walked up the steps. "And you all are?"

"Forgive me," the man who had been taking the lead said. "Heston Chell, of Colevar and Associates. I've brought some of my colleagues, as well as a few dignitaries from the Fuergan embassy. I understand you are carrying some writs?"

"I am," Satrine said, wishing she still had Hilsom by her side for this one. Chell reached out and took the writs from her. He glanced through the sheets, passing some of them to the fellows around him.

"Yes, well, the search warrant seems to be in order, though there are provisions and limitations that will be imposed."

"I'm sorry?" Satrine asked.

"However, I'm empowered to allow you entrance to the household—to you and your people—so you may begin."

He went up the steps and opened the door, leading Satrine and her people through the antechamber into a sitting room. The passel of officials followed close behind.

Sitting on low, elaborately embroidered chairs were Hieljam ab Tishai and her brother-husband ab Orihla. They had a retinue of servants surrounding them, all of them with sheer cloths draped over their heads. On the floor in front of them, a painting of Hieljam ab Wefi Loriz lay flat, surrounded by flower petals, candles, and bowls of water and sand.

Chell stepped over to Satrine. "Now you must understand, this search is explicitly intruding upon the *utiet-kha*, one of the rituals of mourning."

"I've been at two others so far," Satrine said. "I'm almost insulted I wasn't invited."

He lowered his voice. "In this one, from what I'm told by the fine people from the Fuergan embassy, the official transfer of household title of *natir* is being bestowed upon Hieljam ab Tishai, as well as assets, debts, and obligations."

"Fine," Satrine said. "We have—"

"I'm telling you this to make something clear to you, Inspector Rainey. My colleagues and myself, as well as these fine people from the Fuergan embassy, were already assembled in the household for this ceremony. I would hate for you to think that Hieljam ab Tishai and her esteemed family were being anything less than transparent or cooperative in your investigations, calling an army of lawyers to shield her in some sort of way."

"Of course," Satrine said, letting her disdain drip in her voice. "I never considered otherwise." She stepped over to Hieljam ab Tishai. "I've come here—"

Chell slid in front of her. "I'm afraid, as an aspect of the ceremony, Hieljam ab Tishai is unable to speak to you."

"I have a Writ of Compulsion for her, as well as Hieljam ab Orihla."

"Unfortunately," Chell said, in a tone that made it seem like he thought things were hardly unfortunate, "I've been informed by the fine people from the Fuergan embassy that neither Hieljam ab Tishai nor ab Orihla are subject to a Writ of Compulsion. They are, of course, Fuergan citizens with residency in our nation in good standing, and I can assure you their paperwork is impeccably in order."

"Even still," Satrine said, trying to remember exactly what Hilsom had said with the Lyranans. "A Writ of Compulsion can apply to foreign nationals, even ones with good standing. There is precedent—"

"There most certainly is, though I would have to review the relevant statutes in the law, as well as trade agreements, residency code . . . I wouldn't want to bore you, Inspector Rainey."

"Never," Satrine said.

"However, as the *natir* of a *lavark* level family, certain rights and entitlements are bestowed upon Hieljam ab Tishai and her *hriesa*." He indicated Hieljam ab Orihla.

"Really, Mister Chell?" Satrine asked, turning her attention hard on Hieljam ab Tishai. "So now you are Lavark-jai Tishai? Is that what I'm to believe?"

"Inspector Rainey, it really is inappropriate . . ."

She cut Chell off this time. "I have good ears, Tish. And an excellent memory." She pointed over to the dining room. "In there, two nights ago, you said, albeit absently, that you would not become *lavark*. Not enough money. And yet, here you are."

Hieljam ab Tishai did not respond or even react. The servants behind her, though, began to hum a low note.

"Really, Inspector, this is out of the bounds of your applicable writs."

"I'm only speaking while in the household, Mister Chell. I am in the house on a legitimate Writ of Search."

"You aren't searching the household."

"Boys," she said to her half-dozen regulars. "Scour the household for any and all paperwork that may pertain to shipping from and to Imachan. Don't worry if you can't read the language, seize anything that looks promising." She raised an eyebrow at Chell and the rest of the assembled folk. "Now, I will wait here and see what my men find. In the meantime, I'll exercise my own rights, and vocally pontificate key points of the case."

"This is most unseemly," one of the fine people from the Fuergan embassy said.

"And him?" Chell said, looking at Phillen.

"Senior Page Hace is assigned to watch over my health and safety." She gave a sharp glance to him, hoping he would pick up her cue to not object to her giving him a title bump. Phillen probably had a few more months before reaching Senior Page. "Hace, do not let any of these people impose themselves on my person."

"Yes, ma'am," Phillen said, taking his set of irons off his belt. He held them like he would clap them across the skull of anyone who laid a finger on her.

"Now, I'm wondering what's changed here. Everyone I've talked to about this case—as radically different as their stories are from each other, there is one consistent point—everyone agrees that the death of your *isahresa* means a financial loss all around. And your man—Uite? You know he's been talking to us?"

That got something from Hieljam ab Tishai. Her eyes locked onto Satrine, hot and angry.

"Do you not want me to talk about what he said about the money? At least in front of the fine people from the Fuergan embassy?"

Hieljam ab Tishai looked like she wanted to say many things, but she was literally biting on her lip to keep them in. The hum from the servants became even lower—a deep, throaty sound that didn't seem like it could be made by people.

"I can talk about your warehouse, though. The one with

the Imach goods—that sticky sweet stuff? Which you were selling to the Kierans, but the Lyranans stamped off on?"

Tishai glanced at Orihla, just as the servants reached down to the floor and produced a long stole.

"I'm sure you aren't concerned, even though we have that material impounded for now. Because timing wasn't an issue, was it?" Satrine turned to Chell and the other officials. "I mean, I'm sure she showed you all how, on paper, they seem to be solvent. Right? To validate the claim she's making to taking the mantle of *lavark*?"

The fine people from the Fuergan embassy all looked deeply uncomfortable.

"Inspector Rainey," began Mister Chell, "perhaps I've been unclear about what is happening here. This is a sacrosanct ritual of the Fuergan culture, and you are behaving like a wild dog."

"I'm behaving like an inspector in the Maradaine Constabulary, Mister Chell. First rule in looking for a murderer? Ask who benefits." She spun back on Tishai. "Who seems to be benefitting, Lavark-jai Tishai?"

If Hieljam ab Tishai could kill with just furrowing her brow, Satrine would have been dead.

The regulars returned, carrying bunches of paper. "We, um, found this in an office, Inspector. It—seems to be something."

"That'll do, boys," she said. "I'm certain this will help me get to the bottom of things, Lavark-jai. Don't you worry one bit about it. So, we'll take this stuff with us to the party I've put together."

"Party?" Mister Chell asked.

"Oh, right," Satrine said. "You see, perhaps you are protected from my Writ of Compulsion. But I'll tell you who isn't: Kenorax, Hajan, Taiz. I have them and some of theirs all bundled together over at the Tsouljan enclave. I think between all of us, we'll work out the truth of this."

The servants, now chanting words with that same impossible throaty voice they were humming with, placed the stole over Tishai's shoulders. "Khueth hre. Ahmen hre. Lavark hre."

With that, Hieljam ab Tishai lek Lavark sprang to her feet. "I will not let that pack of liars destroy me or the work of my *isahresa*," she shouted.

"Lavark-jai," Chell said, holding up his hands as if to calm her. "You have no need to—"

"And I will not let you disrespect me, Inspector," Hieljam ab Tishai snarled. "I will go to this 'party' of yours, and defend the business of the Hieljam from the jackals and crows who would eat at our dead."

"Well then," Satrine said. "I guess we won't need the lockwagon."

◆————◆◆————

Mirrell scowled at the setting sun. The search for Jinx had been an empty hunt, and the most useful thing it did was fill the streets with sticks, especially in the Little East. That wasn't nothing. The presence was felt. That probably stopped a lot of trouble before it even started.

No riots tonight, despite the fact that regular folk in Inemar were terrified of the Little East, and the folk in the Little East were all on edge. But nothing was breaking out.

Mirrell was annoyed by Jinx's family being out in force with it all, but he had to admit, the help mattered. One uncle was the captain over in Keller Cove, and he brought a few dozen regulars to scour Inemar for Jinx. Another one came over from East Maradaine, and then there were the cousins.

Mirrell had a hard time believing all these folks actually liked Jinx. Maybe because they didn't have to work with him.

Iorrett came back down from the apartment building he had just canvassed. "Ain't no sign of him there, sir."

"Yeah, of course not," Mirrell said. "Ain't no reason for him to go in there, is there? That'd be crazy."

Iorrett gave him an odd look. "You said to canvass it, sir."

"I know," Mirrell groused. He checked his pipe idly. That was pointless, and he knew it. He had been out of tobacco for the past hour. Still some instinct kept him looking in his pipe. "Hey, Jinx smokes, right?"

"I don't know, sir."

"No, he does, I know it." He glanced about. They were right at the edge of Fuergan properties, and there were just a few blocks between here and Keller Cove. Almost no homes or shops in those blocks; all warehouses and factories. Plenty of places to hide. "All feeling like a waste of time."

"Sir?" Iorrett asked. "What are you saying?"

He looked at Iorrett hard. "We've got our own people sticking close to Jinx's family, right?"

"Blazes, yes," Iorrett said. "I even put my cousin—he's a cadet, sir—to trail Corrie. They ain't gonna sneak him home or to the ward without us knowing."

"No, they ain't," Mirrell said. Then it hit him. "Of course, we only got it on their word that he's not there."

"Pardon?"

"Saints, we've been a patch of fools," Mirrell said. "We never actually checked the Welling house."

"Yeah, but they would tell us—"

"If it was your cousin or nephew, Iorrett, what would you do?"

"I ain't got a crazy mage for a relation, sir."

"That ain't—" Mirrell had half a mind to smack this guy. "That ain't the point. We may all be Green and Red, but family is gonna rally."

"I know, specs, we've seen them rally."

"Right, look—point is, we need to check their house for ourselves. Gather me a few regulars from the search.

No whistles, like a Quiet Call. Don't want any of Jinx's family getting word."

Iorrett nodded. "I know who to get and how. I'm on it."

"Good man. Ten minutes, however many you get, and we'll all head up to Keller Cove. And we'll storm that house if we need to."

Chapter 23

THE HOUSE WAS FAR TOO QUIET when Ferah came in. She was used to her cousins being boisterous in the sitting room, Zura and Amalia cooking up a storm, Pop and Timmothen arguing over some point of petty pride.

But there was none of that. Not even the cooking.

"Hello?" she called out. This was very strange. "Who's about?"

"Who's there?" The voice came from up the steps. Granny Jillian.

"It's Ferah, Granny." She bounded up the stairs to find Granny working her way down slowly. "What's going on?"

"All sorts of mess. Haven't you heard?"

"No, what?" Her day had been full of its own mess. Major accidents in the chicken slaughterhouse and the fish cannery, as well as the usual dose of *effitte* wastes who would try to rip her head off when she helped them. That is if they weren't in trance. Brought in two of those today. She took Jillian by the arm and helped her down.

"I don't know all of it, but there's an All-Eyes for Minox. He's apparently lost his senses, throwing magic around and who knows what. Oh, don't flinch at that, Ferah. We all know what he is."

Ferah hadn't even realized she had done that. "So where is everyone?"

"Most everyone is searching through Inemar, trying to find him. Even Amalia. She insisted on going out to Racquin streets."

Aunt Amalia never did that. Ferah knew Amalia grew up in Caxa, but she never went there anymore.

"So it's just you?"

"Me and Zura, but she's locked herself in the basement, praying at that shrine of hers. She's been plum useless since the news hit."

"What about my mother? Surely she—"

Granny Jillian sighed as they reached the bottom of the stairs. "She got hurt—not too bad, mind you—but hurt during some trouble at Ironheart. And . . . Minox might be responsible."

"What?"

"Might, girl. We don't have facts, and we're not going to iron or string up any man without them. Emma and some of the young ones are down at Ironheart with her."

"All right," Ferah said. "I should—"

"Stay here with me, girl," Granny Jillian said. She cast a glance over at the basement door. "I need a pair of hands I can count on, you know?"

"Of course," Ferah said, though it made her uncomfortable. But she would stay, and later have a few choice words with Aunt Zura. "Where do you want to be?"

"Kitchen," Granny said. "Let's see if we can find some decent grub. I'm not used to skipping meals."

Ferah laughed and led her in there, sitting her at the back table. "I'm sure there's some bread, cheese, and dried sausage on hand. I could try to cook something . . ."

"Those aren't your talents, dear," Granny said. "Mine either. Why do you think the cooks of this house are the daughters of other women?" This was something Granny had said over and over.

"Fair enough," Ferah said, taking a jug of cider out of the icebox. She was going to need at least that, if not cracking into the beers.

There was a tapping on the window of the back door.

"What's that?" Granny asked.

"Hold on," Ferah said, moving closer. Who would knock at that door? Who would come around to the back? She opened the door a crack.

Evoy was there, standing a few steps away from the door.

"Evoy?" Ferah said. She hadn't seen him in weeks, and he looked horrible. She had dragged fetid bodies in *effitte*-trance out of abandoned dens that looked better than her brother did.

"Hello," he said, looking down at the ground. "I, um, I was just . . . I'm sorry to be a bother."

"Do you want to come in, Evoy?" she asked. "Maybe eat something?"

"I, um . . . no, I couldn't, because . . . there's a lot of—I am hungry, of course, but . . . no. No."

She held up her hands. "It was just an offer. You can do what you want." Pushing him would probably send him running back in.

"No, I know. I will."

"All right," she said. "But you knocked for a reason, right?"

"Mother isn't there, is she? She'll make me—I don't want to come in and—"

"No, she's not, but . . . I need to tell you something." Ferah moved in closer.

"Arm's length!"

Her brother had reached the point where he refused to let her approach him. "Fine." She stayed in the doorway. "I don't have all the details, but—"

"Mother's been hurt, she's at Ironheart." He said it like he had just realized it, putting whatever pieces he had accumulated together. "That would—of course!"

"Evoy!" Ferah immediately regretted snapping at him, but she needed to bring him back to the conversation. "I know you aren't going to want to go to the ward to see her—"

"No, no, definitely not."

"But perhaps you could write something for her? Some kind words?"

"I could, yes," he said. He turned and went back toward the stable. He got three steps and stopped. "Not why I . . . I came for a reason."

Ferah was getting frustrated. There was a reason why she stopped bothering reaching out to him. "What is it?"

"Minox."

"He's not here right now, Evoy. In fact, he's—"

"He's in the stable," Evoy said. "And he's in very bad shape."

Ferah bounded down the back steps and ran to the stable, barely noticing how hard she checked into Evoy on her way through. She tore open the stable doors, and there was Minox.

Saints, he was in a state.

Minox was a sweaty, sticky mess, stripped down to his trousers. He was babbling nonsense while he made scratch marks on the wall with the chalk in his left hand.

His left hand was truly horrifying. It looked like it belonged on a dead body.

"Minox," she said. He didn't respond.

"Minox!" she shouted.

He twitched in her direction, but otherwise continued his chalk scratching unabated.

She moved closer. He wasn't writing anything of substance—literally just scrawls and scratches.

"He came in here, and he didn't seem right. But then

he got stranger and stranger, and soon he wasn't making any sense at all."

For Evoy to be the one saying that, Minox must have really been bad off.

"Minox," Ferah said, kneeling down in front of him so he'd have to look at her. "It's Ferah. Do you know where you are?"

"Abidada," Minox said, his mouth just flopping and drooling as he spoke. His eyes were dull and glassy. It was like there was nothing of him left in there.

━━━◆━◆━◆━━━

A yellow-haired Tsouljan greeted Satrine as she arrived at the compound with the Fuergans and Hace in her shadow. Bur Rek-Uti, that was his name.

"We welcome you, Inspector Rainey," he said, pronouncing her name in two distinct syllables. "We hope that you are able to conclude your investigation with this . . . collective."

"You aren't the only one, sir."

"Allow me to guide you to this grove of trees. I'm afraid your assembled group will be too large for our huts to fit comfortably. It appears that tonight will be quite pleasant, at least in terms of atmosphere. We have done our best to make you comfortable."

Indeed, a bunch of green-hairs were setting up tables and benches underneath a trio of the sweet-smelling trees filled with purple flowers. Satrine was grateful. This was going to be unpleasant, but at least the setting would be lovely.

Hilsom came up to her from the grove. Satrine waved to her regulars to lead Hieljam ab Tishai and ab Orihla to seats at the table, where Kenorax, Hajan, and Taiz were already in place, each with their own people close by.

"You do have a plan?" Hilsom asked.

"You mean, besides shake them all around until someone confesses?"

He did not look amused.

"Here's what I've got, Hilsom—four groups of people who all had a hand in some shipping venture that came through Maradaine. I've been churning it in my skull now, and I've got a good grip on the whats and whys behind this murder."

"Court of law is mostly interested in the whos and hows. You have to—oh, saints, is that Heston Chell?"

Chell was staying right at the Hieljam's elbows, making sure that none of the regulars went a step out of line with them.

"You know him?"

"We were a couple years apart at RCM," Hilsom said. "I take it he's representing the Hieljam family."

"He tried to keep me from legally compelling them. Fortunately I was able to goad ab Tishai into coming along."

"Eyes on him," Hilsom said. "Cheever is a tabby cat, but Chell has teeth. Be aware you don't overstep."

"My, Mister Hilsom, I wasn't aware of that."

"Don't give me any mouth, Rainey."

Satrine didn't feel any strong need to respond to that, and instead approached her assembled group. They all sat, glowering at Satrine and the rest of the Constabulary. There were several regulars behind them all, including Corrie Welling. She was at the very end, near the Lyranans, her focus more on one of the huts instead of the group. She was also the only one of these regulars who looked like she'd been in uniform for more than a month.

"Welling," she said, coming up to Corrie. "Any word on the All-Eyes?"

"None that I've rutting heard," Corrie said. "I've been here."

"Right," Satrine said. She glanced around to find a

page who wasn't Hace. "You! Do you know where Inspector Mirrell is on his manhunt?"

The page came up, giving her a crisp salute. "I don't, but I can start a running word. We've got a lot of feet in the neighborhood tonight."

"Good," she said. "Tell him I need him and his people to come here." Keep it simple, no explanations. Mirrell would grouse. Let him. She needed some bodies who could handle trouble if it broke out.

And something deep in her gut told Satrine that it was going to. As the page ran off, she turned her attention back to her assembly of interested parties.

"Good evening," she said to everyone. "I'll start by stating that this is an official Constabulary inquiry, invoked under compulsion. This inquiry is being observed by representatives from the City Protector and Justice Advocate. Your statements here are a matter of record and can be presented as evidence in court. Your statements here are presumed truthful and if proven false can be used in charges against you."

Mister Chell cleared his throat. "I would like to assert that Miss and Mister Hieljam are not here under compulsion, and their statements cannot be used in charges of Willful Falsehood."

"So noted," Hilsom said.

"You have us assembled, albeit at force," Heizhan Taiz said. "So what do you wish to ask us?"

Satrine considered this carefully, having drummed over the points and questions in her head all afternoon. She had her finger on the what and why, but not a full grasp. Now to draw the rest out of them, needle them until they led her to the who.

"We have two connected things," Satrine said. "A dead body and a warehouse full of an intriguing shipment."

"And that pertains to me, how?" Mister Hajan asked.

Satrine didn't directly acknowledge him and pressed on. "The dead man—a Fuergan man, here to meet with you, Mister Kenorax—"

"I never came here!"

"But killed with an Imach weapon."

"A Kadabali weapon," Hajan corrected.

"And the body marked with Lyranan writing. And then we have that shipment. Imach goods—excuse me ... Ghaladi goods," she said on Hajan's glare. "Marked to be delivered to you, Mister Kenorax, and paperwork stamped with a Lyranan seal."

"So you've told us, Inspector," Taiz said. "Do you have evidence that these are connected?"

"Well, there is definitely the curiosity that the goods have a Lyranan inspection seal, but not a Druth one. Did we check into that, Mister Hilsom?"

Before he could answer, Hieljam ab Orihla interrupted. "Every shipment cleared Druth customs completely legitimately."

"And that's the thing that really puzzles me," Satrine said, though she wasn't puzzled at all, not on this point. "Because your records showed the goods were scheduled to be sent to Kenorax, who would then send them back to you, to then deliver back to Imachan and Fuerga. The Kierans aren't charged, but rather take a commission."

"Please do not refer to me as 'the Kierans,'" Kenorax said. "I have a name, and I am not a whole people."

"Apologies."

"Are there actual questions here, Inspector?" Chell asked.

"Yes, this is most irregular," Mister Cheever added, giving a small nod to Chell, like they were in union with each other. Chell ignored the man.

Satrine turned her attention to Kenorax. "What were you doing with these goods—the *sukkar*?"

"Nothing, Inspector. As you note, I never received them. I never received the commission from Hieljam ab Wefi or his factors in Maradaine." He indicated the two Hieljam spouse-siblings.

"What were you going to do with the goods?"

"I'm not qualified to answer that."

"Not qualified to say why you're earning a commission?"

"Inspector," Kenorax said, his tone condescending. "I may be compelled to be here, I might have to answer all questions honestly under threat of imprisonment . . . but I'm in no way obligated to give you answers you like."

"All right," Satrine said. She expected hostility. Time to give him a yes or no question. "Does your commission involve a facility you are having built on a plot of land in Shaleton?"

Kenorax looked suitably surprised by that.

"Mister Kenorax?"

"Yes," he said quietly.

"Here's what I think," Satrine said, moving over to the Hieljams and Hajan. "This *sukkar—hsugir—*whatever we call it, is the heart of the matter."

"I hate to interrupt," Cheever said. "But what does it matter if they are doing something with this, how did you call it? *Shu-gar?*"

"What matters is they both were fully invested in it. Isn't that right?" She looked at Tishai and Hajan. "Grown in various parts of Imachan, including Kadabal and Ghalad, and it needs to be processed. I saw one the of boilhouses when I was there years ago."

"You did?" This was Bur Rek-Uti. Satrine noticed for the first time that he, as well as a whole collection of Tsouljans of all four hair colors, were standing to the side observing everything. He sounded shocked.

Satrine didn't answer the Tsouljans. She kept her focus on Hajan. "I'm guessing that Imachan—Ghalad—doesn't have the capacity to process materials that Druthal does. Nor does Fuerga. I asked myself, why bring things all the way out here and then send it back East? And the answer was plain as day. None of your nations matches Druthal in manufacturing goods."

Which was why Shaleton. The whole west side of Maradaine had become factories, workhouses, and canneries for large-scale processing to supply the war in the islands. Most of those had been shuttered when there was no longer a need for regular shipments of uniforms, weapons, and food preserves to go halfway across the ocean. But the structure and technology still existed.

"That's why you're here in Maradaine in the first place, shipping Druth cloth, metalwork, and woodwork as luxury goods back home."

"That was why this one convinced me we had to bring it here," Hajan snarled, pointing at Hieljam ab Orihla. "He said they could increase its value tenfold for our investment! But when he couldn't get it done, his concubine brought in Wefi Loriz to solve the matter."

"You would not respect my title or standing, you impudent swine!" Hieljam ab Tishai spat back at him. "If you had bothered to listen to me, my *isahresa* would not have needed to come!"

"Do not inflate your value, woman," Hajan said. "Neither of you could build the facility you needed on your own."

Satrine jumped back in. "And that's why you went to Kenorax." She turned back to the Kieran man. "You needed something far more than a boilhouse—you needed a—" She struggled for a word.

"Refinery?" Kenorax offered smugly. With his role out in the open, he now seemed quite proud. "And the last thing they wanted was for the Druth to take control of yet another luxury good. So they came to me, yes, so they could have Druth ingenuity without you getting your grubby hands on it."

"Because you had the means to invest in a refinery," Satrine said. She took an educated guess. "But you weren't ready to start the work, that was the problem."

"He didn't—" ab Tishai started to her feet, before catching herself and sitting back down, silent.

"Was there something you wanted to add, Lavark-jai?"

She stayed silent.

"This is very fascinating," Taiz said. "But it really has nothing to do with me or the domain of my office."

Satrine turned her attention to him. He and Nengtaj both sat in their chairs, looking disinterested and haughty.

"You're quite right, Mister Taiz," she said. "I cannot figure out why the Lyranans are involved."

"Thank you," he said. "Then perhaps we may be free to leave."

"No," Satrine said. "I said I can't figure out why. But it is plain that you are. Specifically, that you've decided to involve yourself."

"Because of a seal?" Nengtaj was engaging. "It is a standard inspection that our government performs in the eastern oceans. It is not of Druth concern."

"The seal, among other things. But your government has taken it upon themselves to police the eastern seas."

"There are pirates, smugglers—"

"Yes, fine. But your actions are telling. For example— Officer Welling?"

"Oy, what?" Corrie asked, looking annoyed to be called upon. Her eye was definitely on the hut. Was it possible Minox was there, and Corrie knew? He had said something about coming to the Tsouljans before.

Satrine couldn't focus on that, couldn't interrupt

things to find out. If Minox was here, and if Corrie knew, then they would have to sort that out later. "You were in the riot last night when the Lyranans joined in, yes?"

"Yeah, what of it?"

"How did the Lyranans become involved in the riot?"

"Yeah, well," Corrie said. "The feeks and machs were all smashing each other up, and we sticks were trying to pull them apart. Then a cadre of tyzos marched in, started knocking down everyone in there."

Every one of the assembled suspects flinched and snarled at Corrie's speech.

"A cadre?" Satrine said. "So they appeared to be organized?"

"Yeah, I'd say so."

"So, Mister Taiz, I put the question to you: why have the Lyranans here in Maradaine taken it upon themselves to police the Little East?"

Taiz seemed to give the barest bit of a smile. "Because someone has to, Inspector Rainey. It is not like your Constabulary took much interest until right now." He stood up, and Nengtaj followed his lead. "I believe I am done with this charade."

"Sit down, Mister Taiz," Satrine said, standing in front of him.

He gave a glance off in one direction, and then said, "No, I think I will be leaving now."

He took a step, and the regulars went to grab at him and Nengtaj. Satrine reached out to stop him herself, but then she heard a sound that triggered an instinctive reaction.

She grabbed Taiz by the front of his robe and spun him in front of her, just in time for three darts to strike him in the back. He suddenly went insensate, falling down like a sack of potatoes.

Satrine had no time to deal with that, as Pra Yikenj and a dozen other Lyranans were charging across the field.

———— •—• ————

Ferah put her hand across Minox's forehead. He was scorching hot with fever.

"Saints," she said. "Evoy, help me get him up."

"I . . . I don't think—"

"Damn it, Evoy!" Ferah shouted. "He's going to die unless you help me get him into the house!"

Something clicked in Evoy's eyes, and he ran over, getting under Minox's arm as Ferah took the other side. Minox offered no resistance as they hauled him into the house. Granny Jillian stood at the back door.

"Oh my saints," she said as they brought him in. "What happened to him?"

"That's not what matters," Ferah said. "I need to break his fever or he'll never make it. Bring him to the tub."

They carried him to the downstairs water closet, which included a large bathing tub. They placed Minox inside it. "Start pumping, Evoy."

Evoy got the water flowing on Minox.

"What can I do?" Granny asked.

"My bag is by the door," Ferah said. "Get it for me."

Ferah was back out to the kitchen to pound on the basement door. Now was not the moment for Acserian religious sewage. "Zura! Open the blasted door right now!"

No response from Zura.

"Zura, saints help me, I will knock this door down and drag you up by your hair!" Ferah shouted. Wouldn't be the first time she had to break through a locked door to save a life.

Now she heard steps come up from the basement, and the door unlatched. Zura came out, cold fire in her eyes. "By all that is holy, Ferah, why would you speak so profanely to me?"

"Because Minox is dying. Do we have any ice on hand?"

"No, child," Zura said. "Iceman comes tomorrow. Why do you want that?"

"Minox is in heavy fever," Ferah said, going back to the water closet. Granny had brought her bag. She dug through to find something in her kit that could help. *Doph* wouldn't help. Oil of mesk? That might mitigate the fever, as well as challon root resin. She pulled out the vials and went over to the tub.

"It's worse than I feared," Zura said, kissing her knuckle and rubbing it on her forehead. "He is taken, he is gone."

"Not if I can help it," Ferah said, rubbing the oil on his forehead. She then daubed the resin on his tongue. His face was covered in some sort of gritty grime. Ferah had no idea what it was. She grabbed a cloth and started to scrub it off.

"Look at his hand!" Zura screeched. "He is unclean, I tell you! I knew this day would come!"

Ferah was about to snap back at her aunt when Granny Jillian slapped Zura hard across the face. "We'll have none of that about any of my grandchildren."

Evoy crept over to the tub. "He could do it, I think."

"What?" Ferah asked.

Evoy leaned in over Minox. "Remember the snows last winter, Minox? Don't you want to be in the snow?"

"Too . . . hot . . ." Minox whimpered.

"What are you doing?"

"Planting the idea in his head," Evoy said. "I know it's too hot, Minox. If only it were winter again. If only there was snow."

"How does that help?" Ferah asked. She started to think of other things she could do. How far to Ironheart? Could she get him there in time? For all she knew, more riots were brewing in the Little East. Creedport Ward was closer, but it was a joke. They couldn't do a damn thing. Where did the iceman come from? Their stock was in great houses in the Keller Cove docks, somewhere. Maybe one of the icehouses would be a good place to take him. "We need a cab," she started to say.

"The idea is there," Evoy said quietly. "Now he just needs to be motivated."

Evoy plunged Minox's entire head under the water.

"Evoy!" Ferah shouted. She dove on top of them, trying to claw her brother's hands off of Minox's head. "You're killing him!"

"He needs this!" Evoy shouted.

Granny Jillian tried to grab at Evoy as well, while Zura dropped to her knees in further prayer.

Unable to pull Evoy's hands off—how did he get so strong living in the stable like that?—Ferah grabbed Minox's shoulders to try to pull him out of the water.

"Give us the winter!" Evoy shouted.

Ferah was about to knock her brother in the teeth when she noticed ice crystals forming around her hands. She shrieked and pulled out of the tub, and Evoy did exactly the same. Suddenly all the water became a solid block of ice.

"Too much!" Evoy shouted.

"Minox!" Ferah slammed her fist against the ice. She hit it again and again, and it started to crack.

Then it shattered.

And there was Minox, gasping for breath but alert, eyes taking in the whole room.

"Ferah?" he asked. "Where—am I home?"

"You are," she said cautiously. "How do you feel?"

"Strange," he said. "Hungry. Confused. But . . . present."

"You weren't before?" she asked.

"His hand is still unclean!" Zura shouted.

Minox lifted his hand up and looked at it with a strange regard. "Curious."

Evoy stood up straight. "That's settled, then. Can't stay." He bolted out of the water closet.

"Minox," Ferah said, looking at his hand. It hadn't changed much—still that almost glassy black. But now instead of looking dead and withered, it was flush and active. Minox flexed his fingers while studying his hand, ignoring her. "Minox," she said again. "Do you think you're all right now?"

"I'm not . . . out of balance," he said cautiously.

She touched her hand against his forehead. The fever was gone. "What do you remember?"

He looked about. "I know that I shouldn't be sitting in the tub with the rest of you gawking. Zura?"

Zura's eyes went wide, looking at Minox as if he were a dog that started talking to her. "Yes?"

"Would you be so kind as to bring me a clean uniform and vest?"

She ran out of the room without answering, but she went up the back kitchen stairway, so Ferah presumed she was complying. Granny followed her out.

"Let's get you out of there," Ferah said, grabbing his good hand. He took her assistance ably, standing up and stepping out of the tub.

"The details of my experience are still . . . unclear," he said. "But I remember reaching the stable, and working through some ideas about the case."

"I think you can let the case rest for now, Minox," Ferah said, passing him a towel.

"On the contrary," Minox said. "The pieces are now clicking quite cleanly. Once I'm dressed I must—"

Granny Jillian stuck her head in the water closet. "Hate to trouble you, dears, but right now an Inspector Mirrell is at the door with quite a few regulars at his back. He says if Minox is here, he'll have to bring him in."

Ferah tried to think of what to do—perhaps hide him back in the stable, or down in the basement—when Minox answered.

"Tell Mirrell to come in and sit. I'll be with him as soon as I'm dressed."

Chapter 24

MIRRELL WAS CERTAIN that Jinx was in the house now. If he wasn't, they would have let him in right away to check it out. The Wellings were an old-blood Green and Red family; they'd cooperate, unless they were raising the walls for their own.

"Specs!" A page came running over through the dozen regulars he had on hand. "They're calling for you over at the Tsouljan place."

"Who's calling for me?" Mirrell asked. "Is it Tricky or the captain?"

"It's Inspector Rainey," the page said. "She says she needs you and your search team on hand."

"Well, she's going to have to wait," Mirrell said. He pounded on the door. Of course, he was expecting that old lady to show up again and try to shoo him off.

The door opened again, the old woman giving him hard eyes. "Inspector Mirrell, was it?"

"Yes, ma'am," he said. "Like I said, I'm just here—"

"I know why you're here, son."

He wasn't going to take that attitude, even from the old woman. "If I have to I'll get a Writ of Search and kick the door down. We'll all storm through."

"No such jot," she said. "What are you, Third Class? I may be retired but I still outrank you."

"Ma'am—"

"Ma'am is Inspector First Class Jillian Welling, thank you," she said. "Probably sat at your desk in Inemar House."

He had to chuckle at that. "Yes, of course. My apologies. We are on the hunt for your grandson, who—let me make clear, we're just looking out for his well-being." He didn't really have time for this.

"You've got too much mouth for your own good," the old lady said. "So shut it and listen."

"Yes, ma'am," Mirrell said, almost out of reflex. This woman reminded him too much of his own mother.

"You can come inside, Inspector Mirrell. Just you. None of those babies with crossbows over there."

Mirrell's gut told him this was some sort of trick, but he wasn't sure what that meant. This was still a Green and Red house—they weren't going to jump him or anything. Maybe a ploy for Minox to run away or something.

"Fine," he said. He turned to Iorrett. "Get the house flanked, watch the exits."

"Aye, sir."

Mirrell turned back to the old woman and lifted up his hands. "All right," he said. "You lead."

She backed up enough to let him into the antechamber. "Hang your belt on the hooks," she said, pointing to the hangers on the wall. "You can leave your weapons here."

"You should know I'm not supposed to do that, ma'am."

"I know you aren't coming into my house with a loaded crossbow, son."

Mirrell took off his belt and hung it on a hook. There were plenty of hooks there, but right now no one else's belt was hanging. Probably because every other Welling who had one was out in the streets right now.

She led him to the sitting room and showed him a chair. "You want tea or anything like that?"

"I'm not here to sit and chat. This is—"

"You don't need to be rude, Inspector. I was simply—"

"I am here to find Inspector Welling and make sure he is not a danger to himself or others. I don't have time—"

"Then you've done the former, Mirrell." Welling stood in the doorframe, looking pale and drawn, but far stronger than he had looked earlier in the day. He was dressed in a fresh shirt and inspector's vest, and his hair was damp. Oddest thing of all—odd being relative where Jinx was concerned—he wore a leather glove over his left hand. Mirrell didn't know why anyone would do such a thing in this heat. "I suppose you're going to burden me with proving the latter."

"Give me a good reason why I shouldn't," Mirrell said.

"Thank you, Grandmother," Jinx said. "I'm fine here."

"If you say so," the old lady said, giving Mirrell one more glare. "Call if you need anything. Ferah and I will be right in the other room."

She left, and Jinx came fully into the room, standing at a distance from Mirrell. Mirrell had to admit, he certainly seemed in his proper senses right now, as much as Jinx ever did. But that didn't make Mirrell feel any better. Blazes, he was in his proper senses yesterday, and today he made a thunderstorm in a hospital, and then spent the rest of the day on the run.

"Well?"

Jinx nodded. "Today has been a unique experience for me, one I would not wish on anyone. I was unwell on every level, and I respect that there may need to be consequences for that. Right now, however, I am in charge of my faculties. I will acknowledge that you have every reason to doubt that."

"That's rutting generous of you."

Jinx blinked. "Was anyone seriously injured by my actions?"

Mirrell had to be honest. "You didn't kill anyone. When you—did what you did in the hospital, the ones who got it worst were the machs. And all of them will be on their feet and standing trial in no time."

"That is relieving."

"But somebody could have, Jinx," Mirrell pressed. "Just because this time, things didn't go too badly, it don't mean it won't next time. You're a goddamn weapon, and that's . . . that ain't something you can ignore."

"Are charges laid against me?"

"Not that I know of," Mirrell said. "We ain't exactly had the time to jump on that. We've had to find you, keep the streets safe, the station was attacked by some tyzo—"

"Attacked?"

"Some crazy tyzo skirt came through, took out half the people in the station, and broke out all her friends. Trick and Kellman both got knocked around."

"Inspector Rainey? Is she incapacitated?"

"Nah, you know Trick," Mirrell said. "She was a dog off the leash after that. She rounded up half the East with Writs of Compulsion."

"Has she? So she is still working the Hieljam murder?"

"Unless she's solved it by—" Mirrell stopped himself. He had let himself get drawn off course. "No, Jinx, we ain't doing this. I should take you down to the station-house, put you in front of the captain, and have him start an official Inquiry into your place on the force."

"Perhaps you should," Jinx said. "I know I would do the same in your position, unless new information was brought to light. I presume Inspector Rainey is also at the stationhouse, conducting her compulsion interviews?"

"No, she—damn it, Jinx!"

"I understand your frustration, Inspector Mirrell. What I've been through today, I share it. Do you know where Inspector Rainey is at this moment? It may be crucial for the resolution of the case, as well as her own safety."

Mirrell sighed. Jinx was annoying, but he was at least a straight shooter. If he wasn't going to put up a fight in being taken in, put in for Inquiry, the least Mirrell owed him was honest answers.

"She's at the Tsouljan enclave, with all her suspects."

Jinx's eyes moved back and forth, like he was reading a newssheet only he could see. Then he nodded. "Yes, of course. We must go there in all haste." He headed toward the door.

"We must what?" Mirrell chased after him.

At the antechamber, Jinx was taking Mirrell's belt off the hook. Before Mirrell could object, Jinx had offered it to him. "Despite my addled state for most of today, I've made some breakthroughs regarding the details of the case."

"Jinx, you can't—"

"Bring me in irons if you feel it's prudent," Jinx said, still holding out the offered belt. "But for the sake of the case, we must go to Inspector Rainey."

Mirrell snatched the belt out of Jinx's hands. "Once we're done there, we go back to the station, to the captain, hear?"

"On my word, Inspector Mirrell."

Mirrell put the belt on as Jinx opened the door. They both found themselves greeted by half a dozen crossbows.

"Stand the blazes down, boys," Mirrell snapped. "We found our man, and we all got a job to do."

Jinx didn't wait for them to put their arms down. He walked down the steps boldly, grabbing a crossbow off of one regular and a handstick off another. "I said with all haste, Inspector."

He was already to the street before Mirrell and the rest could get moving.

———◆━◆━◆———

A dozen shaved-headed tyzos came charging across the rutting lawn, led by a skirt with a crazy axe-like weapon, an armored arm, and death in her eyes. That woman dove in on Tricky and the tyzo boss, forcing Trick to let go and jump back.

Corrie didn't waste any time drawing her crossbow and taking a shot at one of the charging tyzos. Her aim was horrible—stupid eye—as she hit a completely different one. He went down, good enough. Another came right at her, and she had no choice but smash his face with her bow.

The rest of the sticks jumped in, going at the mad group of tyzos. Corrie's eye was on that leader, as she was taking hold of that boss like she planned to pull him out. Corrie might have hated every moment in this garden listening to Tricky prattle on, but nobody pulled this sewage on her watch. Certainly not some tyzo skirt old enough to be her mother.

Corrie dropped the smashed crossbow and jumped in on the skirt, swinging a haymaker at her stupid bald head. She only managed to brush her knuckles across the woman's jaw.

Next thing Corrie knew, there was an elbow in her nose, delivered by the arm encased in metal. Then a kick to the knee sent her down to the ground.

And in an instant that lasted a lifetime, that savage ax blade came thundering down to Corrie's chest.

The blade didn't connect. The blow was blocked by a handstick, wielded by the last person Corrie would have guessed.

"I am done with you," Tricky growled at the tyzo. In a flurry she knocked the axe up with her handstick, and then snapped a shot to the kidneys, forcing the woman back.

The tyzo wasn't quashed, though. She came back hard and fast on Trick, who had put herself between the woman and Corrie. Trick didn't give, blocking and taking shots and trading them back as best she could.

And laughing.

Rutting saints, she was laughing.

"Specs!" That page who had been shadowing Trick all damn day shouted. "You can't—" He charged in like a champ, but the tyzo barely wasted a breath clocking him down.

Trick was laughing and turning red in the face now. But she wasn't yielding.

Corrie pulled herself to her feet and brought her best into the tussle with the tyzo, forcing her to deal with the both of them. She was on her game, blocking and dodging attacks from Corrie and Tricky, like she was doing the steps of a dance she had already memorized. This was even with that one arm, which clearly had something wrong with it. Skirt winced whenever she blocked with it. That let Corrie get a few solid hits in. One good one, with her handstick, knocked that axe out of the tyzo's hand.

Then the tyzo got a look on her rutting face, as if to say, "Now I'm done fooling around." Like a cat she snatched Corrie's handstick, and knocked her across the jaw with her own stick, and then did the same to Tricky. All faster than Corrie could blink.

Tricky dropped like a stone, and Corrie wasn't doing much better. She took a wild punch through her daze, but the tyzo blocked it easily and delivered another crack across Corrie's head with her own handstick.

"Let her go!"

Blue fire wrapped around the tyzo, and she was yanked up in the air. She hung in the sky for several seconds, and then came smashing down to the earth, the fire splashing around her.

Then the fire vanished, leaving only the tyzo flat on the ground, and Joshea Brondar standing behind her.

"Corrie, I—"

His hand was outstretched, still glowing blue with flame.

"You're . . . you're . . ." Corrie was still winded. She wanted to say he was a goddamned mage, but she couldn't get the words out.

"I'm sorry," he said. "I didn't—I can't—"

His eyes were full of fear.

This was why he and Minox were friends.

A hand clawed at Corrie's arm before she could say anything. Tricky, trying to pull herself up. Still laughing, face as red as a beet, desperately trying to draw breath.

"I need some rutting help here!" Corrie shouted to anyone who'd hear. "I got an officer going down!"

Satrine held on to Corrie's shoulder like it was the only thing keeping her alive, digging her fingers into the woman's uniform. Her lungs weren't obeying anymore. Only laughter came.

"Anyone!" Corrie shouted. "Get us a Yellowshield!"

Hace came scrambling over, blood gushing from his nose. "I've got you, specs. We're gonna get you help."

"Blazes is wrong with her?" Corrie asked.

Suddenly an old Tsouljan woman, with blue hair, knelt down in front of her. She locked eyes with Satrine, also a rich, vibrant blue.

She didn't seem to speak, but words came to Satrine.

"Calm your heart. Your fear will kill you."

Satrine wasn't afraid, not anymore. She was moments ago. Afraid Yikenj would kill her, kill Corrie, kill everyone here. But her heart was racing. Pounding in panic, as she couldn't get a breath of air. One hand stayed locked on Corrie's shoulder. The other, she reached out and grabbed hold of the Tsouljan woman's arm.

The Tsouljan woman clasped both sides of Satrine's head.

And then, for a moment, she was elsewhere.

She had stepped out to the balcony to watch the snow. Clwythnn winters were usually bitter, but this night was clear and crisp, the cold barely touched her.

This night was the last night she was Quia Alia Rhythyn, Jewel of the Ironroot Clan. Kellin, the dear boy she had watched, guided, and protected now held the Scepter of the Throne as Kelldyshm II, Second King of the First Rule of the Rainstorm Clan.

Exactly as Druth Intelligence wanted.

Kellin came out on the balcony.

"You shouldn't be out here," Satrine said in her High Waish dialect. There were many reasons why, and there was no need to articulate them. Kellin knew them, and so did she. Of course many of the ones he knew were untrue.

"People already talk," he said. "It hardly matters."

"I can't be a burden on your reign." She added the comforting lie, "There's a quiet manor house outside of Donellum waiting for me."

"Not forever," he said. "I promise, once—"

"Don't make me promises," she said. "You shouldn't concern yourself."

"I—"

"Go back in. Dance with the queen." She turned and let herself drink in his sweet eyes one more time. "It's best that no one makes note of me tonight."

"As you say, Alia," he said. He stepped back, gave a slight nod of his head, and returned to the gala.

"Are you there, Lieutenant?" she asked, slipping into Druth Trade for the first time in months.

Lieutenant Dresser, the mage responsible for extract-

*ing her from Waisholm, appeared from the shadows, flesh
forming out of darkness in that disturbing way of his. "I'm
ready when you are."*

"Just another moment," Satrine said, looking out at the
frost-covered rooftops, the two moons high in the sky and
their reflection in the calm ocean. She let herself take a
deep, cold breath in, so the chill of the Waish winter stayed
in her for a little bit longer.

Satrine let out the breath.

Her hand was still clutching Corrie Welling's shoulder, but now she could breathe. Now she could get to her
feet. The Tsouljan woman stepped away.

"You all right, specs?" Hace asked her.

"I'll—I'll be fine. I think," Satrine said. Pra Yikenj was
still lying on the ground, and someone—was that Joshea
Brondar?—stood over her. The blur of the previous
events came back to her. He had stopped Yikenj magically. Uncircled mage, like Minox. She remembered now.

"Let's get a lot of irons on her," Satrine said. She
turned back to her assembled group, most of whom were
in a state of panic. The Lyranans had all been subdued
by the regulars and red-haired Tsouljans. Cheever stood
in front of the Hieljams, Hajan, and Kenorax, as if he
would guard all of them from the Lyranan onslaught.

"I apologize for this . . . unpleasantness," she said to
them. "Mister Hilsom, would you concur there is sufficient cause to arrest Miss Pra Yikenj?"

"Indeed," Hilsom said.

"Mister Cheever, would you object to her being considered a Prisoner of Extreme Peril until her hearing?"

"No," he said. "It's clear that she is sufficiently dangerous that uncommon precautions must be taken. My
office will not object."

"Good." Satrine looked back at the officers who were
ironing Pra Yikenj, who was still insensate. They had put
several sets on her, binding each limb to every other

limb. Normally, this would be High Cruelty, but Cheever's blessing gave them some leeway.

"Are we concluded?" Hieljam ab Tishai asked. "You have your killer?"

Before Satrine answered, Hieljam ab Orihla interjected, "But they wouldn't have!"

"Shush!" Hieljam ab Tishai snapped.

Mister Chell stepped forward. "I believe this has drawn to a close, Inspector. Your officials here seem to be in harmony on the matter. You have your arrest."

"No," Satrine said, speaking from her gut. "Miss Yikenj is being arrested for leading this assault here, as well as on the Inemar Stationhouse. However, I do not believe she is responsible for the murder of Hieljam ab Wefi Loriz."

"That's quite right."

Satrine didn't have to turn to know who spoke, but she did anyway. Inspector Welling came walking across the lawn, with Mirrell and a cadre of regulars at his heels. He looked surprisingly well, compared to this morning. Weary and worn, but no more so than any other day. The only truly odd aspect about him—at least, odd for Minox Welling—was the glove he wore on his left hand.

"Inspector Welling," she said, glancing over to Mirrell. "I didn't think we'd be seeing you here." Mirrell gave a noncommittal shrug in response. He didn't look happy at all, but he also seemed to accept that Welling was here, working.

"Thankfully I am," Welling said. "Not to disparage your considerable skills in investigation, but you will be needing me to solve this case."

Satrine found a warm smile imposing itself on her face despite herself. "And why is that, Inspector Welling?"

"Because of the nature of the true murder weapon." He walked under one of the trees and looked up at it. "Yes, that would be it."

"What true murder weapon?" Satrine asked. "Besides the Imach knife?"

"Kadabali knife," Hajan corrected.

"The knife killed him, no doubt," Welling said, still examining the tree. "But that was almost incidental." He plucked one of the purple flowers off the tree. "Inspector Mirrell?"

"What is it?" Mirrell snarled.

"Please be so kind to reorganize all these assembled parties, somewhere closer to the pond, I think."

"What?" Mirrell asked. "Why?"

"I will make that clear in short order," Welling said, turning to Satrine. "But first I must confer with my partner."

Chapter 25

SATRINE FOLLOWED WELLING into one of the huts. She waited a moment, watching for a facade to drop. If Welling was faking being better, he maintained it in front of her. Not even the slightest hint of relaxation came from him.

"You're all right now?" she asked.

"I am sufficiently improved from this morning," he said. "But I am not 'all right,' and on some level I don't think I ever will be."

"What do you mean?"

He paused, and then removed the glove. His hand was black and shiny, like it was made of glass.

"What happened?"

"I am unable to answer that," Welling said. "I suspect she might have an answer."

He had looked to the door of the hut, to see the same blue-haired Tsouljan who had saved her standing in the entranceway, watching them both with hard eyes.

"Who is she?" Satrine asked.

"Sevqir Fel-Sed. She's an—frankly, I'm not sure what she is. Mystic, priest, mage, all of the above."

"She did something to me," Satrine said. "Triggered a memory or touched my thoughts, but . . . I'm not sure."

"I have a suspicion that the distinctions we make between magic and telepathy and other forms of mysticism are far blurrier to her," Welling said.

"So what happened to his hand?" Satrine asked her.

Fel-Sed didn't respond. She just stared.

"I am not sure what has happened," Welling said, flexing the fingers of his altered hand. "But I can tell you the observable results. This hand is no longer part of my body proper."

"What?"

"I am no longer feeling any sensations from it, other than the flow of magical energy. I can also no longer move it the way I move this hand or any other part of my body." He held up his right hand, looking perfectly normal.

"So how are you moving it?"

"With magic," he said bluntly. "Which is, quite oddly, not difficult at all for me to do. But the sensation is wholly unnatural."

"Why do you think she knows?" Satrine asked.

He put the glove back on. "Because I believe she played a role in my hand becoming like this." He looked at Fel-Sed. "Is that accurate?"

She made a slight gesture that Satrine interpreted as an assent.

Welling looked back at Satrine. "I am telling you this because, as my partner, you have a right to know about potential liabilities in working with me. I will be sharing this with Captain Cinellan, and then I will defer to his judgment beyond that. But I would prefer to maintain my privacy as much as possible."

"Of course," Satrine said.

"You have made headway on this case in my absence," Minox said. "While I've made several realizations on my own, I do not have the full picture. Please brief me as completely as possible."

Satrine quickly ran through the key points: the Fuergan warehouse, the Imach goods, the Kieran refinery in Shaleton, and the Lyranan involvement. She also covered her first encounter with Pra Yikenj years ago.

"So the Lyranans were not involved, but involved themselves?" Welling asked. "I confess, my understanding of both geography and politics of the larger world is limited."

Satrine refrained from detailing the history of the Tyzanian Empire, which at one point touched much of the eastern world as much as the Kieran Empire had Druthal and the other Trade Nations. "Near as I can figure, they've taken the role of policing the eastern seas, and they extended that role to the Little East itself."

"They decided they were the true authority of law in the neighborhood," Welling said, nodding. "I have to concede, it was a failing on our part that they felt the opportunity existed."

"I don't buy that," Satrine said. "They're about control. Control at home and abroad."

"And they wanted control over this market—'sweet tar' is the reference I remember from one of the documents I rifled through. Inasmuch as I truly 'remember' all that."

"I saw that. They all use their own word for the stuff. 'Sugar' is as good a word as any."

"So, the sugar trade. And slaves."

That came from nowhere. "What do you mean, *slaves*?"

"It's purely hypothetical, but—your encounter on the Imach plantation was in 1200, yes? You were sent by Druth Intelligence for a reason."

"Right," Satrine said, not sure where he was going.

"In my examination of my unresolved cases, I found

a strong increase in reports of people disappearing, especially in poorer neighborhoods. The last time there had been such an increase? In 1200."

"You think they're abducting poor Druth people to work as slaves on Imach plantations?"

He glanced over to Fel-Sed, whose expression was unreadable. "My limited understanding of both Fuergan and Imach cultures tells me that they are not morally opposed to slavery, and it would explain our interests when you went there."

Satrine laughed—genuine laughter, not the odd, forced giddiness of the concoction of drugs coursing through her body.

"It is hardly amusing."

"I'm not laughing because of that, Welling," she said. "I'm just . . . thrilled that you are all right."

"I did tell you—"

"Minox," she said firmly. "You are entirely yourself, and for that I am grateful."

"As you say," he said, looking mildly uncomfortable.

"Let's put the slave trade element to the side for the time being," Satrine said.

He nodded. "We hardly have evidence of that, and it is more likely to tangle this case further, rather than illuminate it. I will add that element to my unresolved cases."

"So this 'true' murder weapon you spoke of?"

"It's right here," he said, pulling out the purple flower. "I should know, as it nearly killed me as well. Isn't that right, Miss Fel-Sed?"

<hr />

Minox walked out of the hut, pushing his way past Sevqir Fel-Sed. He half expected her to try to stop him, but she took no action.

The assembled group of suspects and other interested

parties were now over by the pond, away from the trees. Exactly as he needed them to be. Regulars were hauling off the Lyranans who had been apprehended, including Pra Yikenj.

"Leave her and the two other officials," Inspector Rainey told the regulars. "We can throw them in the lockwagons once we finish this matter."

To one side of the group, Joshea stood a few feet away from Corrie. Both of them looked deeply uncomfortable, and clearly for reasons that went beyond their injuries. In Corrie's case, Minox was surprised and proud that she was still on her feet. He approached the two of them.

"I deeply apologize for any inconvenience I have caused," he said quietly. "After I finish all this business, I will make amends."

"You rutting idiot," Corrie said. "You ain't got amends to make to me."

"Nonetheless, I will try," Minox said. Back to Joshea. "I deeply owe you for everything you did for me today."

"I did what was needed," Joshea said. He put on a smile, but he seemed to be hiding some level of shame. "I don't mind you owing me a favor, though."

Minox turned his attention back to the assembled group. Inspector Rainey had come over, and behind her Fel-Sed and a full contingent of Tsouljans had come as well. All four hues of hair were represented in this group, which Minox found oddly intriguing, given his suspicions. Fel-Sed stood at the front, looking on patiently.

"I understand that you are all entangled in the harvesting, shipping, and refining of a substance called 'sugar,'" Minox said. "That appears to be the key element behind the murder of Hieljam ab Wefi Loriz. This is relevant in terms of motive; however, I know that none of you had the means to kill him."

"If you don't believe anyone here is my *isahresa*'s

killer, then why are you wasting our time?" Hieljam ab Tishai asked.

"I am not," Minox said. "However, I will ask that you indulge me a moment. I wish to discuss the crime scene itself for a moment."

"Is that really necessary, Inspector?" This came from a well-dressed man standing with the Hieljam. Clearly their legal counsel.

"It is crucial to understand what has occurred. Hieljam ab Wefi Loriz was killed with a knife plunged into his chest, but there was no sign of fight or struggle. He was already incapacitated when he was murdered."

"Incapacitated how?" This question came from Nalassein Hajan, who looked truly interested in the answer. "Was he poisoned?"

"That was our first suspicion, but our examinarium found no evidence of that. I wondered if it was simply a poison we had no familiarity with. But a far more elegant solution occurred to me—what if it were a poison that isn't a poison?"

"What the blazes does that mean?" Hilsom asked.

"The tea he was served," Minox said. "It comes from the flowers of those trees."

"That tea isn't poisonous." This came from Kenorax. "I've had it many times."

"I believe it is completely safe under normal circumstances," Minox said. "But when magic is applied, it is a different matter."

In demonstration he drew and aimed a gentle stream of raw magic at the trees, doing nothing with the energy. The flowers turned a richer shade of purple, and shook as a haze of a similar color came flying off of them.

"Is that pollen?" Inspector Mirrell asked.

"Normally benign, I imagine," Minox said, removing the magical influence. The color faded, as did the pollen haze. He took the flower out of his pocket. "But when magicked, this flower and its pollen, I believe, become very malignant."

"Can you prove that?" This came from Hieljam ab Tishai.

"I believe so," Minox said. He went up to the gathered Tsouljans. "Suppose one of you eats this flower while I magick it."

"That is not necessary." This came from the yellow-haired Bur Rek-Uti. "I will confirm your theory on the nature of these flowers. The tea, in its natural state, is soothing and relaxing. When its properties are magically activated, it becomes a powerful intoxicant."

"I have realized that, first hand," Minox said. He looked to Fel-Sed. "Every time I came here, I was affected. I was breathing in the pollen, and activating it accidentally. That was what made me sick."

"In part," Fel-Sed said.

"So," Inspector Rainey said, "now we know over what he was killed, and how. There's only the question of who."

"There is no question!" Hieljam ab Tishai shouted. "He was murdered by these very golden-skinned *hshertka* who promised his safety in this place!"

"Blazes," Inspector Mirrell said. "I said that from the very beginning."

Minox had to acknowledge that Inspector Mirrell was correct, but he bristled at the idea of giving him credit for it. That solution was arrived at out of laziness, rather than investigation.

A young green-haired Tsouljan—the gardener boy Minox had spoken to before, stepped forward from the group of his countrymen. "My name is Nuf Rup-Sed. I was born here in Maradaine, and am a Druth citizen by birth."

Minox was about to object, and Inspector Rainey stepped forward to do the same, but the boy spoke louder to drown them out.

"I am responsible, personally, for the death of Hieljam ab Wefi Loriz."

The entire group broke into shouts.

———◆–◆◆–◆———

"Quiet, quiet!" Minox shouted over everyone. He pointed to the regulars closest to Hieljam ab Tishai, who was stalking closer to Nuf Rup-Sed. "Hold her back."

"I have confessed openly and willingly, without duress, in front of witnesses," Rup-Sed said. He looked at Cheever and Hilsom. "You, as representatives of your offices, can attest to it."

"Wait a blazing click," Inspector Mirrell said. "I ain't buying this sewage."

For once Minox found himself in complete agreement with Mirrell.

Inspector Rainey came over to Rup-Sed. "Your confession is incomplete. Anyone could say those words, and might to protect another. Tell us how, and tell us why."

"Why, indeed?" shouted Hieljam ab Tishai, tears streaming down her face. "What reason could you of all people—"

"Me, of all people," Rup-Sed said. "For I am just a gardener, a nearly unnoticed Rup, working with my hands, as is my *linsol*. But I have my ears, and I have my mind. I hear everything. The debts owed by the Fuergan family, the fault of this man"—he pointed to ab Orihla. "The goods in storage for that man"—he pointed to Hajan. "And your rancor for your rival, who is not with us."

"Jabiudal," Minox offered.

"Yes, him." Rup-Sed said. "I knew of this, and more. And I knew my own people here were concerned." He looked to Rek-Uti and the other yellow hairs. "They augured that these trades, this new market, the rival interests in Imachan, and the intrusions of the Lyranans would be the spark that would set the eastern nations ablaze with war."

"We did," Rek-Uti said, his face filled with mortification. "But we spoke only in theory."

"I know what you all said," Rup-Sed said. "Because I listened to all of you!" He advanced on Rek-Uti, but Rainey grabbed hold of the boy and held him back. "Remove the head of the Hieljam, let the Druth discover it, and all would work out. And I did it!"

He turned to Minox and the rest of the group. "He was here alone, to meet with the Kierans, who are always late. So I had ample time. When he drank the tea, I used what skill I have in *ge-tan* to activate it. As he fell, I put him on top of the table, stabbed him with the Imach blade, and painted the Lyranan poem. I then left, unnoticed by all. Moments later he was found, and Constabulary were called."

"Skill in the what?" Rainey asked.

"In magic," Minox offered. "He is a mage?"

"His capacity was limited," Fel-Sed said. "Which is likely why his destiny was always the rup."

Rainey looked put out, but she pulled the irons off her belt. "I am satisfied. Mister Hilsom, Mister Cheever? Any objections?"

They both shook their heads.

Minox watched as she ironed Rup-Sed, reciting the terms of arrest. She handed him off to two regulars, and went to speak with Mirrell and Hilsom.

"Is that all?" Joshea was at Minox's side.

"All that will matter to those assembled," Minox said. He turned and saw Sevqir Fel-Sed watching them lead Rup-Sed off. "Your son?"

"Grandchild," Fel-Sed said in quiet tones, her Trade far less accented than it had ever been. "Though we encircle ourselves to our *linsol* beyond all else. I am fel. His father was vil. And he is rup." She glanced at Minox, and then gave a meaningful look over to Corrie, helping bring the last of the captured Lyranans out to the lockwagons. "But blood is still blood."

Minox held up his hand to her. "You did this to me?"

"No," she said. "You had done damage to it, far beyond my ken. It was dying a slow death, leaking magic."

Minox understood. He didn't feel a need to explain the way his arm had been broken, with Nerrish Plum driving one of the strange magic-draining spikes into it. Clearly its effects were more profound than he had realized. "Which was why the pollen affected me so strongly."

She nodded. "And that made it die faster, which then made you worse. All I could do was channel it, and hope you would find a new balance."

"We need to understand this," Joshea said. "You saw what happened to him. You have to help us."

"There are things I have to do," Fel-Sed said slowly. "But they do not involve you." She walked off toward the hut.

"Wait," Minox said. "There is a problem with your grandson's confession."

"That he could never write an eizhein of such power that it brings Lyranans to tears?" She smiled, as if she had plucked the very thought out of Minox's head. "You will have to consider that unresolved, Inspector. Just as that, for now." She nodded in the direction of Inspector Rainey.

Rainey was standing by the Lyranan woman, Pra Yikenj, reciting the terms of arrest to her with a certain look of grim satisfaction on her face. Yikenj looked at her and smiled, and then said something in a low whisper.

Inspector Rainey stopped her recitation, shock crossing over her face. She shoved Yikenj away, and shouted instructions to the regulars and stalked away.

Minox looked back to Fel-Sed, but she had slipped off.

Rainey came over to Minox. "Looks like we've caused enough damage for tonight."

"What did she say to you?" Minox asked.

"Nothing worth repeating," Rainey said, though her

expression showed she wasn't being truthful. "She's trying to rattle me."

"Very well," Minox said.

"Mister Brondar," Rainey said, looking at Joshea oddly. "Thank you for your help in apprehending her. I know . . . I know you exposed yourself, for my sake and Miss Welling's. I appreciate that, and I will conveniently forget the details on my official reports."

Joshea smiled. "Thank you, Inspector. I just . . . I was glad to do something useful."

"Good." She leaned in closer. "Though you should probably slip off and take that vest off someplace where no one notices you. Hopefully the three of us and Corrie are the only ones who know you shouldn't be wearing it."

"Right," he said sheepishly. "I still need to figure out what to tell my father about all this. Corrie told me she already kicked the hornet's nest over there."

"If you need—" Minox started.

"Don't worry," Joshea said. "Whatever I come up with will be better than an excuse coming from you."

"As you say," Minox said, extending his hand.

Joshea took it. "Though I think we should stay out of each other's path for a few weeks."

"Of course," Minox said. He didn't care for it, but he understood.

Joshea went off, and all signs from the gathered people showed Minox there was little reason to stay at the Tsouljan enclave.

"You're not signed in right now," Rainey said. "So I suppose you could just go straight home."

"Not at all," Minox said. "I promised Inspector Mirrell once this was resolved, we would go to the stationhouse together. There is no cause to delay this further."

Chapter 26

T HE REMAINING PARTIES were given leave to go,
though Satrine noted they were all quite put out. At
some point Hilsom had made it clear to Kenorax that his
holdings were to be put through a thorough audit, and
he looked ready to eat glass. There was also talk of having someone from customs perform inspections of the
various warehouses in the Little East.

Only Hieljam ab Tishai showed any emotion other
than annoyance. She came up to Satrine cautiously. "This
has been a trying time, and emotions have been . . .
heated. I appreciate the diligence and drive you put into
solving the death of my *isahresa*."

"That's my job," Satrine said. "I'm not sure if it's quite
the same for you, but I . . . I've been through similar loss,
with my husband, and—"

"I am not interested," Hieljam ab Tishai said. "It
would be my custom to pay you now, but that is not your
custom. I will honor your way. I hope, in the future, you
show more honor to mine."

Satrine wasn't quite sure what that meant, but nodded
as the retinue of Fuergans and their lawyers left.

"To the stationhouse, miss?" Hace was at her elbow again, despite dried blood caked onto his face.

"Let's take a proper wagon back," Satrine said. "And ride with Mirrell and Welling."

"I've already called for it," Hace said. "I'm not taking any more chances with you for the rest of my shift."

"When does your shift end, Hace?"

"When it does," he said with a shrug. "Or later, if I want. Mostly sleep in the bunks at the stationhouse anyway."

Hace went off to get the wagon, and Satrine shambled over to the street to wait. Whatever Leppin had doped her with had certainly faded, and every part of her body ached.

The wagon arrived and she let herself fall into a seat. Mirrell and Welling did the same, sitting in silence as the wagon trundled off. Satrine was in no mood or condition to force conversation, and let her eyes shut restlessly until they arrived.

Satrine was vaguely aware of the ride, noting they were close when Mirrell told the driver to take them to the front of the stationhouse. As they pulled up, she took more notice of the surroundings, specifically a large group gathered around the front gates of the stationhouse.

"Another riot or protest?" Mirrell asked.

Satrine wondered the same, until she noticed that most of the people were quiet and attentive, and she specifically noticed who they were being attentive of.

Commissioner Enbrain, standing at the main door with Captain Cinellan by his side.

"And it is only through this leadership," they could hear him say as they got out, his voice booming out over the crowd, "and his ability to not only rally his damaged house, but to gather the help he needed from neighboring precincts, that order was maintained in Inemar during this trying ordeal."

"The blazes is he talking to?" Mirrell asked.

"The press," Welling said. "Writers from *South Maradaine Gazette, Maradaine Daily Print, Riverside Standard,* and others I don't recognize."

"The events of the past few days have only solidified the great confidence we all feel in Captain Brace Cinellan. When faced with trials, he has risen to it. Under his command, his inspectors have brought to justice the murderer of a noted foreign dignitary."

He gave a wave of regard to Satrine, Welling, and Mirrell, who were all still standing outside the carriage. Satrine imagined that the press who glanced in their direction must have thought them all dumbfounded.

"That didn't take long," Satrine said as soon as the press were watching Enbrain again.

"That's a lot of butter he's spreading," Mirrell said.

"There *is* an election in a few days," Welling added.

Enbrain went on. "And if the details of this case, as well as these challenging events, prove anything, it is the necessity of an investigative body capable of a wider view. A unit to handle cases just such as these, and capable of going wherever the investigation takes them. That is why I'm announcing the formation of the Maradaine Constabulary Grand Inspectors' Unit. This unit will operate here, out of the Inemar Stationhouse, under the command of Captain Cinellan."

The press people started furiously scribbling in their notebooks.

"Let's go around to the side," Satrine said. "Last thing any of us want right now is to deal with these people."

Inspector Rainey had suggested taking one of the side entrances to avoid the crowd of the press, especially in the light of Commissioner Enbrain's announcement. Minox found, however, that it was hardly possible to avoid a crowd, as many members of his family were waiting in the stationhouse for them.

Uncle Timmothen took the lead, getting unnecessarily physical with Minox as he approached. Timmothen grabbed Minox in a massive embrace, and then held the sides of his head to look at his eyes.

"Are you all right?"

"I am fine, Uncle," Minox said. "I would appreciate you releasing me."

Timmothen did, and then pointed one of his meaty fingers at Mirrell. "And you, you call yourself an inspector, sneaking off to our home!"

Minox held up a hand to put himself in between Inspector Mirrell and his uncle. "Which was exactly where I was, and Inspector Mirrell did right by his duty to seek me there. We could ask no less in his diligence."

"Yeah, but what for?" This came from Edard. "You didn't need hunting down or nothing. Look at you. You're good."

Minox did not want to have this conversation in such a public venue, in the middle of the main work floor of his stationhouse. "I will discuss this at length when we are at home. In the meantime, I hold no enmity toward Inspector Mirrell, and urge you all to do the same. But I do have business which must be attended to, so if this is not your stationhouse, then please go home. I am fine."

His family members, for the most part, went off, all taking a moment to give dark looks at Mirrell or assure Minox that Beliah was fine. Minox thanked them for their pains and went up to the inspectors' floor with Rainey and Mirrell. Two family members stayed right with him, though Minox couldn't rebuke Nyla or Corrie, since this was their stationhouse as well.

"What are you doing?" Mirrell asked Corrie.

"Keeping my one rutting eye on the both of you," she said. "I ain't going to let you run over him with the wagon."

"Corrie, it's fine."

"Like blazes it's fine."

Rainey looked over to Nyla. "Miss Pyle, we have any word on Kellman?"

"He's on the ward floor," Nyla said, not turning her head toward Rainey. "He's expected to make a full recovery, as are most of the men injured in the attack. As you are, I suppose."

Minox fought the urge to rebuke Nyla. He understood her anger regarding Inspector Rainey, and he did not try to convince her otherwise. As long as she remained civil and did her duty, he wouldn't intervene. But her behavior bordered on childish.

Leppin was waiting near the inspectors' desks. He approached Rainey, though he gave nervous glances over at Minox as he did. "How did it go, Inspector?" he asked her.

"Nearly had a bad moment, but it passed," she said. "But I'm more than ready to head home and get proper sleep."

Leppin didn't appear comforted by that. "I didn't think nearly bad was an option. But if you're on your feet, must have turned out all right."

Captain Cinellan came up the stairs with the commissioner, both of them looking rather pleased with themselves. Minox found this distasteful, given all that had occurred.

"Well," the commissioner said. "We've weathered quite a storm here, haven't we?"

"It could have gone worse," Rainey said, her tone guarded.

"Damn near did," Captain Cinellan said.

The commissioner went on. "I want you all to know that everyone of us at Constabulary Plaza are so proud of the work you are doing here. This new unit, it's going to mean a lot of work, but I know all of you, as part of Brace's team here, are up for the challenge."

He shook Cinellan's hand and went for the door. As Cinellan went to his office, Rainey stepped to the side and had a quiet word with the commissioner. Of course, they knew each other—her husband had served out of Constabulary Plaza.

Minox realized that something hadn't been sitting right with him about that announcement—if the commissioner was creating a special Inspectors' Unit to cover the city, he would naturally want to form it out of Constabulary Plaza on the north side of the city. In choosing Captain Cinellan and the Inemar house, perhaps he was signaling that the main headquarters of the City Constabulary was somehow unfit to serve.

Minox filed that in the back of his mind as something that might be important.

Leppin was still standing near Minox, looking expectant. He was about to ask the bodyman what was concerning him when Mirrell interrupted.

"Captain?" Mirrell asked. "We've got—"

"Saints, what time is it?" Cinellan asked. "We should all be getting home. Especially you, Welling." He pointed at Corrie. "You've been working two days straight, put in Ironheart, and you're still here."

"Well, sir, I am on the blasted night patrol," Corrie said. "I should have a horse under me right now."

"Like blazes," the captain said. "You go home, and I don't want to see you here for at least two whole days. Then come in at eight bells in the morning."

"Morning, sir?" Corrie asked.

"Am I not speaking clearly, Welling? Eight in the morning. Dayshift needs a new sergeant on horsepatrol."

Corrie stammered for a moment. "I ain't a rutting sergeant."

"You're not?" The captain stepped closer to her. "You dive into a riot, fellow officer on your shoulder, almost lose an eye, get held hostage, and then knocked in the skull, and what do you do? Change your shirt and get a horse under you." He winked at her. "That's a rutting sergeant in my house. You agree?"

"Blazes, yes, sir," Corrie said.

"Good. Now, all of you, get home."

"Cap!" Mirrell said. "We've got to deal with this."

"With what?" Cinellan asked.

"With . . . Inspector Welling."

"This is not the time, Henfir."

"Begging pardon, sir," Minox said. "I'm afraid it very much is the time. I am an Uncircled mage. I am a source of uncontrolled peril."

"Minox, don't—" Nyla reached out to him.

He raised up his hand—his dead, magicked hand—to ward her off. "It has been gross negligence on my part to act as if my untrained magical ability was of no import to my status as an inspector in this Constabulary House. Today has been definitive proof of that." He looked over to Corrie. "I hurt you and Aunt Beliah."

"Barely," Corrie said. "You'd have to try rutting harder to stop me."

"Not a moment for levity, Corrie," Minox said. "Sir, my lack of control of my magic left me vulnerable, and it put me in a fevered and deranged state. I was a menace, sir. I was the very reason Circle Law exists."

"Hold on, now," Captain Cinellan said. "Henfir, are you saying we need to put charges on him?"

Mirrell hesitated. Despite the antagonism that festered between them, Minox knew Mirrell was not acting out of spite or cruelty. "No, I ain't. But I do think we've got to have a formal Inquiry of Fitness."

"Just a damn minute," Inspector Rainey said, charging back over. "Captain, you can't possibly consider—"

"I'm obliged to consider it, Trick," the captain said. He sat down on one of the desks, rubbing his temples. "Fact is, I've been ignoring the idea as best I could for a long while now."

"And I appreciate that, Captain," Minox said. "There is no greater pride in my life than serving as an inspector in the City Constabulary. But if I am going to do so, I must do it properly, with no question of my right or capacity to serve. Especially in the light of the additional scrutiny you will face with this new Grand Inspectors' Unit."

"Fine." Cinellan looked over to Rainey. "We'll do this by the regs, with an independent investigation, review board, the works. It'll go on for weeks, if not months. You got a problem with that going on while you're partnered to him?"

"I'm certainly not going to walk away from him because of it," she said. "Long as we can do our jobs."

She turned and gave Minox a look that was crafted to say, "I've got your back." But it was craft, albeit excellent craft. There was doubt in her eyes.

"Good," Cinellan said, "because I'm not going to take him off cases until someone makes me."

"Done and done, then," Minox said. "I appreciate your support."

"All right, all of you, get home," Cinellan said. "I'm tired of seeing your faces."

Rainey grabbed her things. "We'll get through this, you hear?" She pointed to his hand. "This, and everything else, it means nothing. You can do this job, and it's what you should be doing."

And in that, there was nothing but honesty.

"Thank you, Satrine," he said.

She sighed. "Three days of running around the Little East, and then a confession drops into our lap." She raised an eyebrow and added, "Unresolved?"

"Unresolved." A weak smile came to his lips. "See you in the morning. A good night to you, Inspector Rainey, and my best to your husband."

She gave him a last nod and headed toward the stairs.

"She really ain't that rutting bad, Nyla," Corrie said, coming up on Minox's left.

"She damn well better have Minox's back, since he had hers," Nyla said. "What does Leppin need?"

Leppin was still standing by Minox's desk. His demeanor was clear—he had something to say for Minox's ears only.

"I'll find out," Minox said. "Allow me a bit of privacy here."

"Keep in sight, Mine," Corrie said.

He approached Leppin, who was now looking quite nervous. "Something the matter, Leppin?"

"Something, I would say," Leppin said. "Been something of a day."

"Indeed. But you have something specific on your mind."

"You were in an altered state today, I understand. Did some strange things."

"Do you have a point, Mister Leppin?"

"Yeah, I do," Leppin said. He pulled an envelope out of his apron pocket. "This morning you wrote this, and had it delivered to me."

Minox had no memory of this whatsoever, but he took the envelope and opened it up. The letter inside was a glimpse of madness, as it was just four words written over and over, written again in the blank spaces at the edge of the paper, in every possible direction.

Where are the spikes?

Minox swallowed the fear that crept up his throat upon seeing this. "I appreciate your discretion in this, Leppin. I apologize, but I was being affected by—"

"Yeah, I heard all about it, Welling. I don't know what

was going on, exactly, but I know you weren't in your proper senses."

"Is this all, Leppin?"

"No, that ain't all." He glanced about and lowered his voice. "It might have been madness, but madness sometimes hits at the center."

"What are you talking about?"

"The spikes from the Plum case—there were eight. One went to Miss Rainey's consultant friend, the other seven we had in lockup. Those seven are gone."

"Stolen?"

"More than that, specs. Near as I could tell, without causing a ruckus, there's no record of them whatsoever. Not in lockup's record, not in the archives, not even my own files. It's all gone."

"How is that possible?" Despite asking that, Minox was not actually surprised by the revelation. If anything, the news was a confirmation of something he didn't even realize he already suspected.

"I don't got the first reckon on that, specs," Leppin said. "Which is why you're the only one I'm telling."

"I will give it all due consideration, Mister Leppin. Which is significant."

Leppin nodded in return and said his good night, slipping off to the back stairs.

Nyla approached, Corrie leaning against the wall in half doze by the stairwell. "Can we go home?"

"Yes, let's," Minox said, taking his cousin's coat for her. "For once, I believe I need a good night's sleep."

Tomorrow was going to be a busy day.

Satrine splurged for the tickwagon to ride across the bridge and back home. Her feet were numb, as were her fingers. It must have been ten bells or later. Missus Abernand would be furious. Satrine would apologize and then fall down on her bed, hopefully for an entire day. She could barely keep her eyes open as she got off the tickwagon and shuffled to her home.

"Been a busy few days," a voice said from the bottom of the stairwell leading to Satrine's apartment door. "I'm not surprised you pulled such a victory out of the fire."

He didn't need to step into the light for Satrine to know who it was, but he did nonetheless. Age had barely touched Grieson, his proud, smooth chin still a defining feature on his smug, handsome face. It was hard to believe it had been fifteen years. Hearing his voice, seeing his face, it blew open a wall in her memory she hadn't even realized was there.

"You're pregnant?" Grieson asked. He didn't seem surprised or concerned. Just asking for information.

"I didn't really know when I went to Kiad," Satrine said. "But the boat ride back made it clear. How the Lyranan woman knew—"

"Never mind about her," Grieson said. "Lyranans aren't our concern. Sounds like she helped our interests this time."

"I didn't think she did it for our interests," Satrine said.

"Of course not. But now we know what we suspected, both about the Imachs and the Lyranans."

"So now. . . ." Satrine said. "I am pregnant. And the father is—"

"Who you put on the Waish throne. So it's in our interest to keep that child safe."

"What?"

"Do you not understand, Agent Carthas? You do recall that Waish customs have a very different view of wedlock and legitimacy than we do. The child in your belly—"

"Would have a legitimate claim on the Waish throne," Satrine finished. She had been aware of that from the moment she had been on the boat.

"So that's your new mission."

"How, exactly, is that my mission?" Satrine asked.

"We'll have a legitimate heir to a foreign throne, but you have to be the one to care for and raise it. You're the proof of legitimacy."

"Did you plan this?"

"Hardly. You're the one who decided to take Kellin as a lover."

That was true, though she sometimes wondered where the line was between what she decided and what Oster put in her head.

He shrugged. "Here's how it'll work. We'll draw up some papers, arrange a stipend for a few months. Officially you will be retired from Intelligence. You'll join polite society—somewhere in the working class, of course. Get yourself ingratiated in one of the Devoted Families. Marry a man in Constabulary or Fire Brigade. Something stable and decent."

"You want me to marry?" Satrine asked.

"Is that any more distasteful than any other orders you've had?"

Satrine had to admit they weren't. "I'll have to be quick about that. I won't be able to hide this very long."

"I have every faith in you."

"You're at my bloody door?" Satrine asked, blood rushing to her head. The exhaustion washed away in a rush. "What the blazes are you doing here now?"

"Because now is when I needed to talk to you," Grieson said. "I'd hardly pop over for a casual visit."

She resisted the urge to knock him across that chin. "Where were you two months ago when I was desperate for money and work?"

"It's not that simple."

"I reached out and got silence."

"Frankly, I wanted to see what you would do, Satrine," he said. "And I'll be damned if you didn't do something amazing."

"Thank you," she said. "I'd like to go in to my home now."

He blocked her passing by him. "You did something amazing, and now we need you."

"You need me, what, as an Inspector Third Class?"

"Yes. We need someone we can trust with access to Enbrain. Especially with his new Grand Inspectors' Unit idea."

That she raised an eyebrow to. "What about the unit?"

He gave her that infuriating smile. "You tell me. You've been close to Enbrain."

"I know the man," Satrine said guardedly.

"So, is he the real thing?"

"In what way?"

"Is he going to use this unit to dig the dirty folks out of the constabulary? Or is he putting up a wall around them to keep them safe?"

That was specific. "How is this the business of Druth Intelligence?"

"We can't do our job if the capital city is filled with rot."

"What will you do about it, though?" The look on Grieson's face bordered on the sinister. She wouldn't put it past him to have a Druth official killed to suit the needs of Intelligence. Blazes, maybe that was the real story behind those Parliament deaths last month.

Instead he just said, "Are you voting in the election?"

"Apparently I'm entitled as a proxy for my husband."

"Your vote is the one I'm interested in." Grieson's eyes bored into hers. "Would you vote to keep Enbrain as constabulary commissioner?"

"I suppose I would, if it really matters."

"Right now, your opinion matters a great deal."

"Are you going to—"

"Just tell me."

"Fine," Satrine said. "Yes, were I voting, I would vote

for him. Yes, I think he is the real thing. He pisses me off most of the time, but not in his devotion to the job."

"Good." Grieson stepped out of her way and strolled up the stairs. "We'll be in touch."

"Hold up," Satrine said. Now she was thinking clearly, possibly for the first time in months, if not years. She wanted to kick herself for not realizing until this moment that Grieson had access to a real solution for all her problems. "You're saying I work for you. Work means money and resources. Something you forgot all about once you let me go before."

"We never let you go—"

"You sent me out pregnant and jobless—"

"Yes, fine, we're terrible people," Grieson said. "I'll make certain that a degree of supplemental income will find its way to you. Discreetly."

"That's not what I want," Satrine said. "You'll still do that, but I need something else. Oster."

"Oster?" He gave her an infuriating grin. "What do you want him for?"

"My husband." She went up the steps to get into Grieson's face. "I want Oster to reach into his jumbled head and get me my husband back."

"Interesting," Grieson said. He shrugged. "Unfortunately, Oster's been dead for years."

"Then some other rutting telepath!" she swore at him. "You can do it, don't pretend you can't!"

He gestured for her to calm down, which only irritated her. "I'll see what I can do, but I'll tell you, the agency will expect your full cooperation."

"Just get on it," Satrine said, turning back to her door. "I've had a long day."

"Always a pleasure, Satrine," he said, and sauntered into the night.

Missus Abernand was not there to chastise Satrine when she came in the apartment. Caribet sat on the couch, reading by the dim lamplight, while Rian cleaned the table.

"Shouldn't you two be in bed?" Satrine asked as she hung up her belt, coat, and vest.

"I told Cari she should go," Rian said.

"I wasn't going to bed until you did," Caribet countered.

"And I wasn't until you came home," Rian said. "We knew you'd be late, and sent Missus Abernand up."

"You knew?" Satrine asked.

"They sent a page," Rian said. "Said you needed to put extra time on the case."

"True enough," Satrine said, sitting down on the couch. "I'm exhausted and famished."

"I've got you," Rian said, going to the icebox.

Satrine pulled her boots off. "I should check on your father."

"I've already done it, Mama," Rian said. "He's all set and asleep for the night."

"Ri, you shouldn't have to . . ."

"I didn't have to," Rian said, coming over with a plate of dried sausage, cheese, bread, and a dollop of something in the corner of the plate. "I just did it."

"What's this?" Satrine asked, pointing to the dollop.

"Jaconvale mustard," Rian said with a proud smile on her face. "It was a gift."

Bells rang in Satrine head. "A gift from whom?" Between Yikenj and Grieson showing up, Satrine wasn't ready for any surprises, even seemingly benevolent ones.

Yikenj. She had let that woman get inside her head.

"From the manager at Henson's Majestic," Rian said. "The store'll be opening the week before Reunification Day. You should see it, Mother, it is grand. There are dresses and shoes, and suits for men, and earrings and perfume, and these wide marble staircases to each floor. Even a seated club with luncheon and ice cream. Everything in one store, Mother!"

"It sounds grand," Satrine said. "Is this your way of telling me you have a job?"

"In gloves and hats!" Rian said. She stood poised in front of the couch. "They said I was exactly the sort of girl they wanted, the sort who could speak like an educated lady—"

"But would work for a half-crown a day," Caribet added.

"Half-crown plus commission," Rian shot back.

Satrine dabbed the sausage into the mustard. She had to admit, it was quite excellent.

"Only for the summer," she said to Rian. "I do not want this interfering with your schooling."

"Yes, Mother," Rian said.

Satrine ate the rest quickly while Rian continued on about her job, and Caribet soon stalked off to bed, clearly annoyed with having heard this all evening.

Satrine got off the couch and put her plate down on the table. "I need to sleep," she said. "And so should you, if you're a working shopgirl."

"All right," Rian said.

Satrine kissed her on the forehead. "I'm very proud of you, my princess."

"You haven't called me that in years, Mother," Rian said.

"I won't make a habit of it," Satrine said. "It'll go to your head."

Rian went to bed, and Satrine went to look in on her husband.

He was well, clean, and sleeping, just as Rian had said. Rian had even shaved him and washed his face. In moments like this, she could believe he was still the man she married, the man she fell in love with, the man who had loved and raised another man's daughter like she was his own without an ounce of hesitation. She kissed him on the forehead and went to the water closet.

The bandages on her chest were thick with dry blood, but her wounds didn't open again when she pulled them off. Washing carefully, it was clear the two holes would leave a scar once they healed, but they would heal. Leppin had done good work for a bodyman. She could have been left with a worse souvenir from her tangles with Yikenj.

That damned Lyranan woman.

Satrine tried to push it from her mind.

But those last words Yikenj whispered before she was taken away drummed through her head.

"You think you've won, but you're the one working with a traitor."

Satrine shook it away. Yikenj was just a spy, not a saint watching from above. She was trying to find another way to beat Satrine, one last time. Rattle her.

Satrine wouldn't let her, because there was no way she was right. Minox Welling could be annoying and off-putting, but there was no chance he was a traitor of any kind.

"You're the one working with a traitor."

Satrine blew out the lamps and crawled into bed next to her husband, who didn't react to her presence. Those words kept hammering at her as she closed her eyes, but she wouldn't let them win. If Berana Carthas's fists couldn't break her as a child, then empty words from a tyzo spy wouldn't either.

Not today, and not tomorrow.

Tomorrow was a workday.

Appendix

Pronunciation Guide for Foreign Terms and Names

All the foreign names and terms encountered in *An Import of Intrigue* are just a small portion of the languages found in their home country or regions. While each language has a wide range of dialects and pronunciation variations, this guide will assist with fundamental understanding of how to read the transliteration of their words.

Fuergan

The Fuergan language is highly aspirated, and the breathy beginnings of many words are transliterated with "Hr," "Hs," "Hl," and so forth.

The Fuergan "j" is much like the Spanish "ll," in that its pronunciation varies widely depending on region, ranging from like the "ch" in champ to the "y" in yam. For the Hieljam, the sound of the "j" is closest to the "si" in vision.

Fuergan vowels are pronounced as follows:

a—as in hat
aa—as in nut
e—as in play
i—as in free
o—as in thought
u—as in bird
ei—as in lane
ai—as in light
ie—as in leer
ue—as in west

Imach

The Imach language is very complicated for easy transliteration, as their alphabet contains twenty-two different vowels and forty-three consonants. The subtle distinctions between many of those vowels and consonants are challenging to distinguish for someone who isn't a native speaker (or a trained linguist), and thus many of them get transliterated the same way—often as single or double l's or r's.

The main thing to note is that Imach dialects do not have diphthongs, so each vowel should be pronounced as individual syllables. Two key consonant rules that should be noted:

> **ch**—as in mechanic
> **ss**—as in mission

Tsouljan

Tsouljan pronunciation is fundamentally easy, as it only has six vowel sounds.

> **a**—as in cot
> **e**—as in day
> **i**—as in free
> **o**—as in go
> **u**—as in run
> **ou**—as in boot

The key thing to note is that all vowels in Tsouljan are pronounced "creaky voice" (also referred to as "vocal fry"). Also emphasis is always on the last syllable in any word, unless syllables are separated with a dash, in which case the syllable before the dash is emphasized.

Lyranan

Lyranan and Tsouljan have similar roots, though Lyranan is far more nasal in both vowel and consonant sounds. Lyranan vowels should be nasalized, with the following pronunciation:

a—as in cat
e—as in bed
i—as in lit
o—as in go
u—as in run
y—as in fear
ei—as in wait
ai—as in write
ao—as in house

Note that "y" is transliterated both as vowel and consonant. At the beginning of a word, such as in Yikenj, the "y" is pronounced like in yam. Use of "ng" in Lyranan should be pronounced as in sing, and use of "nj" should be pronounced as in banjo.

As with Tsouljan, emphasis is always on the last syllable in any word, unless syllables are separated with a dash, in which case the syllable before the dash is emphasized.

Don't miss any of the exciting novels of
Marshall Ryan Maresca

MARADAINE

"Smart, fast, and engaging fantasy crime in the mold of Brent Weeks and Harry Harrison. Just perfect."
   –Kat Richardson, national bestselling author of *Revenant*

THE THORN OF DENTONHILL   978-0-7564-1026-1
THE ALCHEMY OF CHAOS   978-0-7564-1169-5

THE MARADAINE CONSTABULARY

"The perfect combination of urban fantasy, magic, and mystery."
   –*Kings River Life Magazine*

A MURDER OF MAGES   978-0-7564-1027-8
AN IMPORT OF INTRIGUE   978-0-7564-1173-2

And coming soon,
THE STREETS OF MARADAINE
begins with

THE HOLVER ALLEY CREW   978-0-7564-1260-9

To Order Call: 1-800-788-6262
www.dawbooks.com

DAW 213